becoming
the
talbot
sisters

Center Point
Large Print

Also by Rachel Linden and available from Center Point Large Print:

Ascension of Larks

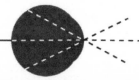

becoming
the
talbot
sisters

RACHEL LINDEN

CENTER POINT LARGE PRINT
THORNDIKE, MAINE

Library of Congress Cataloging-in-Publication Data

Names: Linden, Rachel, author.
Title: Becoming the Talbot sisters / Rachel Linden.
Description: Center Point Large print edition. | Thorndike, Maine :
    Center Point Large Print, 2018.
Identifiers: LCCN 2018008851 | ISBN 9781683248187
    (hardcover : alk. paper)
Subjects: LCSH: Sisters—Fiction. | Large type books. | Domestic fiction.
Classification: LCC PS3612.I5327426 B43 2018 | DDC 813/.6—dc23
LC record available at https://lccn.loc.gov/2018008851

For Sarah.
Sisters are treasures and so are good friends.
I'm so glad you are both.
And for my mother, Adelle,
who taught me courage for the fight.

To have courage for whatever comes in life—everything lies in that.

St. Teresa of Avila

CHAPTER 1

Waverly Talbot gritted her teeth and smiled brightly for the television camera. She could not swear on the Food Network channel, not even if one of her browned butter tarts with a lemon zest–infused shortbread crust was stuck tight to the festive Easter tart tin, not even if she'd warned the kitchen prep team that the daffodil shape was going to be a pain in the rear. The eyes of America were on her, so she smiled her thousand-watt smile for the camera and ignored the perspiration prickling under the arms of her ecru silk blouse. She tried with all her might to look as though she were smoothly professional and not desperately trying to unstick a reluctant tart crust. Which she was . . . on both counts.

"Now, this step can be a little tricky, so watch closely," Waverly cooed, using just the right intonation of warmth and professionalism. It was a tone that hinted at movie star, kindergarten teacher, and sexy housewife rolled into one—a paragon of domesticity, showing a watching nation just how to make the perfect spring treat.

Out of the corner of her eye, Waverly saw her producer, Beau, give her a thumbs-up as Wyatt, the cameraman, zoomed in for a close-up while she carefully dislodged tarts from the baking tin onto the smooth marble surface of her TV kitchen island. Casting a serene smile at the camera, Waverly swallowed hard, struggling to keep her attention on the tarts. The truth was that she was beginning to feel a little queasy. She closed her eyes for a brief second, delighted by the sensation. *Please, please, please, please,* she whispered silently.

Forcing herself to focus on the task at hand, she ignored the slight seasick feeling in her stomach that made her heart flutter with a mixture of apprehension and anticipation. She applied a bit more pressure to the tin. With a tiny pop the tart dislodged, coming out whole except for the tip of one daffodil petal that crumbled onto the counter. The camera moved back, capturing Waverly's slightly flushed face. A curl of soft blond hair fell across her brow, and she swept it back, keeping a calm smile on her pale pink lips.

"Oh dear!" Waverly trilled. "Well, we just have to eat the ones that aren't perfect, don't we?" She winked. "These tarts are wonderful for almost any occasion, and combined with the strawberry-basil limeade we whipped up earlier, they'll have you feeling festively springlike in no time. With a little effort and a little bit of luck, you, too, can design and host a spring-themed garden party that is . . ." She paused for a half second, then delivered her signature line with demure confidence, sweeping her hand over the tarts sitting in a row before her. "Simply perfect."

She picked up a tart, the daffodil troublemaker, and took a tiny nibble, obliterating the mistake. She gazed into the eye of the camera, waited three beats until she heard, "Cut!" and then promptly dropped the offending tart on the counter.

"Great show. This is going to be a popular one." Beau approached the island, scribbling a few notes onto his clipboard. "Especially when those tart tins are featured in the March issue of *Good Housekeeping* next spring. Perfect product placement, Boss."

She brushed buttery crumbs from her fingers and nodded, glad the episode was over. She disliked doing themed episodes for her home entertaining show; they were too gauche for her taste, but audiences loved them. With every pumpkin cookie cornucopia, every patriotic red-white-and-blue ice cream cake, *Simply Perfect*'s ratings climbed. So Beau pressed for at least three a season. In her *Simply Perfect* domain, Waverly Talbot was queen, but public opinion was king.

Waverly untied the frilled turquoise dotted swiss apron she'd worn for the show. Although it was September, it was a warm day and the studio kitchen was sweltering from the lights and the oven. She left the apron on the counter, where an assistant would launder it and return it to the apron closet. Her aprons were as much a part of her image as anything else. She was *Simply Perfect*'s Waverly Talbot, a combination Martha Stewart and Marilyn Monroe, the perfect fifties housewife in the modern world who could sew the button on a shirt cuff, Google instructions for steaming Dungeness crabs, and still look divine in heels and pearls on cable TV. She had over a hundred aprons, all of them custom-made.

"Beau, tell the team to please read *all* of the preparation notes," Waverly instructed with a frown, washing her hands and carefully slathering on a lemon-scented moisturizer. "We can't afford any more mistakes on camera like we had with that tin today. Every detail needs to be right."

"You got it," Beau said, hurrying behind her as she headed back to her office, tucked behind the stage kitchen. Both were located in a renovated carriage house on the expansive Greenwich, Connecticut, property belonging to Waverly and her husband, Andrew Ross. She had begun using the carriage house six years ago because it was free, but as *Simply Perfect* rose in popularity, she chose not to move to a more spacious sound stage. She loved the convenience of walking across her backyard to get to work.

With Beau at her heels, Waverly breezed into her office, a narrow galley space decorated in pale, understated tones. The only color was a series of candy-bright vintage advertisements for fifties kitchenware that dotted the walls, lending a certain air of domestic gaiety to the muted beige-and-cream space. She turned to her producer, intending to ask him to give her a few minutes. She wanted to be alone, to regain her equilibrium and allow herself to explore this new, slightly seasick sensation, and all it could potentially mean.

"Hey, Boss, I wanted to check on a few things for the launch party," Beau said, making himself comfortable on the tufted cream-colored leather loveseat and diving into business before she could speak. "You said you wanted to go with a sort of *Mad Men*–themed cocktail bash here at your place. What still needs to be done?" He held his pen aloft, poised for her reply.

Waverly's new project, a cocktail hour entertaining book, was coming out in just over a month. Publicity was kicking into high gear for the book's release.

She sank into her cream leather office chair and slipped off her high heels with a sigh. Might as well get this over with. She could dwell on the future later. She'd have plenty of time before Andrew came home from his job in the city.

"Sophie has it all under control. Invitations are

already in the mail. I think everything's in hand."

They had decided on a designer cocktail bar with a small jazz band, waiters in black tie, and a select guest list of TV producers, influential cooking blog writers and book reviewers, and a couple of daytime talk show hosts—a glamorous, intimate evening with a few dozen people whose good opinion could propel book sales from average to bestseller.

Beau jotted a few notes on his yellow legal pad, his ponytail bouncing with his energetic scribbling. Beau Beecham was not the sleekest producer around, but he had been with Waverly from the beginning, from her little-watched local television channel show, *Entertaining with Waverly*, to the growing home entertaining empire she presided over now. He was detailed, loyal, and down-to-earth, the right-hand man Waverly relied on to help her keep *Simply Perfect* moving up in the world.

"I think that's all we need to discuss," she said, leaning her head back and closing her eyes. "We can talk about the particulars later."

She let her hand drift over her abdomen as she waited for him to finish writing. Was she really feeling queasy, or had it just been the heat and lights and the intensity of filming? To test herself Waverly pictured a full Thanksgiving dinner— roasted turkey, cranberry sauce, stuffing, gravy with giblets. There. She stopped. The thought of giblets swimming in a sea of brown sauce made her stomach turn over. She definitely wasn't imagining it. She smiled in amazement. All the other times she had never made it far enough to get morning sickness. This was an entirely new sensation.

Beau consulted his notes as he wrapped up the meeting and prepared to go. "Okay, we'll start prep tomorrow at seven and plan to shoot the first segment by nine. We're doing the cardamom quick bread first, is that right?"

Waverly's iPhone buzzed and she nodded in reply, glancing distractedly at the message. She expected to see a text from Andrew announcing that he was held up in a meeting or on his way home. He worked long hours at an investment firm in New York City, commuting from Wall Street to their home on the Connecticut shore. But the text wasn't from Andrew. It was from the hospice caregiver, Jillian.

Mae's worse. I think you'd better come. I'm sorry.

"Oh," Waverly gasped, her heart skipping a beat. She instinctively covered the screen with her hand, blocking out the words. She was not ready. She sat motionless for a moment, shaken by those few words and what they meant. It was too soon. Finally, she stirred herself into action,

15

feeling numb and too slow, as though she were moving through icy water, her usually organized thoughts scattering like marbles.

"Beau, it's Aunt Mae." Waverly spoke slowly, trying to focus and come up with a plan of action. She couldn't just sit there, not when minutes might count, not when she was needed. "They're calling me in," she said, working out the necessary steps in her head as she went along. "I'll go immediately, as soon as I can get a flight to Columbus. Cancel the taping tomorrow and put the crew on hold. I don't know how long I'll be."

Beau gave her a sympathetic frown. Without hesitation, even though they were scheduled to finish taping the entire season in the next couple of weeks, he replied, "Okay, Boss. I'll handle it. We'll take care of everything." He consulted his schedule. "On Friday you were supposed to have Elle Fanning as a celebrity guest. You're making gourmet cake pops together. Want me to see if we can postpone her, reschedule for when you get back?"

Waverly was already on her feet, slipping her aching heels back into her shoes. She paused for a moment, tapping her fingernail against her lips, trying to think clearly. Her mind was already back in a small farmhouse in rural Ohio with the woman who had raised her from the age of twelve. Her heart squeezed at the thought of her aunt. The last time Waverly had seen her, nearly two months ago now, Aunt Mae had been as bald as a newly hatched chick, all pink scalp and wisps of hair, but as full of salt and vinegar as ever. The chemo and radiation had not daunted her. She had been soldiering on.

Waverly swallowed hard. She had thought there would be more time. "I don't know. Let's have a backup date if Elle can reschedule, but let's hope I'm back by Friday." She grabbed her phone and resolutely put aside all thoughts of giblets and queasy stomachs, cake pops and starlets. They would have to wait until later.

"Sure thing, Boss." Beau was already scribbling notes on his legal pad, rearranging the schedule. He would handle everything. He met her eyes for a moment, and in his she read a genuine sympathy. "Hey, I'm sorry. I know how close you were . . . are to her."

Waverly nodded, suddenly focusing very hard on a poster of a smiling housewife beaming over a brand-new shiny silver double toaster. The toaster swam and blurred for just a second, but she blinked back the tears.

On my way.

She sent the text, already moving toward the entrance. She would call Andrew, pack her things, and leave immediately. Beau trotted

17

behind her as she hurried through the test kitchen, where the prep crew was cleaning up and getting ready for tomorrow.

She tossed instructions over her shoulder as she walked. "Get Sophie to book a flight for me, the earliest one I can catch to Columbus today, and have her reserve a rental car for the week. Tell her to get something midsize, not one of those little economy cars. I want something with power windows at least. Oh . . . and Charlie." She stopped, suddenly remembering her twin sister, Charlotte. Of course Charlie needed to know as soon as possible.

Waverly calculated the time difference in her head. Six hours from the East Coast to Central Europe. It was after ten at night over there, but she couldn't wait.

"I'm going to pack a bag. Order a taxi for JFK, and have them here in thirty minutes."

"You got it, Boss." Beau pulled out his phone and started punching numbers.

Waverly didn't look back, confident that Beau would arrange everything. She hurried out the french doors that led from the carriage house and crossed the wide brick entertaining patio and the long emerald sweep of lawn to the main house.

Upstairs in the spacious master bedroom suite, she paused just long enough to call Andrew. He was in a meeting, so she left a message with his secretary and then called her sister's European cell number. Although Charlie was based in Budapest, she traveled almost constantly, and there was no telling what country she was in at any given moment. She worked for an NGO that focused on developing community health programs in post-Communist countries. The last two times they had talked, Charlie had been staffing a women's health drop-in center in Belgrade and riding a night train to Moldova to run a reproductive health seminar in a local high school.

The call went straight to voicemail. Charlie's voice, deeper than her own and less polished, whiskey to Waverly's champagne. "It's Charlie. Leave a message."

"Charlie, it's Waverly. Jillian just contacted me." Her heart was beating so fast she had to stop and catch her breath. "She says . . . she says Aunt Mae is failing. She thinks we'd better come. I'm flying down there now. Call me when you get this."

Her hands were trembling as she disconnected the call. It had been a few weeks since she'd talked to Charlie, maybe even a month. They'd been keeping in contact more frequently since Aunt Mae's diagnosis, their calls mostly centered around health updates. Before that they had talked briefly every few months, on holidays and their joint birthday mainly, but hadn't seen each other in several years. It seemed that they had less in common with each passing year. The path of their lives had forked years ago, and the distance had been widening ever since.

Waverly pulled her trusty Louis Vuitton suitcase from the walk-in closet, opened it, and stared at the empty hull for a long moment, her mind a complete blank. What would she need in Ohio? Finally she threw in a couple of sweater sets and a gray silk dress she liked that seemed funeral appropriate. She didn't want to believe that she would actually need it. Not yet. She snatched her nude pumps and a bag of miniature toiletries she always kept packed and ready. She lingered for a moment over the jewelry. In the end she chose a pair of gold hoops and her Tiffany pearls, a one-year anniversary present from Andrew back when *Entertaining with Waverly* was a struggling local public-access channel show and such a gift was an unexpected luxury. Those pearls were still her favorite. Not the best or most expensive, but the ones that held the most sentiment.

She glanced at the clock. Five minutes until the taxi was due to arrive. Zipping the suitcase, she straightened, smoothed her skirt, and took a deep breath, trying to recall anything she might have forgotten.

And then she felt it—a sharp gripping in her abdomen, like the closing of a tiny fist over her womb. It was a familiar sensation, one that rooted her to the carpet in sudden horror. She swallowed hard, all her attention focused internally, pinpointed on the spot where she had felt the cramp.

"Oh no," she whispered. She felt hot and cold, and slightly nauseated. Outside she heard the crunch of tires on the drive and a moment later the honk of the waiting taxi. And then she felt it again, another cramp, harder this time, unmistakable.

In the spacious pearl-gray master bathroom, Waverly sat down on the side of the soaking tub, her hands clenched tight, willing the sensation to go away, willing herself to be wrong. She waited for one breath, then another. Outside the taxi honked again, but she ignored it. The gripping again, low in her pelvis, so familiar and so shattering.

For a moment she rested her forehead on the ball of her hand, not moving, feeling unutterably weary. The taxi honked again, and then a minute later she heard it drive away. She should call the doctor, she knew, arrange to go to the hospital, call Andrew to meet her there. It was a familiar routine by now. And she needed to contact Beau to cancel the flight and let Jillian know she would not be flying to Ohio tonight. But somehow she couldn't, not this time. Instead, she sat motionless in the quiet calm of the bathroom as the seconds ticked by, paralyzed with disbelief and the dawning realization that what she had longed for and lost so many times before was again being taken. But this time, unlike all the others, there would be no chance to try again.

CHAPTER 2

Cooksville, Ohio

Charlie Talbot sat at her great-aunt Mae's Formica kitchen table, the one with silver tinsel starbursts embedded in the plastic, nursing a jet-lag headache and a cup of cold black coffee. Aunt Mae's funeral was over, and friends, neighbors, and extended family were slowly filling the cramped front rooms of the small white farmhouse that Aunt Mae had called home for her entire life. Waverly was preparing refreshments, and ostensibly Charlie was helping. In reality, Waverly was doing all the work while Charlie sat still and tried to orient herself. She'd arrived from Budapest early that morning, sleep deprived and heavy-eyed with grief and disbelief.

She traced a tinsel starburst with her finger. The table seemed almost retro cool now, though it had been dated even in the early nineties when she'd first laid eyes on it. It reminded her of New Year's Eve fireworks from a bygone era, a little whimsical, a little gaudy. Waverly had never liked it. She'd gotten all the design aesthetic in the family. Today, for instance, she had dressed for the funeral in an appropriately somber but elegant gray silk cocktail dress with a single strand of pearls, looking for all the world like she was starring in a fifties high-society movie. In contrast, Charlie couldn't remember the last time she'd worn a dress. She had found her navy-blue jersey sheath at a boutique at the airport after she landed. She couldn't remember if she'd shaved her legs. She was pretty sure she hadn't.

"Why do people feed grief?" Waverly asked, eyeing the mound of Tupperware containers and Saran-wrapped plates loading the table. All morning before the funeral, there had been a steady stream of people dropping off food.

Charlie shrugged. "Gives them something to do so they don't feel helpless."

Waverly made a *tsk* of disapproval. "Well, I wish they'd bring actual food and not this processed stuff." She picked up a plastic plate piled with mini hot dogs wrapped in refrigerator biscuit dough and wrinkled her nose.

Charlie reached over and snagged one, popping it into her mouth. "But processed stuff is so tasty," she said.

Waverly peeled the foil and plastic wrap off the plates of food, taking inventory. The church had overflowed with people paying their respects to Aunt Mae. Cooksville was a small, working-class town in the southern Ohio foothills of the Appalachian Mountains. Aunt Mae had been

24

born and raised there, and much of the town had turned out to mourn her. Now several dozen guests were packed into the front rooms, spilling from the parlor into the dining room. The twins' second cousin Crystal had offered to preside over the table of coffee and tea set up under the big window. Charlie could hear Pastor Shaw regaling a group of Aunt Mae's friends and neighbors with a story about bagging a huge buck last deer-hunting season.

Waverly's husband, Andrew, was here as well, tucked away in the back bedroom on a conference call for work. He'd arrived just before the service with enough time to envelop Charlie in a warm hug of welcome and murmur a few kind words of condolence, then hold Waverly's hand through Pastor Shaw's eulogy, a crisply ironed handkerchief at the ready if either sister needed it. Charlie hoped she'd see more of him after the crowds cleared. She was fond of her brother-in-law, whose dry wit and calm demeanor added an air of civility to every situation. Besides, she owed him a rematch game of Scrabble. The last time they'd played, more than two years ago now, she'd won by a hair with *ominous,* walking away with a box of gourmet dark chocolate truffles as her prize. She'd shared them with Waverly and Andrew afterward. The pink peppercorn and sea salt flavor had been particularly good.

Oddly, the kitchen was empty except for the

two sisters. People in Cooksville usually gathered in kitchens—commiserating about politics in Washington, DC, the Ohio tornado season, or the disappointing finale of *The Voice*. But now they poked their heads around the doorway, saw Waverly and Charlie, and retreated. Charlie didn't know if they were intimidated to be in the kitchen with the famous Food Network star Waverly Talbot or if they were leaving Mae's girls alone out of respect for their loss.

Charlie scrubbed her hands over her face and ran her fingers through her sandy-blond pixie cut, grown a little shaggy at the edges, trying to keep the creeping fatigue at bay and press the reality of the situation into her brain. It felt unreal to be sitting in the house where they had spent their adolescence. The kitchen still smelled like canned soup and the downstairs bathroom like Aunt Mae, a combination of Irish Spring and Johnson's baby powder.

She took a swig of coffee, pulled a face at the taste, and looked around. The kitchen had not changed in the twenty-three years she'd known it. Small, tidy, shabby at the corners. The counter was the startling yellow of cheap margarine. By the electric oven there was a brown scorch mark on the linoleum where Charlie had dropped a smoking pot of popcorn her freshman year of high school. She'd opened all the windows to air out the stench, and after that left the kitchen to

Waverly. Charlie liked to eat and Waverly liked to cook, so they made a good pair.

In one corner, within sight of the stove and looking incongruously new, sat the flat-screen color television the girls had purchased for Aunt Mae a few years before. Waverly had finally given up buying her aunt luxurious body-care products and satin pajama sets from Bergdorf Goodman after happening upon an entire drawer of gifts still in their iconic lavender shopping bags in Aunt Mae's spare room. That year the twins had split the cost of a new television and a cable channel subscription that they renewed yearly.

The gift was a hit. Aunt Mae hadn't bothered with any channels except the Food Network, where she could watch Waverly's *Simply Perfect* air on Fridays at two, and the Travel Channel, so she could keep up with all the places Charlie traveled for work.

"That Rick Steves sure gets around," she'd said to Charlie the last time they'd spoken, more than a month ago. "He just did a show on Budapest, and I felt like I was right there with you. It sure is a pretty city."

Charlie's heart squeezed with a sudden pang of grief, picturing her aunt cooking a solitary dinner on the stove, her eyes glued to the TV as she tracked her nieces' disparate lives so far away from the tiny square of a kitchen in rural

Ohio. Charlie's job had seemed so exotic to Aunt Mae. She was responsible for organizing health education seminars in schools and community centers around Central Europe, an occupation that kept her on the road many months of the year. She had called every month or so to regale her aunt with another wild tale—her overnight train ride from Kiev in a sleeper compartment filled with Slavic men in white undershirts, the air close and heavy with the scent of sausages. Fighting off a pack of feral dogs on the streets of Bucharest with a furled umbrella and handfuls of pea gravel. Taking a wrong turn in the mountains around Sarajevo and ending up on a dirt road plastered with signs warning about the presence of live land mines in the forest on either side.

When she'd gotten Waverly's initial call, Charlie had been in a village in Moldova running a self-defense seminar for middle school girls. She'd had to wait for a colleague to come from Budapest to take her place, and after that it had taken her over thirty-five hours of travel time to reach Columbus, with long layovers in Munich and DC. She'd barely had time to get changed and ready for the funeral and hadn't had a chance to really talk to Waverly until now. They'd exchanged a few texts, but reception was spotty in rural Moldova. She got the voice-mail from Waverly about Aunt Mae's passing the day after it happened and exchanged texts with her sister between flights at the airports, but just basic information—arrival time, funeral service details. Now was the first time they'd been able to talk alone.

"I can't believe she's gone," Charlie said at last, stunned by the realization. "We're orphans twice over."

Waverly pressed her lips together and nodded, not looking up from arranging a platter of chunks of cheese speared with toothpicks festooned with a fringe of colored cellophane. Party toothpicks for a funeral. Charlie helped herself to a cube of cheese.

Twice orphaned. She couldn't quite wrap her mind around the notion. Aunt Mae had been a rock for them, steady and immovable, since the small plane crash that had claimed the lives of their parents a few months before the twins turned thirteen. In the melee of their parents' death and the ensuing ugly lawsuit and custody case among their mother's extended family, the twins had found solace in Aunt Mae's practical, no-nonsense care. Although they were her nephew's children and she'd only seen them once or twice in their lives before they came to live with her, Mae had never wavered in her devotion and duty to the two awkward girls entrusted to her by the court system. To find her absent now was disorienting, like finding a gaping hole where there had always been solidity.

Charlie kept looking up at the doorway, expecting Aunt Mae to come around the corner wearing one of her polyester housedresses, perhaps the mint-green one with the pussy willow pattern. It had been her favorite. If this were someone else's funeral, Mae would have made her signature sour cream dill spread on Triscuits.

"I didn't know . . . it would go so fast." Charlie cleared her throat, wrapping her hands around the mug of coffee. She didn't particularly like coffee and only drank it out of necessity or politeness or to fight jet lag. She was more of a whiskey-straight-up kind of girl, all bite at the front and a warm caress at the finish. She looked down at the contents of the mug and grimaced at the bitter overbrewed Folgers.

Waverly transferred brownies to a plate, arranging them to look better than they actually were. Boxed brownies were fairly foolproof, but Martha Hanson, the neighbor who'd brought them, was a notoriously poor cook.

"It was a surprise to everyone. Aunt Mae had been failing in the last two months." Waverly spoke evenly, concentrating on arranging the hardened brownies. "But I didn't know it would be so quick, not until Jillian texted me."

Jillian was the personal health aide that Waverly had hired to help Aunt Mae as soon as the diagnosis of pancreatic cancer was confirmed.

Aunt Mae had been only seventy-four, spry and feisty.

"Five months." Charlie shook her head in disbelief. "Is that normal?"

Waverly let out an exasperated sigh. "It's cancer. Is anything 'normal'?" She critically examined a homemade cheese ball coated in chipped ham, the offering from Methodist church pianist Florence Walter for every funeral and Christmas party on record. "Nothing says 1979 like a ham-coated cheese ball," she murmured, sliding it onto a plate and fanning Ritz crackers around it.

Her sister's hands were beautiful as they handled the food. It was like watching a commercial for the crackers. Cue the background music and soft lighting.

Stomach growling, Charlie reached across the table and swiped a cracker from the plate, scooping out some of the cheese ball. She was starving; her body was still on European time, and it was past dinnertime in Budapest. She munched the first cracker and took another.

Crystal poked her head into the kitchen. "Hey, folks are getting hungry in here. Food ready yet?"

In reply, Waverly handed her cousin the brownies and the much-maligned cheese ball, sweeping it out from under Charlie's poised cracker.

31

"Start with these," she instructed Crystal, ignoring her sister's sound of protest.

"Hey, have some pity. I don't even live in this country," Charlie argued.

"That's your choice, so don't complain about it," Waverly said tartly, picking up the mini hot dogs. "Besides, you should eat some real food."

Charlie shrugged and popped the plain cracker into her mouth. "Pretty high and mighty for a girl who grew up on Campbell's soup and canned green beans like the rest of us," she teased, crunching the cracker. "Did you make anything for today?"

"Yes. Can you guess?" Waverly asked.

Charlie surveyed the food on the table, her gaze settling on a dense golden cake covered in perfectly shaped whorls of pale golden-brown frosting. "You made 1–2–3–4 cake with browned butter frosting!" she said in surprise. "Aunt Mae's favorite."

It was a touching gesture. Waverly, who could have made anything in the world for the funeral, had stuck with an old, familiar recipe, almost embarrassing in its simplicity. The cake was so named because it contained 1 cup butter, 2 cups sugar, 3 cups flour, and 4 eggs. Aunt Mae had not liked things fancy.

"She would have been seventy-five in November," Waverly said softly. "I made her a cake every year and sent it to her on her birthday. It seemed fitting to make it now."

Charlie tried to swallow around the lump in her throat. "I didn't know you did that," she said.

"Well, the last few years I had one of the kitchen prep girls make it," Waverly amended. "Here, would you like a piece?" She proffered the cake platter and a fork. Charlie nodded and cut a thick slice. She had learned early on never to turn down Waverly's food. There was a good reason her sister's two books of recipes for home entertaining were climbing the sales charts at a fast clip.

In the three years since Charlie had last visited the States, Waverly's career had blossomed remarkably. Now she made the rounds of the morning talk shows and hosted recognizable Hollywood names as guests in her studio kitchen. Just a few months before, Charlie had stumbled upon a YouTube clip of her sister making homemade pickles with Bruce Willis. Waverly Talbot and *Simply Perfect* were fast-rising stars in the food and entertaining circuit—not yet in the top tier with the likes of Rachael Ray and Ina Garten, but gaining ground in brand recognition and viewership.

Just that morning Charlie had passed a life-size cutout of Waverly in the airport bookstore at Dulles. She'd stopped in to see if they had a Faulkner novel to replace the one she'd accidentally left behind in Budapest. No luck, but as she was leaving she turned around and there was Waverly, clad in a canary-yellow apron with a print of little green finches and holding a glossy lemon drop cocktail. Charlie almost didn't recognize her. When she did, she stopped and stared, disconcerted to see that her own twin sister seemed like a stranger.

No one ever guessed that Waverly and Charlie were twins. Sisters perhaps, but never twins. With her pale blond hair, porcelain complexion, and softer curves, Waverly looked more like their mother, while Charlie's lean, athletic build and smattering of freckles called up their father's side of the family.

They were as different in personality as they were in appearance. When their trust funds were finally released to them on their eighteenth birthday, their lives quickly took markedly different paths. On a whim Charlie booked a ticket to South Africa, desiring to retrace her parents' final footsteps. In Africa she found something she had not even known she was searching for. She had not returned to the US except for brief visits every few years. Waverly, meanwhile, won a coveted spot at the Culinary Institute of America, then went on for additional training in Paris. She launched her first show just a year before meeting Andrew and never looked back.

As children Charlie and Waverly had been

able to read each other's thoughts. A quirk of an eyebrow, the flare of a nostril told them all they needed to know about what was going on in the other's head. That was no longer true.

Charlie looked at Waverly in her expensive dress, the curls falling loose at the nape of her neck as she carefully cut the remainder of the 1–2–3–4 cake into symmetrical slices, and drew a complete blank. With a pang she realized she had no idea what her sister was thinking. A thousand choices, some large, some small, had widened the distance between them. At thirty-five, Charlie felt her sister was more of a polite acquaintance than the inseparable other half of a perfectly fitted whole. The realization was both saddening and inevitable. They had brought the distance upon themselves.

Crystal reappeared, and Waverly handed her two more platters. When she was gone, silence fell on the kitchen for a long moment. Charlie took a big bite of cake, the rich browned butter frosting melting on her tongue. She barely noticed the flavor, however, as she thought about the question she'd been wanting to ask since she'd gotten Waverly's voicemail.

"At the end," she asked finally, "did she suffer? Was it peaceful?" She didn't look up, her eyes fixed on the perfectly sculpted whorls of frosting on her slice of cake. She so wanted Waverly to say yes. Aunt Mae had deserved that, to go out easily. Nothing else in her life had been easy.

"I don't know," Waverly said, her voice strangely flat. "I wasn't there." She didn't look up as she sliced a loaf of chocolate chip banana bread and arranged it on a plate in a fan shape.

"But I thought . . ." Charlie stopped in surprise. "I got your voicemail that she had passed. I just assumed you were with her."

Waverly set the plate down with a clatter and gripped the edge of the table, turning her head away. Her shoulders began to shake. It took Charlie a moment to realize what was happening. Waverly was crying. She stared at her sister in shock. The last time she could remember Waverly crying had been at their parents' funeral. Charlie watched her uncomfortably for a long moment, unsure how she should respond.

"Hey," she said finally. "It's okay if you weren't there. You did your best. I'm sure Aunt Mae knew that."

Waverly raised her head, sniffing away the tears, cutting off Charlie's assurance. "I'm not crying about Aunt Mae." She looked away, facing the porcelain farmhouse sink and the old white refrigerator humming shakily beside it. She took a deep breath. "I wasn't there because I lost another baby."

It took a moment for the words to sink in. Another one. Charlie knew there had been others. "Oh, Waverly," she murmured, at a loss for words. If they had been closer, had seen each other more, had shared in each other's lives, would she know what to say? "How far along?" She felt she had to say something, but every phrase seemed the wrong shape.

"Nine weeks, a week longer than the last one." Waverly blew out a breath, trying to get herself under control. "I was starting to believe, to hope that it would work this time." Her hands were balled into fists. "Except it didn't. And now"—she shut her eyes against the sharp pain of recollection—"my doctor said no more tries. My body can't handle any more. So that's it. I can't have a baby." She bit her lip, although her chin quivered. Tears made silver tracks down her cheeks. "So I don't know if it was peaceful or terrible or if Aunt Mae was in pain. I don't know, because I wasn't here."

Charlie sat in stunned silence. She knew Waverly had been desperate for a baby since her first year or two of marriage, but time and time again her sister's body had failed to hold on to the life she conceived. Waverly had stopped talking about the miscarriages after the third, and Charlie had not asked. It seemed too invasive to inquire.

Waverly took a deep breath and blotted carefully below her eyes with a paper napkin from a stack on the table, wiping away the tears without smudging her makeup. She straightened her shoulders and pasted on a smile that gave no hint to the inner grief and turmoil Charlie had glimpsed just seconds before.

Charlie was aware that people always assumed archetypes about the two of them. They saw Waverly—the soft cloud of pale blond hair, the wide doe-like eyes—and they assigned her the role of the weaker, gentler one who needed to be protected. Inversely, they looked at Charlie, single, direct, and independent, living and working in a region of the world still dominated by men, and they assumed the opposite. But the reality was far more complicated. The truth about Waverly was that under that nimbus of soft hair the color of corn silk, behind those eyes the gentle blue of the new-washed spring sky, lay a shrewd businesswoman, a silken glove with a fist of iron. Since their parents' death she had weathered every setback and heartbreak dry-eyed, with a determination that was truly formidable. Both Charlie and Waverly were strong-willed, independent, resilient—character traits they had forged amid the loss of their parents and their drastic change in circumstances. Although they differed in many ways, at their core they shared a common strength and grit.

"There's nothing left to try," Waverly continued after regaining her composure. "So that's it. We're done. I can't have a baby." She looked up at her twin, her gaze open and bleak, as though all hope had been scooped from her world. That look frightened Charlie. She had never seen Waverly so raw, so resigned.

"What about adoption?" Charlie asked, grasping for any idea that might give her sister hope.

"Andrew won't consider it," Waverly said. "He doesn't feel the need for a child the way I do. He has Katie." Andrew had been married before and had a fifteen-year-old daughter who lived most of the year with her mother in Atlanta.

"There's nothing else you can do?" Charlie asked, feeling awkward even asking the question.

Waverly shook her head. "Our only other option would be a surrogate, but the specialists say there's something wrong with me, with my eggs, and I can't imagine another woman carrying a baby that's half of Andrew and none of me. I want to know that a baby is supposed to be ours, that I'm meant to be its mother. I want a connection somehow." She looked up at Charlie, her eyes swimming with unshed tears. "I've longed to be a mother more than anything in the world," she said finally, "but it seems like it just isn't meant to be." She blew out a breath of air, then confessed. "You know the saddest thing? We're here and I should be mourning Aunt Mae, but I'm mourning my own loss instead." She looked down at the crumpled napkin clutched in her hand, her expression sad. "Aunt Mae deserves better than that."

Charlie opened her mouth to reply, to utter some reassurance, but no words came out.

At that moment Pastor Shaw stuck his head around the door.

"Charlotte, Waverly, we're going to have a few minutes where people can share memories of your aunt. We're waiting for you to join us." His soft brown eyes turned down at the corners, and his hair was thinning in the back, making a bald spot the size of a teacup saucer. He gave the sisters a sympathetic look. "You girls all right?"

Waverly nodded, turning quickly away from him. Charlie caught his eye. "Just give us a second," she said. He nodded in understanding and withdrew.

Girls. Charlie smiled ruefully. They were grown women now, successful and strong, but around here they would always be Mae's girls. When they first showed up at Aunt Mae's doorstep on the cusp of adolescence, they were grieving and stunned by the monumental changes in their lives, bereft not only of their parents but of their entire world. Gone were the elite private girls' academy and Joe, their stern-faced driver who picked them up from ballet and classical violin lessons. Gone, too, were the white mansion in Roland Park and the proper Sunday tea with Grandmother Helen, the Boston Brahmin matriarch of their mother's family.

The tiny town of Cooksville, Ohio, was their

father's childhood home. After he left for medical school at Johns Hopkins, he chose to stay and build a life and a successful career in Baltimore. Although he never moved back to Cooksville, he retained a fondness for the humble, working-class town of his childhood. For the girls, however, although their paternal roots were sunk deep in its soil, Cooksville had been a place as foreign as Singapore or Bombay.

In the blink of an eye their privileged, rarified world was replaced by a rural, blue-collar community of people whose lives were markedly different from their own. The first week of deer-hunting season they stared in horror at the carcass of a deer strung up to bleed in their neighbor's front yard. They strained to understand the rural southern Ohio accent, where people instructed them to "warsh up for supper" and where *tin* and *ten* and *pin* and *pen* sounded exactly the same.

Each week they navigated the aisles of Walmart, helping Aunt Mae compare prices and check the sales fliers. They learned the value of thrift—cleaning their dinner plates and counting their pennies. What Waverly missed, she confided to Charlie, was the gleaming granite and stainless steel kitchen of their childhood home and her set of monogrammed baking dishes from a gourmet cooking store in New York City. She longed for Mademoiselle Amelie's ballet studio where she'd been taking lessons for many years.

Charlie didn't mind the financial constraints of their new life, but she struggled with the feeling of geographical limitation. Most residents of Cooksville were born and died within the town limits, their view of the world shaped largely by their small community. Charlie felt hemmed in by the small-town life, aware of a wider world but removed from it. The knowledge made her itchy to break free from Cooksville, to see something bigger. At the first opportunity she had done just that, kicking the Appalachian dust from her heels and setting out for more exotic destinations.

The girls had been welcomed by the community with a practical, unspoken kindness, but even so, they had never really felt at home there. In some fundamental way their sense of home had died with their parents. Once grown, they had built lives for themselves far away from this poor little pocket of the world. Now returning out of necessity, they found themselves embraced once again, welcomed back with the same warmth and kindness, as though they had never left.

"You ready to go?" Charlie asked gently.

Waverly took a deep breath, smoothing her dress, composing herself. "Yes, of course."

They went in together.

CHAPTER 3

Charlie awoke at two in the morning, coming out of the black well of sleep with a suddenness that disoriented her. For a moment she could not place herself. She looked around the room, at the dim outline of the white wardrobe and matching dresser, the little square-paned window where the silver glimmer of moon made an outline on the wood floor. *Aunt Mae's house.* The words floated through her mind, surprising her. For the space of several seconds, she was thrown backward in time, a teenager again in the small gabled room. Was it time to get up for school?

With the thought came a memory so vivid she could taste it—waiting for the lumbering yellow school bus in a light drizzle of rain, the chilly autumn air heavy with the smell of wet brown leaves and woodsmoke. Waverly standing beside her in a mustard-yellow pleated cheerleading skirt, a brown bag lunch in her hand, calling out, "Here's the bus, Charlie. Finally! I can't feel my toes anymore."

Charlie glanced over at the other twin bed, but the white chenille bedspread was smooth and tucked taut across the empty pillow. In an instant she was back in the present. Aunt Mae's death. The funeral the day before. Waverly looking up at her with a desolate expression Charlie had never seen before. "There's nothing left to try," she'd said, tears glistening on her cheeks. "So that's it. We're done. I can't have a baby."

Charlie sighed. It had been a brutal day.

Wide-awake, jet-lagged, and thirsty, she swung her legs over the edge of the bed and grabbed the book she'd been reading before she fell asleep, a dog-eared copy of *The Grapes of Wrath* left over from her high school AP English course. She made her way barefoot down the creaking stairs to the kitchen and flipped on the humming overhead light. She set the book on the table. She always carried a book with her, just in case she got bored or had a travel delay, which happened frequently in her line of work.

She was alone in the house. Waverly and Andrew were ensconced in the Hide-a-Way Inn in town, the only establishment of its kind in tiny Cooksville. It leaned heavily toward animal-head trophies and tartan, a combination that was intended to conjure up a Scottish Highlands vibe but instead managed to look both shabby and tacky at the same time.

Charlie ran a glass of cold well water from the tap, the pipes under the sink groaning in protest as she turned off the faucet. She sat down at the table, now stacked with a tidy set of empty washed Tupperware containers labeled by owner, waiting to be picked up. She took a long swallow of water, savoring the familiar taste of the minerals.

For a moment she was lulled by the surroundings into a sense of contentment, but it was followed closely by a sharp pang of grief when she remembered who was missing. Aunt Mae didn't feel dead, just absent, as though she'd run down to the basement to fetch some canned beets but would return any minute. Charlie half expected to see her stumping up the creaking stairs, Mason jar in hand.

Charlie drained the water in one long gulp and got up to refill her tumbler. On the counter by the sink sat a stack of unopened mail and two scratch-off lotto tickets, unscratched. Mae's next-door neighbor Ed Waters must have brought them to her before she died. Charlie picked up the tickets.

Her aunt had possessed a firm and deep-seated belief that one day the Good Lord would pay her back for all her earthly trials by letting her win the lottery.

"I don't need to win much," she'd claimed, "but one day I'm going to win me enough to go to Hawaii. I'm going to sit on one of those black sand beaches and drink piña coladas out of a coconut and watch the sun set over the Pacific

Ocean." She set aside five dollars a week for the tickets she favored—games like 10X the Money or Emerald Riches. She never made it to Hawaii. Waverly had been planning to take her to their time share in Kauai for her seventy-fifth birthday as a surprise, but after the cancer diagnosis Aunt Mae had declined more rapidly than anyone had expected and there had been no time. Charlie frowned, saddened by the memory.

Aunt Mae kept a bottle of bottom-shelf bourbon in the cupboard behind the flour container and took two fingers of it on ice every Friday evening when she scratched off the tickets, waiting to see if her luck would change. On a whim Charlie opened the cupboard and rooted around, finding the mostly empty bottle of Rebel Yell. She poured herself two fingers of the stuff, dropped in an ice cube, and took it back to the table with the lotto tickets. She took a sip, grimacing at the raw taste, and then scratched off the lotto tickets. First Cash Blast and then Gold Fish. No winners.

"Well, maybe you've already won the jackpot," Charlie murmured. Despite ten years of Sunday school at All Saints Episcopal Church in Baltimore as a child, Charlie remained mostly agnostic about the concept of heaven. But if there was one, she was sure Aunt Mae was enjoying herself somewhere in the Great Beyond. Mae had not been a saint by any textbook definition, but she had been pious in her own earthy, salty way.

She'd believed that generosity was the marrow of humanity and that the greatest goals in life were to sacrifice for others and to be faithful and uncomplaining no matter what the Good Lord saw fit to give you. Her favorite story in the Bible was about the widow who gave two small copper coins at the temple. Rich people in front of the widow gave large sums out of their abundance, but she gave all she had to live on. Aunt Mae had taken that story to heart.

"Whatever the Good Lord puts in your hand you give back to others," she'd told the twins more times than they could count. It was the Gospel According to Aunt Mae.

Her words had been good precepts to live by, ones that had benefited Charlie and Waverly far more than they realized in their teen years. Only now in adulthood could Charlie see the value in them, see what she and Waverly had gained by those simple virtues. She could only guess what it must have cost Aunt Mae to stick to them so faithfully.

Charlie raised her glass in a silent salute and took a sip, closing her eyes against the burn of the liquor. She was struck with a sudden regret. Why had she not come sooner, when Aunt Mae had still been living, standing in the kitchen in her blue terry cloth house slippers, watching the television and imagining herself on that black sand beach with a tropical drink in her hand?

Why had she come only now, when it was too late, when she was alone in this house with only the memory and shadow of Mae?

"I'm sorry," she said aloud, penitent. "I should have come sooner." She didn't know if Aunt Mae could hear her, but she had to say it all the same.

"I just . . . Work was busy," she said, aware that those words rang hollow, both true and now irrelevant. Work was always busy. That was no excuse. She had no excuse.

She knew Aunt Mae had not expected her to come, and somehow that made it worse. A woman who had sacrificed as much as she had, raising two orphaned girls through their tumultuous teen years, working a tedious shift job at the local mattress factory just to keep them in cereal and tampons and winter coats. And she would not have expected them to come. Charlie tightened her hand around the tumbler, struck by a sharp sorrow. It was too late. She could not make this right.

Somehow time had flown by and she had not even realized it. In seventeen years she'd returned only a handful of times. When she left South Africa for good six years ago, shattered and disillusioned and desperate for a change, she had not returned to Ohio. She had gone instead to Budapest, and the years in Central Europe had sped by without her even really counting them. How long had it been since she'd touched

American soil? Two years? Three? She couldn't quite remember.

Restless with guilt and suddenly ravenous, Charlie jumped up and rummaged through the refrigerator. It was stocked with leftovers from the funeral, but she passed them by, looking for something simple and familiar. A few slices of American cheese sitting in their cellophane sleeves caught her eye. Beside them sat a loaf of sliced white bread.

With a sudden dart of nostalgia, Charlie pictured sitting at the kitchen table with Waverly on school nights, eating grilled cheese sandwiches on discount white bread, dipping the edges in creamy bowls of canned tomato soup, watching *Wheel of Fortune* with Aunt Mae as she stood at the stove pressing a plastic spatula into the tops of the sandwiches to make the cheese melt faster.

"Try an *H*," Aunt Mae would advise the contestants and then shake her head when they chose an *R* or *L*. "Of course she didn't get it," she'd mutter as she turned the sandwiches. "Should have bought a vowel."

Charlie pulled the bread and cheese from the shelf, snagging the plastic tub of Kroger-brand margarine as she closed the door. At the stove she heated a small skillet and buttered the outside of two slices, layering two squares of cheese on the bottom slice. She found the plastic spatula and pressed down on the top of the sandwich. It gave a satisfying sizzle as the bread began to fry.

How many years had it been since someone had made a grilled cheese sandwich for her, frying the bread so that it didn't burn but turned crispy and golden, layering the American cheese two deep and melting it just so?

"You got to butter the bread all the way to the edges like this," Aunt Mae had said. "That's the secret." It had been a little thing, but somehow it had meant everything, Charlie realized. She bit her lip, thinking of Aunt Mae at the stove night after night, cooking for the girls after a long day on her feet at the factory. One at a time her aunt's little acts of kindness might seem insignificant— a grilled cheese sandwich, a bowl of poached eggs in milk over buttered saltines when one of the girls caught a chill. Those actions were like copper pennies, small enough to be overlooked, but all together they were the currency of life. Charlie had not seen it until now.

Standing at the stove in the shabby, familiar kitchen, her grilled cheese sandwich browning too quickly at the edges as the cheese slowly melted in the pan, Charlie felt a piercing sense of loss, a longing so strong she almost choked on it, a longing for someone to take care of her, to smooth the hair back from her forehead and check for fever, to make poached eggs in milk and pour it over buttered saltines.

She was not only longing for Aunt Mae, Charlie

realized, but for her mother, gone more than twenty years, for her pale, cool hand on Charlie's brow. There was no one to come home to now. Aunt Mae was dead, and Waverly . . .

Charlie felt another sharp pang of regret when she thought of Waverly. She missed her sister, she realized, missed the closeness they had once shared.

"My two little peas in a pod," their mother had called them fondly. Two peas in a pod. Charlie had not thought of that nickname in years.

As she slid the slightly scorched sandwich onto a plate and sat down at the table, she felt the distance keenly for the first time in a long time. Although Waverly was sleeping just a few miles down the road, tucked up at the Hide-a-Way Inn, she might as well have been sleeping on the moon. But what could Charlie do? She could not turn back the clock on their relationship. Their lives were an ocean apart. She had no idea how to bring them closer together.

She took a bite of her sandwich, satisfied as the crunch of the fried bread gave way to rich, melted cheese. Waverly wouldn't approve of any part of this sandwich. Charlie could hear her sister's voice in her head, not Waverly's smooth, slightly sexy *Simply Perfect* voice, but her scolding one, the one she reserved for her loved ones.

"That is all just plastic food," Waverly said disapprovingly. Charlie glanced at her sandwich and couldn't disagree. She knew it was plastic food, but she didn't care.

"This is pure comfort," she told the imaginary Waverly, her words gooey with melted cheese.

Charlie pictured Waverly, her beautiful, willful sister who didn't know how to take no for an answer, who was used to aiming for something and achieving it through sheer determination and perseverance. Waverly seemingly had the perfect life—a glamorous career; a handsome, successful husband; a huge house on the Connecticut shore; even a sailboat—but not the one thing she really wanted most: a baby. Charlie didn't think she herself had a maternal bone in her body, but Waverly had always wanted to be a mother. What must it mean to her, to be denied the thing she most desired? When they were children Waverly had swaddled and nursed and carried her Cabbage Patch Kid with her in a tiny pink satin pram while Charlie had taken hers adventuring in the woods behind their stately house and then left it out in the rain.

Taking another bite of her sandwich, Charlie sighed and shifted in the hard kitchen chair. She was not by nature particularly introspective. She leaned more toward practicality and action. The quiet of the house unnerved her, made her long for something to do. She reached instinctively for her book, then set it down unopened. Wasn't that the problem, that she had been too busy to see what was really important? And now it was too late. Aunt Mae was gone.

Charlie finished the sandwich, poured another finger of bourbon, and forced herself to sit still and take stock for the first time in a long while.

What did her life consist of now? she asked herself. A few dozen boxes of books, a rented apartment in Budapest, and, if she were honest, an occupation that allowed her to constantly improve other peoples' lives but not really build one of her own. Her entire existence could be packed into a few suitcases. She wanted it that way. By traveling light she had less to lose.

The memory of what she had lost in Johannesburg was still stark after more than six years, seared into her consciousness—a heartbreaking mixture of good intentions and failure, the still-bitter taste of burnt idealism sharp on her tongue. She had taken the job in Budapest because it was useful and she was good at it, although it was not work she was passionate about. It was good enough. Her life was good enough.

But now, sitting in her dead aunt's kitchen at two in the morning, Charlie was regretting her choices. She was not frightened of being alone. She had lived with the dull ache of isolation for six years since moving to Budapest, drifting through a culture not her own. It had been her choice—the disconnection, a benign numbness she really did not mind. She liked the utter control she had over her life, her ability to pack a suitcase at a moment's notice and go anywhere. She liked living with few connections and few constraints. But there had always been something to come back to. Aunt Mae had acted as a touch point of sorts. Now that she was gone, Charlie felt strangely vulnerable. She had no anchor anymore, no center from which to arc away, knowing she could always return.

She swirled the bourbon around in her glass. She could not bring Aunt Mae back, could not turn back the clock and be fifteen again, sitting at this table watching the contestants spin the wheel and buy a vowel. "Any fool can see what that phrase is. It's 'a blessing in disguise.' " Aunt Mae shook her head as the contestants looked puzzled. While Vanna White turned the letters, Aunt Mae turned the sandwiches four times so that they browned evenly and didn't burn.

Those days were gone. Charlie had left them behind by her own volition. They would never come again. Aunt Mae was gone. Only Waverly was left, and she felt so far away.

Well, don't just sit there feeling sorry for yourself. Do something about it. It was Aunt Mae's voice, as clear as though she were sitting across the table. Charlie looked up, startled, half expecting to see her aunt sitting across from her, but the kitchen was empty.

"Like what?" she asked cautiously, casting a glance at the remaining bourbon in her glass. Just how much had she drunk?

There was no answer.

"Like what?" she asked again. What could she possibly do now to erase the years and distance, to bring back her sister, to make amends to Aunt Mae? What could she do to create a center to her world again?

Whatever the Good Lord puts in your hand you give back to others. Again Aunt Mae's voice, repeating her well-worn words to live by. Charlie furrowed her brow, trying to decipher just what she had that could be beneficial to Waverly. She didn't have time for the copper pennies of life, the tiny gestures of affection and care that built slowly over time. She and Waverly led lives that were too different, too far apart. If she wanted her sister back, she needed something big.

And then a thought popped into her head, bright and fleeting as a spark of electricity, and just as shocking. She could give Waverly a baby.

Charlie laughed, almost dismissing the notion out of hand. It was crazy. But then she paused, considering the idea. As far as she knew, she had two good ovaries she had no intention of using for herself. What if she offered to be a surrogate and carry a baby for Waverly? What if Charlie could give a gift so big that it would mend the years of silence and distance between them?

What if she could make them a family again?

The thought was terrifying and a little thrilling. It made sense to her in some instinctual way. She knew there were a multitude of things to consider if she went forward with this notion— the practicalities of work and geography and physiology—but she didn't bother to think through the details immediately. Those would come later. She just went with her gut. This was right; she could feel it.

"Okay, Aunt Mae," she murmured, tossing back the last of the bourbon. "Let's see if we can put these ovaries to good use after all."

CHAPTER 4

The next morning at the bustling Early Bird Café in downtown Cooksville, Charlie planned to drop her bombshell of an idea on Waverly. It was just the two of them at breakfast. Andrew was on an early-morning call with London and had stayed back at the inn.

The café was crowded, but Barbara, the long-time waitress at the Early Bird, had managed to clear a table for two near the open kitchen just for them. Waverly was a hometown celebrity in Cooksville. She even had a Cooksville fan club, a group of retired ladies who called themselves the Perfectettes and FedExed Waverly a pineapple upside-down cake on her birthday every year.

The sisters ordered, and a few moments later Barbara brought their food, well ahead of anyone else's in the restaurant. Waverly's had been garnished with a radish rose perched on a bed of cucumber slices carved into leaf shapes. She thanked Barbara with a gracious smile, and then as soon as the waitress moved on to another table, carefully moved the lopsided embellishments to the side of her plate.

Charlie quirked a smile. "Oh, the perks of being a celebrity," she observed.

The café was warm and thick with the scent of frying breakfast meat and pancake syrup. In the background a country music station played hits from the nineties—Tanya Tucker and George Strait warbling plaintively behind the clatter of plates.

Charlie tucked into her Coming Home breakfast platter, scooping up a fried egg and a bite of maple bacon, and considered how to introduce her grand idea to her sister. She noticed Waverly eying her enormous plate of bacon, sausages, fried eggs, and waffles with unveiled jealousy. Waverly had ordered two poached eggs and a fruit plate with a side of cottage cheese and a cup of green tea. As fraternal twins they did not share the same metabolism. Charlie had always been lean and wiry no matter what she ate, while Waverly had softer curves and had to watch her weight carefully.

Charlie gestured to her plate. "Help yourself," she said, her mouth full of egg. She offered a slice of thick-cut bacon to her sister.

Waverly sighed and sipped her tea. "No, you got the fast metabolism in the family. I have to look at myself on television, and I look better without bacon around my middle."

Charlie shrugged and poured a generous helping of maple syrup onto her waffles. She glanced at her sister, who was slicing her cantaloupe into perfect bite-size pieces. Maybe it was best just to come right out and say it. She took a deep breath. "I've been doing some thinking since Aunt Mae's funeral," she said. "I want to have a baby for you."

Waverly froze, a spoonful of cottage cheese and cantaloupe halfway to her mouth. "You what?" She put the spoon down very slowly, cottage cheese curds falling to the plate below.

"I want to have a baby for you," Charlie repeated slowly and distinctly, as though Waverly were hard of hearing.

Waverly had gone very still. "Is this a joke?" she demanded, her tone indignant.

"No," Charlie insisted, a little piqued that Waverly would think she would joke about such a serious matter. "I have two good ovaries, as far as I know. I might as well put them to use. I mean, we'll have to get everything checked out medically, obviously, just to make sure everything's in good working order. But if it is, I'll carry a baby for you."

Waverly just stared, unblinking, as though she'd been turned to stone. Her face was blanched of all color.

"Everything all right, girls?" Barbara stopped at their table. "I think word got out that you're here. There's a TV crew coming through the door." She nodded toward the entrance.

Charlie glanced over to the door. Indeed, a cameraman and a reporter were headed straight for them. The redhead wearing a fuchsia suit and holding a microphone looked slightly familiar, and in a moment Charlie placed her. Jessica Archer. Head cheerleader of the Cooksville Wildcats their senior year of high school. If Charlie recalled correctly, Jessica and Waverly had competed both for that position and for prom queen. Jessica won head cheerleader; Waverly was crowned queen. Neither had been particularly fond of defeat or of each other.

"Look sharp," she murmured. "We've got company, and it's a blast from the past."

Waverly turned to see Jessica headed straight toward her, and in half a second she transformed, slipping instantly into her *Simply Perfect* persona. She straightened, brushing her hair back over her shoulder, and pasted on a gracious smile.

"We're not done with this discussion," Waverly said through gritted teeth, her smile bright and unwavering. "And for the record, I think you're crazy." Then she turned to the approaching news crew with practiced ease.

"Good morning, I'm Jessica Archer for Channel 9, your only local news station for Athens County." Apparently already on the air, Jessica maneuvered herself to neatly block Charlie from the camera and focus her attention on Waverly.

Charlie scooted her chair away from the table a

little, sat back, and watched the interchange with amusement.

"I'm here this morning with our own local Food Network star Waverly Talbot. And may I say she is looking simply perfect." Jessica tittered at her own joke. The camera swung from Jessica to Waverly, who smiled and gave a little nod as though she'd been expecting to be ambushed at breakfast, indeed that she welcomed the attention. Only Charlie noticed the tightness at the corners of her smile.

"And what brings Cooksville's very own celebrity chef to the Early Bird Café this fine fall morning?" Jessica trilled.

Waverly waved away the compliment gracefully. "Just enjoying a healthy breakfast to start my day off right," she said. "It's always a pleasure to be back in Cooksville."

Charlie smirked at the blatant lie, and Waverly shot her a sideways warning look.

"And how is Ernie's cooking this morning?" Jessica asked, shoving the microphone into Waverly's face, so close her lips brushed the foam cover.

Waverly backed away a few inches. "Like coming home," she said with a glance at her sister's breakfast platter. Charlie chuckled.

"Well, word on the street is that *Simply Perfect* is now ranked in the top one hundred shows on the Food Network." Jessica smiled sweetly, emphasizing the number *one hundred,* and Charlie thought her tone held a hint of malice. So, the old high school rivalry might not exactly be dead.

"Number nineteen, to be exact," Waverly replied just as sweetly.

Charlie looked around the café. A small crowd was beginning to form outside the door, locals peering through the large plate glass window to see what the television van parked outside was all about. Every patron in the restaurant was watching the exchange in fascination, their forks poised motionless over their plates.

"Well, Waverly Talbot, we wish you and *Simply Perfect* all the best. Perhaps this is the year you'll finally outrank *The Pioneer Woman.* We're rooting for you, although those biscuits of hers are hard to beat." Jessica turned to the camera after delivering this zinger and signed off. "This is Jessica Archer with Channel 9, your only local news source for Athens County." She closed the segment and lowered her microphone, then turned back to Waverly. The cameraman lowered his camera and fiddled with the settings.

"What brings you back to little old Cooksville, Waverly?" Jessica asked with a smile as cold as an ice cube. "A special occasion?"

Waverly met her gaze with an equal lack of warmth. "A death in the family," she said calmly, taking a sip of green tea.

"I . . . hadn't heard," Jessica stammered, having the grace to look embarrassed.

Charlie scooted her chair back to the table, edging around the reporter, and speared two bites of her now cold waffles. Waverly turned back to her own breakfast, and Jessica stood beside their table awkwardly for a moment.

"Well, we really should go. Come on, Kevin." Jessica gestured for the cameraman to follow her. She gripped her microphone. "We're covering a landmark city council meeting on waste management at ten," she told Waverly. "Tune in tonight on channel nine to see your interview. If it doesn't get bumped by something more important."

"Like waste management," Charlie offered around a mouthful of waffle.

Jessica had barely cleared the door when Waverly rounded on Charlie.

"What do you mean you want to have a baby for me?" she demanded, leaning in so she could not be heard by the other diners around them.

Charlie took a sip of orange juice, surprised by Waverly's reaction. Charlie had assumed, deep down, that her sister would be grateful for the offer, or delighted, or both. She'd imagined her disbelief melting to joy, the distance of the past years fading away in the light of her gratitude. But Waverly didn't look grateful. She looked borderline furious. Her mouth was pursed like a pink prune.

"Order up!" Ernie yelled from the kitchen. Barbara brushed past them, her arms laden with plates of biscuits and sausage gravy.

Charlie leaned closer as well. "It makes sense, doesn't it?" she urged. "You said you couldn't use a surrogate that would be half of Andrew and none of you. Well, I'm as close as you can possibly get without being you. We can use a sperm donor if that would make it feel less weird, you know, with Andrew being my brother-in-law and all. Let me do this for you. I'll make a baby for you, and you can raise it." She sat back and reached for her orange juice.

Waverly narrowed her eyes and stared at Charlie for a long moment. "We're not talking about growing carrots or cucumbers, you know," she said tightly. "This is a person you're talking about making. Do you have any notion what this entails?"

Charlie shrugged. "Not really, but that's okay. A stranger would do it for money. Why can't I do this for my own twin sister?"

Waverly poured more hot water onto her green tea leaves and squeezed a lemon wedge into the cup. Her brow was furrowed, a sign that she was deep in thought. She was trying to act brusque and businesslike, but Charlie could see a hint of longing beginning to soften the corners of her mouth.

Charlie took a deep breath, trying to embed

into her memory the scent of hot coffee and frying bacon and a wisp of clean, cold air when a customer opened the door. Soon she would be back to the smell of old paving stones and bus exhaust, baking apple strudel and urine, smells that had also come to be familiar. But these scents awakened memories long dormant. It smelled like her teenage years.

"Why?" Waverly finally asked. "Why would you do this?" She searched Charlie's face as though trying to delve past her words to the deeper meaning beneath them.

Charlie leaned back in her chair and considered her response.

"Do you remember the day we went to court, the day the judge assigned us to Aunt Mae?" she asked.

After their parents' death the girls had been thrust into the middle of a nasty family feud among their mother's kin, used as pawns in a convoluted war involving money and power and their dead parents' estate. Their father had no family to speak of. His parents were dead, and his only brother, Uncle Billy, was a kind but absentminded confirmed bachelor and not a suitable candidate for the girls' guardian. Uncle Billy had watched helplessly as the twins were fought over like a scrap of meat, but he had not been able to offer any practical solution. The feud ultimately landed the participating family members in court with a judge tasked with assigning custody of the girls and sorting out the entire sordid mess.

"I was terrified that the judge wouldn't like us and that we'd end up in foster care. I was so afraid they'd separate us." Waverly looked pained at the recollection. "What made you think of that?"

"I was just remembering something Aunt Mae said to us that day. We still thought we might have to go live with Aunt Audrey and Uncle Stephen." Charlie frowned, remembering the terrible uncertainty of that time. No one on their mother's side had been particularly warm or engaging, but their mother's sister, the human icicle, was the worst. She had only wanted custody of the girls as a way to access their property holding and inheritance, which was sizable. "It was right before we went into the courtroom. Aunt Mae told us, 'You girls stick close together, you hear? Family's the only tie that don't break.' "

"Sounds like something she would say," Waverly agreed. She was ignoring the remainder of her breakfast, focusing all of her attention on Charlie.

Aunt Mae had shown up at the trial unexpectedly, alerted to the situation by Uncle Billy. She had no interest in the family squabble, but had driven from Ohio to Maryland in her dyspeptic blue Chevy Chevette just to support the girls, whom she had only met a handful of times. After interviewing all members of the family, the judge surprised everyone with his ruling. He awarded custody to Aunt Mae but left the handling of the estate to their uncle Stephen, an attorney.

The judge had meant well, and his ruling had removed the girls from all the power plays and family drama over their parents' money and placed them in a stable and loving, albeit completely unfamiliar home, but it had unforeseen consequences. As soon as the court case was over, Stephen refused to release any funds for the care and maintenance of the girls. He made sure to keep the beautiful house, the hefty bank account, and all the tangible assets within his control.

Aunt Mae had neither the money nor the business savvy to fight him, and so she took the girls and raised them on her own dime. By the time the twins turned eighteen and were entitled to the estate, there was little left. Their uncle had squandered most of it on bad business decisions and underhanded dealings. The only things that remained were their trust funds, protected by law until the girls came of age.

Charlie leaned forward. " 'Family's the only tie that don't break.' Aunt Mae didn't just say the phrase, she lived by it. She took us in and cobbled us together into a family of sorts, the three of us. And now she's gone. That leaves only you and me. And we aren't exactly living in the same universe." Charlie looked down at her plate and swirled a bite of waffle around in a pool of butter. "I don't want this to be the end of our family, of us," she admitted. "I want her to be right."

Waverly dabbed at her mouth with a thin paper napkin and met Charlie's eyes. "Are you sure you want to do this?" Her tone was sharp and serious. "I don't know anyone else who would even dream of doing such a thing for me."

Charlie was not sure, but she knew she was going to do it anyway. She felt a sick jolt in her stomach as though she were about to take a swan dive off a cliff. She'd felt that way before, but she'd been standing on the Victoria Falls Bridge above the Zambezi River on the border between Zimbabwe and Zambia, about to bungee jump straight down to where crocodiles circled in the river more than 350 feet below. She was not a particularly impetuous person, but she could be bold when she knew something was right. She had that feeling now.

Still, she hesitated for a long moment. She was signing a blank check with no way to know the outcome, how it might change her life or Waverly's. She thought of Aunt Mae, lying newly buried in the Oakview Cemetery.

She imagined her sitting at the table with them, chewing a slice of maple bacon and listening in to the conversation. What would she say about this rash promise? Charlie couldn't decide if she'd think her niece was crazy or if she'd be proud.

"I'm sure," Charlie said finally, diving headfirst into thin air.

CHAPTER 5

How's your puzzle going, darling?" Waverly asked, peering over at Andrew as he methodically worked through the *New York Times* crossword. She settled beside him in their sagging queen-size bed, trying to avoid the dip in the middle of the mattress. Andrew *hmm*ed absently but didn't look up, his forehead creased as he tried to decipher a clue. Waverly and Andrew were spending a quiet evening in their junior suite at the Hide-a-Way Inn. Misnomers abounded at this particular establishment; the Double Comfort bed was anything but comfortable, and the only nod to a suite were the two chairs and small pine table in one corner of the room with a Mr. Coffee and two white diner mugs perched on top.

Outside the sliding glass doors all was dark and quiet. Their room was lit by lamps attached to the wall on either side of the bed, casting pools of yellow light onto the shiny red-and-black tartan comforter. On the opposite wall, mounted on a wooden shield, hung a taxidermied deer head sporting an impressive rack of antlers. Waverly tried to ignore the glassy eyes that seemed to follow her wherever she went in the room. It was decidedly creepy.

She tucked her legs under the comforter on her side of the bed and peeled the foil from a snack-size pudding cup, scooping up a cold, sweet spoonful of pudding with the little silver teaspoon she always carried in her purse. It was one of the set from her parents' wedding silver. The entire set had been gone by the time the twins reached adulthood, sold by Uncle Stephen to pay off some debt, but Waverly had the single teaspoon left. She'd been eating a bowl of the nanny's home-made rice pudding in her bedroom the day before her parents died, and when she hastily packed up a suitcase with her favorite things before leaving with Aunt Mae for Cooksville, she'd taken the spoon with her. It was her favorite keepsake, a memento of a happier time. She savored the spoonful of pudding, letting it roll over her tongue. Butterscotch, her favorite.

"Hmm . . . a three-letter word for heat," Andrew murmured absently. He usually did the crossword over breakfast, finishing it most days before he'd drained his second cup of coffee, but they'd spent most of the day sorting out matters of Aunt Mae's estate.

Waverly didn't bother to guess the answer. Andrew and Charlie were the linguists in the family. She could never beat either of them when it came to word games, and she didn't really want to try. Her husband and her sister had a long-running Scrabble war between them, playing a game or two on the rare occasions Charlie returned from Europe, complete with gourmet prizes for the winner. Waverly never joined in, preferring to flip through cookbooks or research new show ideas rather than be soundly beaten by both of them.

Besides, Waverly had other things on her mind at the moment. Her sister's offer was tantalizing. She could feel the stirring of hope in her breast, and it made her nervous. Hope was a dangerous emotion. She had learned that the hard way.

Looking for distraction, she clicked on the television and searched through the channels until she found the Food Network, her home turf. *Cupcake Wars* was just finishing. She settled back against the headboard, setting the now empty plastic carton of butterscotch to the side, and carefully peeled the foil from the top of a vanilla. She scooped up a heaping spoonful, enjoying its bland creaminess.

It was a dirty little secret that *Simply Perfect*'s Waverly Talbot loved grocery store pudding. She kept a stash on hand at home, hiding the little plastic tubs in the back of her dry goods cabinet as though they were pornography, shameful and yet titillating somehow. It was pure comfort food. When the girls were in high school, if there was a coupon in the weekly flier and Kroger was having a sale, Aunt Mae would buy the pudding cups as a treat, tucking a cup into their school lunches as a surprise. So little had been happy in those early years that the little plastic cups had been a bright spot for Waverly. Vanilla, double chocolate, or pistachio—they all tasted like nostalgia to her now.

"Ire!" Andrew exclaimed, looking over the top of his reading glasses at the TV and then penciling in the answer. Waverly scooped another spoonful of pudding, letting it slide off the spoon onto her tongue little by little, savoring it as she watched a contestant frantically frost a seemingly endless supply of cupcakes while her teammate tossed edible glitter on dozens of already frosted ones.

Waverly turned her attention from the show and gave her husband a sidelong glance. She wanted to tell him about Charlie's proposal. But what was the best way to go about it? She should wait until he finished his puzzle and she had his attention. She was afraid to speak the idea aloud, nervous that the tiny flutter of hope would be extinguished by Andrew's clinical practicality.

She took another spoonful of pudding. With his crisp, pin-striped blue cotton pajamas, his close-cropped hair, and clean profile, Andrew reminded Waverly of a man from another era, the fifties perhaps, an investment banker for the Rat Pack.

He was the CEO for the New York branch of a large and venerable investment firm, seven years older than Waverly, with hair a distinguished gray at the temples and a lean physique he toned playing golf and tennis. Born and raised in London, he had finished university at Cambridge and chosen a job in international banking. After working for a few years in London, he'd been transferred to New York. He'd never returned to the UK. He was bicultural now, with a smooth, plummy Oxbridge accent and a penchant for a pint of Old Hooky bitter, but with a love for the Yankees and the *New York Times*. They'd met at a charity gala for lung cancer research. Waverly was a guest host for one of the tables, and Andrew had sat at her right, his manner sweet and a little shy. By the end of the night, he'd asked her to go sailing, and she had accepted immediately, sensing a kind, intelligent soul under his reserved exterior.

Waverly knew what people had thought of them at first. That Andrew was getting a trophy wife and in return Waverly had snagged a sugar daddy to support her dreams of stardom. Her entertaining empire was still just a struggling local access show back then, and Andrew was a recently divorced man. But the skeptics were wrong. Theirs was a love match, not a marriage of convenience. Andrew was steady, thorough, a good man with a dry sense of humor and a quiet confidence that was unshaken by his wife's rising career. Waverly leaned on him for support and strength. He was her rock, and she needed him in a way she did not let herself need anyone else. In turn, Waverly added the sparkle and glamour to Andrew's predictable and often high-stress life, coddling and prodding him to enjoy a world outside of his job and routine. There had been ups and downs in the past eight years, but overall they shared a happy marriage. They were partners, equals, each other's closest ally.

"Here's one for you," Andrew remarked. "Slow-cooked Italian dish. Two words. Four letters each."

"Hmm, I have no idea," Waverly demurred, reaching for another pudding cup, this one double chocolate. She was going to have to eat plain salad tomorrow to make up for three pudding cups in one evening, but they were helping to calm her nerves.

Andrew paused, considering the clue. "Maybe Charlie will know. I'll ask her in the morning."

Cupcake Wars ended and a rerun of *The Pioneer Woman* came on. Waverly frowned but didn't change the channel as Ree Drummond promised to show viewers how to make a simple and filling hamburger soup fit for ranchers and hungry teenagers. Waverly made a *humph* sound. Ree Drummond, the warm and down-to-earth star, was Waverly's personal nemesis. She thought the redhead's flat midwestern vowels and slow-talking, *aw shucks* demeanor seemed a little rehearsed. Waverly had sat beside her at a charity event once and could have sworn that Ree's accent was actually that of a regular New Yorker. What's worse, *The Pioneer Woman* had snagged the weekly Food Network spot Waverly had been hoping for.

Waverly licked her spoon slowly, tuning out Ree rhapsodizing about the homey hamburger soup, and tried to calculate how best to broach the topic at hand with Andrew. It was a touchy subject for both of them after so many years and so many failed attempts. They had weathered the storm year after year, but every miscarriage, every failed try, had taken a toll on their relationship.

In truth, Waverly suspected that Andrew wanted to lay the idea of a baby to rest and set about enjoying their childless lives. He had never said it, and she had never asked him. She was afraid to face his honest answer, afraid that it would compel her to give up her dearest dream. She could not let it go. She was supposed to be a mother, longed to be a mother with an ache that sometimes felt overwhelming. It was a basic and instinctual desire, this visceral hunger to hold a child to her breast and breathe in the innocent smell of that little warm head, knowing that the baby was hers to love and care for. Sometimes she felt that the longing for a baby was so strong it might pull her heart from her chest.

She scraped out the last bit of pudding from the cup and tapped the spoon against her teeth. On the television Ree was stirring oregano and cayenne pepper into the soup, delivering instructions with her typical slow smile. Waverly frowned at the screen.

"Waverly, what is on your mind?" Andrew asked without looking up from his paper, penciling in another word.

Waverly turned to him, startled. "What do you mean?"

He turned, peering at her over the top of his reading glasses, and raised an eyebrow, his mouth quirking with the hint of a smile. "You've eaten three pudding cups in the last twenty minutes and you're sitting over there fidgeting and boring a hole in my head instead of watching that gingery woman make soup." He put his paper down and regarded her patiently. "So what is going on in that lovely head of yours, my dear?"

Waverly clicked off the TV and turned to her husband, her heart in her throat. What if he said no? She had to find the words to show him that this could be the answer to their many years of loss, the key to her heart's deepest desire.

"Charlie made an incredibly generous offer to us today at breakfast," she said slowly, watching

77

Andrew's face carefully. "She wants to be our surrogate."

Andrew looked puzzled. "Our what?"

"She's willing to carry a baby for us, since I can't attempt another pregnancy." Waverly looked at Andrew, her eyes shining. "This could be our chance to have a child, darling. It could actually work this time."

Andrew slowly laid down his pencil and the newspaper and met her eyes, his own grave. "I thought we were done with this," he said quietly.

She felt the tension rise up instantly between them—all the frustration and sadness and fatigue of the past eight years. So many tries and so many failures. She folded her arms across her rose silk robe, across her empty belly. "We never said we were finished," she countered, a touch belligerently.

Andrew sighed, a tired sound that frightened her more than if he'd been angry. "But your doctors said we had to be. They said it was the end, that this last time was the last try."

"And now Charlie's given us another chance," Waverly said. "Just think about it, Andrew," she urged. "Doesn't it seem right?"

He took off his glasses and folded them up, massaging the bridge of his nose. "Are you actually considering this?"

Waverly hesitated. "Yes, I am." Her voice caught and she stopped, swallowing hard. She struggled to keep her tone steady. She wanted to discuss this calmly, to help Andrew see all the reasons it could work. But in the end she just spoke the words that bubbled up from her heart.

"I can't give up, Andrew. I can't let this be the end. I need a baby. I'm supposed to be a mother. I know it. I've never been more sure of anything in my life." She reached over and took his hand, touching the heavy platinum wedding ring, lacing her fingers through his. "Please," she pleaded quietly. "Promise me you'll at least consider it? For me?"

He didn't meet her eyes, but finally he nodded, his mouth set in a stoic line. "If it really means that much to you . . . I'll consider it," he said. "I'm not saying yes, but we can explore the possibility."

"Thank you," Waverly whispered fervently, on impulse planting a kiss on his knuckles. "This could be the best thing we've ever done."

Andrew reached over and rested his hand on her head for a moment, stroking her soft curls. "I hope you're right," he said quietly, his tone weighty with resignation. "I hope you're right."

While an elated Waverly headed off to shower, Andrew sat for a long moment on his side of the bed, unsure what to do after his wife's pronouncement. Charlie had offered to carry a baby for them? Andrew shook his head in bewilderment. He didn't even know quite what to say. It seemed like such a drastic measure, to have another woman carry their child, even if she was Waverly's twin.

He was surprised Charlie had even suggested it. Frankly, she'd never struck him as the maternal type. She was more of a lone wolf, strong and independent. He would have bet ten pounds sterling on her passing her childbearing years without a backward glance. But this idea of theirs . . . He sighed, feeling immensely weary and a little ambushed.

He got up and rummaged through the mini bar, coming up with a small bottle of Famous Grouse Blended Scotch Whiskey. He thought longingly of the elegant eighteen-year-old Macallan with its subtle notes of sherry and fruitcake sitting in his study at home, then poured the Famous Grouse into a tumbler and got back into bed. He could hear the water running in the bathroom and Waverly singing a Celine Dion song. Celine was her favorite chanteuse for shower serenading. He cocked his head and listened.

Waverly warbled in her high soprano about the new day that had arrived.

Andrew smiled ruefully. The song reflected Waverly's renewed optimism so perfectly, almost exactly the opposite of how he felt. In truth, though he would never admit this to his wife, Andrew had been relieved when the doctor had said there would be no further tries. There had been so many years of hopes and disappointments in Waverly's journey toward motherhood. Andrew had already fathered a child, and while he loved his daughter deeply, he had no strong desire to repeat those early childhood years—so many bleary sleepless nights, so much poo, the mess and chaos and sheer exhaustion, the sticky surfaces and tiny fingerprints everywhere. It was a chapter of his life that he had enjoyed while it happened but did not particularly miss.

He would have given up long ago, decided a baby was not in the cards, and settled down to enjoy the life they had together. It was a good life, a satisfying life, but Waverly could not see that. And so they had tried again and again, each time ending up in a sterile doctor's office or hospital room with Andrew trying to comfort her as she grieved another loss.

Andrew was tired of the tries, of the perpetual second chances, of seeing his wife's optimism repeatedly crushed. He wanted . . . What did he want? To take the Catalina out sailing on sunny Sundays, Waverly's wicker picnic basket stuffed with tasty tidbits she'd whipped up. To make love to his wife without either of them thinking of ovulation cycles or optimum windows of time. To look across the table at her and see his entire world sitting there, and to have her look back at him the same way.

Andrew sighed. She had never looked at him that way. Waverly loved him deeply. He knew that. But there was always a hint of sadness in her eyes, a longing for something just over the horizon. He had often wondered if it had to do with the death of her parents so young. Was she trying to regain something . . . family, stability, a sense of her place in the world? He could only guess at the deep recesses of his wife's heart. He didn't know for sure, and he suspected that Waverly might not even be aware of it if he asked her. He sighed again. There were no easy answers.

The shower and the serenade had both ended, and a moment later Andrew heard the muted roar of the hair dryer in the bathroom. Sipping the disappointingly unrefined whiskey, he clicked on the television, searching through the channels with no particular aim in mind except to distract himself from the troubling issue at hand. Perhaps he could catch a bit of tennis or some cricket if the channels were available, which he very much doubted. He found the Food Network and a couple of reality shows, and then a local news channel. He was about to pass by when suddenly Waverly appeared on the screen. She was sitting in a café being interviewed by an aggressive redhead in a shockingly bright pink suit. The clashing red hair and pink suit were eye-catching, but Andrew could not tear his gaze away from his wife.

"And what brings Cooksville's very own celebrity chef to the Early Bird Café this morning?" the reporter asked Waverly, edging in next to her breakfast table. Andrew caught a glimpse of Charlie's knee in the corner of the screen.

Waverly smiled graciously, although she had obviously been surprised into an interview. He could see her food still on her plate. "Just enjoying a healthy breakfast to start my day off right," Waverly said. "It's always a pleasure to be back in Cooksville."

Andrew watched his wife admiringly. Even interrupted midbreakfast, Waverly was as cool and collected as ever. It was one of the most attractive things about her. When he had first met her, he'd found her to be an irresistible combination of soft-spoken good breeding and hardheaded business savvy. She was remarkably beautiful to boot. He had fallen for her before he'd even known what hit him, shocked by the ease with which she had made a bright, soft place at the core of his stiff, ordered routine of a life.

On-screen the reporter was continuing her interrogation. "And how is Ernie's cooking this morning?" she asked, shoving the microphone into Waverly's face. "Like coming home," Waverly said, flashing her winning smile for the camera.

Andrew felt his defenses crumble once again. He had never been good at denying her anything she set her heart on. He stared at the lovely, poised façade she presented in the interview, the professional Waverly Talbot, and remembered holding her time and again as she curled against his chest, shaking with grief, dry-eyed but devastated by yet another loss. Her heart's desire had proven so elusive. And now she had been given another chance. A crazy, unexpected last chance.

He took a large gulp of the whiskey, feeling it burn down his throat along with the truth he could not yet bring himself to admit. He would give anything to make Waverly happy, to mend the sorrows of her heart, to fill the hole no amount of his love had ever been able to fill. Charlie's offer was no exception. He sighed and poured himself another shot of whiskey, downing it in one swift swig, steeling himself to face what he already knew was coming. They were going to give a baby one more try.

CHAPTER 6

October
Greenwich, Connecticut

Charlie lay on the examination table in a blindingly white room, staring fixedly at the ceiling as the doctor prepared to perform the insemination procedure. The process so far had been surprisingly simple. Charlie stayed with Waverly and Andrew for the couple of weeks needed for the health evaluations, blood tests, and sperm analysis. After many hours of thought and discussion, Waverly and Andrew had opted for a sperm donor. That way the child would carry neither of their genetic material. It seemed fairer that way. They had chosen a donor and made all the arrangements.

During the few weeks of waiting for all the details to be taken care of, Charlie and Waverly dealt with Aunt Mae's affairs—arranging for the farmhouse to be cleaned out and sold, paying the funeral and burial expenses. Waverly's attorney was handling the legal details for the estate. After the funeral expenses were covered and the bills paid, there was very little left to do.

It seemed surreal to Charlie, lying there as the doctor completed the job with a syringe of washed and concentrated sperm. It was all so clinical, so hygienic and sterile. In normal life a baby was usually the result of an act of love and passion, but here there was no emotion at all. It was tidy, precise, devoid of any direct human element whatsoever. After she remained reclined for a few more minutes, the nurse told her to dress.

"You can take a pregnancy test in two weeks. If you aren't pregnant, we can repeat this procedure up to six times," the nurse explained briskly. "If the pregnancy test is positive, you should seek immediate care with a qualified care practitioner."

Charlie slipped on her jeans, pausing for a moment to reorient herself. That was it? She felt no different, completely normal, in fact. She tried not to visualize the biological activity taking place in her body at that very moment. She wasn't prudish by any stretch of the imagination, but she found the idea of several hundred million of a stranger's sperm making a mad dash for her ovaries a little unsettling.

Waverly insisted they celebrate that night with dinner out at a well-reviewed restaurant where she knew the head chef. "He did a guest segment for the show and made the best pots de crème once," she explained.

She was almost giddy, though Charlie felt a

little dazed and Andrew seemed a bit subdued. Charlie had noticed that during the entire process of the last few weeks, he had seemed less enthusiastic than Waverly. She hoped he wasn't having second thoughts. If he was, it was too late now.

Seated in a brick and candlelit alcove, Waverly held aloft her glass and offered a toast. "To the future," she said, beaming at Andrew and Charlie by turns. They clinked glasses and Charlie took one swallow of her sparkling water, trying not to think of eggs and sperm.

"What's a ten-letter word for hopeful?" she whispered to Andrew as Waverly consulted the menu.

Andrew wrinkled his forehead in thought. "Optimistic," he guessed after a moment.

Charlie nodded, impressed. "Your turn."

Andrew glanced at Waverly, who was thoroughly quizzing the server about how the daily fish special was prepared. "What's an eight-letter word for 'no choice but to accept'?" he asked quietly.

Charlie thought for a second. "Resigned?" she asked, quirking a brow at him.

He raised his glass with a rueful smile and toasted her. "Cheers," he said. "I'll drink to that."

Two weeks later Charlie sat on the toilet in Waverly and Andrew's immaculate guest bathroom, staring at the little plastic stick in her hand.

There were two pink lines in the white window of the test. Charlie checked the directions again, then glanced back at the two lines, confirming. She was pregnant. She stared at the second pink line, vivid against the white oval window. There was no turning back now. She was having a baby. She took a deep breath and paused, waiting for it to feel real.

It didn't. Not at all. She felt no different, although her hands were trembling. She felt only a vague sense of relief that she would be able to return home now, back to her apartment and job, back to her normal life.

Later it would become real, she assumed, but for now it felt far removed from reality, this pregnancy a fact that bore no physical witness in her body except for a dull tenderness in her breasts. She stared at the gleaming subway tiles of the bathroom and swallowed hard, wondering what had possessed her to suggest this. Well, she could not turn back now. She was committed for better or worse. She sincerely hoped it was for better.

She washed her hands slowly in cold water and smoothed back her cropped hair. She needed to tell Waverly. This news affected her sister even more than it did her. Nine months or so and her work was done, but it would change Waverly's world for good.

Charlie studied the test for another long

moment, thinking of the mysterious processes already hard at work in her body, a series of events she had set in motion and no longer had any control over. *This is the beginning of a whole new life,* she thought, not sure if she meant the baby's or her sister's or her own. Maybe all three. She opened the door and went in search of Waverly, holding the positive pregnancy test before her like a peace offering or a flag of truce. Whatever it was, she had a feeling that nothing would ever be the same.

The party was still in full swing when Waverly slipped into her bedroom and closed the door behind her, not bothering to turn on the overhead light. Through the tall windows came the soft yellow reflection of the strings of lights lacing the patio below. She could hear the muted tones of the jazz band beneath the hum of conversation. Really, she should be down there mingling with the crowd of influential guests, shimmering and charming them in her champagne bias-cut gown. It was her book launch, after all. But she was up here instead. She had been struggling to concentrate on the party or care about the book or anything else. All she could think about was the pregnancy test Charlie had handed her before breakfast, those two pink lines clear and bright in the little window. Two pink lines. A baby. Her baby.

She took a deep breath and crossed to her closet, standing on tiptoe in her nude high heels, reaching into the back corner of the top shelf for the narrow silver box she had hidden there. Pulling it out, she carried it to the bed. She sank down on the tufted velvet bench at the foot of the bed and set the box carefully beside her. It had been her grandmother's and then her mother's before her death. Now it was Waverly's, and it held her most precious possessions, the ones no one knew she'd kept, the ones that had brought her such joy and such heartache.

She opened the lid, running her fingers over the beautiful, ornately carved brush and mirror set inside. There was a horsehair brush, an ivory comb set in sterling silver, and a mirror whose glass had the speckled patina of age. She moved the comb aside. Beneath it lay six positive pregnancy tests nestled into the soft satin, their pink lines faded but still visible. She pulled them out and spread them across her lap, staring at them. Six pregnancies. Six losses. Six babies she would never get to hold in her arms. She pulled out the corresponding ultrasound photos from beneath the mirror, each image grainy and blurry in black and white. Once a blighted ovum. Three times embryos with no heartbeat detected. And twice little hearts that had stopped just a few weeks after they started beating. Those had been the hardest. To see the miracle of the tiny flutter on the screen, bright and rapid as a point of light, and feel the surge of hope that this time, this time it was going to work. She had gripped Andrew's hand, elated by the good news. And then a few weeks later to see that the little heart had gone still, the doctor's sympathetic murmur that there was nothing to be done . . . It felt each time as though her own heart had stopped beating too.

"Hello, little ones," she said softly, studying each of the photos. It still hurt to see them. She had carried each little life for such a brief time, had just begun to hope and dream about the person developing within her, and then every time there had come the crushing weight of disappointment. After the first one she had tried to convince herself to remain detached, to wait and see if this time it really worked, but she could never quite manage it. There was too much hope, too much longing in her heart.

She gathered the pregnancy tests in her hand, cradling them gently, a blighted bouquet of promises unfulfilled. They were all that was left, the only proof that she had created and carried life, that she had really been, for such a brief and bittersweet time, a mother.

And now . . . she thought of the pregnancy test that Charlie had shown her with its two pink lines, another promise, a tantalizing, daring sign of possibility. Again. She was afraid to trust, afraid to hope once more. But this time it was different. Maybe Charlie could do what she could not. Maybe Waverly really was destined to be a mother, just not to a child she carried in her body.

She considered the thought. Did it matter to her that she would not carry this child? She shook her head. No, it didn't. She would have been delighted to complete a pregnancy, to cradle a child within her body for all those months and bring him or her into the world. But at the end of the day, the method by which a child arrived in her arms was far less important than the baby itself. She was supposed to be a mother. She knew it. There was a child she was supposed to raise. She felt it, the rightness of it, in the marrow of her bones. And now, just possibly, the time had come. She put her hand to her abdomen, experiencing again the first soft flutter of excitement, effervescent as champagne bubbles floating up in her stomach.

"Waverly?" It was Andrew's voice, calling up the stairs. Waverly jumped at the interruption. She had to get back to the party. "They're expecting a speech from you, my dear," Andrew reminded her.

"Coming," she called back. "One moment."

She pressed her fingers to each ultrasound photo. "I won't forget you," she promised, replacing them in their resting spot. "You are still my babies."

• • •

Late that night, after the guests had stumbled to their cabs and limos, after the staff had swept the patio of fallen leaves and gathered the last discarded cocktail glasses, after the patio lights had gone dark, Waverly slipped into bed next to a slumbering Andrew. He roused slightly at the movement but didn't wake as she tucked herself under the goose down duvet, fanned her curls out over the satin pillowcase, and closed her eyes. The party had been a success, but she was exhausted, both from the evening and from the emotional roller coaster of Charlie's positive pregnancy test. She felt herself slipping into sleep, but just before she drifted off, in the moment between wakefulness and slumber, an image flashed before her eyes, quick and vivid as a snapshot.

She was standing on a train platform in one of the cavernous, historic railway stations in Paris. She thought it might be the Gare de l'Est. It seemed familiar from her time living in Paris. Before her idled a train ready to depart. A young girl of about five years old, with curly dark hair and solemn brown eyes, perched on the steps of the train, holding on to the metal handrail with one hand. She wore a dark blue polyester puffy coat and scuffed pink sneakers. Somewhere a bell sounded, signaling a departure. The girl turned and looked straight at Waverly. She had a dark red birthmark on her right cheek in the shape of a strawberry. She did not smile.

"I'm waiting for you," she called in heavily accented English. "Come and find me." And then the train pulled slowly from the platform, carrying the girl away.

Waverly woke with a start. She blinked in the darkness of her bedroom, puzzled by the dream. Where had she seen the girl before? She seemed so familiar. Waverly shook her head, unable to attach any meaning to the scene, and allowed herself to drift off to sleep.

CHAPTER 7

Budapest, Hungary

In the gold glow of late October, Budapest looked tired but grand. Charlie watched the city blur past the window of her taxi from the airport, the urban sprawl gradually changing from square, uniform Communist block apartments, ugly and identical in their utilitarian brutalist architectural style, to stately rows of five-story-tall buildings in an Austro-Hungarian design. The old buildings were still beautiful, their soft paint colors and lavish embellishments lending a slightly shabby but elegant air to the city. Charlie leaned her head against the window and smiled with contentment. It was good to be back.

The city was divided into twenty-three districts that spiraled clockwise in widening circles from the historic center. The mighty Danube River separated the two sections of the city, the older, hilly Buda from the flat, more modern Pest. Near the center of Pest lay the Fifth, Sixth, and Seventh Districts, and the taxi headed there, dodging its way through the congested traffic.

There was something noble about Budapest,

Charlie reflected, watching the city blocks pass by slowly. It had maintained its dignity through two world wars, multiple bombings, and countless occupations. Each time, the stalwart Hungarians rose up to regroup and rebuild. It was a refined, cosmopolitan European capital with a thriving arts scene and a vibrant café culture, often compared to Paris in the 1930s.

The taxi headed down the wide *korut*, the main artery of the city that arced away from the Danube River like a bow from its string. It turned onto Andrássy út, the tree-lined grand boulevard modeled on the Champs-Élysées in Paris, where chic cafés and designer stores like Armani and Burberry surrounded the imposing neo-Renaissance Hungarian Opera House. Another turn onto a side street and they pulled up to a renovated historic five-story building overlooking the leafy-green Liszt Ferenc Tér, a square dedicated to the Hungarian composer Franz Liszt. As the taxi stopped, Charlie noted that this late in the season the cafés on the square were starting to roll up their awnings and put away their outdoor tables. After the frigid winter months, they would reappear with the new buds in spring.

Although Charlie's building was technically in the Sixth District, the square it was on butted up to the edge of the seventh, the old Jewish ghetto of Budapest. After World War II the

96

Seventh District had fallen into disrepair, but in recent years it had undergone a revitalization as hipster bookstores and trendy wine bars cozied up to kosher restaurants and the second-largest synagogue in the world.

Charlie liked the Seventh District with its rough-around-the-edges artistic vibe. She felt more at home there than she did walking along the chic splendor of Andrássy út. There was always something interesting happening in the Seventh, though the district still carried an air of sadness beneath the pulsing beat of the young hipster and tourist crowd . . . the whispered echoes of its former inhabitants who had been shipped off to Auschwitz before the end of World War II, most never to return. The district, like so much of Budapest, carried the weight of its history heavy on its back. It was moving proudly into a bright future, but remnants of tragedy and struggle were everywhere, if you knew where to look.

Charlie paid the driver and lugged the huge brand-new designer roller that Waverly had insisted on sending with her and her own small carry-on suitcase through the building's grand entrance hall and past the wide, sweeping stone staircase to the ancient elevator in its black iron cage. The elevator lurched hesitantly to the second floor, and Charlie fumbled with her keys, finally letting herself into her apartment and bolting the tall double wooden doors behind her with a sigh of relief. She was home.

She kicked off her shoes and donned her house slippers without thinking. In central and eastern Europe, wearing shoes indoors was simply not done. She hadn't understood it when she had first moved to Budapest until she began to pay attention to the amount of dog urine, cigarette butts, and sticky substances on the sidewalks. Then slippers had seemed like an eminently sensible idea.

She turned up the heat and prowled through the chilly apartment, taking stock. It was a simple, spacious one bedroom/one bath with a kitchen, living room, and an additional half-size room where she kept her computer and a futon for the guests she never had. The ceilings were high, at least twelve feet, and the floors were wood parquet. It was a typical Hungarian apartment in the city center; the entire space exuded an air of melancholy graciousness from a bygone era. Tall windows looked out onto the square, where a few of the cafés and coffeehouses still had out tables for al fresco dining. In the heat of late summer, she would fall asleep with the windows open to the sounds of clinking wine glasses and cutlery and sometimes, late at night, a Hungarian song or two after guests had imbibed too much *egri bikaver*, Hungary's famous "bull's blood" wine.

In the tiny kitchen Charlie opened the cupboards filled with standard-issue white IKEA plates, bowls, and cups, and then the diminutive refrigerator, knowing she would find nothing more than a moldy rind of soft cheese and a few wrinkled apples. She was not hungry exactly, but she felt off-kilter, as though she had been thrown across the ocean into a different time and place so quickly her soul had not had time to catch up with her body. She threw the apples and the moldy cheese away. All that was left were a squeeze tube of mayonnaise and a half-full bottle of *eros pista*. She stared at the spicy Hungarian pepper paste, suddenly feeling queasy. She put her hand over her mouth, surprised, and then bolted to the bathroom to dry-heave into the toilet.

"Well, that's unexpected," she murmured, hunched over the gleaming white porcelain. After a few moments the nausea passed, and she sat up. She wondered what else she could expect. In one way, she was not concerned about the pregnancy. Her body had been created for it. It was a natural process carried out by millions of women. After all, there were seven billion people on the planet and all of them had been in utero at some point. But, Charlie realized, sitting on the cold tile floor, she was woefully unprepared for that natural process to happen to her. It was one thing to see glowing pregnant women on the metro or at the *piac*, her district's local fresh fruit and vegetable market. It was quite another to be growing a human being inside of her own body. She wondered what exactly was going on in there, what biological sequence of events was at work without her knowledge or consent. She gently laid her hands on her still-flat abdomen. It seemed surreal that there was a little life growing there. She knew it in her head, had seen the pink lines on the two additional pregnancy tests Waverly had insisted she take. The doctor had confirmed it. But that didn't make it any more real.

"Hello," she said softly, wondering at what age babies could begin to hear in the womb. Amid a dizzying array of pregnancy-related paraphernalia, Waverly had sent a pair of expensive headphones and a compilation of Mozart CDs to help the baby's brain develop optimally. Charlie had no intention of sitting around with headphones on her stomach, but she realized how little she knew about prenatal development. Maybe the small library of books Waverly had sent was going to be more helpful than she'd thought.

Charlie hoisted herself off the floor and wiped her face with a damp towel. The woman in the mirror looked haggard, with blue circles under her eyes and dark blond hair gone flat at the back. Charlie frowned at her reflection but didn't bother to freshen up. In her bedroom she dug through the roller until she felt the hard edge of a book and pulled it out. *A Woman's Complete Guide to Pregnancy*. Perfect. She flipped to the index at the back, searching for "morning sickness," and read the listed section of symptoms, possible causes, and tips for coping with it.

Remember to keep something in your stomach at all times. Eat small meals to help stabilize your blood sugar. Hmm. She frowned, thinking of the empty shelves of her fridge. First thing to do was buy some groceries. The Klauzal Tér Market Hall was still open. She could walk there in just a few minutes. Her favorite fruit and vegetable vendor, Atilla, always slipped in an extra tangerine or apple free of charge after he weighed her kilos of produce.

An hour later Charlie arrived back home from the market and tucked herself into bed with a carton of Greek yogurt, a bowl of tiny yellow pears, and all the books Waverly had sent. She stared at the table of contents in one for a long moment, not quite sure where to start. Finally, she turned to the section on early pregnancy symptoms.

Fatigue, nausea, increased sense of smell, dizziness or faintness . . . She stared at the list in astonishment. It wasn't new information; she'd skimmed an online article on early pregnancy a few weeks before, but it was one thing to read a list in a clinical, purely informational way and quite another to then experience those symptoms word for word. After an hour of reading, Charlie could barely keep her eyes open. She yawned so hard her jaw popped.

Fatigue: the number one early pregnancy symptom, she read. No kidding. She felt like her arms and legs were made of lead. She dragged herself to the bathroom and brushed her teeth while trying to hold down her gag reflex. *Increased gag reflex: early pregnancy symptom number six.* With a muffled groan she fell into bed, the lights still on and the bowl of pears half eaten beside her. *This is a whole new world,* she thought as she slipped into a dreamless sleep.

When Charlie woke, bright-eyed and feeling refreshed at three in the morning, she abandoned any attempt at sleep and embraced the peculiar energy that accompanied jet lag. It was a sensation she knew well. Some of her most productive times had been in the early hours of the morning a day or so after an international trip.

Grabbing a bowl of muesli, she decided to unpack. She dispatched her carry-on in a matter of minutes, tipping most of it into the dirty clothes bin in the bathroom. Then she returned to the living room to face the enormous roller stuffed with items Waverly had deemed necessary. Charlie would have chosen to leave most of it behind, but the sisters had struck a compromise of sorts.

Initially Waverly had pushed for Charlie to remain with Andrew and her until after the birth. "Just until after the baby comes," she argued as she passed Charlie a white chocolate and cranberry scone and a cup of tea. They were having afternoon tea in the formal living room on Sunday, the day after Charlie learned she was pregnant. "You could take a leave of absence. No one's going to die from not learning how to properly use a condom for a few months. Sugar?"

Charlie had stared at Waverly, her hackles rising. While technically true, Waverly's point was infuriating in its dismissiveness toward her life and work.

"Waverly, offering to have this baby for you doesn't mean I intend to put my entire life on hold for nine months. I have a job in Budapest. I'm going back." Charlie set down her teacup and the warm scone, ready to square off against her sister and fight for her independence.

Andrew had cleared his throat. "My dear," he said mildly, stirring milk and sugar into his tea. "Charlie is giving us an enormous gift by carrying this baby, and we should do whatever we can to make this time comfortable for her. If she wants to return to Budapest, I believe we should help her in any way possible."

Outnumbered, Waverly huffed her disapproval but relented. Over a second cup of tea and another scone, they agreed that Charlie would stay in Budapest until a month before the birth and then return to Connecticut.

After giving in to Charlie's wish to return home, Waverly had thrown herself into equipping her sister for the next nine months. When she was not filming the last of the next season's episodes for *Simply Perfect*, she'd been preparing and purchasing for the baby, requisitioning her assistant, Sophie, to devote herself fully to baby research.

In the end the result had been an enormous, expensive suitcase filled with a mind-boggling amount of paraphernalia, including prenatal vitamins, various herbal teas that were deemed safe for pregnancy, several sets of designer maternity wear, a hefty library of books for pregnant women, some giant elasticized belly-support bands, and a long list of websites and telephone numbers of prenatal experts compiled by Sophie.

Charlie planned to ignore most of the items, although the designer maternity stretch jeans from Paige Premium looked appealing. She pulled them out of the suitcase and held them up. She wasn't showing yet, not even a hint of softening in her flat tummy. It would be awhile before she needed them. She quickly unpacked the rest, storing all the baby-related items in her guest room/office.

From the depths of the suitcase, Charlie pulled out a plastic Kroger bag containing a few things she had selected from Aunt Mae's home, mementos that reminded her of Aunt Mae and of her childhood. There was Aunt Mae's red patent leather purse, the one she only used on Sundays. Charlie opened it and found a Methodist church bulletin and a half-eaten roll of wintergreen Lifesavers. She popped a Lifesaver into her mouth and shut the purse, feeling thirteen again. Charlie had loved to see Aunt Mae carry it. She thought it was jaunty, a rare statement piece for a woman who worked too hard to worry much about fashion.

Next was a set of porcelain salt and pepper shakers in the shape of mushrooms—one bright yellow and one red. They'd graced Aunt Mae's kitchen table every day since Charlie could remember. She set them on her own simple wood table and resumed unpacking.

With a fond smile she pulled out her Pound Puppy Ralph, one ear tattered where she'd rubbed the soft fabric every night for years to fall asleep. Farther down in the bag she found the Glo Worm toy she'd used as a night-light and a blue Smurf Pez dispenser.

She held the Pez dispenser for a moment, struck by a memory. She'd won it at a carnival with her dad on her eighth birthday. Their parents had divvied up the girls on their birthday that year. Waverly and their mother had attended a fancy-dress high tea at a posh downtown hotel. Charlie had begged to go to the carnival instead, and her father had taken her, just the two of them. They'd stayed out well past her bedtime, Charlie giddy under the brightly colored lights, the loud carousel music making her ears ring. She'd fallen into bed after ten p.m., sticky with cotton candy, feeling slightly sick from a caramel apple and a corn dog but euphoric from the evening spent with her father. He'd let her play all the carnival games, and in a lucky turn at ring toss she'd even won a live goldfish in a plastic baggie of water. It died a week later, and she'd been left with only the Pez dispenser. Her dad had won that for her at the balloon and dart toss. He'd been a surgeon with steady hands. She pointed to the one she wanted and he dutifully popped the balloon. He had seemed at that moment like the strongest man in the world.

Charlie carefully set the Pez dispenser at eye level on the bookshelf in her living room, right in front of Tolstoy and Kafka. Next she shuffled through a couple of Bruce Springsteen and Bob Dylan CDs she'd found in the dresser she and Waverly had shared. They were still her favorites. She slid one into her laptop and was immediately transported to southern Ohio in 1996 with the first strains of "Hungry Heart." She let the music play as she finished unpacking.

Digging down into the bottom of the bag, she pulled out the last item, a beautifully illustrated children's book with a big gold seal on the front declaring it to be a Caldecott Medal winner. *St. George and the Dragon*. It had been her favorite as a child. She'd been entranced by the tale of the courageous Red Cross Knight, who slew a dragon, and the good and beautiful Princess Una, whose kingdom was terrorized by the dreadful beast. Charlie had not known as a child that the tale was based on Edmund Spenser's epic poem *The Faerie Queene*. She had just liked the story—the brave knight, the beautiful princess, the wise hermit, and the terrible dragon bent on destruction and ultimately vanquished by the knight's courage.

In the background Bruce Springsteen was singing about going down to the river, about the harsh reality of life, about disillusionment and the passage of time. Charlie hummed along absently as she flipped through the book, skimming passages of the story and admiring the beautiful illustrations. It was like seeing an old friend again. She smiled as she looked at the pages, feeling equal parts fondness and resignation.

Once she had wanted to be like St. George, to go into the world a courageous knight, to slay dragons and rescue those in need. She had pretended that she was a knight, fashioning a cardboard sword and shield and slaying an imaginary dragon in the back garden every after-noon for months. It had been youthful idealism, fueled by fairy stories and naiveté. She felt a pang of nostalgia as she looked through the book. Where had that girl gone, the one who had believed she too could go boldly into the world and slay dragons? Time had shown her otherwise, time and harsh experience. She was no knight. She was just a woman, tired and a little jaded, cut down to size by the harsh realities of life. With a small frown of regret she slipped the book onto her bookshelf, wedging it between an Edith Wharton novel and her collection of Hemingway. Best to leave it there where it belonged, in the realm of fiction.

CHAPTER 8

The next morning before work, again feeling slightly nauseated, Charlie took the bus to Első Pesti Rétesház, the First Strudel House of Pest, intent on a slice of sour cherry strudel. Considered by some to have the best strudel in the city, the restaurant boasted a variety of fresh strudel and an excellent breakfast offer—coffee, orange juice, and two pieces of strudel for a modest price. It was situated near the magnificent Catholic basilica, Szent István Bazilika, where for two hundred Hungarian *forint*—less than a dollar—you could view the shrunken, gold-dipped hand of Hungary's most venerated king, his digits now housed in a small lit-up case in a side room.

"*Jo regelt.*" Kinga, the young waitress on duty, called out good morning in Hungarian as Charlie walked in the door. Her eyes lit up when she saw Charlie. "Charlie, I haven't seen you in a long time."

"Hey, Kinga." Charlie returned the greeting, slipping off her vintage cropped leather jacket. "I was in the States. Just got back."

Usually she dropped by the strudel house about

once a week, often on a weekend, to enjoy a slice or two of raspberry, cheese, or sour cherry strudel. Over time she'd gotten to know the waitstaff. Kinga was her favorite, a petite hipster with a thick, dark auburn ponytail, chunky yellow glasses, and a pair of black Converse she wore with everything.

A few customers were seated in the restaurant with coffee and plates of strudel in front of them. The entire place exuded a calm cheer and smelled delicious. It had an old-world vibe, with real tablecloths and lots of dark wood and antique objects on display, Hungarian with just a hint of kitsch. Charlie liked it. Although she usually avoided anything that smacked of tourism, for some reason she didn't mind this place. It was welcoming and uncomplicated. The world just seemed brighter with a piece of strudel in front of her.

She approached the glass display case and surveyed the selection. Good, they had sour cherry. They also had apple, cheese, apricot, and *mak*, a traditional strudel stuffed with a dense layer of poppy seeds. She made a face at the mak. The gritty texture was not her favorite. She was about to order just a breakfast special for herself but then reconsidered. Perhaps she should cushion her arrival back to work with strudel. If she brought a box of pastries, maybe it would deflect any serious questions about her lengthy absence or anyone noticing something different about her, like a certain glow. It seemed like a good preventative measure.

"I'll take four of the four-piece boxes to go," she told Kinga, listing her flavor choices. "And a strudel breakfast—one sour cherry and one cheese, please." She sat down at a table for two and waited for her order.

In a few minutes Kinga brought the strudel, along with orange juice and a cup of coffee. Charlie set the coffee aside. It came with the breakfast, but she had no intention of drinking it.

"How's school going?" she asked.

Kinga was in cosmetology school and was hoping to get a job abroad when she was done.

"I'm finished." The girl beamed. "And my cousin texted me yesterday that he has a job for me in Munich. I go in a few weeks." She placed the boxed strudel at the empty place across from Charlie.

"Munich, huh?" Charlie glanced up at Kinga, her hair pulled back in a ponytail with a fringe of bangs at the front, looking impossibly young to be setting off alone to work in another country. Charlie smiled at the thought. She must be getting old. She'd been younger than Kinga when she bought a ticket to Johannesburg and never came back.

She lingered for a few moments over her breakfast, enjoying the warm, muted bustle of the restaurant, the happy clink of forks on plates. With a glance at her watch, she realized she was going to be late to work. She waved Kinga over and paid her bill.

"Send me a postcard from Munich, and have fun," she said, spontaneously adding a large tip to the amount of forints for the strudel.

Kinga ducked her head and grinned sweetly. "Okay. Thanks, Charlie."

Charlie picked up the to-go boxes of strudel. "Just be careful," she added as an afterthought.

Kinga nodded cheerfully and handed Charlie her copy of the receipt. "You sound like my grandma." She laughed.

Charlie shook her head in consternation, hoisting the boxes of strudel in one arm. "I really am getting old," she said with a rueful smile, then hurried out the door to catch the bus.

"Morning." Charlie pushed through the tall double doors of Care Network's office twenty minutes later, armed with strudel. She opened the boxes and set them on the long conference table in the main room, and the few colleagues who were already there clustered around, greeting her but largely focusing on the pastries. Charlie grinned, helped herself to a slice of cherry cheese strudel, and settled into a seat at the table. It was good to be back.

Care Network's Budapest office occupied a

worn but spacious apartment on the top floor of a shabby Austro-Hungarian building. The block of flats, which had once housed the Budapest gentry, stood near to the ornate Keleti train station in the somewhat dubious Eighth District. At night Roma prostitutes patrolled the corners around the station, wearing black vinyl jackets and fishnet stockings. Homeless drunks slumped in the doorways of the ground floor shops, drinking cheap beer from liter plastic bottles and smoking. It was not the pretty part of the city, although it had once been grand, but the rent was cheap and many of the problems of the Eighth District were the problems Care Network was trying to address.

Charlie had been working for the NGO since her move to Budapest six years before, immediately after her abrupt departure from South Africa. She had been drawn from the start to the organization's purpose statement—"To provide training and resources to promote whole person health and wellness to underserved individuals and communities in central and eastern Europe." With a full-time staff of twelve, plus interpreters and local workers in various permanent drop-in centers and youth programs, Care Network ran over fifteen programs around the region. It wasn't the flashiest or most glamorous charity around, but it met a need and was an effective organization.

"Well, if it isn't Charlie Talbot. You're a sight for sore eyes." Duncan Cameron, Care Network's personnel coordinator, dropped into the chair beside Charlie, holding a slice of apple strudel. With his effortless boyish charm, an Edinburgh accent like golden syrup, and a smile that would melt the coldest heart, Duncan was the perfect person to coordinate personnel and volunteers for Care Network in the ten countries where they had a presence.

"Thanks, you too," Charlie said, genuinely pleased to see her favorite colleague. "What did I miss while I was gone?"

She leaned back comfortably in her chair and ate her strudel, waiting for Duncan to fill her in. She and Duncan often worked closely together, and she enjoyed his wry sense of humor and perpetually cheerful disposition. He could, quite literally, charm his way into or out of almost any situation. His affable personality, combined with a keen-eyed intelligence and blunt honesty, made him an excellent coworker.

Duncan took a big bite of strudel. "We canceled the Christmas care package delivery to the orphanages in eastern Serbia."

"Why? Donors love that one. It's always one of our most successful programs." Charlie finished her strudel in a few bites and debated taking another slice, but a glance told her the box was already empty except for the poppy-seed-filled ones. She frowned, wishing she'd saved another slice of sour cherry for herself. Was it her imagination, or was her appetite picking up already?

"Turns out the orphanage staff were taking some of the gifts home to their own kids and selling the rest." Duncan licked the last of the apple strudel from his fingers. "We're trying to figure out how to make sure the kids actually get the presents, and then we'll start up again next Christmas."

Charlie rolled her eyes. Corruption was a constant problem in Central Europe, one that filtered down through so many layers of bureaucracy left over from Communism.

"I was sorry to hear about your aunt." Duncan gave her a sympathetic look. "Did you get everything taken care of with her estate?"

"All squared away." Charlie nodded, feeling a small pang of guilt. She had no intention of telling anyone at work the real reason she had been gone so long . . . not until she couldn't hide it any longer.

The problem wasn't her coworkers. It was Ursula, her boss, an icicle of a woman from Stuttgart who was a stickler for rules and took great pains to enforce them. She had landed the director position just two years ago and had proceeded to whip things into shape—her shape—with a brisk efficiency that had alienated her from the rest of the office. She'd taken a particular dislike to Charlie after a confrontation over Ursula's decision to cancel self-defense courses for middle school girls. Charlie had won the argument and the courses were reinstated, but she had made an enemy by disagreeing with her boss. They had kept each other at a prickly distance ever since.

Charlie was certain that Ursula would frown on having a single female staff member pregnant in a region where many countries were still quite traditional and conservative. Especially a staff member who taught reproductive health courses. Charlie would look like a walking advertisement for what not to do.

"Anything else I missed?" she asked.

Duncan shrugged. "Oh, some rumors of budget cuts. Nothing confirmed, but looks like we might have to let one or two staff go."

"Really?" Charlie asked, dismayed by the thought. With a small staff, losing anyone would hurt, and there was always the possibility that she could lose her job in the cuts. Then where would she be—camping out in the spacious guest suite at Waverly and Andrew's house, getting rounder by the day? That was a depressing thought.

"Hey, you guys ate all the good ones already?"

Charlie and Duncan both turned at the question to find Arben, their Albanian staff member in charge of transportation and logistics, peering at the remaining strudel selection in disappointment.

"Sorry, mate. You're too late." Duncan shrugged and grinned.

Arben grumbled but picked out a piece of mak strudel and ambled over to them. He was a popular member of the staff, a warm, bluff man with three young kids under the age of six.

"Hey, Arben," Charlie greeted him. "How are Luljeta and the kids?"

"They're good," Arben said around a mouthful of mak. "Making me crazy as always, but good."

He pulled a face, and Charlie and Duncan both laughed. Arben liked to complain, but he was a family man to the bone, deeply dedicated to his wife and children.

"Is Ilir around?" Charlie asked. "How's he doing?"

Arben's younger brother, Ilir, lived with their widowed mother and sister in Albania but often visited Arben, staying for a month or two at a time. He helped Arben with logistics part-time, and his carefree personality and cocky, youthful humor made him a staff favorite.

"He's doing okay." Arben shrugged. "He needs new friends. He's going to come stay with us next week. Maybe it will help." Much to Arben's dismay, his brother had become increasingly zealous for the pro-Albania cause, supporting politicians with aggressive rhetoric and surrounding himself with people Arben considered to be radicals.

"Ursula alert, incoming. Just saw her out the window." Kate, Care Network's pert and efficient office manager, bustled into the room with a pot of fresh coffee and a warning.

Immediately the tone of the office changed. People straightened up, brushing strudel crumbs off their clothes and turning intently to their work. Arben clapped Duncan on the back, gave Charlie a little nod, and found an empty chair farther down the conference table.

A moment later the door opened and Ursula swooped in. With her severe gray suit and chopped blond bob, she was all business. She clapped her hands once, and the staff sprang to attention like well-trained spaniels. Charlie exchanged a look with Duncan, and they slowly turned their chairs in her direction. Kate slid into a chair on the other side of Charlie, her eyes fixed on Ursula.

"*Guten morgen.*" Ursula spied Charlie and gave her a brief nod. "Charlie, I see you are back with us again."

"Don't get too excited," Duncan murmured out of the corner of his mouth.

Ursula glanced sharply at him, and he smiled back innocently. She raised an eyebrow but didn't reprimand him. Even the rock-hard Ursula was not immune to his charms. Kate stifled a giggle and shot a look at Duncan, blushing when he winked at her.

Charlie rolled her eyes. Duncan was as charming as could be, but he could be a complete idiot about matters of the heart. He seemed oblivious to the fact that Kate had been smitten with him since her arrival from Toronto almost eighteen months before.

Ursula fixed the entire table of staff with a stern look, and Charlie composed her face into an expression of polite interest.

"I have two items of business to communicate," the boss announced. "The first is that Dr. Harrington is no longer an employee of Care Network, effective immediately. We are searching for a suitable replacement."

A low hum of surprise zipped around the conference table. Care Network employed a licensed medical doctor as a consultant for all of their programs to make sure that the information they gave was medically accurate and up to date. Dr. Harrington had held the position for the last decade.

Kate turned to Duncan and Charlie, leaning in. "Want to know why he got the sack?" she queried in a low whisper. "I heard it all through the office door when Ursula finally fired him."

"Well, the man drank like a fish, even on the job," Duncan offered. "He smelled like a distillery at nine in the morning."

Kate nodded. "I know, but that wasn't it. His medical license had been suspended in the UK for years, and we just found out about it. You should have heard Ursula. I thought she was going to pop a blood vessel."

Charlie leaned back in her chair. The boozy doctor would not be particularly missed; he had been both incompetent and somewhat boorish. Perhaps they could get someone more qualified this time around.

Ursula cleared her throat to regain the room's attention. "Now I have some bad news," she said. "As some of you are aware, we have recently lost a portion of our funding from private donors. This means that we will be forced to reduce our staff by at least one person."

A ripple of concern spread through the staff, and she held up her hand.

"This decision will not be made lightly. I will be reviewing every staff member thoroughly before making my decision. We will keep the most qualified, most productive, most dedicated staff members. If you do your job well and are a benefit to us, you have nothing to fear."

Duncan raised his hand. "When will the cuts be made?" he asked. He looked completely unconcerned. Ursula liked him, and his role in the organization was indispensable. He probably had more job security that anyone in the office.

Ursula nodded briskly. "A good question. We

will make the final decision by the middle of April. That is when our current funding runs out, and this will give me enough time to make a thorough and accurate assessment of staff."

Charlie listened with a sinking stomach. A little more than six months away. Enough time to be totally and unquestionably visibly pregnant. Enough time to allow Ursula to find an excuse to let her go. Charlie needed to be on her best behavior. She ticked off the time on her fingers. Six months and she could be out of a job. She couldn't let that happen, but what could she possibly do to stop it?

CHAPTER 9

December
The *Simply Perfect* television studio
Greenwich, Connecticut

I knew from a very young age that I loved to cook," Waverly said in answer to the *Good Housekeeping* interviewer's question.

They were sitting in staged comfort around the French provincial kitchen table in Waverly's studio kitchen, sharing tea and some buttery stem ginger shortbread they'd baked as part of a photo shoot for the article. Outside, snow lay on the ground, and Michael Bublé quietly crooned Christmas favorites in the background. Afternoon sunlight slanted in through the french doors.

Waverly took a sip of tea from one of her special collections of teacups and continued. "I lost my parents tragically quite young, and I have always felt that cooking was a way to keep my mother close to me. She was an excellent cook. Most of my mother's friends employed someone to cook for them, but my mother loved to cook, so she did it all herself. She taught me so much. I have a distinct memory of helping to stuff dried apricots with a teaspoon of camembert and a whole toasted walnut for a fall party. I sneaked bites when she wasn't looking. I couldn't have been more than five or six." Waverly smiled at the memory.

The interviewer, an earnest young woman named Emily, paused from tapping out notes on her laptop and looked sympathetic.

"Yes." Waverly took another sip of tea. "I think it all started with those apricots."

"And does it work?" Emily asked, pausing with fingers poised over the keyboard. "Do you feel your mother is with you when you cook?"

"Yes, I do. Sometimes I imagine what she would have thought of this dish or that recipe, but I can't really know. It was so long ago. Now I have only the memory of her and my father. Everything I do honors their memory and the love they gave me."

"You miss them?" Emily asked.

Waverly didn't hesitate. "Every day," she said truthfully, wistfully. "Every hour of every day since the day I lost them."

They wrapped up the interview with a few puff questions, and then the photographer requested more shots of Waverly at work in her studio kitchen. She tied on one of her favorite aprons—lemons and green citrus leaves on a white linen background with ruffled eyelet trim—and set about whipping up a simple salmon mousse while the photographer circled her, taking shots.

It was a novelty not to have to narrate every step and interact with the TV audience as she usually did. She removed the chilled baked salmon fillet from her Sub-Zero refrigerator and moved it to the counter with the other ingredients.

The photographer crouched on the other side of the island, snapping away. "Just act natural," he instructed. "I'll get the shots I need as you work."

Waverly nodded and continued her preparations. As she worked, her hands on autopilot, her thoughts wandered to her mother. Margaret Talbot had been only thirty-six when she died, a year older than her twin daughters were now. What had she thought when she kissed them good-bye and followed her husband to South Africa? None of them had imagined it would be the last time they saw each other.

Their father, Robert, was an oral and maxillo-facial surgeon, a vigorous and hearty man with a booming laugh and a ready smile. He donated two weeks a year to patients in the shantytowns around Johannesburg who had no other hope of treatment. He'd been doing it for years and had finally convinced his wife to accompany him. They were supposed to be gone for the usual two weeks, with a safari weekend tacked on to the end to celebrate their fifteenth anniversary. The twins were being cared for by their nanny.

And then the unthinkable happened. The

charter plane to the park went down outside of Johannesburg with no survivors. The twins were just shy of thirteen. It was the greatest loss of Waverly's life, devastating at such a tender age. In some way she felt she had never recovered. The miscarriages, heartbreaking as they were, had somehow served to intensify her grief over losing her parents, each loss building upon the last, every one hollowing out her heart just a little more.

"Beautiful. This lighting is perfect," the photographer called out, stepping back to capture a series of shots. Emily, the interviewer, sat at the table with Sophie, watching the shoot.

Waverly ignored them all, intent on her task. She scraped soft cream cheese into the blender with the chilled salmon fillet and added a dash of olive oil and some salt and pepper. She dumped in the prepared juice and zest of a lemon and some fresh chopped dill, and blended the entire concoction until it was smooth and creamy pink.

"Looks delicious." The photographer moved in for a close-up.

Waverly remembered what it was like to have her mother close to her—leaning her head against her mother's soft bosom clad in a pale peach satin brassiere, listening to her talk on the telephone while she traced her lips with Dior Grege 1947 lipstick. Waverly had worn that lipstick in homage to her mother for every show since *Simply Perfect* began. It was her signature shade, as iconic as her aprons, but it was her little secret. No one knew it wasn't her shade at all. It was Margaret Talbot's, and Waverly was just a little girl playing dress-up with her mother's makeup box.

Waverly spooned the mousse into a pastry bag and set out a dozen of her homemade cracked black pepper and sea salt oatcakes. Meticulously she piped a swirl of mousse onto each one, making sure that each swirl was uniform in size and shape.

The photographer circled her, the click of the camera the only sound in the quiet space. What would it be like to be a mother, Waverly wondered for the thousandth time. When she thought of holding the baby, smelling the downy little head, pressing the tiny body against her own heartbeat, she couldn't breathe. She was made for motherhood. It was her destiny. And in just a few short months, her dream would come true. It seemed surreal to her, standing piping salmon mousse onto oatcakes, that right at that very moment, far away in Budapest, her baby was growing in her sister's womb. Perhaps it was awake right now, stretching tiny fingers and toes, squirming in the dark warmth.

"Can you turn toward me just a little so I can see your face?" the photographer asked, and

Waverly complied, turning a few degrees but not breaking the rhythm of her work.

She had signed up for daily fetal development updates on her iPhone, complete with ultrasound photos and detailed descriptions. In quiet moments alone she would stare at the screen until her eyes blurred, taking in the miracle of fingers and tooth buds and the tiny beating heart. She had an app that compared the baby to fruits and vegetables. Week seven, a small blueberry with a strong heartbeat. Week nine, a cherry with a developing digestive tract and reproductive organs.

This week Charlie and baby were out of the first trimester. Most of the danger of miscarriage was past now, and both Charlie and baby were doing well. Charlie reported that her fatigue and nausea were lessening, and her energy was back. Waverly had breathed a sigh of relief and ordered a beautiful crib from Restoration Hardware in celebration.

When the photo shoot was finished, Waverly handed out the salmon mousse canapés to Emily, the photographer, and Sophie.

"A reward for a job well done," she said with a warm smile, setting out a plate with the extras on it. "Enjoy!"

While they clustered around the black marble island and devoured the fruits of her labor, Waverly slipped into her office and took out her phone. She felt a thrill of anticipation as she clicked on the update for week thirteen. Baby was about three inches long, about the size of a peapod, fully formed, with fingerprints. The baby could now even suck his or her thumb. She stared at the last ultrasound photo Charlie had sent, the giant bobblehead and tiny rounded fingers, thinking of the baby in Charlie's belly, growing by leaps and bounds, oblivious to the outside world or to the fact that an ocean away its mother was waiting with breathless anticipation.

She had a million things to do for work, but the baby was all Waverly could think about. While she was in front of the camera filming a short promotional video for the Food Network, showing the audience how to make the perfect dumplings for Chinese New Year, she was weighing the merits of various orthodontic pacifiers and organic baby wraps. During the photo shoot for her new book jacket photo, she had posed at her studio kitchen island and considered which was superior, the Munchkin Warm Glow Wipe Warmer or Prince Lionheart Ultimate Wipes Warmer.

"Hey, Boss." Beau knocked and poked his head into the office. "Heard it was a great interview. That salmon mousse was fantastic, and you know I don't even like fish."

"Thank you," Waverly said absently, still staring at the fetal update.

"You have any plans tonight?" Beau asked. "Some of the crew are heading down to the White Lantern. Wyatt's band is playing there tonight. Thought you might like to join us."

"Oh." Waverly looked up, considering the invitation for a moment. Andrew was working a long day in the city and wouldn't be home until late. For a moment she was tempted to say yes, and then she remembered. Charlie had gone to a doctor's appointment that afternoon and had not yet e-mailed or called with the results. It was late evening in Budapest, but perhaps she would contact Waverly before she went to bed. "I think I'll stay home and get some work done tonight, but thank you."

With a nod of farewell, Beau withdrew. Waverly knew full well that she wouldn't be working. What she was actually going to do was make herself a cup of ginger tea and spend the hours until Andrew came home trawling high-end baby stores online. She was spending more and more time in this way, trying to prepare for the big event. It allowed her to feel closer to the baby growing so far away in her sister's belly.

Charlie was trying to include her in the process as much as she knew how, Waverly understood, but she was busy with work and travel, and growing a human took time. For days on end there was nothing much to report. Charlie called once a week or so and e-mailed with every doctor's appointment, relaying every detail of new pregnancy symptoms or telling anecdotes about Hungarian culture in regard to babies.

"My doctor tells me I should drink some red wine because it's good for the baby, but I can't take a bath or eat foreign foods. I'm not sure he realizes that for me, everything here is technically a foreign food," Charlie had told her, chuckling. The calls were usually brief and sometimes a little awkward. There had been so many years of distance between the sisters that trying to bridge it now felt like plowing ground that had long lain fallow. It was hard work for both of them.

Waverly chafed at each day that passed without news. She was restive, counting down the days to July 11. It seemed so far away. Sometimes she would pinch herself, unable to believe that it was actually happening. She was going to have a baby. At last.

"Hello, little one," she said softly, gently pressing a fingertip to the ultrasound photo. The baby looked undeniably human now, with a cute profile, its arms outstretched and feet like little paddles. She checked her e-mail again and her cell phone. Nothing. She would have to wait until tomorrow to hear how the appointment went. She sighed, disappointed.

"Who will you look like?" Waverly asked, studying the blurry black-and-white outlines of its face.

Perhaps the baby would have Charlie's lithe frame and freckles, or the pert nose and soft blond hair that Waverly had inherited from their mother.

Whatever the combination of genetic traits, Waverly knew she would love this child. It was her family, almost her own flesh and blood, destined to be in her arms. Close enough, she told herself. Close enough to look like her, to seem familiar, to be family, to be her own.

"Grow big and strong, sweet one," she murmured. "We can't wait to meet you."

That night as Waverly slipped into sleep, she dreamed that she was sitting at the antique white French dressing table in her mother's bedroom, the place where Margaret had put up her hair and applied her makeup every morning. Waverly looked at her reflection. She was an adult, the fine lines at the corners of her eyes made her look a little tired. She was wearing her mother's long peach silk negligee. The dressing table in front of her was littered with perfume bottles and bobby pins. She reached for a tube of lipstick, her mother's ever-so-familiar Grege 1947, and uncapped it. She puckered her lips and glanced up at the mirror, then froze. A little girl was standing behind her, watching her with solemn dark eyes. She had curly dark hair and a red birthmark on her cheek in the shape of a strawberry. It was the same girl she had dreamed about before at the train station in Paris. The girl looked at her for a long moment and smiled shyly.

"Come find me," she said, holding out her hand. Then she turned and disappeared.

Waverly woke with a start and sat bolt upright, her heart pounding. The dream had seemed so real. She put her hand to her chest, feeling not the slippery glide of peach silk but the reassuring feel of her own more sensible poplin pajama top. She was in her own bed with Andrew snoring softly beside her. She turned on her side but did not close her eyes.

Why did she keep dreaming of the same little girl, a child she was sure she had never seen before? She bit her lip. What if it was a premonition, a taste of the future? What if Charlie was carrying a little girl and somehow Waverly was getting a glimpse of her child? The girl certainly bore no resemblance to either Charlie or Waverly, and they'd chosen a sperm donor with similar physical characteristics, but still, genetics were funny things. Perhaps the sperm donor had dark-haired and olive-skinned relatives. Maybe Waverly was dreaming about her future daughter.

She shivered at the thought, equal parts delighted and unnerved. She took a swallow of water from her bedside carafe and settled back down in bed, but she couldn't sleep. She lay staring at the ceiling as the minutes ticked by and thought about her future as the mother of a daughter. It felt so very right.

CHAPTER 10

January
Budapest and a Serbian village

"Just the breakfast special this morning." Charlie slid into a seat at an empty table for two at the First Strudel House of Pest and ordered her usual from Tamas, one of the regular servers. She glanced around the restaurant but didn't see Kinga. On impulse she swapped her usual raspberry strudel for raisin with a slightly crumbly sweet cheese.

She was leaving the next day on a two-week work trip through Romania and Serbia. The two slices would have to tide her over until she returned. She had not been to the strudel house for a few weeks. In fact, all of December had passed since she was last there. The Christmas holidays had gone by in a whirl of work parties, events with friends, strolls through the quaint outdoor Christmas markets dotting the squares around Budapest, and long, lazy evenings reading in her pajamas by the glow of candles and Christmas lights.

Now it was early January. The weather was

gray and bitter outside, with a crust of ice on the puddles and leaden low clouds over the Danube. People scuttled past the restaurant, their stoic faces burrowed in scarves and thick fur coats to ward off the icy wind coming off the river. Inside, however, the restaurant was cheerful and warm and smelled deliciously of baking pastry. A few businessmen sat at tables, deep in conversation, empty plates with crumbs in front of them. A family of Japanese tourists, still bundled in puffy down coats, took photos of themselves eating strudel, posing and looking up at their phone attached to a selfie stick.

Tamas brought her order to the table.

"Is Kinga here this morning?" Charlie asked. "Or did she already leave for Germany?"

"She left a week ago, right after New Year," Tamas confirmed. "Her cousin found a job for her in Munich." He slid the plate of strudel and a fork down in front of Charlie, along with the accompanying orange juice and coffee.

"Does she like it?" Charlie asked, eyeing the strudel, her mouth already watering in anticipation.

Tamas shrugged. "No one has heard from her. I texted her last week but she didn't text me back."

Charlie took a sip of orange juice and picked up her fork. "When you do hear from her, tell her I said hello. I hope it goes well for her." And then she turned her attention to the waiting strudel.

• • •

"So you slip the condom over the tip of the penis like this." Five days later Charlie was bending over a spotted brown banana, showing a group of high school Romanian girls how to properly apply a condom, and botching the job fairly soundly. The banana was too ripe and she was having difficulty rolling the condom down its flaccid sides.

It was sweltering in the school classroom, although outside a January frost was still white on the grass. These Communist-era block buildings had fiercely overefficient heating systems with no temperature control. She wiped her sweaty hands on her jeans and took a second attempt at the banana while Monica, her translator, soldiered on, elaborating to give Charlie time to get it right. The skin on the banana split, and soft banana oozed out the side onto her hands. The girls broke into a chorus of dismayed giggles, and even Monica cracked a smile.

Care Network was doing a two-week-long series of reproductive health education seminars in local schools in rural Romania. Sex was a subject not talked about in Romanian culture, and the rate of teen pregnancies reflected the lack of any sort of thorough sex education.

Charlie could hear Duncan in the next room giving a similar demonstration to the boys. From the gales of laughter filtering through the wall, he was either doing an amazing job or completely botching it. Charlie couldn't tell which. Probably the former. Duncan was as smooth as butter. She forced the condom down over the last inches of the banana and triumphantly held it aloft to demonstrate. The girls tittered nervously as Monica wrapped up the presentation.

When Charlie glanced toward the back of the room, she was surprised to see that a guest had slipped in sometime during her demonstration. He was standing at the back of the classroom, hands in the pockets of his brown corduroy trousers. He wasn't tall, just a couple of inches taller than Charlie, but solidly built, with a brawler's body and thick auburn hair cut short at the sides. He wasn't handsome in a classical sense, but he had a pleasant face, sturdy and open. He looked dependable, like someone you would want on your side if you were in a tight spot. Charlie squinted, trying to place him. He looked familiar, although she couldn't quite say why.

He met her eyes, and his supple mouth twitched. It looked like he was trying to tamp down a laugh.

She handed the classroom off to the teacher, who began a wrap-up speech in Romanian. A few minutes later class was dismissed and a torrent of dark-haired girls poured from their desks, blushing and giggling behind their hands. Charlie was at the front, gathering up her supplies and vowing to bring her own very green and firm bananas next time, when the familiar stranger approached her.

"That was quite a demonstration." He smiled, showing square white teeth. He held out his hand. "Dr. Johan Kruger at your service."

Reaching to shake his hand firmly, Charlie froze, his accent transporting her in a moment back to South Africa . . . the intense heat of the afternoon sun on her neck as she sipped bottled water and surveyed the long line of people seeking free medical exams in one of the many townships that sprang like mushrooms out of the parched dust.

"Johannesburg," she said abruptly.

He looked surprised for a second and then nodded. "Yes. How did you know?"

"I know you." She realized she was still gripping his hand and released him, trying to think that far back, to pinpoint where exactly she had last seen his face. A hazy image of him in a white lab coat directing an ant hive of doctors and nurses to various stations—immunizations, infant checkups, HIV testing. "At a health camp for one of the townships, nine or ten years ago. I was finishing a degree in public health from UNISA and it was a practicum. You were there helping run the camp, if I remember right. I'm Charlie Talbot."

"Is that right?" He surveyed her with a sudden interest. "I thought you looked familiar but I couldn't place you. Now I remember. You were volunteering with the women's health clinic, weren't you?"

Charlie nodded and chucked the offending banana, still sheathed in its cheerful hot-pink condom, into the wastebasket by the teacher's desk. She didn't want to talk any further about Africa.

"What can I do for you, Dr. Kruger?" She wiped her hands on her jeans and picked up the box of supplies.

"Call me Johan," he urged, offering to take the box from her hands. "And more to the point, what can I do for you? I'm your new medical adviser. Anything you need me to help with today?"

So Dr. Johan Kruger of South Africa was now on the staff of Care Network in Central Europe? What a small world.

"Nothing I can think of for now." She led the way out of the classroom. "Our last medical consultant approved this material, which isn't saying much, but I think it's pretty sound. We've got three more classes to do this afternoon, but I've got to find some less ripe bananas."

"Might keep the demonstration a bit more on track," he agreed with a wry smile.

"How long have you been in Europe?" she asked, amazed by the coincidence and a little shaken by the connection to her past. Anything that reminded her of her years in Africa brought a mixture of emotions—many good, but a few still so painful.

Johan followed her into the next classroom, carrying the box of supplies. "Only a couple of months. I've made a commitment for a two-year term, and then I'll see how it goes."

"Are you here alone?" Charlie thought she remembered that he had been married when she'd last seen him. She had been engaged at that time, a brief mistake with a gentle, earnest environmental activist named Shane.

"Ah, yes, just me." Johan cleared his throat. "Been divorced about six years now. And you, any family here?"

"No, still single," Charlie said briefly. She hardly thought of her engagement or Shane anymore. The fact that the breakup had not bothered her much spoke volumes on how ill-fitted they really had been for each other.

"When we met I think you were working on a concept." He frowned, trying to remember the details.

Charlie did not offer any help. She didn't like to be reminded.

"You were going to open a health clinic for women in one of the townships, isn't that right?"

"Yes."

"Did you ever get it going?"

"No," she said, looking away. "I never finished it, and then I had to leave."

"Pity. It sounded like a good idea."

He studied her face and she turned away, not wanting him to see how raw it still was, how much the failure still hurt her.

"So how do you like Europe so far?" She motioned for him to set the box on a desk and pulled out the jumbo package of neon-colored condoms.

"A bit tame after Africa," he confessed with a shrug, "but it's growing on me. Nice to be able to get a good French cheese and a pint of Belgian ale without paying an arm and a leg."

"Well, Doctor," Charlie said, handing him another squishy banana and a condom in electric yellow. "How about taking the next session? Let's up your excitement level a little."

Unfazed, he took the items from her. "Sure, I'll take a crack at it."

Johan did an admirable job, seemingly unperturbed by the impromptu nature of his assignment or the room full of fifteen-year-old girls giggling behind their hands every time he talked about male anatomy.

Charlie watched from the back of the room. She remembered this about him from before, the air of capable calm that surrounded him. Even in the midst of a frenzy—a medical emergency in one of the white tents, the frantic voices of a hundred people all clamoring to be heard—he moved purposefully and steadily, creating a bubble of stillness around him in the midst of chaos.

It had been reassuring for those like Charlie who had been new volunteers to the medical camps, unprepared for the intensity of working with such large numbers of people in need. She had liked him and instinctively trusted his leadership. She felt the same way now, watching him at the front of the class. He seemed so familiar, an unexpected visitor from a period of her life she had once loved. She still felt the loss keenly, but seeing him reminded her of the many good times, so many years of good memories. Only the end had gone so very wrong.

Charlie finished up with the last class of the day. Johan sat in the back with a cup of coffee and watched her. Strangely, she didn't feel at all awkward in his presence. Halfway through the class, though, she began to feel queasy.

"First you open the packet like this," she said as Monica translated in rapid, lyrical Romanian. Everything sounded so dramatic and poetic in Romanian, a close cousin to Italian.

"Then you slip the condom over the tip of the penis like this." She struggled with the banana. It was so hot in the room. A bead of sweat rolled down her back and she swallowed, becoming acutely aware of both the squishy texture and the too-ripe smell of the banana. The sickly sweet, almost rotting smell was overpowering. Her stomach heaved and she swallowed hard again, forcing down bile. She had not eaten lunch, too busy to stop. That had been a mistake.

Monica glanced at her questioningly as Charlie faltered, but Charlie rallied after a moment, determined to soldier on. "It's important to make sure that the condom does not break," she said loudly. Her stomach was definitely roiling. The room tilted a little and blurred.

"Charlie?" Monica asked, giving her a worried glance. Charlie dropped the banana on the desk, vaguely aware of Johan getting to his feet and starting toward her from the back of the classroom, his face registering concern.

"Sorry," she said, then bent over and vomited into the wastebasket amid the horrified shrieks of twenty adolescent girls.

In a moment Johan was there, bending over her, holding the wastebasket as she retched. She didn't protest. She was shaking and too nauseated to care who was watching.

Charlie glanced up to see Monica staring at her in shock. She waved a hand to her translator, urging her to continue the talk, and after a few stunned seconds Monica started in again, wrapping up the presentation alone. Charlie suspected that her impromptu performance had ruined the class's attention span.

"Not here," she managed to say to Johan, and

he obliged her, helping her down the aisle to the door, his arm strong around her waist, his other hand clutching the soiled wastebasket.

In the slightly cooler and empty hallway, Charlie regained her bearings a little. Assuring Johan that she was fine and blaming the hot room and low blood sugar, she slipped into the empty bathroom and bent over the sink, leaning her head against the cold white tiles. Her stomach gave another heave, but there was nothing left to bring up. She splashed water on her face and then tried to remain still until the nausea passed.

After a few minutes she pulled open the bathroom door to find both Duncan and Johan standing outside, wearing identical expressions of concern. She joined them in the hall, embarrassed by the attention. The wastebasket was nowhere to be seen.

"Charlie, what happened? Are you feeling okay?" Duncan took her elbow. "You look a bit peaky."

"I'm fine," she said, trying to brush off his concern. "I must have eaten something for breakfast that didn't agree with me, and those rooms are hot as an oven." She felt embarrassed, vulnerable somehow.

Johan was watching her with a furrowed brow and an intent look. "How long have you been feeling this way?" he asked.

She didn't answer him directly, not wanting to

say anything that could give her away. Ursula had been watching the staff like a hawk, making notations, holding the entire office hostage with the thought of the layoffs. Charlie had no intention of giving her fodder until it became unavoidable.

"I'm fine. I probably just need to eat something and cool off," she said, dodging his question and not making eye contact.

"I've got some bananas," Duncan offered.

Charlie gave him a murderous look and bolted back into the bathroom just in time.

CHAPTER 11

A Serbian village on the Bulgarian border

The high shriek of shearing metal woke Charlie, followed by the long skid of locked tires and then a sharp bang. She sat upright in the single, hard bed of the rented apartment, heart pounding. Through the sliver of open window came a draft of icy air and silence.

Fumbling under the bed for her house shoes, a pair of Birkenstock clogs, she slipped them on, ears straining for any other noise. Had she imagined the terrible sound? No, in the room next to her she heard Monica stirring. Sliding from under the duvet, Charlie went to the window and pulled back the curtain, surveying the main road. It looked like dozens of other main streets in tiny villages across Serbia—a narrow strip of faded asphalt flanked on either side by clusters of stucco, red-tile-roofed houses and tidy yards with beds of straggly dormant roses and bare fruit trees. The village lay less than twenty kilometers from the Bulgarian border.

The road was empty, the houses dark. She was probably the only person in the village sleeping with her windows open even a crack in January. Central Europeans had a deep abhorrence for drafts, which they believed could cause sickness. Maybe no one else had heard the noise. She hesitated for a moment, considering whether it was wise to venture out and investigate, but concern won out over caution. Someone might need help.

Charlie grabbed her down coat and the flashlight she always carried with her when she traveled and threw open the door. Monica was already in the hall, pulling a wool coat over her pajamas.

"Did you hear that?" Charlie asked. "It sounded like a crash."

Monica nodded, dark eyes alert. "I think it came from past the village."

Charlie switched on the flashlight. "Let's go see."

Together they hurried out into the dark, sleeping town. They were staying in an apartment over a tiny convenience store near the edge of the village. A few houses down from the store the buildings ended abruptly next to a shallow creek, and beyond that, flat black harvested fields stretched into the distance until they blended with the snowy, rolling forested hills.

It was the last village on their two-week trip. They had finished the reproductive health education seminars in Romania and then crossed into Serbia, driving south to preview potential seminar locations for the following year. Duncan and Johan had parted ways with them after the final Romanian seminar, traveling by bus to southern Romania to meet with a new partner organization. Charlie and Monica planned to finish the trip through Serbia and then drive the Care Network van and materials back to Budapest in a few days.

Charlie shivered in the night air; it was thin and piercingly cold and smelled of frost. All her senses were on high alert, her breath coming fast in her chest. The moon was bright in the clear sky, washing the road before them in a pale silver light. As they passed the last cluster of houses, she swept her flashlight over the narrow road, illuminating the cause of the sound. A small white transport truck had barreled through town and miscalculated the bridge, running into the stone wall. It lay half on its side against the wall, lolling crazily, one headlight shining into the gurgling creek below.

Charlie broke into a trot. "This could be bad." She ran toward the driver's door, Monica right at her heels, and tugged it open. Inside, the driver lay against the steering wheel, unconscious but breathing, an ugly gash pouring blood from his forehead. Charlie laid a practiced hand against his neck, checking his pulse. "He's ali—" she started when they both heard the same noise. A bumping and whimpering from the back of the truck.

The two women looked at one another in alarm. "Animals?" Charlie guessed aloud.

"Maybe," Monica said, casting a nervous glance behind her. The bumping had become a rhythmic hammering sound, as though whatever was inside was trying desperately to force its way out.

Charlie hurried around the back of the truck and unbolted the back door, swinging it open a crack and shining her light inside. The beam of her flashlight caught a glimmer of dark eyes. She swung the door wider, sweeping the light across the truck's cargo. It was not animals. It was women.

Sitting packed shoulder to shoulder, they flinched away from the flashlight's beam, blinded by the glare. They were young, early twenties at most, bruised and disheveled from the crash.

Monica swore softly in Romanian at the sight of their frightened faces. Charlie said nothing, stunned into silence. She stood motionless for a moment, staring at the faces before her. The young women stared back with wide eyes. Each sat with her hands in front of her, bound together with a long plastic zip tie.

"Are you okay?" Monica called softly into the truck. She repeated the phrase in Romanian, Serbian, and Hungarian.

The girls were beginning to stir as they recovered from the shock of the crash. One of them sitting near the door caught Charlie's eye, a swarthy girl with short, dark hair. She wiped her hands across her mouth, leaving a smear of blood on her cheek. She stared at her bound hands in the dim light, then touched her split lip gingerly. Her eyes were wide with shock. No one answered the question.

"Hey, are you okay?" Charlie asked her, trying to elicit some response. The girl nodded slowly, still not speaking.

Monica glanced uneasily back down the road, hunching down into her coat. Nothing stirred. "Charlie, we don't have much time. The men who own this truck will come looking for them," she said. Her teeth were chattering, whether with cold or fear Charlie couldn't tell.

"Do we call the police?" Charlie asked, doing a quick head count. She thought there were six. In the dark it was difficult to be sure.

Monica shook her head and laughed drily, a black sound. "The police are probably part of it. They will return the girls to those who are selling them. The police get bribes at the borders to let them cross, no questions asked. This truck is probably heading for Bulgaria."

"What do we do with them?" Charlie asked. "We can't leave them here." Her hands were shaking and she tucked them under her arms, trying to remain calm, trying to act like a professional. She glanced over her shoulder, but nothing moved along the road. She was sweating, although the temperature was in the low twenties. There was a sharp, metallic taste in her mouth—the taste of fear. She had not experienced it since that last, horrible night in Johannesburg. She pushed the unwelcome memory away. Not here, not now.

"We have to get them out of here," Monica said, her voice low and urgent. She stepped forward, speaking rapidly in Romanian. A second later one or two voices answered her, and the girls began to shift toward the open door.

"I told them we will help them," Monica murmured to Charlie. "We will take them to the apartment. I'll go ahead to make sure no one sees them. You get them ready." Not waiting for an answer, Monica slipped into the darkness, going back into the village the way they had come.

Charlie paused, at a loss as to how to proceed. "Hey, can anyone speak English?" she called softly into the dark recesses of the truck.

"Yes, a little," said a shaken voice from the back.

"Come up here and translate for me, please," Charlie said. "Hurry. We don't have much time."

A girl scrambled awkwardly to the door of the truck. She was petite with auburn hair pulled back in a ponytail and heavy bangs that fell across her brow. She turned and the beam of the flashlight hit her face, illuminating chunky yellow plastic glasses. Charlie stared at her for a moment in stunned disbelief.

"Kinga?" she gasped. The girl squinted against the glare of the flashlight, and Charlie dropped the beam, stepping toward her. Kinga flinched involuntarily, shrinking back from Charlie's movements.

"Hey, it's me, Charlie, from the strudel shop." Charlie held up the flashlight so Kinga could see her face.

"Charlie?" Kinga met Charlie's eyes. Tears began seeping from behind her glasses. She was shaking so hard her teeth chattered.

"Hey, hey, it's okay," Charlie said, reaching up and touching her arm. With Charlie's assistance Kinga clambered from the truck, stumbling as she hit the ground, unable to right herself because of her bound hands. Charlie grabbed the girl's elbow, steadying her. Kinga pulled away quickly from Charlie's touch.

"Are you hurt?" Charlie asked in a low voice.

Kinga shook her head, pushing her glasses up her nose with her bound hands. "I'm okay."

"How many girls are in the truck?" Charlie asked, glancing over her shoulder back down the road.

"Six." The olive-skinned girl with the cut lip spoke for the first time. She swung her legs over the edge and joined Kinga and Charlie. "There are six of us. You know her?" she asked Kinga, jerking her head toward Charlie.

Kinga nodded. "From Budapest. She's a friend. She'll help us."

"What's your name?" Charlie asked.

"Simona," the girl replied. She touched her split lip again and winced. The blood was smeared on her chin.

"Where are you all from?" Charlie peered into the truck.

"Bulgaria, Romania, and Hungary," Simona replied, glancing around her warily. Her body was tensed. "I am from Bulgaria."

"Do any of the others speak English?" Charlie asked.

Kinga shook her head. "I don't think so. Only Simona and me."

"I don't speak good English," Simona said. "I speak good Bulgarian and Romanian."

"Okay, you and Kinga can help me translate then," Charlie said. "Tell the others that my colleague Monica and I are going to help you."

She and the girls both froze as they heard a loud groan from the cab of the truck.

Charlie swore softly. "Quickly, get the girls out of the truck and be quiet," she instructed them. "Then wait for me."

Kinga nodded. She said something to Simona, who translated into Bulgarian and then

Romanian, addressing the other women. Kinga followed with a Hungarian translation.

Charlie flicked off the flashlight and slid quietly along the side of the truck to the cab. Her heart was pounding a frantic staccato beat in her ears. She didn't think, just acted. She didn't know yet how she and Monica were going to help the women, but she knew that they could not afford to have the driver conscious or mobile.

She approached the cab as quietly as she could, then peered around the side, her heart hammering in her ears. The driver was still slumped over the steering wheel, but he was stirring. Hands shaking, Charlie didn't stop to think. She reached past him and gently turned the keys in the ignition. The headlights cut out instantly. In the near darkness she could hear the man's ragged inhalations. He groaned, turning his head. Slowly, slowly she slid the keys from the ignition, holding her breath, willing him not to awaken. If he did, she didn't know what she would do. He smelled of sausages and sweat, and she had to force herself not to gag.

Keys in hand, she paused, unsure what to do next. Then she heard a ringtone blare from the floor of the cab. A cellphone lay next to the driver's feet, flashing an incoming call with the beat of a European techno song. Frantic to stop the sound, she scrabbled for the phone, then dropped it on the pavement and ground it into the asphalt with her clog, stomping on it again and again until the music stopped and it broke into pieces. Breathing hard, she wiped her trembling hands on her pajama pants. She was sweating, although the air was bone-chillingly cold. Adrenaline was coursing through her veins, icy and electrifying, heightening every second, every sound and movement. She took a deep breath, willing herself to think, to calm down. The important thing was to buy the women time and get them somewhere safe.

She waited for a long second, but the driver did not stir again. Flicking the flashlight on, Charlie looked around the interior of the cab for anything that might prove useful. In the beam of the flashlight she found a dozen or more long plastic zip ties scattered around the seat of the cab and a box cutter on the floor. She slid it out of the cab quickly and opened it, feeling better to have some small protection in her hand, though the thought of using it was absurd. She'd never been in a knife fight in her life.

"Here," a voice said from behind her. Charlie whipped around. Simona was standing beside her. She reached out her bound hands and gestured impatiently to the box cutter. "Cut me free."

Charlie awkwardly sawed through the plastic, and a moment later Simona's hands sprang free. As soon as she was released, Simona pushed past

Charlie, reached around the driver, and carefully grabbed two zip ties from the front seat. With brisk efficiency she secured the man's wrists to the steering wheel. He moaned and stirred again. Simona stepped back hastily, shutting the door of the cab with a *click*.

"He goes nowhere now," she said grimly. She massaged one wrist and then the other for a moment.

Charlie handed her the box cutter. "Free the others."

With a quick nod, Simona took the tool and disappeared toward the back of the truck.

Charlie hesitated for a moment, looking at the truck keys in her hand, and then finally tossed them overhand into the stream. They made a long, lazy arc into the darkness and landed with a distant splash.

When she came around the truck again, all the women were huddled by the open doors, shivering in the cold. Simona was working her way methodically through the group, cutting the zip ties. Kinga had her arm around one of the girls, who was cradling her elbow and crying softly.

Monica reappeared then, beckoning them to follow her. Silently they did, winding down the road and up the stairs to the apartment. Charlie brought up the rear, keeping a sharp eye on the houses they passed and praying that no cars would come through. Nothing stirred, not even a curtain. Everything remained dark and quiet, but Charlie knew that didn't necessarily mean that no one was watching.

Once in the apartment, Monica shut the door and bolted it, then turned to Charlie. "We have to get them away from here before the men who did this come looking for them," she said, her tone quiet and urgent. "Charlie, these men, the kind who sell girls, they are very bad men. And these girls cost them a lot of money. They will come to find them, and when they do . . ." She didn't finish her sentence, just glanced over Charlie's shoulder to where the young women were sitting silently on the couch and floor, hunched over in self-protection and fear.

"What if we took them to the drop-in center in Belgrade?" Charlie offered, assessing the young women from the corner of her eye. "The center staff will know how to help them."

Care Network ran a day center for women and children in Belgrade, Serbia, offering a hot lunch, job training, and basic medical care.

Monica bit her lip, thinking. Then she nodded. "Yes, good, but we need to go now."

Charlie was already moving. "You get the van," she said. "I'll triage any injuries and get them ready to leave. We can call the center staff on the way so they know we're coming."

Monica slipped out the door and down the stairs like a ghost. Charlie surveyed the girls for a moment. They stared back at her, dazed, traumatized, and quiet.

"Simona, Kinga." Charlie looked around the small room, spotting the two who spoke English, and beckoned them over. "I need you to translate. Tell the girls we have to leave immediately. We are taking you to Belgrade, to a place where you'll be safe. Is anyone hurt?"

Simona asked the question in rapid Bulgarian and Romanian. Kinga repeated it in Hungarian. The girls stared at Charlie, eyes wide. One by one they responded, their voices barely above a whisper.

"They're okay, just some little cuts. But this girl, Gabi, says her arm hurts." Kinga motioned to the one cradling her elbow.

Charlie nodded. "Okay, I'll be right back and look at her arm." She headed for her bedroom and hastily stripped out of her pajamas, throwing on a pair of jeans and Keds and slipping back into her down coat. She spent a few minutes frantically stuffing items into her suitcase, then did the same in Monica's room, thankful that the interpreter had already packed most of her items for their departure the next day. Rolling suitcases bumping behind her, she came back into the living room.

"Where's Gabi?" she asked. The girl came

forward. She was slight, with pale-green eyes and a curtain of straight dark hair.

"*Szia*," Charlie greeted her in Hungarian.

Gabi looked startled but answered after a moment. "Szia."

"Can I check your arm?" Charlie asked. Kinga translated the message in rapid Hungarian. Gabi looked uncertain but nodded slightly.

Charlie examined her arm. She thought it was just a bad sprain, but she noticed a row of cigarette burn marks that swooped across the girl's collarbone like a necklace. It made Charlie feel ill to look at it. Her hands were trembling as she made the examination, and she had to force herself not to go back to that dark place— the lonely road, the taste of blood and dust in her mouth, the fear, paralyzing, suffocating her more than the weight of her assailant. She jerked herself back to the present, forcing a deep breath out through her nose. This was not her story, not her trauma. Not now. She had to be strong for these young women who needed her help.

"Who did this to you?" she asked, but the girl just stared at her, uncomprehending.

Simona overheard her and came over. "They promised us jobs," she said in halting English. "Good jobs in Germany." She shook her head. "But this is not what we get." She made a spitting motion on the ground and muttered something under her breath. "They trick us and hurt us very much. They tell us lies."

"Who told you lies?" Charlie asked her.

Simona shrugged. "My uncle promised me good job in Frankfurt, but his friends take me to Belgrade instead." She balled her hands into fists. "I trust him because he is family. He says he gets good job for me to help my little girl."

"You have a daughter?" Charlie asked, surprised. Simona looked young, barely in her twenties.

Simona nodded. "She is four years old. I leave my little girl with my mother and go for good job in Germany, but my uncle, he lies. He gets money for me," she said angrily. "First we go to Belgrade to break us. Now they sell us to Turkey for work in club for sex."

"They told you that?" Charlie asked in disbelief.

Kinga shook her head, joining the conversation. "We heard them talking. They sold us to the men who gave the most money. We were going to Turkey."

Charlie stared at Kinga, remembering the last time she had seen the girl at the pastry shop, how excited she had been at the promise of a new adventure in Germany, how sparkly and full of life. It had seemed so innocent and enticing, a bright future discussed over slices of sour cherry strudel. Now Kinga was drawn in upon herself, her eyes hooded. She looked bruised, haunted, as though she had seen things she could not easily erase.

A soft knock came at the apartment door. Charlie opened it a crack, checking to make sure it was safe, and then opened it wider. Monica slipped in.

"The van is downstairs. We must go." She motioned the girls forward.

"I got your stuff," Charlie whispered, handing her the suitcase.

"Wait." Simona stepped in front of the door, arms crossed. She looked from Monica to Charlie and back again. "Where do you take us?"

Monica frowned, then rattled off an explanation in Romanian. She turned to the other girls, raising her voice slightly at them. After a moment she turned back to Simona and motioned for her to come. Simona hesitated, glancing back at the other girls.

Kinga stepped forward and stood beside Charlie. "I trust her," she said firmly in English. "She will help us. I am going with her." She repeated the words in Hungarian to Gabi.

Simona looked at Charlie again, seeming to weigh her options.

"We will help you," Charlie reassured her. "We will take you somewhere safe. I promise. Don't you want to be able to get back to your daughter?"

Simona narrowed her eyes and studied her for a long moment, then nodded once and followed Monica and Kinga down the stairs. The other young women trailed in a silent line.

Once they were all seated in the van, Monica drove slowly through the silent town with the headlights off. Charlie kept glancing back over her shoulder, sure that they were being watched, that someone would stop them at any moment. But the town remained dark and quiet.

When they reached the town limits, Monica revved the engine and switched on the headlights, flooding the narrow road with a soft white glow. All around them were dark rolling hills and long open fields. With a glance in the rearview mirror, Monica accelerated, putting as much distance as she could between them and the scene of the accident.

Charlie kept her eyes on the rearview mirror for the first few miles, still expecting to be pursued. After twenty minutes she sighed and sat back.

"I think we got away," she murmured to Monica. "I'll call the center." She pulled out her phone and punched in the number. "When will we get to Belgrade?"

Monica shrugged. "At least a few hours," she said. "Maybe more because it is dark and some of the roads are not good."

Charlie placed the call, alerting the drop-in center staff to their arrival, then handed back a box of Band-Aids and some antiseptic wipes from the first-aid box. She followed the basic supplies with bottles of water and a few packages of cookies and granola bars they had left over from the trip. The girls were spread out over the two rows of seats. They all swayed back and forth as Monica took the turns as fast as she dared.

Charlie studied the young women in the dim dome light as Kinga handed out supplies and issued instructions. They were young, probably between sixteen and twenty. A few were pretty. Most looked as though they'd lived hard lives. They were just ordinary girls. If Charlie had passed them on the street, she would have thought nothing of it. But she had not passed them on the street. She had found them locked in the back of a transport truck, about to be sold like cattle.

She shuddered as the reality of what they had been headed for sank into her brain. She knew that human trafficking in Central Europe was a major problem. Anyone who worked with aid organizations in the region was aware of the issue. Men and women were promised a good job in another country, then coerced into prostitution or forced labor, kept as slaves and physically or sexually exploited. Thousands of people a year disappeared from their villages in Romania, Bulgaria, and Hungary, lured by the false promise of work. It was a silent problem, shadowy, tied to organized crime in a very efficient but almost invisible system. Charlie had glimpsed it now and then in her time with Care Network, but just the corners, the edges, the tail end. She had never stared it in the face until now. She glanced at Kinga in the rearview mirror, at the girl's drawn, blank stare, and something shattered inside of her.

"How often does this happen?" she asked Monica, pitching her voice low so the others couldn't hear her. "How often are women trafficked like this?"

Monica tapped the brakes as a stray dog ran across the road ahead of them. She sighed and shrugged. "No one knows for sure how many, but many girls. Thousands. It is all so secret. One day a girl is just gone. You talk to her family and they say she got a good job in Germany or Moscow, but no one ever hears from her again."

"Do they ever come back home?" Charlie asked.

Monica shook her head, her expression bleak. "No. They disappear. Like they never existed."

"But how can this keep happening?" Charlie protested, horrified. "Why doesn't someone stop it?"

Monica shifted gears and gained more speed as they reached the top of a hill and began the descent. There was nothing as far as the eye could see, no lights or other vehicles, just their white van and a long stretch of road.

"It's the money," she said matter-of-factly. "The girls want to make money. They see the TV—the Kardashians and *Desperate Housewives*. They want to be like the West, but there are no jobs in their villages, no way to make money. Everyone is desperate, very poor. Maybe they have a child to support, or a sick parent. All different reasons but all the same desire: a good job when there are no good jobs. So they go to other countries. Everyone does it, goes to London or Madrid, and sometimes it is okay. There are real jobs there. They work in a hotel or as a house cleaner. But sometimes . . ." She inclined her head toward the girls. "Sometime you just disappear and no one knows what happened to you."

Charlie swallowed hard. She remembered Tamas's words the last time she'd bought strudel. How he'd shrugged and said that no one had heard from Kinga. If not for the accident tonight, no one would have ever known the truth. She would have vanished like so many others. Charlie would have thought of her occasionally when she went for strudel, wondered how Kinga was liking her new life in Germany. She felt sick at the thought.

"So what happens to these girls now?" she asked.

"There is a safe house in Belgrade," Monica said. "Run by Baptist missionaries. I think probably the girls will go there. The people who run the safe house will help them get home. But in a year or two they may try to take another job. It could happen to them again." She hesitated. "Charlie, these people, the ones who sell girls . . ." She stared out the windshield into the darkness, frowning. "They are very bad men, and they have lost a lot of money tonight. If they find out what we've done, who we are . . . We need to be very careful."

Charlie nodded, instinctively glancing back at the road behind them. She put one hand on her stomach, over the gentle swell of the baby. She had not considered the danger she might incur by rescuing the young women. But what else could she do? It was unthinkable not to help them escape. She watched the road in the rearview mirror for several more minutes. Nothing moved. There were no cars anywhere in sight. No one could possibly know where they were taking the girls. They were safe. They had gotten away. But even as she tried to reassure herself, she could not shake a lingering sense of unease.

CHAPTER 12

February
The *Simply Perfect* television studio
Greenwich, Connecticut

O h, I'm glad that's over," Waverly sighed, kicking off her red stilettos and curling up in her ample office chair. She took a sip of the signature Valentine's Day hot chocolate drink she had concocted for a special five-minute segment that would air on *Good Morning America* the following week. The show had called just a few days before with a cancellation by another Food Network celebrity, and Waverly had jumped at the chance to fill in. Her video clip would be featured on the show to promote her cocktail-hour entertaining book. It was a golden opportunity, but the last-minute nature had the entire team scrambling. She took another sip of the hot chocolate, considering the elements—bitter Peruvian dark chocolate, whipping cream, cinnamon, a touch of cayenne pepper, and manuka honey—all served in a martini glass with a dollop of whipped cream on top. It was a traditional French drinking chocolate with a warming twist. She called it Honey Bee Good. It was decadent and delicious.

On the cream leather couch across from her, Beau sat with his ever-present clipboard, ready to discuss the coming week. Fatigued from the hectic morning prepping and shooting the impromptu video, Waverly closed her eyes and took another sip, basking in the glow of a job well done.

"Boss, we need to talk."

Waverly's eyes popped open at his serious tone. She set her glass down. "I'm listening."

Beau laid his clipboard aside, clasped his hands together, and leaned forward, looking ill at ease. "I got a call from Susan at the Food Network today."

Waverly watched him curiously. What was going on? Was there bad news? "Yes," she said slowly, prompting him.

"There's buzz about *Simply Perfect* from the higher-ups." Beau glanced down at his hands and wouldn't meet her eyes.

"Buzz?" Waverly asked, mystified.

"Some people, Susan wouldn't say who, but some decision makers at the network feel that *Simply Perfect* isn't as . . . fresh as it once was. They feel like we might have peaked." Beau hazarded a glance in her direction.

"Peaked?" Waverly was offended by the very notion. "Except for that little dip last quarter, we've been showing steady growth in viewership every quarter for the last five years," she protested. "The new book is selling well. *Simply Perfect* is a successful show." She stared at Beau indignantly.

He held up his hands as though warding off her ire. "I know, I know. But, Boss, television isn't what it used to be. There are so many choices now; it's a viewer's market. And cable networks are getting nervous, they're looking for sure bets. They want rock-solid ratings and superstar shows—Rachael Ray plastered on every Walmart cookbook end cap. That sort of thing." He sighed in resignation. "*Simply Perfect* is a good show, a solid show. It's just not the biggest show around, and the network, well, they're not taking the chances they used to. Susan was just giving us a heads-up. We need to be thinking about how to bump the show up another level, boost ratings and visibility. We need to go from good to great if we want to stay in the game."

Waverly sat back in her chair. It was true that *Simply Perfect*'s numbers had dropped slightly last quarter, but so had a lot of good shows. And their two-part Christmas entertaining special had been very popular, the highest viewership yet. Surely the network wouldn't drop them, not when they were growing, not when things were going so well. But still, she knew Beau was right; viewers had hundreds of options now, all vying for their precious minutes. Was *Simply Perfect* dynamic enough to capture their interest and hold it? If she were honest with herself, Waverly had to admit that she wasn't sure. Neither was the Food Network, apparently.

She leaned her head back and massaged her temples, where a stress headache was beginning to bloom behind her eyes.

"Don't worry yet. Nothing's for certain," Beau said, trying to placate her. "Susan called as a personal favor to me. It was a warning, okay? Not a done deal. But we need to think about our strategy."

"What can we do?" Waverly asked, still baffled by the turn the conversation had taken. She sat up straight. "Did you tell Susan about the *Good Housekeeping* endorsement?"

"Waverly, Boss." Beau laced his fingers and leaned forward. "We have to do better," he said bluntly. "That's all there is to it. We need to kick it up a notch or two, or this time next year they may not renew *Simply Perfect*."

His words slowly sank in. If the network chose not to renew the show, there would be no more *Simply Perfect*. It was as simple as that. Oh, they could maybe get picked up by a smaller cable channel somewhere, or go back to being regional. But it would be a slow slide from there into obscurity and eventual cancellation. The implosion of everything she had worked so hard for, had dreamed of and fought for and created from scratch with sheer grit and determination. Her mind flashed to the dozens and dozens of aprons hanging in her studio wardrobe. What in the world would she do with those if the show were canceled? Who would she be without *Simply Perfect*? It would be the end of everything.

"Well then," she said, her tone determined and calm, betraying none of her inner turmoil, "we have to do better. Let's start today." She picked up her hot chocolate and took another sip, her mind already working to solve the issue at hand. The problem was, she had no idea how.

At one in the morning Waverly awoke, instantly alert. Her mind was racing, going over and over the conversation with Beau earlier that afternoon. Lying in the dark, she thought of a dozen compelling, articulate arguments for the decision makers at the Food Network channel, mouthing them soundlessly as Andrew snored softly beside her. At last, frustrated and nerves jangling, she got up and went down to the kitchen to putter.

She didn't turn on the overhead lights, preferring the soft under-the-cabinet lights by the sink. The room was quiet except for the gentle hum of the refrigerator. The backyard through the white french doors was dark and silent. Waverly tied on her mother's apron over her pajamas. She had dozens and dozens of aprons for the show, but in her own kitchen she wore only one, Margaret Talbot's cotton frilled apron, an ivory with peach-colored rosebud print. It was worn soft and supple, and stained in a few places, but Waverly wouldn't think of wearing anything else. For those few minutes she was embraced by the spirit of Margaret Talbot. For those few minutes she could almost imagine her mother perched on a stool beside her, smiling approvingly and giving advice.

Suitably clad, Waverly set to work. She was formulating a show centered on tapas that were a fusion of Spanish and Moroccan cuisine. At her spacious granite island she rubbed the spices between her fingers, reveling in the fragrant, exotic blend—cumin, ginger, cinnamon, coriander. She pictured Moroccan marinated chicken and olive tapenade in puff pastry bites. After working on the filling for a few minutes, she grew frustrated. She was too distracted. Nothing was coming together quite right. The flavors were a little bitter, just slightly off. At last she gave up.

She made herself a cup of ginger root tea and sat down at the kitchen table with her laptop to check her e-mail, hoping for a message from Charlie. It had been almost a week since the last one. Her sister had most recently been sending funny anecdotes about second-trimester pregnancy symptoms, namely, bladder incontinence when she coughed and a strange penchant for paprika-flavored potato chips. Waverly read each e-mail several times, greedily scooping up the images and stories, trying to vicariously connect with the baby through the words and grainy black-and-white photos.

There—a new message from Charlie. Subject line: *Genetic ultrasound results—call me.* Waverly's heart skipped a beat. She reached for her phone.

Charlie picked up after two rings. It was seven thirty in the morning in Budapest, Waverly realized belatedly. Perhaps a touch too early to be calling a pregnant woman.

"Well, good morning to you. What are you doing up in the middle of the night?" Charlie asked.

She sounded like she'd just woken up, her voice husky with sleep. She also sounded perfectly at ease. Waverly relaxed slightly. Nothing terrible had happened to the baby, then.

"I couldn't sleep. I just got your e-mail and called to make sure everything's okay." She sounded strained even to her own ears. She so desperately wanted this baby to be healthy and well.

On the other end of the line, Charlie yawned. "Yep, Junior and I are all good here. I can't button my pants anymore, so now I'm wearing those stretchy-topped ones you bought me.

173

They're actually really comfortable. I might never go back to regular pants again. I had the twenty-week ultrasound yesterday. Everything looks great. Baby has the right number of fingers and toes and lungs and other organs. Dr. Nagy says it's a perfectly healthy baby."

Waverly closed her eyes, awash with relief. The baby was healthy and strong, a boy or a girl, her child. There was no cause for alarm. For a moment she thought she might burst into tears. Charlie sounded so close, as though she were in the next room and not a continent away with an ocean between them. She wished Charlie were sitting at the table with her, keeping her company. She would make Aunt Mae's poached eggs in milk over buttered saltines for her sister. The protein and calcium would be good for the baby. She hoped Charlie was eating enough.

Charlie was still talking, and Waverly tuned in to the conversation again.

"The doctor couldn't tell if it's a boy or a girl. The baby seems to be very modest—had his or her legs crossed. I'm sending you some images now. Next time Dr. Nagy said they'll do a 4-D ultrasound, whatever that means. Do you want to know the gender if they can tell us?"

"Oh." Waverly put her hand to her throat, feeling her pulse start to return to normal. Did she want to know the gender? What an amazing question. "Yes, yes, I'd love to know," she clarified.

"Okay, I'll tell them at the next appointment and see if the baby will cooperate." Charlie yawned again.

"Are you okay? Do you need anything?" Waverly had to tamp down the intense urge to mother her sister, the mother of her child. "Are you eating enough? Getting enough good nutrients? Are you taking the fish oil supplements I sent with you?"

She realized how desperate she sounded in her own ears and abruptly stopped talking. She wanted to control every last little detail, make sure that everything humanly possible had been done to ensure the safety, health, and well-being of the baby and Charlie. But as she'd learned so many times before, some things were out of her control. Some things happened despite your best efforts.

Charlie laughed, assuring her gently, "This baby is going to be just fine. It will be mostly made out of strudel, but we're both doing great."

"Okay." Waverly blew out a breath. She had to let it go, had to trust the natural process of Charlie's body and her sister's good sense. Charlie had good sense. It was one of her strongest points.

"Hey, I've got to get ready for work. I just sent you those ultrasound photos." Charlie was rustling on the other end of the line.

"Okay," Waverly said, reluctant to end the call. "If you need anything at all . . ."

"You'll be the first to know," Charlie promised.

"Well then . . ." Waverly didn't know what else to say. "Thank you." Those two little words encompassed so much she didn't know how to express.

"You're welcome," Charlie said, and Waverly sensed that her sister understood without the words being spoken.

When they ended the call, Waverly immediately opened the new e-mail from Charlie, complete with attachments. She clicked on the ultrasound images one after another, tracing the baby's profile—upturned nose, the egg-smooth curve of the skull, skinny arms with tiny fingers outstretched. In one the baby was sucking its thumb. In another it appeared to be reclining comfortably, as if poolside in a chaise lounge.

Waverly studied the pictures greedily, her heart squeezing with both gratitude and longing. Her professional life might be unexpectedly teetering precariously, but at least this remarkable gift from her sister was still going right in her life.

"Please, please, please," she whispered, squeezing her eyes shut, saying a little prayer of health and safety for Charlie and baby so far away, not even quite sure what she was asking for, but asking all the same.

CHAPTER 13

Late February
Budapest

C harlie almost believed they had gotten away
with it. It had been more than five weeks
since she and Monica had rescued the girls, and
all had been quiet since then. The night of the
rescue, they arrived in Belgrade in the dark early
morning. After a few hours' wait at the drop-in
center, the girls had been transferred to the safe
house on the outskirts of the city. They would
stay there until they could be repatriated to their
respective countries. Charlie and Monica had
waited until daylight at the drop-in center and
then headed back to Budapest. Before the girls
left for the safe house, Charlie gave Kinga her
cell phone number.

"If you need anything . . ." She trailed off,
not sure how to put into words her concern and
care for the young woman. She pressed some
crumpled euros into Kinga's hand and made
her promise to call if she needed anything at
all.

"Be careful," she said. "Stay safe." Charlie

hated to leave her. A cell phone number and twenty euros felt like so little, but it was all she could think to do in that moment.

Kinga had nodded, her eyes wide and frightened, and a few days later Charlie received a text from her, letting her know that all the girls were safe and doing well. Kinga said she was hoping to come home soon.

Charlie found her mind returning again and again to that frigid black night. Something had changed in her when she'd opened the door of the transport van and seen the girls sitting there; it had broken open a place inside of her that had been long sealed off. She tried to return to her usual patterns—work, socializing with colleagues on Friday nights, reading in the evenings, or watching a documentary—but she felt unsettled, restless, the sensation stinging like nettles along the surface of her skin.

Unsure what to do about this change, Charlie focused on the tasks at hand, specifically work and the baby. She was still keeping the pregnancy a secret at work, although it was becoming harder and harder. She had resorted to wearing baggy sweaters over the maternity skinny jeans Waverly had gotten for her. She just looked like she was getting a little chubby.

Posing in front of her bathroom mirror one workday morning, Charlie snapped a quick photo of the bump to send to Waverly. She knew her sister loved any piece of information Charlie could give her. It was difficult with the distance and time difference and their busy schedules, but Charlie was doing the best she could. Without question the sisters had connected far more in the last few months than in the previous six years combined.

When Charlie left for Africa the first time, Waverly had driven her to the airport. She would be leaving in a few days herself for the Culinary Institute of America in Hyde Park. The sisters had stood at the boarding gate as Charlie's flight was called, facing one another, unsure how to say good-bye. Looking at Waverly, Charlie had suddenly realized what it meant to board that plane. She was heading across the ocean. Waverly was driving to New York. For the first time in their lives, they would be apart. She bit her lip, unsure that she wanted to leave. Since the death of their parents, they had been each other's constant. It was destabilizing to think of waving good-bye to Waverly. Perhaps Africa could wait after all. They called her section of the plane and still she hesitated.

"You should go," Waverly said. "That's your row." She raised her chin and gave Charlie a tight smile that wobbled at the corners.

"Are you going to be okay?" Charlie asked, wanting to say so much and yet unsure how to put any of it into words. "New York seems so far away."

Waverly laughed and sniffed back tears. "Not as far as Africa." And then, "Of course I'll be okay. This is what we both want, isn't it?"

Charlie nodded, but she wasn't convinced. Something was about to change permanently. She could sense it. If she set foot on that plane, there would be no going back.

They issued the final boarding call, and still she lingered.

Waverly stepped forward and pulled her into a fierce hug, then propelled her toward the gate. "Go," she said firmly, her eyes suspiciously pink. "It's just a few weeks. I'll see you when you get back. You can come visit me in New York."

Charlie had boarded the plane. When she looked back, Waverly was standing there alone, her hand raised in farewell. *It's just a few weeks,* Charlie told herself, but she sensed the change even then, before the heartbreaking beauty of Africa captivated her, before she purposefully missed her flight home.

In the ensuing years she and Waverly had kept in contact, at first almost daily, and then gradually a bit less as they both became absorbed in their separate lives. Charlie had visited Waverly in New York and then Paris. Waverly had never come to Johannesburg. There were a few visits back home together for Christmas, but the time between the twins' calls and e-mails and visits lengthened with each passing year.

When Charlie left Africa, her heart and her life in pieces, and took the job in Budapest, the silent spaces stretched even longer. In the midst of her brokenness, Charlie had no capacity for connection with her sister. She did not tell Waverly what had transpired in Johannesburg, why she had left, and her omission made the distance between them even greater. That was the turning point, the place where their relationship had stalled. Without honesty there had been no capacity for growth.

Charlie shut herself away, and Waverly, newly married to Andrew and on the cusp of *Simply Perfect* stardom, seemed too busy to realize the gradual change. If she had noticed, she'd done nothing to remedy it. So they had continued in polite distance for six years until Aunt Mae's death, until Charlie's offer and the baby changed everything again.

"Let's send your mama this photo of you growing," Charlie said to the baby, then sent the photo to Waverly, adding a few lines to let her know everything continued to be okay. Then on impulse she googled *How to keep pregnancy secret?* She knew it was just a matter of time until someone at work figured out the truth and her cover was blown.

"Anyone have any fabulous suggestions?" she

murmured, scanning the online articles and blogs for inspiration.

Bring your own coffee to work so you can drink decaf instead, one article suggested. *If anyone asks why, just tell them you're trying to save money.*

If you go out for drinks with friends, order at the bar and just get a virgin drink. No one will ever know, another advised.

Layers, layers, layers. You can get away with just looking like you've gained a few pounds if you strategically layer clothes, at least for the first couple of months.

Bolstered by the ideas, Charlie decided to employ all the suggestions. She chose an outfit, then turned sideways and scrutinized her reflection in the bathroom mirror. She was wearing a pin-striped button-down man's shirt over her skinny maternity jeans and a blazer she'd bought after watching *Annie Hall* but had never worn. If she squinted, she just looked a little thicker around the middle. Too much strudel, maybe? Because her natural frame was lean and wiry, even at twenty weeks her swelling belly was fairly small. Still, she would only be able to hide it for a limited time.

She sighed and tried to suck in her tummy. "Well, pal, this will have to do. Hope it's good enough." That was how she thought of the baby—as a little pal, a sidekick along for the ride. They still did not know the gender, but Charlie had a strong feeling that the baby was a boy. She found herself talking to him more and more, feeling a little foolish but liking the companionship in some strange way. She was a solitary creature by nature. Since her broken engagement with Shane, she'd always lived alone. With her traveling lifestyle she could not even keep a houseplant, let alone a pet. But there was the baby now, bobbing along with her on trains and buses and in the Care Network van, a tiny traveler in a tummy suitcase. She found his presence strangely comforting.

"Hat or no hat?" she asked him, slipping a fedora, also never worn, onto her head. "Too much? Draws too much attention? I think you're right." She abandoned the fedora and left the blazer unbuttoned, hoping the loose lines would disguise the baby belly for a little longer.

She was running late for work. The number 6 train where she got on idled mysteriously for more than ten minutes. Eventually a woman made an announcement through the intercom, and the passengers grumbled quietly in response. Charlie spoke only basic Hungarian, enough to catch a few key words. Delays due to maintenance on the tracks. She sighed. She was not going to make the morning meeting. Great, just what she needed. Something like this, even if it was just a missed meeting, begged Ursula's scrutiny, which was the last thing she wanted right now. She was trying to fly below her boss's radar, keep her head down and do her job. She tugged the blazer over the gently rounded swell of her belly.

The passengers slowly filed off the train, streaming toward the sidecar. Apparently the number 6 was indefinitely delayed. She texted Duncan to let him know the situation and then joined the masses on the sidewalk, weighing the length of time it would take to walk to work or to find another means of transport. She decided to walk. The exercise would do her good.

"Sorry I'm late," Charlie said, hurrying into the main office room twenty minutes later. She sank down into one of the office chairs around the conference table, a little out of breath. A few of the other staff looked up from their laptops and mumbled greetings.

"You look a bit done in," Duncan observed, turning his chair and looking her up and down. "Busy weekend?" He grinned cheerfully and winked.

Charlie laughed. "A little," she said dismissively. "Nothing too exciting. What did I miss? Fill me in."

Duncan shrugged. "Not much, just a report on the new projects for the summer." He leafed through a stack of papers.

"I've got the kettle on. Anyone want a coffee or tea?" Kate asked, pausing on her way to the tiny cupboard that passed for a kitchen. She made the offer in general but was looking at Duncan as she spoke.

He nodded without looking up from the report. "Thanks, love. Black tea, one milk, two sugars."

Charlie pulled her thermos from her satchel and patted it, employing tip number #4 from the "How to Hide Your Pregnancy" article. "Brought my own, thanks. I'll take some water, though." She was thirsty all the time. It was hard work making a person.

With a backward glance at Duncan, Kate disappeared to get the coffee, looking a little crestfallen.

"Duncan," Charlie said, making a snap decision to intervene. "You know you're my favorite colleague. I think you're brilliant at your job, but sometimes, personally, I think you're an idiot."

Duncan looked up from the report in puzzlement. "An idiot? What's brought this on?"

Kate reappeared at his elbow and slid a mug of tea in front of him. He thanked her with a quick smile and turned back to Charlie, who shook her head, half amused, half irritated on Kate's behalf. She waited until Kate was out of earshot before saying, "When it comes to women, you can be completely blind. Our office manager has been mooning over you since her first day on the job. She's cute as a button, efficient, makes a great cup of tea, and thinks you hung the moon. If I were you, I'd take a second look."

Duncan looked surprised and glanced over his shoulder at Kate as she delivered a cup of coffee to Arben. "Is that so?" he said. He considered for a moment and then nodded. "I'll give it some consideration."

"You do that." Charlie unscrewed her thermos and poured herself a cup of rooibos tea, then turned to the task at hand. "Now fill me in on what I missed in the meeting."

They chatted through the morning and skipped lunch, discussing the new summer programs and the immediate steps they needed to take to get the initiatives off the ground.

As they discussed the summer schedule, Charlie felt a growing sense of unease. The baby was due July 11, and she would most likely be off work for most of the summer. She needed to tell her coworkers soon so they could arrange a replacement. They were counting on her help with the busy summer programs. Unfortunately, there was the matter of Ursula and the layoffs. Their boss wasn't even subtle, making notations on her tablet and generally creating a sense of uneasy tension in the office.

While Kate, Duncan, and the other Western staffers would no doubt be supportive when Charlie finally had to tell them about the pregnancy, the reality was that many of the countries they worked in and the local contacts they had there were quite traditional, especially in the Balkans. In a region where women married young, an "older" single woman was already considered to be an unlucky novelty. Adding a pregnancy to the mix was going to complicate things exponentially. And if anyone discovered the real reason for the pregnancy, well, there would most likely be no recovering from that. Pregnant by a sperm donor? Giving the baby to her sister?

Charlie had not fully considered the implications when she had hatched the plan. In the middle of the night, sitting at a Formica table in the kitchen where she had grown up, mourning the loss of the woman who raised her, the way forward had seemed so clear and simple. But afterward, back once more in her real life, she had become gradually more aware of the complexity of the decision she'd made. If she lost her job, she would not be able to afford to continue living in Budapest. Her salary was modest by any standard, her trust fund long ago swallowed up by the fiasco in Johannesburg. She had very little financial cushion should something go wrong. She needed to make it through the round of staff cuts, then announce her pregnancy and arrange for time off for maternity leave. As soon as she gave the baby to Waverly, she would be free to return to work as usual. This was the plan. Hide the pregnancy as long as possible. Manage to keep her job until she could get her life back to normal.

Since finding the girls in the back of the van, however, she had to admit that her idea of normal had shifted radically. She was trying hard to keep this job, needed to keep this job, but there was a growing suspicion in the back of her mind that all her efforts were becoming increasingly unsatisfying. Did she really want to spend the rest of her life putting condoms on bananas?

She thought of Kinga and the other young women in the back of that van. She thought of the zip ties tightly binding their wrists and Monica's voice on the dark drive to Belgrade when Charlie had asked how often this sort of thing happened.

No one knows for sure how many, but many girls. Thousands.

Do any ever come back home?

No. They disappear. Like they never existed.

Those words haunted her. How could she sit by when this was the daily reality? She needed to help in some way, but she had no idea how.

Charlie zoned back into the conversation just as Duncan finished describing the new roster of volunteers.

"Dr. Kruger will be heading up the health programs for mothers and babies this summer. Charlie, he wants to talk to you about helping him. He'll be in sometime in the next hour," Duncan concluded.

"Great," Charlie said, unsure what she was agreeing to. She squinted out the window and took a sip of water, wishing she'd brought a sandwich or a snack. All she'd had that morning was the rooibos, and now she was feeling a little light-headed. The office seemed too hot.

A few minutes later Ursula swept into the office and convened a two-hour budget meeting that Charlie had forgotten about. Her heart sank as she scanned the lengthy agenda. She desperately needed a snack and either a nap or a brisk walk in the fresh air, perhaps both. She was feeling more unwell by the minute. Her blood sugar must be low. She'd read about it as a common pregnancy symptom. She dredged the bottom of her bag, hoping for a bag of almonds or a forgotten apple, but came up empty.

The meeting seemed to drag on interminably, the room growing warmer by the minute. After almost forty minutes, Charlie's cell phone dinged with a text message. Ursula paused midsentence in her discussion of transportation costs in April and shot her a stern look. Charlie glanced at her cell phone as she silenced it. A text from Monica.

Charlie, call me. We have a problem.

Alarmed, Charlie murmured an apology and escaped to the bathroom in the back hall, locking the door behind her.

In the bright light of the tiled bathroom she sat down on the toilet and called Monica immediately.

Monica answered on the first ring. "Charlie." Her voice sounded strained.

"Hey, what's going on? Are you okay?" Charlie whispered. Leaving a meeting to use the toilet was acceptable. Leaving a meeting to make phone calls in the bathroom was definitely not. She hunched forward on the seat, intent on Monica's voice.

"I can't talk right now, but we need to meet as soon as you can. Someplace safe." Monica sounded panicked, her words coming in a rush.

"Safe? What do you mean?" Charlie asked, her pulse quickening. "Safe from what?"

"Charlie," Monica said. "The men who sold Kinga and Simona, they found me."

"What? How?" Dread curdled her insides in an instant. She tried to draw a deep breath. "What happened? How did they find you?"

Monica cleared her throat nervously. "I can't talk now. Meet me at Szimpla as soon as you can. I'll explain everything." She hung up.

Clutching the cell phone, Charlie tried to think. Her heart was hammering in her ears. Should she go to the police? But what if they were in on it? She knew that corruption was rife in Central Europe. Hungary was no exception. Nowhere seemed safe. The traffickers had found Monica.

It was probably just a matter of time until they found out about Charlie's involvement too, if they didn't know already. What could she do?

Someone knocked on the door.

"Occupied," she called out. She shut her eyes and leaned over, putting her forehead on her knees. Her head was swimming and her pulse was rapid in her ears. She thought she might pass out. She had locked herself in the bathroom. Another stupid move. If she did pass out, no one would be able to help her. She needed to open the door. She needed a snack and a place to lie down and let her blood sugar stabilize. How had they found Monica? Her thoughts were whirling around in her head at an alarming rate.

Someone rapped on the door again, firmer this time.

Annoyed and light-headed, Charlie stood up, staggered to the door, and managed to turn the lock, pushing open at the same time as the person on the other side pulled it. She lost her balance and toppled forward. Someone grabbed her as she fell. All of a sudden she was steadied against a barrel chest, and a strong arm clamped across her back, keeping her upright. Startled, she glanced up, finding herself almost eye to eye with Johan Kruger. He smelled warm and spicy, like southern sweet tea and cinnamon.

"Hello there," he said.

She was standing very close to him. The

smooth, round contour of her belly was poking into his middle.

He stared hard at her for a long moment, eyes narrowing in sudden comprehension. She opened her mouth but no sound came out.

"Charlie, are you all right?"

She heard his voice from a great distance as her vision narrowed to a pinpoint and then was swallowed into a warm blackness. The last thing she felt was Johan's arm supporting her as her knees buckled.

A few minutes later she came to. She was lying on the cold bright blue tiles of the bathroom, her head pillowed on her lumpy bag. Johan knelt next to her, his fingers on the pulse in her wrist.

"Easy there," he murmured as she tried to sit up. "Better lie back for another minute. I sent Kate for something to eat. You'll feel better once you've got something in your stomach."

Obediently Charlie lay back. The tiles were uncomfortably hard, but she didn't want to risk passing out again. She looked up. Johan was watching her with a thoughtful expression.

"How far along are you?" he asked.

She didn't bother to deny it. "Just past twenty weeks."

He nodded. "Did you eat anything recently?"

She shook her head. It felt strange to finally admit that she was pregnant. Oddly, she didn't feel exposed by his knowing. He didn't seem surprised.

"I thought you might be pregnant back in January in Romania. The bananas." He smiled slightly, cocking an eyebrow.

She nodded. "Nobody knows except you. I need to keep it a secret."

"You've seen a doctor." It was not a question.

She nodded again. "The baby's doing great. I just don't want anyone from work knowing yet. It's complicated."

"It almost always is," he agreed ruefully.

She laughed. He probably thought the father was a work colleague. Perhaps the result of a wild weekend tryst in Montenegro with Duncan. The truth was far more convoluted and bizarre.

"I'm okay," she assured him, struggling to sit up. "I just need to eat something."

There was a knock at the door, and Kate poked her head in. "Here's the sandwich and a yogurt I had in the fridge." She handed both to Johan, looking curiously at Charlie. "You feeling okay?"

"Yeah, just low blood sugar. Should have eaten breakfast, I guess." Charlie drew her blazer across her middle and managed a weak smile as Kate withdrew, shutting the door behind her. Johan insisted on staying with her while she ate the yogurt and all of the sandwich. She found she was ravenous and devoured the mozzarella, tomato, and basil panini in a matter of moments.

Johan was easy company. He sat with her on the bathroom floor and asked her questions about her time in Budapest, filling her in on what he had been doing since they'd worked together in Johannesburg. She struggled to keep up her end of the conversation. All her inner focus was bent on the call from Monica and their impending meeting. Her heart skipped a beat every time she thought of it.

At last Johan declared her well enough to get up, although he recommended she take the rest of the day off, a decision she gladly agreed to. She couldn't possibly work now, not with Monica waiting for her, not with this impending feeling of doom.

Johan helped her to her feet, his hand warm and strong. He didn't let go for a moment. "You all right?" he asked, scrutinizing her. "You look pale."

She smiled shakily and nodded. "These hormones are crazy."

He nodded, looking sympathetic. "So I hear. Take care of yourself. Rest, drink plenty of fluids."

"Yes, Doctor." She gave him a mock salute.

Johan gave her another assessing look. "You sure you're okay?"

"I'm sure," she said without much conviction. She tried to shrug it off, straightening her shoulders and smiling briskly.

"If you run into trouble," he said, looking her in the eye firmly, "I hope you will consider me a friend."

She clutched her cell phone in her hand, thinking of the panic in Monica's voice. What could he possibly do about that? But still, it was kind of him to offer.

"Thank you," she said, and meant it.

CHAPTER 14

When Charlie arrived at Szimpla Kert, Budapest's iconic "ruin pub," Monica was waiting in the cave-like entrance. Housed in a formerly condemned factory, Szimpla was an enormous warren of derelict rooms, crumbling staircases, and patios that abounded with dim nooks and overlooked corners. It was entirely decorated with recycled furnishings—a seating area made from an old Trabant car, a lamp crafted out of half a bicycle. It smelled of stale cigarette smoke and spilled cheap beer. And at this hour it was almost deserted.

Charlie and Monica found an unoccupied corner with two mismatched chairs huddled against a narrow wooden table. Charlie went to the bar and returned with peach juice for herself and the shot of plum palinka, Hungary's iconic fruit brandy, that Monica had requested.

"What happened?" Charlie asked immediately, sliding Monica's drink over to her side of the table.

Monica cast a nervous glance over her shoulder and leaned forward. "I got a package in the mail today," she said quietly.

She pulled a manila envelope from her handbag and shook the contents onto the table. In the dim light from the floor lamp beside them Charlie squinted to see clearly. She froze, a tendril of fear snaking down her spine as she saw the items. Two plastic zip ties cut in pieces and a smashed cell phone.

Charlie's pulse quickened as she stared at the objects on the table, and she tasted again the fear, silver in her throat, as cold and sharp as the January night it had happened.

Monica cast a look around and then pulled a folded scrap of paper from her pocket. "This was in the envelope too." She spread the paper out on the table. In bold black scrawl it said, *Să nu scoți o vorbă!*

"What does that mean?" Charlie asked.

" 'Don't say a word,' " Monica said.

Charlie stared grimly at the words on the paper. "How did they track you down?"

Monica shrugged. "I'm sure it wasn't hard. The girls go missing in a tiny village in the middle of the night, and the next morning we are gone too."

Charlie sat back and cursed softly. She'd thought they were safe, that they had escaped detection. She glanced over her shoulder but the room was empty. Still, she felt eyes on her.

"What do you think they want with you?" Charlie asked finally. "Why did they send you that message?"

Monica leaned forward, over the pieces of plastic. "I think it's a warning not to talk about what we saw." She looked down and toyed with her shot glass of palinka. "A lawyer called me yesterday. She works with the safe house where the girls are. Remember the girls who helped us, Kinga and Simona?" She glanced up briefly at Charlie, who nodded. "The girls knew who their traffickers were. Kinga was sold by her cousin. Simona's uncle tricked her. The lawyer told me that they are taking the men to court. Both men were arrested last week in Serbia in a police raid, but they are claiming the girls were going to Turkey willingly. Kinga and Simona say they were forced to go. And we're the only witnesses who can prove they were taken against their will. Their lawyer wants me to testify about what we saw that night. I think she will contact you too." Monica licked her lips nervously.

"You told her about me?"

"I didn't have to. Kinga and Simona already had."

Charlie shifted in the hard chair and stared at the pieces of plastic, feeling the weight of this new information. They were in the middle of something extremely dangerous.

She crossed her arms over her swelling belly, a gesture of protection. "What are you going to do?"

Monica sighed heavily. "I've been thinking

about this," she said finally, "and I cannot testify." She carefully scooped the cut pieces of zip tie and the smashed cell phone into the envelope, not meeting Charlie's eyes. "I'm going home to Romania," she said. "And I'm going to keep my mouth shut."

Charlie stared at her incredulously. "Are you serious? You're just giving in to them?"

Monica looked up, her expression scared and a little sad. "Charlie, you don't understand. These people . . . They will stop at nothing to get what they want. They know who I am. My father is dead. I am the only one left to take care of my mother. My sister has two little girls. These people could hurt my family. I can't risk it. I already told Ursula that today is my last day. I am taking a night bus to Medias tonight."

Charlie was dumbfounded. Monica was leaving, going home to Romania, just like that?

"What should I do?" she asked, feeling suddenly very alone.

"Whatever you think you have to do," Monica replied simply. "If you keep your head down, maybe they won't figure out you were there too." But her tone of voice was doubtful. She stood, threw back the shot of palinka in one swallow, and grabbed the envelope from the table. She hugged Charlie hard for a long moment, whispering in her ear, "Be careful, my friend." A moment later she was gone.

In disbelief Charlie watched Monica hurry down the grimy hallway toward the stairs. She did not glance back. So that was it? They had worked together for more than three years. She considered Monica a friend. And now, just like that, Monica was leaving.

Stunned, Charlie gripped the edge of the table. Tendrils of panic were spiraling through her chest like cigarette smoke. She breathed in and out hard through her nose, trying to remain calm and in control. But the truth was that she was spooked. It had been years since she'd felt this vulnerable, and the memory of that night in Johannesburg and its aftermath still haunted her in unexpected moments. Charlie shook her head. She felt so alone. She had no idea what to do next.

Outside of the ruin pub, Charlie walked slowly down the narrow street, turning her back to the sharp wind. The sky was leaden gray and low over the closely crowded buildings. The air smelled like car exhaust and snow. Without thinking she headed toward home. Around her flowed pedestrians—Hungarian businessmen in long overcoats carrying briefcases; short, sturdy matrons in brightly dyed fur hats with small nervous dogs on leashes; the occasional cyclist weaving through the press of bodies. A hunched Roma woman in a head scarf and flowing skirt lay prostrate by a bakery entrance, begging with her hands outstretched. A paper cup with a few twenty-forint coins sat in front of her.

Charlie's cell phone rang, and she glanced at the screen. A Serbian area code. With a sense of inevitability, she turned away from the crowd and ducked into the doorway of a closed boutique to answer the call.

"Hello, I'm looking for Charlie Talbot." The voice was female and American, brisk and businesslike.

Charlie cleared her throat. "This is Charlie."

On the other end of the line the woman introduced herself. "My name is Sandra Ling. I'm a lawyer representing Kinga Varga and Simona Antonova. I work for a not-for-profit organization that provides legal representation in cases of exploitation and injustice. Kinga and Simona have both filed charges against the men who sold them, and the men will stand trial, but the defendants are claiming that the women went with them willingly. I understand from Kinga and Simona that you and your colleague Monica were the ones who discovered the girls in the back of the truck. Is that correct?"

"Yes." Charlie's pulse was pounding in her ears.

"I've already contacted Monica about testifying," Sandra said.

"She won't." Charlie interrupted the lawyer. "I

just talked to her and she said she won't testify at the trial. She's going home to Romania tonight."

"Oh, I see," Sandra said, her tone measured but disappointed. "Did she tell you why not?"

"She's scared," Charlie said. "She got a threat in the mail today."

"A threat? What was it?" Sandra asked. Charlie heard her typing in the background.

Charlie described the contents of the packages and the slip of paper, glancing over her shoulder to make sure she was not being overheard. No one was paying any attention to her.

"And has anyone contacted you or threatened you in any way?" Sandra asked.

"No. I don't know if they know I was involved." Charlie realized her hands were trembling and tucked one under her arm, trying to steady herself. She was usually so strong, level-headed, but the zip ties and smashed cell phone had rattled her. *Să nu scoți o vorbă*! She was not obeying the warning.

"I see. So someone's concerned about what Monica saw and could testify about in court. That's good. Ms. Talbot, even if Monica is not, are you willing to testify?"

Charlie hesitated. That was the million-dollar question. "What happens if I don't?" she asked.

Sandra sighed. "Most likely the traffickers will go free. Without your testimony it's just Kinga and Simona's word against theirs. The other girls who were with them are too scared to press charges or to testify. They all have families back home who might suffer if they speak up. We're up against a corrupt and flawed judicial system. Sometimes the justice officials are being paid off by the traffickers. The amount of money people make from human trafficking is staggering, and a lot of people stand to gain from making sure it's allowed to continue." She sounded weary.

"So, if I do testify, will it make any difference?" Charlie asked. A large Korean tour group passed her, the tour guide holding aloft a bright-red umbrella, a stream of middle-aged Koreans shuffling along behind him, cameras at the ready. Charlie bent away from the press of people, trying to hear.

"There's a strong possibility that it could," Sandra said cautiously. "With your testimony we would have a good case. More and more often we are winning these cases, and it makes a difference every time. Each trafficker who is sent to prison isn't just one more criminal off the streets. He's also a deterrent to all the others who are looking for easy money. The threat of prison can be its own deterrent."

Charlie said nothing, caught in indecision.

"Ms. Talbot," Sandra said after a long moment of silence, "you could be the difference between Kinga and Simona winning their cases or their traffickers going free to continue exploiting other women. Are you willing to give your testimony about what you saw that night?"

"I don't know," Charlie said finally. "I need to think about it." She felt pressured to make a decision and paralyzed by anxiety. She needed space to think through her choice and what it could mean.

"Okay," Sandra said, sounding resigned. "Well, please consider your decision carefully. If you do decide to testify, we will need you to appear in person in court for both trials as a witness. The trials will be in Belgrade. It's where the girls were sold first. We don't have dates yet, but it could be anywhere from a few weeks to a few months from now."

"Okay, I understand," Charlie said. She just wanted to get off the phone and be alone. She wanted to go home and make some toast and curl up on the sofa to think. She glanced behind her nervously. Was she being watched? No one was looking in her direction, but she felt exposed all the same.

"I'll be in touch when I know more," Sandra Ling told her.

Charlie disconnected the call and started to walk briskly, eager to be home, but at the last moment she changed her mind and headed instead for Castle Hill, needing to be high above the city, somewhere she could gain perspective. Everything was moving too fast, the ground shifting under her feet. She needed to regroup and to breathe.

Twenty minutes later Charlie reached Castle Hill by bus and made her way across the almost deserted square to Fisherman's Bastion, an enchanting series of white stone terraces and towers set high on the hill overlooking the city. She had it all to herself except for a South Asia family who were bunched together in the cold, snapping photos of Matthias Church, their colorful saris and white tennis shoes poking from beneath their down coats. She ducked into one of the turrets in Fisherman's Bastion and braced herself against a pillar, looking out over the stone parapet to the Danube below. Although it was only late afternoon, the daylight was fading and the lights along the river were just coming on, golden and soft in the quiet air. It started to rain, an icy mist that drifted and settled slowly like the breath of clouds. Charlie huddled closer into her down coat.

She felt removed from the situation, a little numb, unable to believe that this was really happening. She was shaking with adrenaline, but her mind was clear and clinical. She wished she could have a drink. A shot of whiskey to steady her nerves would be welcome right about now. Charlie shivered, feeling at once vulnerable and alone. No, not alone. She put a hand to her stomach. She was vulnerable, but she was not alone. And that made the situation infinitely more complicated.

She pictured the baby bobbing about placidly in the warm darkness of her womb, sucking his thumb or toes, safe and content. It was not just about her and the trafficked women. She thought for a second of calling Waverly but dismissed the notion in the next breath. She could imagine her sister's reaction—demanding that she return immediately to the States so she and the baby could be safely cocooned in their enormous house until the danger had passed. She would harangue Charlie until she got what she wanted. Waverly could be astonishingly stubborn. Well, so could Charlie. No, she decided, she would not consult Waverly. This was her mess, her decision.

Placing a hand on her stomach, Charlie asked softly, "So, pal, what do we do?" In response there came a flutter, quick and delicate like a minnow darting through a stream. She froze, marveling at the sensation. It was the first time she had felt the baby move.

"Hello," she murmured, forgetting all else for a moment in the wonder of feeling the little person inside of her. She poked her belly where she'd felt the movement. The baby moved again, a tiny motion that felt a little ticklish and a little queasy. She had not imagined it, then. She laughed, delighted. She felt nothing more, but it didn't matter. He was in there. He was really in there.

The knowledge both amazed and terrified her. She was aware of a growing responsibility for him, and a new, fierce desire to keep him safe. She'd never felt this way about another human being before. She was his guardian, his protector.

"Do you have any idea how to fix this mess?" she asked aloud, but there was no response. Charlie tapped her fingers on the cold stone of the railing, trying to think rationally and logically, trying to ignore the icy lump of fear lodged high in her belly, right above the hard swell of the baby. What was best for the baby, for her, for the rescued women? It was a muddle. Could one solution fix all three? It seemed unlikely.

The safest course of action would be to simply slip away as Monica had done, run from Budapest, keep silent and disappear. She could take a leave of absence and return to the States until the baby was born. Waverly and Andrew had enough money and clout that she had no doubt she would be safe. She would probably lose her job, but she would ensure the safety of both herself and the baby. And yet she found the notion distasteful. It didn't feel right, to run to safety and leave the girls to face their traffickers alone. It felt cowardly. What if her testimony really did make the difference between very bad men being put behind bars or being allowed to continue preying upon vulnerable young women? There could be serious implications if she did not testify. Didn't she have a moral obligation to speak up?

Charlie pictured the young women that night in Serbia—the beam of her flashlight illuminating their terrified faces, Kinga shrinking from her touch, a far cry from the carefree girl of a few months before with her dreams of a job in Germany. Charlie saw again the chain of cigarette burns ringing Gabi's neck, the thick white plastic zip ties binding Simona's wrists, pulled so tight they left ridges in her skin for hours after she had been freed.

The images made Charlie nauseated, the fear sparking up in her gut quick as a struck match. It brought back other memories too, ones she had thought long buried, ones she had worked hard to cover and control. The taste of grit ground into her lips and rasping against her teeth, the bruise on her windpipe for weeks afterward, purple and ugly and big as a fist. They rose to the surface now, leaving her heart pounding in her ears. She glanced behind her, as though afraid the past was creeping up at her back. The stone archways were empty and glistening with rain. The question of what she would do was inextricably linked to her own past. Her current dilemma had nothing to do with her years in South Africa and yet everything to do with them too.

Charlie closed her eyes, shutting out the golden glow of the magnificent parliament building, its massive Gothic Revival dome rising over the Danube, the shimmer of lights reflecting on the dark river through the misting rain. She swallowed hard and wrapped her arms around herself, trying to stop trembling, but she could not seem to get warm and she could not stop the shaking. The memories she'd tried so hard to suppress were rattling her bones, rising in her mind like ghosts resurrected. They would no longer keep silent. She had to let them speak.

CHAPTER 15

Seventeen years earlier
Johannesburg, South Africa

Charlie had never intended to travel to Africa and not return. It had been an almost spontaneous trip, born out of longing and a long-held grief. When the girls' trust funds were finally released to them on their eighteenth birthday, Charlie looked at the number of zeros in her bank account and felt at a loss as to her next step. She could go anywhere now, do anything. The world was open to her.

"So what do you want to do?" Waverly had asked, standing at the yellow counter in Aunt Mae's kitchen, neatly cutting out circles of biscuit dough with a crimped cookie cutter. She had already applied for and been accepted to the Culinary Institute of America. Her path was chosen. In a few months she would leave for New York.

Charlie twirled an ice cube in a glass of iced tea and considered the question. What *did* she want to do?

All she knew was that she wanted to see the

place where her parents had died. There had been no remains to repatriate, no coffins at the funeral. Robert and Margaret Talbot had vanished from the earth in the blink of an eye, or so it had seemed to Charlie at the time. In that moment her life had veered drastically from its expected course. She didn't know how to move forward now, but perhaps if she started from the place where it all had ended, she would be able to see a way.

She booked a round-trip ticket to Johannesburg, intending to stay for two weeks. Once there she hired a guide to take her east to the site of the crash. A few hours into the drive, just before they reached Kruger National Park, the guide veered off the dirt road and stopped the tired Land Cruiser.

"There." He gestured across a field.

"Where?" Charlie shaded her eyes and looked out across the sweeping land. All she saw were rocks, dirt, and trees. It was greener than she'd pictured. She'd imagined a desert somehow, the wreckage of an old charter plane sticking up out of the sand. This was peaceful, bucolic.

The guide shrugged, his face a blank. "I don't know. It was a long time ago, miss."

Charlie felt a sharp stab of disappointment. "Isn't there a marker or something? A memorial? Is there anything left?"

The guide shook his head. "It is all gone now."

She looked out across the landscape again, searching for something—a token, a feeling of completion or closure, something to make this trip worthwhile. She was standing so close to where her parents had died and yet she felt nothing. They were just gone, the landscape of her heart as empty as the green plain before her. She got back in the Land Cruiser, disappointed, and headed back to Johannesburg.

What Charlie had hoped to find at the sight of the crash she discovered quite unexpectedly the next day, when she visited the medical and dental clinic where her father had spent time volunteering each year. Located in a crowded township outside of Johannesburg, the tidy white concrete building sat solidly in the midst of the shantytown sprawl. The receptionist, a young black woman in a crisp white uniform, looked at her curiously when Charlie asked to meet with the administrator.

"And what is the nature of your meeting?" the young woman asked formally.

"It's about my father," Charlie said hesitantly. "He used to volunteer here when I was a child, but he was killed in a plane crash. It was years ago. I just wondered if there was anyone still here who knew him." She looked around the clinic, feeling lost and discouraged.

The young woman gave her a sympathetic look and asked Charlie to sit, then disappeared into a back room. A few moments later an older white woman appeared. She was tall and blond, an Afrikaner, with a short, choppy haircut. She looked Charlie up and down.

"You've grown," she pronounced. "The last time I saw a picture of you, you were just elbows and freckles."

Charlie stared at her, taken aback by the familiarity of this woman she had never seen before. "You know who I am?"

"Yes, Dr. Talbot was your father, wasn't he?" The woman cocked her head to one side and surveyed Charlie. "You look like him."

Unexpectedly Charlie felt her eyes well up with tears. Here was what she had come seeking, memories she did not have, someone who remembered her parents in a way she could not.

The woman smiled at her kindly. "I'm Dr. Coetzee. Come back to my office and we'll have tea."

As she followed Dr. Coetzee back through a narrow doorway, Charlie felt it, a flash of closeness. Her father had been here, within these walls. This was one of the last places where he had talked and laughed and breathed. Somehow it felt to her that he was here still. She put a hand out, touching the cool wall, overcome with a sense of familiarity, of things coming full circle. It felt like destiny.

Charlie came back to the clinic every day for

a week, drawn by the sensation of her father's presence. Dr. Coetzee gave her a cup of rooibos tea each morning and put her to work cleaning out the storage rooms. By the second week Charlie began to notice the people—a pregnant mother with three young children clinging to her skirts; an old man with one remaining tooth coming to have the rotting stump pulled. The steady stream of humanity captivated her, especially the women and older girls. They were strong and gracious, steadfast in the face of immense difficulty and suffering. In the midst of grinding poverty they had dignity and perseverance. She saw what the clinic could offer these women and so many others in need, and she was enthralled. So this is what had drawn her father back year after year. She understood it now, the desire to help with your own hands, the painful truth that you could never do enough.

When it came time for her return to Ohio, she found she could not tear herself away. Despite the brutality of life in the slums around Johannesburg, the opportunity to help these people called to her. The afternoon of her flight back home she watched a plane cleave the sky over the township, climbing higher and higher as it carried its passengers far away. Then she turned back to the clinic and got to work.

One month turned into one year and then another. After several years volunteering full-time at the clinic, she started a course of study, earning a degree in public health from the University of South Africa. Two years into her program she got engaged. Shane was a kind and decent man, who worked with an environmental awareness NGO operating out of Johannesburg. He had been sweet, with his long hair and devotion to sustainable agriculture, intelligent and idealistic enough to appeal to her. But it had taken them less than a year after their engagement to realize how ill-suited they really were. He was a dreamer, too soft for Charlie, and she was too practical, too hard and stubborn for him. There was nothing dramatic in their parting, just a dawning mutual understanding that they were categorically mismatched and that the engagement had been a mistake. They ended it amicably enough, although Shane immediately transferred to his organization's Kampala office. They never spoke again.

Toward the end of her studies at UNISA, Charlie volunteered at a mobile clinic for women. It was a shambling old bus that rotated through the townships surrounding Johannesburg, offering basic exams and contraceptives for women who did not have access to medical care in their communities. The care the mobile clinic offered was rudimentary and often insufficient, but it was certainly better than nothing.

During her time at the mobile clinic, Charlie

heard firsthand the shockingly commonplace accounts of rape and sexual abuse, and saw the terrible toll HIV/AIDS and ignorance of sexual health took on women and girls. After graduation she returned to the mobile clinic and spent several years working specifically in the area of women's health. Slowly she began to formulate an idea, a vision that gave direction and meaning to her life. She had gone back to her apartment after one particularly difficult appointment with a girl, just thirteen years old and pregnant from being raped by her uncle, and stared at her bank account with its long line of zeroes. She could do something to help. She could make a difference.

Armed with her public health degree and fired by a new zeal and determination, she set about planning a full-service women's health center. It would be based in one of the largest townships outside of Johannesburg, a place that currently had no permanent clinic, and would offer health screenings, contraceptives, a sexual abuse and rape hotline, and counseling for women on a range of health-related topics. It would be the most comprehensive clinic for women in any of the townships.

"I feel like this is what I was born to do," Charlie told Waverly on one of their infrequent calls. "I just wish Dad could see it when it's finally up and running. It's going to help so many women here."

Charlie worked tirelessly on the project for almost two years, determined to help these vulnerable women, many of whom she considered to be friends. She waded through mounds of paperwork, curried favor with local bureaucrats, and recruited volunteers. She hired a local business manager to handle the financial end of things, freeing her to concentrate on the programs and services the clinic would offer.

At last the clinic was set to open in a month's time. There would be a ribbon-cutting ceremony; a girls' choir would sing. Charlie carefully crafted the free packets of information about their services that she and a handful of volunteers would give out to every home in the township before the opening.

And then it all fell apart.

Charlie first got wind of the problem with a call from her bank in the US. They had noticed a series of overdraft charges. Was she aware of the issue? Sure there had been a mistake, Charlie logged on to her account. Sitting at her kitchen table under the stark light of a single bulb, she stared at the diminishing columns of numbers in her bank-balance history, confused. Where had the money gone? She'd started with well over two million dollars, and now there was a deficit in the account. The last several large charges had been rejected for insufficient funds.

Puzzled and uneasy, Charlie walked over to

the clinic and let herself into the tiny office where her business manager had been handling all the budgets and accounts. She sat down and began sorting through the papers and combing the books, trying to make sense of the numbers. It took hours to unravel the mess. There were glaring errors. Unexplained receipts and a stack of unpaid bills. Over the course of a long evening she slowly pieced together a history of the past financial year. At last she sat back, stunned, the reality of the situation gradually seeping into her brain.

It was gone. All gone. Every penny and then some. And she had not known. She had trusted the money to someone else, and her trust had been misplaced. The clinic was bankrupted before it even opened. Sick with dismay, she put her head in her hands, papers strewn about her in crumpled white drifts, and tried to think, to come up with a plan. She called the business manager's cell phone, but the call could not be completed. The phone number was no longer in use. She decided to walk to the woman's house, to confront her in person. Perhaps there had been some dramatic mistake. Perhaps this could still be rectified.

It was well past dark when she locked the clinic door, her head pounding, her heart heavy. She walked the ten minutes briskly, aware that she was a single female out alone after dark.

She never went out by herself after dark in the township; it was too dangerous. But these were desperate times. She was on the verge of her entire dream collapsing around her.

When she finally reached the business manager's home there was a light on inside. Relieved, she pounded on the door. A woman, whom she vaguely recognized as an aunt or a cousin, answered. Charlie greeted her politely and then asked to see her business manager.

The woman wouldn't meet her eyes. "She's not here," she said, her gaze straying over Charlie's shoulder.

"Where is she?"

The woman shrugged. "I don't know. She said she had business in the north."

"When will she return?" Charlie asked with a growing sense of desperation.

Still the woman would not meet her eyes. "She will be there a long time."

"Do you know how to reach her? I need to speak with her. It's urgent." Charlie raised her voice a little, insistent.

Another shrug. "No, there is no way."

Charlie knew stonewalling when she saw it. She would get nothing useful from this woman. Indeed, she was quite sure the business manager would never be seen in the township again. She was gone, and so was Charlie's money. There was little Charlie could do. She could go to the police, but nothing fruitful would come of it. The woman had taken the funds and fled.

With a sinking heart Charlie turned away from the house. She had no idea what to do next. Among other things, she discovered that the clinic had not been properly licensed. And the mortgage on the property had gone unpaid for the past few months. The business manager had smoothed over important details and embezzled money earmarked for those essentials. There was not enough to even open the clinic. And she was completely broke.

Charlie started toward the main road in the darkness, dazed and disheartened. She needed to find a taxi, get back to her apartment and try to muster her resources. Already she felt the courage of her convictions draining from her. How could she possibly succeed now? She walked down a dusty side street, paying scant attention to her surroundings. Halfway to the main road she realized she was being followed. She was on a stretch of dirt lane with no houses, just a high wall on either side. There were no lights and no one around. She picked up her pace, trying to reach the nearest cross street, hoping for people or at least a little light, but it was too late.

She never saw her attacker's face, just felt the crushing weight of an arm hooked across her windpipe as he grabbed her from behind.

She inhaled the acrid smell of him, stale sweat and cigarettes. She was strong, but he was far stronger. She struggled and kicked at his shins.

He grunted. "Scream and I snap your neck." He lifted her to her tiptoes, cutting off her air until she went limp in acquiescence, then he forced her down into the dust of the road. Something sharp dug into her back and she tried to twist away, but he held her fast, struggling to undo his trousers and keep her pinned down at the same time. She broke free for a second and opened her mouth to scream, but he choked her again, livid and reeking of alcohol. He clubbed her in the side of the head with his fist so hard she saw fireworks. And there was no one to hear her anyway.

When he was gone, she scrambled up and sat in the dust for a few minutes, trembling, in shock. He had taken everything—her bag and phone, even her shoes. Bleeding and barefoot, she stumbled to the nearest house and banged on the door, begging to borrow a mobile phone. The occupants of the house, a sturdy older woman and a thin young man, her son, took her in and treated her kindly. The woman gave her rooibos tea laced with sugar and then sent the young man with her in a taxi to the hospital. As Charlie left their home, the woman slipped her own house shoes on Charlie's feet. Her eyes met Charlie's for a moment.

"You are strong," the woman said, her eyes kind. "In a little while this suffering shall pass away." The shoes were too large, but Charlie was grateful for the gesture.

In the ensuing hours, as Charlie was examined at the hospital and interviewed by a jaded police officer, she sat dry-eyed and stunned, unable to comprehend how things had changed so quickly. She was penniless, alone, and violated. Her beloved clinic was unlicensed and bankrupt. She wanted to be brave, to be bigger than the violence and the corruption that was robbing her of so much. But she could not undo the damage. That night broke something inside of Charlie, something that she could not repair no matter how much she wanted to. A week later she left South Africa. She never went back.

Charlie opened her eyes and shivered in the wet cold seeping through the stones of Fisherman's Bastion. It had begun to rain harder. By morning it might turn to snow. She had run far and long, but it had all come back to face her once again. Not the same story, but a similar one. Violence against the vulnerable, corruption, greed, the loss of innocence. It was a story she had wanted so badly to forget, but she was learning she could not.

It just keeps coming back to find me.

Since that night in Johannesburg, she had

been running from her failure, hiding in plain sight from the pain of her shattered idealism. The attack had violated her body, but the loss of her beloved clinic had scarred her even more deeply. She had lost her vision and her sense of purpose. She had not been strong enough to stay, to save herself and the clinic despite the crippling setbacks. She had buckled under their weight, and that failure sat in her stomach like a stone, bitter as wormwood, hard as granite.

If I could have been a little stronger, better, I could have made it all work. Charlie shook her head. She would have been able to offer so much through the clinic, benefit so many women. But instead, she had turned tail and run, leaving everything behind. With that decision Charlie had lost her vision for the future. In that act of running, Charlie had lost herself.

Feeling again the weight of the old grief, the stale sense of shame, she stood for a long time looking out at the beautiful golden glow of the city she had come to for refuge. How she wanted to rewrite history, to be stronger than the circumstances, stronger than the perpetrators who had robbed her of so much. But she had fled to Budapest and hidden away with a job that required little of her heart and a life she shared with no one. It was safe—safe and sterile.

In an instant she remembered again what had been taken from her, with a stab of grief so white hot it made her grit her teeth not to cry out. How was this her life—her half-empty apartment with no art on the walls; her nonexistent love life; the bookshelves groaning with books, a replacement for relationships and friends. She felt as though she had wandered into some other person's life. Surely she was meant for greater things. She had done her best to forget, but here it was again, the same quandary wrapped in a different set of circumstances. And she was faced again with a question, *the* question.

"What do I do now?" she asked aloud, the question ringing off the stone arches. She had run once. Would she run again? Or would she have the courage to face the darkness, to square off against those who inflict violence and pain on the vulnerable? In Africa she had not stood against the ones who had inflicted it on her. Instead, she had run to Budapest. But the darkest places of human nature knew no borders. She had seen it again on that road in Serbia; she would face it in the world wherever she went. She could not outrun the evil that flourished in the dark recesses of the human heart.

For a moment she pictured her hero, the Red Cross Knight. How she had idolized him and admired his bravery. As a child she had wanted to be brave, imagined herself to be as brave as he. But when she had faced her own dragon, she had dropped her sword and run.

Charlie thought of Aunt Mae, of the words she had lived by. "Whatever the Good Lord puts in your hand you give back to others." It had been her guiding principle, her gospel. There was no doubt in Charlie's mind what Aunt Mae would do if she were faced with this dilemma. Charlie had only a little in her hand—a few words to speak before a court of law, the truth about what she had seen that frigid night on the road in Serbia. It was not much, but perhaps it would make a difference. Perhaps it would be enough.

She stood looking out at the city for a long while, weighing the dilemma and the possible consequences. She stood waiting for a flash of inspiration, waiting for salvation in whatever form it might take. But none came. This was her decision, her chance to choose a different path if she dared.

Okay then. Charlie sighed, feeling tired to her core but no longer afraid. She knew what she had to do. There was really only one good answer, only the conviction that seeped like liquid metal into the marrow of her bones, giving her strength.

She had been running for too long; it was time to turn and face her dragons. She did not have a brilliant plan, only the sure conviction that she must speak up in defense of those who had no other voices to speak for them—and that she must protect the baby from whatever her courage cost her.

I will keep you safe, she promised, cupping her hand over her belly in a gesture of protection, *but it's time to stand and fight.*

CHAPTER 16

March
The Bahamas

I do believe there's nothing in the world a little Caribbean sunshine won't cure," Waverly mused, tipping her face back and drinking in the strong, lemony March light.

Andrew glanced up from his paper and smiled at his wife across the breakfast table, noting the look of delight on her face. "You may be correct in that belief, my dear." He took a sip of his coffee, strong and black, and continued to browse the financial section of the paper for any interesting articles.

They were enjoying a leisurely breakfast on the veranda of the Paradise View Hotel on New Providence Island. Their table looked out over the brilliant shimmer of blue water, stands of coconut trees, and a strip of sand as soft and white as icing sugar. A few other tables were occupied but set at a discreet distance away. They had one corner of the veranda all to themselves.

Andrew and Waverly had stayed at the hotel twice before, once when they'd been engaged and then again a few years after their marriage. Although he preferred vacationing in cooler temperatures—skiing in Verbier, for instance—Andrew enjoyed the Bahamas. They offered excellent sailing, a strong enticement for him. Waverly adored the islands and this hotel in particular, with its long cotton-candy-pink main house festooned with a wide white second-story veranda and a tranquil sea view.

The sun was warm on the crown of Andrew's head and a fresh breeze was blowing in from the water, bringing the salt smell of the ocean. Even with his British bones, which were leery of the sun, he had to admit that it felt like a balm after a particularly frigid New England winter.

"My dear, thank you for arranging this little surprise getaway," he said, meeting Waverly's eyes over his coffee cup and smiling. "It is both an unexpected and a much-needed reprieve."

"It's perfect," Waverly agreed, buttering a fresh croissant and taking a small bite. She vigilantly monitored her carbohydrate intake, but Andrew knew she had a particular weakness for fresh croissants. "Truthfully, I've missed you," she admitted. "You've been so consumed with work and I've been so worried about *Simply Perfect*'s future that I feel like we've barely seen each other. And of course I've been preparing for the baby, which has taken quite a bit of time."

"Ah, yes, I suppose that's true," Andrew murmured, shifting uneasily in his very comfortable deck chair. He *had* been busy with work, but only because he had no idea what to do in his own home life anymore. In some way he felt as though he'd lost his wife. They saw each other so little, and when they did her conversation centered entirely upon either excitement about the baby or concern over the show. She and her team spent hours each week brainstorming ways to boost *Simply Perfect*'s ratings and save its future. Half the time if Andrew awoke in the night and went to the kitchen for a glass of water, he would find Waverly bent over her recipe books, furiously scribbling ideas. And when she wasn't preoccupied with her show, she was browsing baby blogs, buying items online, and getting ready for their new arrival. There was little room left for him, it seemed.

Frankly, he found this new dynamic worrisome. He missed his wife. He was lonely in his marriage. And the baby hadn't even arrived yet. He felt both trapped and a bit resentful. But he didn't know how to change anything, and he certainly didn't know how to bring it up to Waverly. His lack of enthusiasm and growing concern over this child would shatter her.

"Isn't this just heaven?" Waverly sighed, smearing homemade marmalade over her buttered croissant. Andrew *hmm*ed his agreement but did not look up. He needed to just keep his chin up and endure it, he told himself firmly. He had, after all, agreed to the baby, or so he kept reminding himself. With strong reservations, it was true, but he had agreed. But when he thought of the next years, truly thought of how this baby would change their lives permanently, he felt only a cold, leaden dread. How could he possibly bear this feeling through so many days and weeks and months and years? How could he continue living a life he was more and more uncertain he wanted? He should tell Waverly, but he couldn't find the words.

Waverly watched Andrew perusing the paper across the breakfast table and frowned. She'd planned this trip to be a reconnection point, but so far her husband seemed distant and pre-occupied, much as he had since before Christmas, actually since around the time of Aunt Mae's funeral. He was courteous with Waverly as always—she couldn't imagine Andrew any other way—but he was not present. She missed him.

She toyed with a bite of her grilled red snapper, nibbling a tiny piece. It was delicious, rubbed with fiery goat peppers and spritzed with lime juice. Andrew had opted for a very traditional Bahamian breakfast of corned beef and grits, but it sat on his plate untouched.

"Aren't you hungry?" she asked him.

"Not very," he replied from behind the paper.

"I got an e-mail from Charlie yesterday," she said, taking a sip of freshly squeezed orange juice.

"Oh yes?" Andrew said politely.

"She sent us a surprise. Do you want to see?" Waverly took the photos from the petal-pink Fendi purse at her feet.

Andrew laid his paper aside.

"She sent me the ultrasound photos in 3-D." She slid the photos across the table to Andrew. "I had the hotel print them off this morning. I couldn't wait to show you. This is our baby, darling."

Andrew picked up one of the photos, studying it with a furrowed brow. The image was of the baby's face in profile, clear although strangely orange, as though he or she were sculpted from butterscotch pudding.

"Isn't she beautiful?" Waverly asked, picking up another of the images, tracing a finger down the button nose and across the plump lips.

Andrew didn't say anything, just gazed at the photo in his hand.

"The doctor still couldn't tell the sex because of the placement of the umbilical cord. It's annoying to still not know, but he thinks it's a girl," Waverly confided. "He said 70 percent sure. Charlie thinks it's a boy, but I agree with the doctor." She thought of the handful of dreams she'd had—the little girl with dark hair and eyes the color of cocoa. Somehow she suspected she was seeing her daughter.

Andrew was still studying the ultrasound photo. He looked sober.

"Isn't it amazing to see her sweet little face?" Waverly asked. "It makes her seem so real." She gazed out at the water where a sailboat was bobbing gently across the waves. "Can you believe it, Andrew. In just a few months, we're going to be holding our baby in our arms."

Her voice caught, and she swallowed the lump in her throat. After so much heartbreak and loss—to see that little face, hold a warm little loaf of newborn baby in her arms and then take that baby home with her, not have to give it back to the mother with a fierce jab of longing. To *be* a mother herself—it seemed surreal. Her heart felt as though it were inflating in her chest, a pink balloon filling her with joy lighter than helium. She touched a finger to the photo again, tracing the little hand. It was real, this baby who would soon be hers.

"I've been thinking about nursery colors," she said, pulling a few fabric samples from her purse. "I'm thinking of doing it in sherbet shades—tangerine, lemon, raspberry, lime. That way it's cheerful and fresh. What do you think?" She pointed to the strips of color she'd selected.

Andrew cleared his throat, barely looking at the

color swatches. "Waverly, we need to talk about this."

She glanced up at his grave tone. He was holding the ultrasound photo. He was looking at her and he wasn't smiling.

"All right," she said calmly, as a frisson of unease skittered down her spine. She laid the swatches on the table next to the other ultrasound photos.

Andrew set the picture down by his untouched plate and gazed out at the view for a long moment. When he spoke, his voice was quiet, thoughtful. "My darling, I don't know if I can do this. I thought I could. I so wanted to for your sake, but I'm just not sure I can."

Waverly stared at him for a moment. "Do what?" she asked blankly.

Andrew looked at her soberly. "Be a father to this baby. I was against the idea from the beginning, but I went along with it because I love you, and you were so determined to have a child. But, Waverly, I feel as though from the moment the baby came into our lives, even just in theory, I lost you. And I'm afraid that when the baby comes into our home for real, it will just get worse. I thought that by giving you a child, giving you the desire of your heart, you would finally feel complete. I thought it would bring us together, but every day I fear I am losing you more." His eyes on hers were gray and bleak. He was begging her to understand. "I'm lonely lying next to you, and the thought of living this way for so many years . . . It feels impossible."

"Impossible." Waverly stared at her husband, aghast. "What are you saying?" she managed to choke out. "It's too late. We have a baby. This is our baby." Her eyes darted wildly from his face to the ultrasound photos. How could this be happening? "What are you saying?" she asked again.

"I don't know," Andrew admitted, his voice quiet.

That scared her more than if he'd shouted or raged. Andrew never raged. But the sorrow in his voice sounded final, as though he had already made a decision without her knowledge or consent.

Waverly gasped for breath, too stunned for words. She pressed the flat of her hand against her chest where a sharp pain was blooming, squeezing the air from her lungs. It was a panic attack. She knew the symptoms, had suffered them for years. She tried to breathe slowly in and out through her nose, but all she could hear was Andrew's voice in her head, shattering her dreams. He was still talking. She caught fragments of his sentences, his tone calm and measured. She felt like she was watching him through a long black tunnel as a sense of helplessness enveloped her, the shock humming in her ears.

"But our dream for a family . . . ," she managed.

"Was never my dream," he said gently. He reached across the table and took her hand. She stared at their clasped fingers, at the swatches of nursery colors splayed beneath their hands like a delectable sherbet rainbow. She tried to draw a full breath, to stop the panicked feeling rising in her throat, cutting off her oxygen.

"What do we do?" she asked helplessly.

His gaze upon her was a mixture of confusion and pain. It hurt her deeply to see that look, to know that fulfilling her heart's greatest desire was causing him such grief. She was still reeling, trying to grapple with the implication of his words. How could they ever figure out a compromise?

"I love you, my darling," he said finally. "I will always love you. But we do not want the same future, and I don't know what we can possibly do to change that."

Waverly bunched her Burberry trench coat against the window of the plane and nestled the wad of fabric into the crook of her neck, watching the aquamarine water shimmering below as they gained altitude. She shifted again, trying to put as much distance as possible between herself and Andrew sitting next to her. He was reading the paper, his expression stoic and sad.

The weekend had gone exactly the opposite

of how she had envisioned it. Andrew's honest confession had blown a hole right through the middle of her dreams for the future. After the stalemate of the breakfast conversation, they had discussed the matter again that evening with a similar result. At the end of the conversation, when their words had trickled down into an unhappy silence, Andrew had made a suggestion.

"Perhaps we should take a few weeks apart to think things through," he said, looking pained. "I can go to the cabin. You can stay at the house or go to that wellness spa in Vermont you like."

"I don't want to be apart," Waverly said instantly, panicked at the thought. How had it come to this so quickly? How had she not seen the cracks in their relationship, the telltale signs of his deeper unrest?

"I need a little time and space to clear my head," Andrew said, "and think about the future."

His words petrified Waverly. What was there to think about? Everything had been going so well. She didn't want a separation, but she couldn't offer a better option and so she reluctantly agreed to his request. Maybe it would do them both good to have space to think through their priorities and their future. She hoped with a little time apart Andrew would either warm to the idea of the baby or one of them would come up with a brilliant compromise, whatever that might entail.

She shifted against the hard window, trying

to get comfortable as she felt her life dissolving around her. It seemed she was being asked to make a choice between the husband she deeply loved and the baby she desperately craved. Not only that, but what about Charlie? It was not a hypothetical baby they were discussing. It was a flesh-and-blood child, Andrew and Waverly's flesh-and-blood child. Well, technically it was an anonymous sperm donor and Charlie's flesh-and-blood child, but Waverly didn't like to consider the minutia of eggs and sperm and DNA. Charlie had agreed to carry the baby for them, but from the beginning the understanding was that she was just the vehicle, the vessel. The baby was Waverly and Andrew's.

Waverly pressed her forehead against the cold glass, trying to ease the pounding in her temples. She turned the dilemma over and over in her mind, but nothing changed. It seemed like an impossible puzzle. Any way she looked at it, she lost something precious.

She closed her eyes, exhausted and heartsick and more than a little angry at Andrew. How could he change his mind now, now that they had already committed to a life together as a family with this baby? She had no idea how this whole messy situation could possibly be made right again.

The minutes ticked by in the quiet airplane, and despite her agitation, Waverly began to feel the effects of her sleepless night. After a few more minutes, she felt herself drift into a restless doze.

In the first hazy moments of sleep, she found herself standing in front of a towering Corinthian column with the winged archangel Gabriel in bronzed glory at the top. Behind him were two curved monuments with statues of robed figures set in stone alcoves. It was evening, and the lights from the monuments cast a soft glow over the immense plaza spreading around her. A light rain speckled the plaza, the patter of drops on the ground muffling all other sound. A little girl in a bright pink raincoat stood at the base of the column.

Even before the girl turned, Waverly knew who it was. The girl met Waverly's eyes and pulled back the hood of her coat, the rain beading on her dark hair, running down her cheek with its strawberry birthmark. "I'm waiting for you," she called. Waverly put her hand out, but the girl was already gone.

Waverly blinked in the stale air of the plane. Andrew turned a page of his paper. The flight attendant rolled a cart down the aisle, collecting garbage. She had been asleep just a few seconds, but those seconds had changed everything. She knew where the dream had taken place. It was Heroes Square in Budapest. Charlie had sent her a postcard of it once. Waverly still had it pinned on her bulletin board in her office.

She glanced over at Andrew. The lines of his face had deepened to a tired frown. She could not convince him to embrace a dream and a life he did not want. Neither could she abandon the baby she was meant to raise. She didn't know how to make it all come out okay. But she knew what she had to do next.

CHAPTER 17

Late March
Budapest

When the door buzzer rang, Charlie was expecting the pizza delivery man. She pushed the button down, calling into the receiver in English, "Come on up, first floor, door number four," and hung up. A few minutes later, at a sharp knock on the door, she swung it open, already counting out forint.

"Szia," she said absently, intent on the bills and coins in her hand. "One thousand eight hundred and ninety forint and . . ." She looked up, trying to calculate an appropriate tip, and stopped, the words catching in her throat. Waverly was standing in the doorway, a large suitcase next to her and one hand raised to knock again. The sisters stared at one another for a moment.

"Surprise," Waverly said, flashing a bright smile.

Charlie blinked at her, the forint forgotten in her hand. Her mouth was hanging open just a little. She stared in speechless shock at her twin standing in the doorway of her apartment.

"Can I come in?" Waverly asked. "The flights were brutal, turbulence all the way and no decent white wine."

Charlie stood back and let Waverly pass. "What are you doing here?" she finally managed to ask.

Waverly rolled her suitcase into the spacious hall and unwound a blush-colored pashmina scarf from around her neck. "I came to see you and the baby," she said matter-of-factly. She unbuttoned her trench coat and hung it and the scarf on a coat hook. "You look wonderful, by the way. The bump is so darling, like you've swallowed half a cantaloupe. You're glowing. Pregnancy becomes you."

"You didn't tell me you were coming." Charlie was still staring at her sister in disbelief. "You're lucky I'm even here. I'm almost never here."

Waverly nodded, looking unconcerned. "You e-mailed me last week with the ultrasound pictures and said you were around until May. I knew you were in town." She looked around the entrance hall and attached kitchen, taking in the high ceilings, parquet floors, and gracious open spaces.

"Very nice," she said approvingly. "May I use your bathroom?"

Charlie shook herself, as though awakening from a dream. She was finding it hard to formulate sentences. "First door on your left." She cast another disbelieving glance as Waverly disappeared into the hall, then addressed her retreating back. "I'll go make up the futon."

A half hour later they ate dinner sitting across from each other at the dining table in the corner of the living room. Neither spoke as they shared Charlie's rustic goat cheese and red onion pizza and a bottle of Theodora sparkling mineral water. As they ate, Charlie watched her twin's every move as though trying to solve a particularly perplexing puzzle. There was something off about Waverly, but Charlie couldn't pinpoint exactly what. Something was going on under the surface—she'd lay money on the fact.

"How long are you planning to stay?" she asked finally.

Waverly shrugged and topped off her glass of mineral water. "A week or two, if that's all right with you?"

"What about the show?"

"We finished taping the next series of episodes ages ago. Beau has it all in hand. I'm taking a holiday."

"Where's Andrew?"

At the mention of her husband's name, Waverly hesitated, a shadow flitting across her face.

Aha, thought Charlie. *That's it.* She eyed her sister with a prickle of unease. She was genuinely fond of her brother-in-law, not to mention the fact that she was currently six months pregnant with Waverly and Andrew's baby. What was going on with Andrew?

"Everything okay?" she asked, watching her sister's face carefully.

Waverly took a sip of water and smiled, slipping into her *Simply Perfect* persona in an instant. Charlie saw her do it, the perfect mask falling firmly into place.

"Of course. Why do you ask?"

"You've never visited me before," Charlie pointed out. "And now you just show up with no warning. Are you sure everything's all right?"

"Why shouldn't it be?" Waverly asked, but there was the slightest edge to her voice. She met Charlie's eyes, her own guileless and open as a spring sky. "I couldn't stay away any longer," she said simply. "I had to come for you and the baby."

After dinner Waverly retired to the office to unpack her suitcase and settle in. Charlie knocked on the door, armed with a stack of fresh towels. When Waverly answered, Charlie caught a peek of her sister's Louis Vuitton suitcase splayed open on the bed. Half the space was taken up with Waverly's expensive vintage-looking clothes in the pastel shades she favored, but the other half was packed tight with cases of Snack Pack and Handi-Snacks pudding cups. Charlie said nothing but shot Waverly an assessing look. Grocery store pudding was her sister's go-to comfort food, her culinary security blanket. If Charlie had needed further proof that something was not right in the simply perfect world of Waverly Talbot, this clinched it.

Waverly saw Charlie's look. "I brought you some pudding," she said smoothly. "I thought you might want something familiar from home. And it's a good source of calcium. Do you mind if I pop these in the refrigerator?"

They both knew that Charlie didn't like pudding cups. She found the consistency gluey. It reminded her a little of mucus.

"Sure, put them anywhere you find space," she said. She looked at Waverly for a long moment. Waverly looked back.

"Well, I'd better get my beauty sleep," Waverly said, breaking the silence. "I'm sure we have lots of exciting things to do tomorrow. I'm so looking forward to exploring this beautiful city."

Charlie nodded and backed out the doorway. For the present she would leave Waverly and her pudding cups in peace.

Over the weekend Charlie tried to be a good host, taking Waverly to see the most iconic sights, playing tour guide all over the city. They took in the breathtaking view of the city from Castle Hill where Waverly oohed and aahed over the fairy-tale splendor of Fisherman's Bastion and Matthias Church, then strolled down Andrássy út, stopping for coffee and cake at one of the elegant old-world coffeehouses sprinkled around the city center.

They did not speak of the most important things in their lives, but instead discussed the flavors and textures of the famous Hungarian cakes and the grandiosity of the architecture. Charlie made no mention of the potentially dangerous situation with the trafficked women or of her conversation with Sandra Ling, but she was wary and alert whenever they went out, keeping her eyes open for anything suspicious. When she'd called Sandra to say she would testify, the attorney had given her a warning about her safety.

"Be careful and very vigilant. Now that you have agreed to testify, it may mean you will become a target of threats like Monica was." The attorney's tone was grave. "Or this may not happen at all. Even if the traffickers know of your involvement, it's possible that they may choose to leave you alone. Often we find that people from powerful Western countries like the US do not suffer the same harassment as those from other, less-privileged countries."

"Like Monica," Charlie clarified.

"Yes, unfortunately, like Monica. A Western passport and the money, power, and political clout behind it may shield you from becoming a target. Just be alert, and let me know immediately if something happens."

Nervously, Charlie had agreed. Since the call she had been on high alert, wary of every shadowy man in the entrance to the metro stations, scanning the crowds of people on the street for anyone who might be following her.

For her part, Waverly seemed to be thoroughly enjoying her stay. She bought trinkets for her staff, declared repeatedly that she was delighted to be close to the baby, and gave every indication that she was simply doing what she'd said she'd do when she first arrived—enjoying a holiday in Budapest with her sister. But Charlie knew her too well. Several times she caught Waverly studying her growing belly with a pinched look of worry. There were no phone calls from Andrew. In fact, Waverly didn't mention him at all, a troubling sign, glaring in its omission. And then there was the stack of pudding cups taking up most of the vegetable drawer in the refrigerator. Waverly ate them at night after Charlie went to bed. Charlie found the rinsed and empty containers in the recycle bin each morning. But Waverly said nothing about it, and neither did Charlie. Each kept her own secrets and pretended all was well.

On Monday when Charlie returned to work, she gave Waverly a map, a guidebook, and her office number and left her to her own devices. When she arrived home from work that afternoon, Waverly was just taking a pan of some delicious baked good out of the oven. Charlie had smelled it all the way from the elevator. Waverly was also talking in a low tone on her cell phone. When Charlie walked through the door, she quickly hung up with a reluctant murmur.

"Was that Andrew?" Charlie asked, shrugging out of her cropped leather jacket and hanging it by the door.

"Yes," Waverly said. She didn't elaborate.

"Everything okay?" Charlie pressed a little, trying to gauge her sister's reaction.

"Of course. He's decided to head up to his cabin in the next couple of weeks to do some fishing and . . . contemplate his life choices," Waverly said with a measured tone. "Are you hungry?" she asked brightly, changing the subject. "I made cheese scones. They're still warm."

Charlie decided not to push. She would have to figure out another way to gain information about what exactly was going on with her sister and brother-in-law. "I'm always hungry," she said, eyeing the delectable-looking scones.

A hefty side benefit of having Waverly as a guest was her cooking. Since her arrival Waverly had been whipping up delicious meals every night, proving that there were definite perks to having a celebrity chef as a sister.

"I'll get you a plate." Waverly waved Charlie into the living room. "But don't get too cozy. I decided not to cook tonight. We're going out." She came into the living room a moment later with a glass of milk and a piping-hot cheddar scone on a plate, a pat of butter melting temptingly down the sides.

Charlie accepted it gratefully, breaking off the end and savoring it. This was what she had been missing, living alone so many years. It was what she had mourned when Aunt Mae died, the little acts of kindness, those shiny copper pennies doled out one by one by someone who loved her. It was why she had hoped the baby might mend the cracks in their sisterly bond and bring them back together. She needed to care for someone other than herself. She needed someone to care for her.

Charlie put her feet up on the arm of the couch, stifling a groan as she devoured the scone. She was beginning to feel the aches and pains that so many pregnant women complained of—a twinge in the lower back, swollen feet from the added weight of the baby. She was still small for being six months along, with a perfectly rounded tummy that stuck out like half a melon, but she felt the presence of the baby keenly. He—Charlie still thought of it as he, although the doctor had pronounced himself almost certain it was a girl—was active, especially at night, somersaulting and kicking energetically. Sometimes Charlie would awaken with the motion and lie in the darkness as the baby performed gymnastics in her belly. More and more she found herself talking to him throughout the day, brief comments about some news article she read on the BBC or an opinion on a matter from work. She was comforted by his presence, silent though he was. She liked to think he was listening to her.

While Charlie polished off the scone, Waverly prowled around the living room, finally stopping to peruse the heavily laden bookshelves.

"You don't have one book here I want to read," she observed with a frown. "Not a single romance or a fluffy British chick lit novel."

"I just read what I like," Charlie answered unapologetically around a mouthful of scone.

"Well, I wish you'd like something a little lighter and more fun. Oh, look." Waverly brightened and pulled a book from the shelf. "Isn't this the one you loved when we were kids, about the princess and the red knight?"

"Red Cross Knight," Charlie corrected, taking a sip of milk. "*St. George and the Dragon*."

"You wanted to be a knight when you grew up," Waverly reminisced, smiling. "Do you remember? I wanted to be a movie star named Lilah Thorne and you wanted to be a knight."

"Lilah Thorne sounds like a porn star," Charlie said, "and yes, I do remember I wanted to be a knight. Some dreams die hard, I guess." She licked the tip of her finger and concentrated on picking up every last crumb of the scone off her plate.

Now that she'd mustered her courage and decided to testify in the trials, she'd thought she might feel a little more like the Red Cross Knight—brave and noble. Instead, she just felt jumpy and scared. It didn't feel very knightly, but she was mustering all the courage she had to face this dragon.

Waverly turned the book over in her hands. "Oh, this takes me back to when we were little. Remember Daddy always telling us we could be whatever we wanted? 'The sky's the limit for my girls.' Do you remember him saying that?" She smiled fondly. "Do you think they'd be proud of us?" she asked after a moment.

"Who? Mom and Dad?" Charlie set her empty plate aside.

Waverly nodded. She leafed through a couple of the book's pages. "If they saw us now, do you think they'd be proud?"

It was a deep question, the kind they hadn't asked each other in a long time. Charlie tucked a pillow under her knees and thought for a moment. Years ago, before the debacle that ended her time in Africa, she would have answered with an unhesitating yes. She was following in her father's footsteps, fulfilling his legacy. How could he not be proud of her? She pictured Robert Talbot—that strong-boned, good-humored face, the powerful rugby-player build, the laugh that boomed up from his broad chest. Oh, she missed him still.

"I hope so," she answered truthfully. "I went to South Africa to find them. Did I ever tell you that's why I went? I wanted to honor them, to honor how they lived and how they died. And I stayed because I found myself there, in the places they had been, in the things Dad loved. It just fit somehow. But when I left . . . I didn't leave well. And I think that would make them sad. I think I've been running for a long time." She stopped, surprised by her self-revelation.

Waverly paused, the book open in her hands, and looked at her sister. "Running from what?" she asked curiously.

"My own failure, I guess." Charlie couldn't meet her sister's eyes. "Do you think they'd be proud of you?" She turned the question around, shifting the spotlight from her own discomfort.

Waverly pursed her lips. "I like to think so." She paused. "It's only half past five and our dinner reservation isn't until seven thirty. I'm a bit hungry. Would you like a pudding cup?"

Charlie shrugged. "Sure, why not?" Something sweet sounded appealing. Waverly disappeared into the kitchen and returned a moment later with two cups and two spoons. Chocolate for Charlie and French vanilla for herself. Charlie peeled the foil from the top and tasted a spoonful.

"Oh, wow, this takes me back to about 1997." She took another spoonful. "Not too bad, actually."

"And it's good for the baby," Waverly added, scooping up a large spoonful. "It's chock-full of calcium."

They ate their pudding cups in companionable silence. For a moment Charlie almost believed time had turned back twenty years and they were sitting together about to watch *Dawson's Creek* or *Roswell* while Aunt Mae pulled a double shift at the factory. On those nights Waverly would cook dinner and they would watch their favorite shows, the ones Aunt Mae disapproved of. She liked old shows like *Bonanza* and *Dallas*.

Waverly took a spoonful of her pudding and savored it. "In a way I think everything I've done has been a tribute to Mother and Daddy," she said, returning to their previous conversation. "An attempt to preserve the memory of our family, our childhood. I wanted to create a beautiful thing to celebrate the life we shared with them, however brief it was."

She finished her pudding and set the spoon in the empty container. "I didn't see it that way for the longest time. I just did what felt right. But I think I've always been looking to recapture our childhood somehow." She looked down at the empty pudding cup in her hands. "I think *Simply Perfect* has really always been about them, and about us before . . . before we lost everything. I still miss them," she said softly. "And I like to think they'd be proud of what I've created in their honor."

Charlie felt a lump rise in her throat. She tried to imagine what Robert and Margaret would think if they were able to peek into her living room and see their twins, grown to mature women now. The sisters had each made choices in the light of their loss. Those choices had led them far apart, but now it seemed that perhaps they were finding each other once again.

"How rustic," Waverly declared a few hours later, surveying the traditional Hungarian restaurant with satisfaction. She and Charlie were sitting in uncomfortably large carved wooden chairs at a table made from a slice of tree trunk. The restaurant had white stucco walls and heavy wooden beams and was packed with diners. Waverly had reserved the last available table for the evening.

When the waiter brought their meals, she took a bite of hers. "This is absolutely delicious," she said in surprise. She nibbled the forkful of grilled chicken breast topped with goose liver, mushrooms, and ewe's cheese, analyzing the flavors. The cheese was unique, earthy and slightly tangy. She tried to think where she'd encountered the flavor before. It was reminiscent of a sheep cheese she'd tried last summer from an artisan cheesemaker in Vermont. Andrew had not cared for it, but Waverly had bought a chunk of it anyway and served it with a brandy fig jam.

"Mine is great too. Good choice of restaurant," Charlie said, her mouth full of savory chicken paprikash.

"What is in this?" Waverly shut her eyes and tasted another forkful of her dinner, trying to separate the individual components. She had an uncanny ability to pinpoint flavors and ingredients and then replicate the dish. When they were in high school she'd managed to recreate the distinctive flavors of KFC's secret fried chicken recipe, Aunt Mae's favorite, and then made it for every Sunday dinner for an entire year.

"Can I try yours?" Waverly reached her fork over without waiting for her sister's assent. She tasted the chicken paprikash and made a sound of approval. The classic Hungarian dish consisted of savory chunks of chicken swimming in a hearty paprika and sour cream sauce over homemade noodles. The sauce was rich and creamy, and the noodles had a pleasantly chewy texture. She savored the flavor for a moment. "Oh, this is decadent." She helped herself to another bite and said, "Why isn't Hungarian cooking more well known?"

Charlie shrugged. "I don't know. Most Hungarians know how to make these dishes.

Any decent home cook can recreate them. Even I know how to make goulash." She sat back, adjusting the band of her maternity jeans.

Waverly eyed her sister with a twinge of jealousy. Charlie looked as toned and fit as ever. She seemed to be sailing through pregnancy the way she sailed through life, with a pragmatism and ease that made Waverly feel high maintenance and fussy. Had she been sitting there six months pregnant she probably would have been as big as a balloon with cankles and acid reflux. But she still would have traded places with Charlie in a heartbeat.

With a sigh she turned her attention back to the food. She shouldn't regret what she could not have. Better to celebrate the fulfillment of a long-held dream, even if the child was coming to her in a way she had never imagined.

"Someone should introduce the world to this food. It's too good to be a secret." No sooner were the words out of her mouth than she sat up straight, fork in hand, struck by the glimmer of a marvelous idea. "Oh," she said, looking around the restaurant speculatively. She tapped her fork against her lips, eyes narrowing.

"How's the show going?" Charlie asked, scooting her plate out of reach of Waverly's fork.

"Hmm?" Waverly turned her attention back to her sister. "Oh, not that well, actually," she said. "The network is feeling skittish. They're afraid we may have peaked. We need to strengthen our viewership and prove that we're still fresh, or it's possible that *Simply Perfect* may be canceled." The thought gave her a twinge of panic every time she pictured it.

Charlie paused, her loaded fork halfway to her mouth, and gaped at her twin. "Canceled? Are you serious? But what would you do?"

"I don't know." Waverly looked down at her meal and speared a chunk of goose liver. She didn't want to contemplate what she would do. She just wanted to make sure it didn't happen.

"Isn't there some way to save it?" Charlie asked.

"Believe me, I've been wracking my brain for months trying to find a way to boost ratings, and I'd about given up. But I just had an idea that I think might actually work. Want to hear it?" Waverly sat up straight in her chair, excited by her new notion and its potential.

"Sure." Charlie took a hefty slice of soft white Hungarian bread from the basket at their table and wiped her plate clean with it, sopping up the last of the creamy sauce.

Waverly leaned forward, a predatory gleam in her eye. The idea she was concocting was good. A fresh angle and a chance to snag a new segment of viewers while keeping her loyal fans too.

"We take *Simply Perfect* on the road here in Central Europe. We do episodes with local cooks in their own homes. It's still make-at-home recipes and home entertaining tips—the things that are signature *Simply Perfect*—but with an international flair." She sat back triumphantly. "It's *Simply Perfect*'s formula but with a fresh angle that could appeal to a whole new group of viewers."

She pulled out her iPhone and started tapping out a text to Beau. This could really work. She could feel it, the stirring of excitement in her stomach, the possibility that it could be the answer they were seeking.

"We've already taped the spring episodes, but I think we should abandon them and go with something fresh," she said aloud, although she was talking to herself. "We'll need to bring the crew over and the equipment, although I wonder if we could rent some of it here." She tapped furiously at the phone. "And my aprons. I'll need at least a dozen of my aprons." She looked up and frowned, calculating the numbers in her head. "No, make that twenty." She glanced around the restaurant speculatively. "We'll start here in Budapest. I like this restaurant. It's very charming. I wonder if the owners would let us film a program in their own home kitchen. Then maybe we could do something in . . . What countries are nearby?" She tried to remember her geography, but it was hazy at best. Where was Ukraine? Was that close?

Charlie sat watching her sister's machinations, munching a second slice of bread. "Romania, Bulgaria, Czech Republic, Slovakia, Serbia," she offered.

Waverly's phone pinged a reply from Beau. She scanned his text, then typed a reply. This was going to be so good, she could feel it.

"What about Andrew?" Charlie asked, breaking into Waverly's stream of consciousness. "Won't he be expecting you to come home soon?"

Waverly paused, her finger hovering over the phone. She went very still, not sure how to reply. She hadn't wanted to broach the topic with Charlie and had avoided any mention of their troubles altogether. But Charlie wasn't a fool. She knew something was wrong.

"Andrew and I are spending some time apart right now," she said finally, evenly, her voice betraying no emotion. It felt like a stab to the heart to say those words.

Charlie's eyes flew to her sister's, a concerned look on her face. "Why?" she asked.

Waverly frowned, resenting the question that pried into her marriage difficulties. In one way it wasn't any of Charlie's business, but considering that she was at that very moment growing a child for Waverly and Andrew, in another way it was very much her concern.

"He's . . . reassessing," Waverly said in a measured tone, looking down at her phone.

"Reassessing what?" Charlie asked, folding her arms across her middle, over the baby, as though to brace them both for bad news.

"His priorities," Waverly said flatly. She met Charlie's eyes, her mouth pressed into a thin line. That was all she was going to say on the subject.

Charlie tilted her head, studying her twin for a long moment, but Waverly met her eyes with an obstinate silence. She could be Fort Knox when she wanted to be. Charlie sighed and shrugged, looking around for the waiter and letting the subject drop, at least for the moment.

"I'll get the bill," Waverly said, waving her hand to attract the waiter's attention from across the room. "My treat."

She was glad for the reprieve but sensed it wouldn't be the end of it. At some point she was going to have to confess everything to her sister. So far Andrew's stance seemed unchanging, but Waverly was still hopeful that he would come to see things differently before the baby arrived. If not, she had no idea what she would do.

CHAPTER 18

G et another light over here. We want to be able to see the food," Beau bellowed to the Hungarian TV crew, who scrambled to obey the order.

Waverly looked around the traditional Hungarian kitchen happily. It was all coming together so well. Beau and the *Simply Perfect* crew had flown in just two days before, after a whirlwind week of planning, haggling, and paring down to make the impromptu road show feasible.

Besides Beau and the Hungarians he had hired as muscle, the crew consisted of Wyatt, the cameraman, a hastily procured Hungarian sous chef who was in charge of setting up the kitchen for the show and having all ingredients at the ready, and Sophie, who was acting as makeup artist, travel coordinator, and all-around errand girl.

Their very first show was set to begin filming in just a few minutes in the home of the woman at whose restaurant Waverly and Charlie had dined the week before. The kitchen, a large square room with two deep stainless steel sinks, an ancient gas stove, and bright orangish-red tiles on the walls, was a flurry of activity. Charlie stood against the far wall looking like she was just trying to keep out of the way.

By the kitchen island Sophie was making the owner of the restaurant camera ready. Barely five feet tall and stout, with a pouf of hair dyed a bold maroon, Erzsi was clad in a crisp, new white apron. The apron was too long for her and hung below her knees. She obediently closed her eyes as Sophie lightly dusted her face with powder.

"To reduce shine for the camera," Sophie explained.

Erzsi nodded without comprehension and shot a sidelong glance at the camera, drawing herself up to appear taller.

Waverly held up two aprons and considered them against the backdrop of the red tiles. "What do you think, Charlie?" she asked, pursing her lips speculatively. "Is the pink dotted swiss too garish with the tiles?"

"Everything's too garish with those tiles," Charlie observed dryly.

Waverly threw her a look. "It's charmingly atmospheric," she corrected. "The audience will love it, and love her."

She nodded to Erzsi, who was squinting at Sophie and repeating her one scripted line, "Eets *Zimply Perfect* in Budapest," over and over in heavily accented English.

"I'll go with the yellow, since the pink clashes," Waverly announced to no one in particular. She folded the frilled canary yellow apron around herself, tying a neat bow at the back. "So, first we're making sour cherry soup, correct?" she asked Erzsi, who was standing at attention behind the kitchen island, her head barely clearing the top.

"Can somebody find us a stool?" Beau yelled. "We actually want the audience to be able to see the cook."

"*Meggyleves?*" Charlie translated to Erzsi. "Cherry soup?"

Erzsi's face lit up, and she nodded vigorously. "*Jo, jo.*"

Waverly surveyed the kitchen island where the ingredients sat at the ready—glass measuring cups filled with sour cream, sugar, and red wine, and small fragrant heaps of cinnamon and cloves. Off to one side sat a large glass bowl shimmering with ruby-red sour cherries. This was the part she loved best, taking beautiful ingredients and turning them into something even better.

"Cold fruit soup," she mused, shaking her head. "It's so retro it's going to seem fresh all over again. This is going to be a treat."

One of the Hungarian crew appeared with a wooden stool, and suddenly Erzsi's head popped up over the top of the island. She squinted in the bright lights and smoothed her apron self-consciously as Wyatt and the rest of the crew prepared to begin filming.

"Ready on set," Beau called.

Waverly tweaked the bow of her apron, gave Erzsi a reassuring nod, and closed her eyes for a brief moment, sending up a prayer for favor, asking that this be the solution for the show's precarious future. She took a deep breath, calming her nerves, then opened her eyes, slipping into the world of *Simply Perfect* in a heartbeat, the feel of it as familiar as breathing.

"Aaaaand action." Beau gave a thumbs-up and stepped back to let Waverly work her magic. She turned her thousand-watt smile to the camera.

"*Yow naypowt*," Waverly crooned in her best attempt at a Hungarian greeting. "I'm Waverly Talbot, and today marks the beginning of an exciting adventure as we embark on a culinary journey through the kitchens of some of Central Europe's finest home cooks. Our first stop is beautiful Budapest, Hungary, as renowned cook Erzsi Szabo shows us the secret to making a deliciously decadent sour cherry soup that will have your guests licking their spoons and eager for more."

She passed a practiced hand over the island, showcasing the ingredients, then looked up at the camera again. "Thanks for joining us as we venture into kitchens across Central Europe to explore new recipes and local foods that are"—she paused one beat and then smiled winningly—"simply perfect."

Taking the show on the road proved to be a smart decision. Over the next week *Simply Perfect* filmed several full-length episodes in Budapest using contacts that Erzsi had provided. They also created a series of three short teaser clips featuring local Hungarian food and wine. Beau sent the clips to Susan at the Food Network, who passed them on to her bosses. A few days later she reported that those in charge were intrigued and cautiously optimistic about *Simply Perfect*'s new angle. They were looking forward to seeing more.

Beau grinned as he told Waverly the good news. "This may be our ticket, Boss. Your idea could save the show!"

He and Waverly quickly made the decision to extend the trip another few weeks to allow for more episodes and feverishly began scouting locations.

Charlie watched the hustle and bustle with a bemused interest. So this was what Waverly's life was like. It seemed so fast paced, texts and phone calls and viewership number predictions flying through the air like missiles. Everyone even talked faster. Charlie kept herself on the periphery, focusing on work as usual, content to let Waverly be in the midst of the hubbub. She would much rather curl up with a good book at the end of the day than always be working, always be on point. But it suited Waverly. Even in high school she had wanted to be at the apex of the action, the queen bee at the center of the hive. Charlie had watched from the sidelines, happy to be solitary and free of encumbrance.

"Would anyone you work with have good contacts for filming a show?" Waverly asked at breakfast the morning after she and Beau decided to extend the tour. She slid two perfectly done sunny-side-up eggs onto Charlie's plate along with a homemade English muffin, already generously buttered.

Charlie took a bite of the muffin and closed her eyes for a moment as the pools of melted butter oozed from the toasted crevices. "I don't know, but I can ask around," she said, mouth full.

"I packed you a lunch, just a few slices of the stuffed pork tenderloin and roasted root vegetables from last night." Waverly handed her a plastic container with a fork and knife taped to the top.

Charlie mumbled her thanks around another mouthful of muffin.

"And before I forget, I got you a present." Waverly set a little square box by Charlie's plate. "A small thank-you for hosting me and being so helpful with the show."

Wiping her buttery hands, Charlie opened the

box. Nestled against the red velvet was a small carved medal on a delicate silver chain. Charlie squinted, trying to make out the figures on the medal. It was a knight on a horse, pinning a squirming dragon to the ground with a long spear. Above the figures were the words *St. George* and below them the plea *Pray for us*.

"That's very . . . Catholic looking," Charlie observed. It was a strange gift, especially by Waverly's usual gift standards. She tended toward designer boutique presents—expensive items in gorgeous packages that smelled like French perfume.

"I found it in a little antique shop around the corner," Waverly said happily. "It reminded me of your knight and dragon book. The owner told me that St. George is the patron saint of courage, so it seemed like fate." She lowered her eyes. "I got it for you and the baby."

Touched by the explanation, Charlie slid the medal from the box. It was small and heavy, the figures softened from age and wear. She imagined someone's thumb rubbing the medal daily and whispering a prayer to St. George, the patron saint of courage. She liked the thought. Courage was something she certainly needed more of these days. She had not heard back from Sandra Ling, but the upcoming trial and the threat of danger were always in the back of her mind, a constant dark possibility, putting her on edge.

She undid the clasp and slipped the chain around her neck, tucking the medal under her shirt. It lay against her chest, a reassuring little weight. She felt strangely warmed by its presence.

"Thank you," she said, and meant it. It was a surprisingly fitting gift.

When Charlie got to work, she dutifully asked her colleagues about any contacts they might have for an episode of *Simply Perfect*. She had not anticipated the response when news of her celebrity sister spread through the staff. Ursula was out for two days of meetings with other charities in the city, so the mood in the office was primed for festivities. Productivity ground to a halt as people began googling Waverly online.

"She's your twin? You don't look anything alike," Duncan observed, studying a clip of *Simply Perfect* he found on YouTube. "She's a real fox." He whistled slowly through his front teeth.

"Thanks," said Charlie dryly. The other staff gathered around Duncan, urging him to find more videos.

"Tell me she's single," Duncan said, watching Waverly frost maple-glazed carrot cupcakes. "She can frost my cupcakes anytime."

"Hey." Charlie slapped Duncan's shoulder in reprimand. "Watch it. That's my sister you're talking about. She's happily married," she added, hoping that was still true. Waverly had not said anything more about her and Andrew's time of separation except to offer a vague and not entirely reassuring, "Hopefully he'll come around."

"Come around to what?" Charlie had asked, but Waverly had waved her hand dismissively and not answered. Charlie had e-mailed and texted Andrew several times, but he had not replied. She found his silence even more worrying than Waverly's evasive answers.

"Has your sister really been a guest on *Good Morning America* and hosted a benefit dinner for AIDS research with Elton John?" Kate asked, scanning Waverly's Google search results. "Says here she's written three cookbooks. She's properly famous." Kate looked impressed.

"Not cookbooks. Home entertaining books," Charlie muttered, trying to concentrate on her work e-mails. It was a useless endeavor. She shut her laptop with a sigh. Waverly and *Simply Perfect* were going to dominate the day, and Waverly wasn't even present. She didn't envy her sister her fame or recognition, but sometimes the hubbub around her celebrity status annoyed Charlie just a little. Waverly breathed admiration like oxygen, and at times it felt as though there was no room left for anyone or anything else.

"How come we've never heard of her?" Kate asked, scrolling through Google images of Waverly. "Is she really famous in America?"

"Sort of." Charlie shrugged. Truth be told, she avoided thinking about Waverly's professional success. Not because she was jealous, but because she was unsure how to reconcile the Waverly she had known since they shared a womb with the sparkly diva of home hostessing. The perfect makeup and hair and scripted lines made Charlie feel alone, as though she had lost her twin sister and a glossy stranger had taken her place. She never watched Waverly's shows, and currently she was using Waverly's first two home entertaining books to prop up the dresser in her bedroom where it was missing a leg. She preferred her sister in the flesh, with all her strengths and foibles, not airbrushed and perfect. That was the real Waverly, the one who drove Charlie nuts, the one she still loved deeply despite their differences.

"What are you talking about, guys?" Arben came through the door to the office and joined the entire staff gathered around Duncan's chair. His younger brother, Ilir, a slender, darkly handsome nineteen-year-old wearing a tracksuit and matching bright blue athletic shoes, followed close on his heels. Arben and Ilir peered over Duncan's shoulder curiously.

"Hey, I know her." Ilir pointed to the screen.

"My mom and sister watch this show all the time."

"*Simply Perfect* is in Albania?" Charlie asked, surprised.

Ilir nodded. "Yeah, Albanians love this show. They dub the voices in Albanian. This woman is . . . How do you say it? Sexiful?"

"Sexy, or successful?" Charlie wasn't sure which compliment he had in mind.

"That's Charlie's sister," Kate piped up.

Ilir looked suitably impressed. "Wow, she's famous. And hot."

"So I'm told," Charlie muttered. "Wait till Waverly hears that she's famous in Albania. She's going to love this."

"You should bring your sister to the office tomorrow," Duncan suggested. "Show her around the place." His idea was greeted enthusiastically by the rest of the staff, who badgered Charlie until she capitulated. They were all eager to meet Waverly in the flesh.

"I'll see if she can make it tomorrow," Charlie agreed finally. Since she had promised to help Waverly scout locations for filming, it seemed likely that bringing the star herself to the office might open some doors for *Simply Perfect* in Central Europe.

"Can she take a picture with me for my mom?" Ilir asked.

"I'll ask her," Charlie said with a sigh.

• • •

Waverly descended on the office the next morning like a conquering hero, bearing two pans of homemade cinnamon rolls heavily festooned with cinnamon cream cheese frosting.

Duncan took one bite and rolled his eyes heavenward. "Where have you been all my life?" he groaned.

Waverly giggled. The rest of the staff were equally enthralled as she doled out the treats and a sizable dose of the Simply Perfect Waverly Talbot charm.

Charlie quirked an eyebrow when she saw that Waverly just happened to have a few headshots in her handbag. "Really, do those come in handy that often?" she asked.

"You'd be surprised," Waverly said, autographing one with a flourish and handing it to Ilir for his mother. She was delighted to discover she had a sizable following among Albanians.

Charlie gave up on work entirely for the morning and instead hosted Waverly, showing her around the office and introducing her to all the staff. The office atmosphere felt festive after the addition of the cinnamon rolls and Waverly's charisma.

Midway through the morning Johan dropped into the office, and Charlie waved him over so that she could introduce him to Waverly.

"Dr. Kruger and I worked together when

I was in South Africa," Charlie explained.

Waverly offered him a generously portioned cinnamon roll and smiled winningly. "Tell me a story about Charlie," she cajoled. "I never get to see this professional side of her."

Johan took a big bite of the cinnamon roll, his eyes widening in appreciation. He made a satisfied *mmph* sound and then looked thoughtful as he chewed.

"To be fair, we really didn't know each other well," he prefaced. "We only worked together for a few weeks, but I remember one thing that stuck with me about your sister. She's got guts. Once we were at a camp outside of Johannesburg, and we had a stampede on a supply truck. Mothers had been queuing for hours in the sun waiting for baby formula, and when the truck finally came the women crowded around it, panicked that they wouldn't get anything. It was chaos. Some were actually in danger of being trampled. The rest of the staff were intimidated and backed off, but not your sister. She waded into the mess, clambered up onto the back of the truck, and by some miracle managed to restore order.

"She was shouting at the top of her lungs and brandishing a can of baby formula." He demonstrated with the remaining half of his cinnamon roll, holding it aloft and shaking it. "She wouldn't back down. And unbelievably, the crowd calmed down. The mothers got back into a line, and Charlie started handing out the entire contents of the truck. No one got hurt, and everyone got a portion of the goods. It took courage to do that, and dedication, and from what I've seen, your sister has both in spades." He nodded at Waverly and gestured with the cinnamon roll. "This is delicious, by the way."

"Thank you." Waverly dimpled.

Charlie flushed at Johan's praise, feeling uncomfortable. She didn't blush easily, but she was taken by surprise by his detailed recollection of the incident and his admiring words. She remembered that day. She hadn't felt particularly courageous at the time. She had just done what needed to be done. She had been more impressed with the women who had responded to her calls for calm and order, who had tempered their panic and fierce desire to provide for their babies with restraint and self-control. No one had left that supply truck empty-handed.

Johan took his leave with an apology, late for a meeting. After he left, Waverly elbowed Charlie in the ribs. "My, he's a charmer. And those broad shoulders . . . Mmm. Is there a Mrs. Kruger?"

"Was. They're divorced," Charlie said around a mouthful of her second cinnamon roll. She couldn't seem to stop eating these days. She was gaining weight little by little, all her normal lean, sharp edges softening and curving in new directions.

"Hmm." Waverly shot her an arch look. "And he thinks you're courageous . . . and dedicated." She somehow managed to make the last word sound suggestive.

Charlie ignored the insinuation. It was true that she found Johan Kruger attractive, very attractive if she were honest with herself, but she wasn't about to confess that to her sister. She'd never hear the end of it. When Waverly got an idea in her head, she could hold on like a pit bull. A very pretty pit bull, but still . . .

Waverly spent the rest of the morning bewitching the staff into giving her useful contacts, and by lunchtime she had a list of potential home cooks for the rest of the episodes she wanted to shoot.

"What a helpful group of people," she commented as she and Charlie stepped out to get a quick bite to eat at a nearby café. "And some of their contacts sound very promising. Duncan has a friend in Sarajevo who runs a little restaurant specializing in meat. Doesn't that sound quaint?"

"They all specialize in meat. It's the Balkans," Charlie muttered, scrutinizing the menu board to see what was on special for the day. Garlic cream soup and a pork schnitzel.

"And Arben has an aunt in Kosovo who can show me how to make a traditional dish called *adjvar*," Waverly said happily. "Apparently you make it over a wood fire and roast peppers for hours. It sounds so rustic. This is going to be wonderful. I have such a good feeling about all of this."

While they waited for their soup at the café, Waverly's phone beeped with a text message. She checked it, frowning as she read.

"Is there a problem?" Charlie asked.

Waverly shook her head. "No. It's just Andrew. He's heading up to the cabin tomorrow." A brief troubled look slipped across her face before she schooled her features into a pleasant smile and slid her phone back into her purse without responding to the text. "Now, how about that soup?"

When they returned from lunch, it was to a very subdued office environment.

"The bear is in the house." Kate muttered the warning as she sailed by on her way to the copy machine.

Charlie stopped. Ursula was back early from her meetings. Charlie turned toward the entrance, intent on sending Waverly out the door before her boss saw she'd brought a family member into the office, but it was too late.

"Charlie, do you have a guest?" Ursula was standing at the door to her office, watching them in disapproval. Technically they were not supposed to bring guests into the office, but when Ursula was away, the staff tended to be very loose with this rule.

Charlie reluctantly turned back. "My sister, Waverly Talbot," she said, deciding to make the best of it. She'd told Waverly that the pregnancy was a secret at work and had made her promise to keep mum, but she hadn't explained about her tenuous employment position.

She stuck out her chin, aware that the entire office was watching the unfolding drama, and chose a white lie. "Waverly was interested in knowing more about our work here. She and her husband generously support many charities and are considering a donation to Care Network."

Waverly looked surprised by this unexpected news of her altruism, but Charlie shot her a warning look and her sister stepped forward and extended her hand, smoothly covering her initial reaction.

"Waverly Talbot. Thank you for all your hard work. It's a marvelous organization, such useful services to the public."

Ursula looked disgruntled for a moment but shook her hand. "Thank you for your interest in our organization," she said stiffly and then, with a stern look at Charlie, said, "but we don't allow guests in the office. It is a policy to protect the clients' sensitive information."

"Of course, I understand," Waverly agreed, widening her eyes just a little. "I begged Charlie to let me tag along and see the important work you do here. I'm just going now. Would you care for a cinnamon roll?" She pulled the container from her bag and offered Ursula one of the last ones.

"I don't eat white sugar," Ursula said, eyeing the cinnamon rolls. "It poisons the body."

"Of course," Waverly reassured her cheerfully. "No matter. Since Charlie's eating for two now it certainly won't go to waste."

Charlie gaped at her sister, then glanced at Ursula, who was looking at her and frowning.

"Eating for two?" the boss said slowly, puzzled. "What do you mean?"

Too late Waverly realized her mistake. "Oh, Charlie's always had a big appetite," she said, backpedaling. "Even when we were kids. She eats like a grown man."

For a moment Charlie thought they might get away with it, but then Ursula's gaze sharpened, zeroing in on her stomach, camouflaged as usual in a baggy man's dress shirt.

"Charlie, are you pregnant?" she asked sharply. "I thought you were just getting fat."

Charlie opened her mouth, realized she couldn't lie, especially when it was soon going to be very obvious that she was indeed very pregnant. "Yes, I'm pregnant."

She glanced over her shoulder and saw the look of shock registering on the faces of her colleagues. Duncan raised his eyebrows and mouthed, *What? Who?* She ignored him and turned back to her boss.

Ursula's mouth compressed into a thin line. "I think it is best if you leave now with your sister. I will see you tomorrow morning at ten o'clock in my office to talk about this."

Charlie nodded, feeling a mixture of resignation and chagrin. This had not gone at all as she had wanted it to. Ursula turned on her heel and disappeared into her office with a click of the closing door.

Waverly caught her eye and said, "Sorry," with a guilt-stricken expression.

Charlie scrubbed a hand over her face, suddenly very weary. She wanted a hot bath, a nap, and another cinnamon roll. Make that two cinnamon rolls. She was probably going to be unemployed by noon tomorrow. When she thought about the possibility of being fired, she wondered more and more if she'd even really mind. Perhaps it would be for the best.

"Come on," she said to Waverly, not looking at her colleagues, who she was certain were riveted on the dramatic scene. "And don't even think about putting that container away. Just hand all the cinnamon rolls over to me right now. It's the least you can do."

CHAPTER 19

All in all the meeting with Ursula could have gone worse, Charlie reflected, walking home in a heavy drizzle before noon the following day. She had not been fired on the spot, although she cringed, imagining the number of black marks now beside her name in Ursula's ledger of employee misdeeds. The boss was leaving for a series of seminars in Germany for two weeks, and they had agreed to discuss the matter further once she was back. Until then Charlie would be taking an unpaid leave of absence, since, "We can't have an unmarried pregnant woman teaching school sexual education classes," as Ursula so bluntly put it.

Charlie had readily agreed to Ursula's conditions. Maybe in those two weeks she could come up with a strong case to keep her job, if she still even wanted to. Or perhaps she should use the time to figure out what it was she actually wanted to do. At the very least she would have more time to make a contingency plan in the very likely event that she found herself unemployed in a few weeks' time.

"Well, pal," she sighed, putting her hands over

her belly and talking to the baby as she waited at a crosswalk, "I think we'd better start preparing for a change in employment status." The light turned green, and she crossed hastily. Thinking of making a change was disconcerting, but at the same time she felt a stirring of excitement. Perhaps it was time to start looking for something new, something that allowed her to engage in a bigger way, something that related the zeal and indignation she felt every time she thought of Kinga and Simona and that bleak winter night in Serbia.

Free for the rest of the day, Charlie dropped by the final Budapest filming of *Simply Perfect*; it was taking place near Vigadó Tér, a small but lovely park situated along the Danube, with curved stone benches ringing a beautiful fountain. The show was being filmed in the home of a pair of Hungarian sisters in their twenties. Their family had owned an esteemed cake and coffeehouse in the Sixth District for four generations before it was confiscated under the Communist regime. Their grandmother passed on all the family recipes to the sisters, and they had recently reopened the coffeehouse to carry on their family's tradition.

Charlie rang the buzzer for the apartment and a moment later was buzzed in. It was a small but airy third-floor space with a balcony and a lovely view of the park and the river. The open kitchen/

dining room area was humming with activity as the crew arranged the finished desserts. The sisters, both petite with dark hair the color of chestnuts, flanked Waverly as she tasted their finished creations at the sleek, modern IKEA kitchen island.

"Oh, these are delicious," she exclaimed. Waverly saw Charlie out of the corner of her eye and gave a little wave, gesturing and mouthing, *Almost done.*

Beau motioned for Charlie to keep quiet, and she nodded, tucking herself into a corner of the dining room as Waverly wrapped up the show. It was centered on a famous Hungarian dessert—*dobostorta*—a decadent chocolate buttercream-layered sponge cake topped with crystallized caramel.

On camera Waverly took a fork and cut the tip off a slice of dobostorta, then put the morsel in her mouth, savoring it for a long moment. She smiled and delivered her signature line.

"Aaaand cut," Beau yelled just as Charlie's cell phone rang. He shot her an annoyed glance, and she ducked out the door leading from the dining room to a small wrought-iron balcony. It was raining steadily, fat, cold drops falling from the eaves of the building, and she pressed back against the door, trying to avoid getting soaked. The sky was a leaden gray with clouds so low they almost seemed to touch the rooftops. Far below, a taxi splashed through puddles, narrowly avoiding a pedestrian walking a black puli. Vigadó Tér was empty, the stone benches glistening in the rain.

"Hello?" She bent her head, trying to hear against the dull patter of rain on stone and the distant sounds of traffic.

"Ms. Talbot, this is Sandra Ling."

Charlie's heart skipped a beat. "Yes?" She clutched the phone tighter and glanced behind her, through the glass door and across the dining room to the kitchen, where Waverly was laughing and chatting with the camera crew, handing out slices of cake all around. In the hustle and bustle surrounding her sister's visit, Charlie had almost managed to forget about the trial and the constant looming threat of someone discovering her participation. Almost. She was always alert, always watching people around her from the corner of her eye, but she'd begun to relax a little, to believe that perhaps nothing would happen after all. Now it all came back to her in a rush. Nothing sinister had happened since Monica had left, but she wasn't naïve enough to assume that was the end of it. She glanced around uneasily. The balconies on either side of her were empty.

"We have a date for the first trial," Sandra informed her. "It's Kinga's. The judge has set it for the seventeenth of April, a little more than two weeks from now. Will you be able to come to Belgrade to testify on such short notice?"

Charlie hesitated, frozen to the spot with sudden indecision. All her rhetoric and bravado was well and good, but now she actually had to do something. Could she? She thought of that last cataclysmic night in Johannesburg and swallowed hard, her heart speeding up in her chest. Would she give what she had in her hand? Was she brave enough to risk again?

"Ms. Talbot, can we count on you to testify at the trial?" Sandra asked again.

Charlie took a deep breath. She touched the medal of St. George, hidden under her shirt, weighty and warm against her skin, and her fingers brushed the words emblazoned there. *St. George, pray for us.* She shut her eyes and offered up a quick but fervent prayer. *Let me be strong enough. Let it make a difference.* She opened her eyes. Nothing had changed, but she felt stronger, ready.

"Yes," she said finally, firmly. "I'll be there."

The next day Charlie arrived home after running a few errands. It was suppertime and already growing dark, the sunny afternoon giving way to the lengthening shadows of early evening.

Waverly was in the shower singing the theme song from *Titanic* in a high soprano. "My heart will go on . . . ," she warbled over the sound of the running water. Waverly and her crew were leaving the next day for a two-week *Simply Perfect* gastro tour of the Balkans.

Charlie shrugged out of her leather jacket and was just slipping her feet into her house shoes when the door buzzer rang. She picked up the receiver. "Hello? Szia?"

There was no one there. She could hear the background noise from the street below through the receiver, but no one spoke. She hung up, and a moment later it buzzed again.

"Hello? Who is this?" Charlie asked, but again there was no answer. Feeling a prickle of unease, she hung up and quickly put on her slippers, padding to the tall windows in the living room that overlooked Liszt Tér and the front of the building. There was no one standing at the door on the street below.

Charlie scanned the square, her gaze following a couple of students hurrying home, a few tourists standing in front of the vibrant, oversize bronze statue of composer Franz Liszt, his mane of hair flying, his hands poised midchord. There. Over by the café next door, a man was leaning against a metal support for the café awning. Dark-haired and scowling, he had his hands in the pockets of his heavy wool coat, but he did not look relaxed. He was staring up at her building intently. It seemed almost as though he were looking at her window.

Charlie gasped and backed away, her heart skipping a beat. Was this it? Had they found her? She sat down hard in a chair and forced herself to take a few deep breaths. Stress was bad for the baby. Of course, so was being targeted by human traffickers. Maybe it was just a fluke. Perhaps he was simply standing outside waiting to meet someone. Charlie waited a few moments and then sidled close to the window and peeked out from the side. The man was still there, waiting, watching her building. He lifted a cell phone in her direction, and it looked as though he took a picture. Charlie hastily scooted away from the window again, heart pounding. She needed to call Sandra Ling.

Dimly she heard the water in the shower turn off. Waverly would be out any minute. Charlie couldn't let her know about any of this or she'd be on a plane to Connecticut before she knew what hit her. She fumbled for her cell phone and punched in Sandra's number.

The lawyer answered on the second ring. "Charlie, is everything all right?"

Her calm voice was reassuring, and Charlie took a deep breath. "I think I'm in trouble," she said, straining to sound logical and not panicked. "I think they've found me." Her words tumbled over themselves as she described the man.

"Okay," Sandra said when Charlie finished. "Whether it's a coincidence or not, I think it's best you don't stay in the city until the trial. Is there anywhere you can go for a while, just to lie low?"

"I'll find somewhere," Charlie said, her mind racing with possibilities.

"Good," Sandra said. "I would recommend that you not leave your apartment while the man is outside, but I think it's a good idea if you leave the city as soon as possible. Be careful, and call me if you see anything else suspicious."

After Sandra hung up, Charlie thought for a moment. Where could she safely hide out until she could testify at the trial? She could go to one of Care Network's field locations in Serbia or Romania, or perhaps Slovakia. But if the traffickers knew she was affiliated with Care Network, they could easily track her down at any of their locations. And then she had a brilliant idea.

When Waverly came out of the bathroom, wafting the scent of French rose soap and Dior perfume after her, Charlie was ensconced in her favorite armchair eating a huge slice of leftover *dobostorta*. She wasn't sure if the man was still out there. She had drawn the curtains and double-bolted the door.

Waverly glanced pointedly at the cake. "Giving the baby a sugar high, are we?"

"And hopefully me too," Charlie said unrepentantly. She took a big bite of cake. Waverly disappeared into the kitchen and emerged a moment later with a Swiss Miss creamy vanilla pudding cup and a silver spoon. She sat down on the sofa and peeled the top off the pudding cup.

"What would you think if I came with you on tour?" Charlie asked around a mouthful of cake.

"You want to come with us?" Waverly looked surprised. She scooped up a spoonful of pudding. "Well, that would be lovely. Would you really like to?" She slid the spoon into her mouth and closed her eyes.

"Sure. I haven't been to Sarajevo in a couple of years. I can just bum around with you for a while. I have a meeting in Belgrade in about two weeks anyway." Charlie spoke with a nonchalance she did not feel. Her palms were sweaty as she gripped the fork, and she had to fight the urge to run immediately, run fast and far away until she knew the danger was past. She was determined to do it differently this time around. She would be brave. She'd take care to keep a low profile until she could testify, but she would not run away from the fight. Not this time.

She took another large bite of cake. Joining the *Simply Perfect* gastro tour, surrounded by the glitter of a camera crew, was the best option she could think of. No one would notice her if Waverly was around. All she needed was a couple of weeks before she could testify. Surely she could hide in plain view until then.

CHAPTER 20

April
Sarajevo, Bosnia

W hat a picturesque city," Waverly observed, twirling to take in Sarajevo's old city center. Beau and the film crew were setting up the shoot for the next morning and didn't need her for the evening, so Charlie had offered to play tour guide. Waverly followed Charlie down a cobblestone street and then through a narrow alley lined with shops selling mounds of ornately decorated engraved copper and silver platters, boxes, spoons, and bullet shells.

"It's one of my favorite cities in Europe," Charlie said. She agreed with her sister. Sarajevo was charming, a city with a vibrant soul and a tragic history, a little cousin of Istanbul with strong ties to its Ottoman past. She slowed her pace, pointing out the beautiful old green-roofed mosque behind a tall stone wall overhung with spindly rose canes.

"Here." She stopped beside two pipes jutting out from the high wall surrounding the mosque. Water poured from the pipes into a grate set in the street. "Try this." Charlie cupped her hand under the pipe and took a deep drink of the sweet spring water.

Waverly looked skeptical. "Is it safe?"

"It's perfect," Charlie replied, taking another draft. Waverly hesitated, then stepped forward and copied Charlie, tentatively trying a sip.

"Legend has it that if you drink from this fountain you'll always return to Sarajevo," Charlie said. She dried her hands on her jeans and gazed around them at the contented hubbub, a mixture of tourists clutching shopping bags and taking photos with iPads, Bosnian families with dark-haired children in snowsuits, and old men strolling with their hands behind their backs. It was difficult to believe that less than twenty-five years before, Sarajevo had been under a brutal and extended siege by the Army of Republika Srpska, with almost every building damaged and thousands of civilians killed by shelling and sniper fire. The citizens of Sarajevo had rebuilt their beloved city in the aftermath of the war, determined to carry on despite the pervasive wounds from the past. Some buildings still had holes, but the city had done a remarkable job of picking up the pieces and remaking itself. Bosnians were tremendously resilient.

Charlie shook her head, struck anew by the complex reality of Bosnia and its neighboring countries. If you didn't know to look, you might never glimpse the underlying web of ethnic and religious conflict that lay beneath the Balkans, a gridlock of mismatched puzzle pieces with no clear solutions.

The two sisters wandered through the old city, through the maze of streets crowded with low red-tile-roofed shops and restaurants. Waverly stepped inside a shop to browse, and Charlie waited outside for her. She shivered, pulling her leather jacket closer around her. The air was colder here, and wet. While Budapest was warming and budding for spring, Sarajevo was still chilly with the long touch of winter. The city lay in a long valley surrounded by mountains on every side. The location was perfect for skiing, and Sarajevo had hosted the 1984 Winter Olympics. Charlie wrapped her arms around herself and wished she'd remembered to bring her winter coat. A few minutes later Waverly returned and showed off her purchase, a pair of rose-colored Turkish house slippers elaborately embroidered with gold thread.

"Come on, let's go get some supper," Charlie said, eager to be somewhere warm. She briskly set off toward her favorite *cevapi* place, ready to introduce her sister to the wonders of Bosnian grilled meat. It was growing dark, but the old city was bustling, the shops spilling warm light out onto the smooth sand-colored paving stones of the ancient streets. They squeezed their way into

Cevabdzinica Zeljo, a small restaurant crowded with wooden tables and chairs. A couple of Russian tourists were just leaving, and Charlie grabbed their spot by the window. It was warm in the restaurant from the open grills of the kitchen, the steamy air laden with the mouth-watering smell of grilling meat. Waverly sniffed appreciatively as she slid into the chair across from Charlie.

"Whatever that is, it smells heavenly," she called to her sister, pitching her voice above the loud chatter of other diners.

A hard-faced waitress approached them with two plastic-coated menus, but Charlie waved them off, giving an order for the both of them. The woman nodded and headed for the grills at the back of the restaurant. In a few moments she came back, sliding two metal plates onto their table. Each held a fresh hot pita stuffed with chopped raw onion and cevapi, the fast food of the Balkans, finger-size skinless minced-meat sausages grilled to perfection. A white substance that looked like cream cheese lay mounded on the side of the plate.

"Wait till you try this." Charlie grinned, cutting a chunk of pita and cevapi and smearing it with the white spread.

"What is it?" Waverly asked, pointing to the spread.

"*Kajmak.* It's like butter and cream cheese had

a love child." Charlie chewed and swallowed, closing her eyes to better enjoy the experience.

"Oh my. It's delicious. So creamy." Waverly rolled a bit of cevapi and kajmak around in her mouth, analyzing it. "Maybe we should use this on the show."

Someone tapped on the glass behind Charlie's head, and she turned, mouth full of cevapi, staring for a moment in incomprehension at the handsome, dark-haired young man waving at her through the window. Then she recognized him: it was Arben's brother, Ilir. He grinned, and Charlie motioned him in.

Ilir slipped into the crowded restaurant and found an empty chair at another table. He dragged it over to them and straddled it backward. "I found you," he said proudly.

"What in the world are you doing here?" Charlie said, pitching her voice loudly to be heard over the noisy din of other diners.

Ilir shrugged. "I came down with Arben yesterday. He's got a meeting about a Roma kids camp, and I came along. I ran into your producer in town, and he told me you were in the old city."

"So you just wandered around until you found us?" Charlie asked.

Ilir nodded, looking pleased. The waitress stopped by their table and scowled at him, waiting for his order.

"A Coke," he said, unfazed by her glower. She

returned in a moment and thumped the glass bottle onto the table.

"I found a great location for your show," Ilir said, taking a swig. He seemed jittery, full of nervous energy. He tapped his foot against the leg of the chair, looking from Charlie to Waverly expectantly.

Waverly leaned forward, instantly intrigued. "Tell me about it."

Ilir grinned. "My cousin's getting married this weekend, and she says you can film the whole thing if you want. My aunts are making traditional food, and you can watch them and learn. It will be great—real Albanian food, dances, crazy Albanian traditions. The Americans will love it. You want to see the real Albanian culture? This is your chance."

Waverly's eyes lit up. She put down her fork and looked at Ilir with a calculated expression. Charlie could see her sister already estimating the viewership numbers that an Albanian wedding could draw for her show.

"Where is it?" Charlie asked, trying to think about logistics. She needed to make sure she could make it back to Belgrade from wherever they were in time for the trial on the seventeenth.

"Near Tirana," Ilir announced proudly. Seeing her hesitation, he assured her, "But don't worry. I've got a van. I'll take you."

In the end Waverly and Ilir prevailed. It was

too good an opportunity to pass up, Waverly insisted when Charlie tried to convince her to stay closer to Belgrade. But there would be music and special food at the wedding, maybe some shenanigans they could capture on camera. It was a golden opportunity, one Waverly didn't want to miss.

"This wedding could help save the show," she wheedled, trying to cajole Charlie into saying yes. "Anything we can do to draw viewers is a step toward securing *Simply Perfect*'s future. Come on, it will be fun."

"Okay," Charlie reluctantly agreed, "but I have to be back in Belgrade by April 17. No exceptions."

"Of course." Waverly waved away her sister's concern. "We'll just go for the weekend, and then you're free to be wherever you need to be. Ilir says it's only a few hours away."

Charlie raised her eyebrows, unconvinced. "Nothing is only ever a few hours in the Balkans," she muttered, but Waverly was already texting Beau about the change of plans.

Two days later they were waiting in the lobby when Ilir arrived. He rattled up to their hotel in an ancient blue Ford Transit. Charlie yawned, a bit bleary-eyed, watching as he parked in front of the entrance. Waverly was texting instructions to Beau, who would follow the next day with the rest of the crew after they finished shooting additional footage of Sarajevo. Waverly and Charlie were going on ahead to meet Ilir's aunts, scout out the wedding location, and start brainstorming the new episode.

Ilir honked his horn twice, and when they came through the hotel door, he jumped out of the driver's seat and helped load Charlie's small backpack and Waverly's massive rolling suitcase into the back of the Transit. He seemed less sociable than he had a few days before, more distracted, almost curt. Charlie shrugged it off. Maybe he wasn't a morning person. She could sympathize. Waverly was remarkably chipper in the mornings, bright-eyed and inquisitive, going full speed ahead as soon as her eyes opened. Sometimes it was a little too much to handle.

Although Charlie had initially been reluctant about the entire trip, she had to admit that it was probably time to move on from Sarajevo. Albania seemed like as good a place as any to hide out. Staying in one place for more than a few days felt too risky; she already had a feeling they'd stayed in Sarajevo too long. It was a small city where gossip traveled fast. And Waverly and her film crew weren't exactly inconspicuous. Charlie was glad to be headed somewhere new, somewhere she could hide before heading to Belgrade for the trial.

"Should we be concerned about riding in this?"

Waverly asked sotto voce, casting a skeptical look at the rusted body of the van.

Charlie shrugged. "No more than anything else you'll find around here. It will probably get us there okay." She climbed up onto the passenger seat and beckoned to her sister. "Come on. Albania's waiting."

They sped south out of Sarajevo toward Montenegro, Ilir pushing the van as fast as he dared on the narrow winding roads. The drive was taxing, hours of sharp, never-ending turns as they climbed mountain after mountain and descended into one valley after another. It was also breathtakingly beautiful, with sheer rock walls, deep green lakes, and jagged cliffs rising above them. When they reached a summit, the world spread out around them in a panorama of snowcapped peaks as far as the eye could see.

While the vistas were stunning, the ride was by no means comfortable. The van was drafty and creaky, the suspension bone-jarring. Waverly and Charlie talked little, by turns staring out at the gorgeous scenery and hanging on for dear life to avoid being thrown sideways as the Transit rounded yet another hairpin turn at startling speeds. Luckily neither of them was prone to motion sickness, but even so, Charlie was feeling a bit queasy by the second hour. She stared straight ahead, concentrating on a fixed point in the distance, willing the ancient vehicle to stay on the road, willing the minutes to fly by faster.

Several hours in, Charlie asked Ilir to pull over so she could relieve her full bladder. There was nothing around them, just a vast expanse of sky above the gray boulders and shrubs on the top of yet another mountain. They were in Montenegro and had not passed a town in a long while. Occasionally they would see a house in the distance, perched on a rocky incline, smoke curling from the chimney. But nothing else existed except the gray ribbon of road and the seemingly endless mountains. Charlie crept behind a boulder and crouched to relieve herself. When she was done she joined Waverly at the nose of the van, both of them pausing to stretch their tense muscles. Ilir stepped away and pulled out his cell phone. Amazing, thought Charlie, that in the middle of such desolation there was still cell reception.

"There's nothing here," Waverly mused, taking in the vast, empty landscape. "I've never felt so alone in the world."

Charlie yawned, nodding. The fresh air was settling her queasy stomach. "When the Ottomans came through they took one look at these mountains and decided whatever was on the other side wasn't worth the trouble," she said, joining her sister on the edge of the cliff. "I can see their point."

Ilir rejoined them, texting on his phone. He

looked up. "We should go now," he said, heading back to the van. "We're late."

"Late for what?" Charlie asked. She'd been unaware they were on a time schedule. Ilir slammed his door shut as Waverly and Charlie clambered into their seats, Charlie riding shotgun and Waverly on the bench seat behind them.

"We're meeting friends," he said briefly. "They are helping with the show."

As he started the van and pulled back onto the road, Charlie surveyed him for a moment. He was just nineteen, handsome and cocky, with a bit of a swagger and an endearing smile. There was something effortlessly charming about Albanian men, a confidence and warmth that could be thoroughly disarming. Although Charlie knew Arben had been worried about his brother in recent years, disapproving of the company he was keeping, Ilir was one of her favorites around the office.

After driving for an hour on another almost deserted stretch of road, they stopped in a small town in the south of Montenegro. It was just a dot on the map, a handful of tired houses, a gas station, and a restaurant with a bar. Ilir pulled the van into the parking lot of the restaurant, a squat building with one other vehicle parked outside, an ancient blue Lada. In the restaurant window was a yellow sign for *Jelen pivo*, a Serbian beer. Out front by the road on a long spit was what looked like the carcass of a sheep roasting over a bed of live orange coals.

"We eat here," Ilir announced. "The owner is the father of my uncle's wife."

Waverly peered between the front seats at the spit. "What is that?" she asked. The animal took another rotation over the coals. With its legs trussed together, it looked as though it were making a graceful leap over the grill.

Ilir shrugged. "Maybe lamb. Come on, food is inside."

It took a moment for their eyes to adjust to the dim and smoky interior. Three large Balkan men were hunched over a square table, sharing a platter of food and bottles of Jelen. As they passed the table, Charlie glanced over at them. One of the men met her eyes. He was huge, with a shaved head and a tattoo of a double-headed eagle on his neck. She looked away from his unfriendly stare, down at the platter on the table. It was the partially eaten head of a sheep, its face bald and beaky with one wide, blank eye turned toward the ceiling. Waverly saw it too and let out a muffled exclamation, hurrying to follow Ilir. The men cast stony glances in their direction, and Charlie didn't look back. She could feel the men's eyes following her as she walked away.

Once they were seated at a corner table, the proprietor shuffled over, greeting Ilir familiarly with an embrace and a kiss on both cheeks, then handed them all sticky plastic menus. Ilir spoke to him in Serbian and the man nodded and replied, eyeing Charlie and Waverly with an air of tired disinterest.

"I told him who you are," Ilir explained. Two of the men at the table with the sheep's head were smoking cigarettes, and the smoke drifted lazily across the room.

Waverly wrinkled her nose. "Are they allowed to smoke in here?" she hissed to Charlie. "It's bad for the baby."

Charlie only nodded, not bothering to explain to Waverly that cigarettes and most Balkan men were inseparable. Many had been smoking since puberty or before. She studied the menu, trying to make out the Cyrillic letters. She could read a little. Most of the dishes were variations on grilled meats—stuffed with cheese or plain—with sides of bread and pickled peppers. She recognized *csevapcsicsa*, the Montenegrin version of cevapi.

"I'm feeling a little light-headed from the road," Waverly announced, scanning the menu even though she had no chance of understanding anything on it. "Do they have anything light—a vegetarian option or a salad?"

Ilir consulted the menu, then beckoned the proprietor over and questioned him. The man rattled off a reply, and Ilir shook his head at

Waverly. "Unfortunately, they do not have salads. Only peppers in vinegar. And *ajvar*."

"Ajvar?" Waverly looked confused.

"It's a condiment," Charlie muttered. "The one with the roasted red peppers you were so excited about."

"Oh." Waverly looked disappointed. "Well, how about some fresh fruit? A fruit salad maybe?"

Ilir asked the question and translated the reply, although the proprietor's nonverbal was a giveaway. He was looking at Waverly suspiciously from underneath bushy gray brows.

Ilir relayed the message. "He says fruit is for children."

"Well, what do they have?" Waverly asked, scanning the menu.

"They have meat," Ilir explained, gesturing to all of the items. "And chicken."

Waverly looked nonplussed. "Isn't chicken a kind of meat?"

Ilir shrugged. "It's different. And they have sausages."

Charlie raised her menu slightly to cover her smile and ordered the grilled pork stuffed with cheese. Waverly gave in and ordered chicken with ajvar and a side of pickles.

During lunch Charlie noticed the table of men watching them. They had finished their shared sheep's head and were sitting smoking and drinking another round of beer. She bent over her meal and ate quickly, eager to leave. There was a lonely air of menace about the place. If something happened here, the outside world might never know. For the first time she realized how alone she and Waverly were. If not for Ilir, they could easily disappear off the map.

When she looked up, the men were gone. No one else came into the restaurant. The proprietor was behind the long wooden bar, smoking a cigarette and watching a grainy television mounted in the corner high on the wall. When they had finished the meal, he reappeared with the bill and a tray with three shot glasses of clear liquid.

"Homemade *rakija*," Ilir explained. "From plums in his garden. You have to try. It's the best."

"It's like strong brandy," Charlie said, taking a shot glass from the tray but not tasting it. "Everyone has a cousin or uncle who makes it in their basement."

Waverly took a glass and eyed it skeptically. "Is it safe?"

Charlie shrugged. "Usually." She pushed her glass over to Ilir. "I can't because of the baby," she explained, gesturing to the mound of her stomach.

Ilir addressed the proprietor, and wordlessly the man took back Charlie's shot glass, returning a moment later with a small open bottle of pear juice. "For you." Ilir nodded to her. "For free."

"*Hvala*." Charlie thanked the man in her very limited Serbian and took the bottle. She didn't really want pear juice, but it seemed rude not to accept it. She took a few sips as Ilir and Waverly clinked their shot glasses and downed their drinks in one swallow.

"Oh my goodness, that is potent." Waverly coughed and sputtered, eyes watering. "It's like drinking gasoline."

Ilir stood. "I need to make a call," he said, pulling out his cell phone. "I'll be back. Stay here." He lingered for a moment at the table, and Charlie had the impression that he was waiting for something. After a minute he headed toward the front of the restaurant and went out to the parking lot. Charlie craned her head and peered out the window behind her. The three men who had been in the restaurant were still in the parking lot, sitting in the old blue Lada. Ilir crossed to the car, and the driver rolled down the window. Ilir bent down and gestured to the restaurant, talking to them.

"That's odd," Charlie murmured. "I wonder what he's doing." She turned back around, feeling a little woozy. The room was shifting strangely. She glanced up and found the proprietor watching her, his face expressionless. Behind him the TV was showing an image of a man running across an open field while bullets pinged the earth around him.

"Charlie." Waverly's voice sounded strained. "I don't feel well."

Charlie turned to look at her sister, but the room spun and everything went topsy-turvy. The last thing she remembered was the proprietor's large, calloused hand on her head as he laid her cheek down gently on the tablecloth beside the half-empty bottle of pear juice. Her vision narrowed to a pinpoint of light, and then everything went dark.

CHAPTER 21

Somewhere in the Balkans

Waverly was wearing someone else's slippers. It was the first thing she noticed as she came to consciousness slowly, hazily in the dimness of an unfamiliar room that smelled of cigarette smoke and floral dryer sheets. Her Jimmy Choo wedges were nowhere to be seen, and instead she was wearing a pair of hand-knit booties in a neon pink, nubby and slightly misshapen. She blinked twice, shaking her head, trying to clear it. Her thoughts were sluggish, and she had a piercing headache. Her tongue felt too large for her mouth and fuzzy, as though it were made of felt.

She looked around, turning her head slowly, feeling confusion and a vague concern. She was lying on a narrow single bed, covered with a heavy acrylic blanket that was pulled up to her chin and tucked neatly at the sides. She squinted in the dim light coming through the single shuttered window on the far wall, struggling to orient herself, trying to remember how she had come to this unfamiliar place.

The room was bare and spacious, with an orange tile floor, a spindly wooden table, and two molded plastic chairs. Across the room against the far wall Charlie lay motionless on the other twin bed, the round swell of her pregnant belly poking up under the blanket.

Waverly struggled to sit up, wincing against the throbbing in her head, and still wearing the ridiculous booties, unsteadily padded across the room to check on her sister. Her eyes were closed and she was breathing rhythmically. Waverly bent down and touched Charlie's forehead gently, just resting the tips of her fingers against her sister's freckled skin. She was warm to the touch. Waverly put her hand on Charlie's belly and after a moment was rewarded with a kick from the baby. Slightly relieved, she stumbled back to the other bed and sat down, gripping the edge of the bedframe to steady herself and try to piece together the afternoon.

She remembered stopping at the rundown restaurant somewhere in Montenegro. She had a vague memory of eating chicken and then toasting with Ilir, tossing back a liquid that burned and tasted like plums mixed with gasoline. A face flashed across her mind, the silent proprietor watching them with a guarded expression as he offered them his homemade liquor.

Waverly licked her dry lips. It must have been in the drinks—the liquor and the pear juice. It would have been so easy, really. A slip of the hand as he poured her shot and popped open the slim glass bottle of juice for Charlie. Drinks on the house.

Although she had no previous firsthand knowledge, Waverly suspected they'd been roofied. How long had they been out? And where in the world were they? Where was Ilir, for that matter? She hoped nothing bad had happened to him.

With a growing sense of unease, Waverly walked woozily across the room, which seemed to tilt ever so slightly back and forth, and tried the door handle. Locked. So they were not guests. Someone did not want them to leave. A gap at the bottom of the door let in a strip of light and the muted sound of a television coming from another room. She rattled the handle again, but it wouldn't budge. Pressing her ear to the door, she tried to make out sounds but couldn't decipher anything clearly. Someone was smoking, though. The smoke was drifting lazily under the door, just a hint of it.

"Hello," she yelled loudly, her speech a little slurred. She rattled the handle. "Hello, let us out!" But there was no response. Huffing in frustration and alarm, she tried the window next, unlatching the shutters to reveal rusted bars across the opening. She stared at them in dismay. They were truly prisoners. The view was of a bare patch of land with a few twisted fruit trees and a decrepit tan car sitting on blocks. No other houses were in sight.

On the table were two tumblers and a pitcher of water in an incongruously cheerful orange polka dot print. Waverly hesitated but poured herself a glass of water, her thirst overtaking her caution about drinking unclean water. She took a sip. It tasted like nothing. Hopefully filtered. She sat down in one of the hard, plastic chairs and pressed the cool glass to her forehead, trying to think.

Her pulse was racing and her head felt light. Must be the effects of the drug. She took another sip and tried to concentrate. It appeared to be close to evening. No one knew where they were. Not her camera crew or Beau, not Andrew far away in the US. She thought of her husband with a sudden stab of longing. His calm, even presence made everything manageable. She missed him so much. How had she not realized it before? She had been waiting, hoping he would come to his senses. And now he was an ocean away, completely unaware that his wife was currently being held captive for reasons unknown somewhere in the Balkans.

She drank her glass of water and poured another, feeling marginally more lucid. How did a television star simply vanish? Like this, that's how. She shook her head, disbelieving. The reality of their situation was gradually dawning on her. In a hyper-interconnected world of smart-phones and GPSes and satellites, how could this happen? Surely someone would come looking for them. But where would they look? Beau knew that she'd left Sarajevo, but it could be two days before he realized she had not arrived at the intended location in Albania. And even then no one would know where they'd gone. They could simply disappear.

She cast an uneasy glance around the room, assessing the situation. Who knew their where-abouts? Only Ilir? Presumably he knew what had happened to them. Perhaps even now he was going for help. Ilir was related to a colleague of Charlie's. What was his name . . . Arbor? That didn't sound right. But regardless, Arbor would notice his brother missing if Ilir didn't reappear in Budapest, wouldn't he? And Beau would know soon that Waverly and Charlie were gone too. Whatever the circumstances of their disappearance, someone would realize they were missing and come for them eventually. Waverly nodded, slightly comforted.

Still, she wondered who in the world had taken them. What possible reason could someone have to drug them and hold them captive? Unless there had been some mix-up, some misunder-standing. Waverly brightened considerably. Yes, that seemed likely. Probably this had nothing to do with her and Charlie. Waverly thought of the three men in their tiny car. Hadn't Ilir been talking to them in the parking lot right before she and Charlie passed out? This must have something to do with Ilir and those men, then. That was probably it. A misunderstanding, a matter of an unpaid debt. Perhaps he had gotten himself in trouble with them. It could be Mafia related. So much was in this part of the world, Charlie had told her. Probably just a misunderstanding, nothing a wire transfer from the States wouldn't fix in a jiffy.

Somewhat cheered by this thought, Waverly finished her glass of water and sat back to wait for whatever came next. She was looking out the window at the decrepit car, thinking of Andrew, when Charlie stirred, coughed, and asked drowsily, "Where are we?"

Waverly turned to the bed, a slight smile on her face. "I've no idea," she said cheerfully, "but I think we've been kidnapped."

A look of incomprehension crossed Charlie's face, quickly replaced by panic. She put her hands on her round belly and struggled to a sitting position. Her feet skittered across the floorboards, searching for her Keens.

"Gone," Waverly informed her. "Everything's gone—shoes, purses, everything. But don't worry. I think there's been a mix-up. It's probably just about money. I think Ilir owed a debt to those men at the restaurant. I'm sure we can get it sorted out with a wire transfer from my bank."

Ignoring her sister, Charlie hoisted herself up with a groan and tried the door. Finding it locked, she joined Waverly at the window, peering out at the depressing yard. A few chickens pecked the dirt and a stray dog paused to urinate on one of the fruit trees. Charlie cursed under her breath, gripping the windowsill so hard her knuckles went white.

"This is not good," she murmured to Waverly, then called out the window loudly, "Hello? *Zdravo*?" She swayed unsteadily and closed her eyes for a moment.

Nothing. The chickens paused, then resumed pecking at the scrubby weeds.

"*Upomoc!*" Charlie yelled. "Help!" And when that elicited no response, she tried again, sounding a little more desperate. "*Trebam ici u wc?*" She clutched her abdomen.

"What is it? Is it the baby? Is something wrong?" Waverly asked sharply, suddenly concerned. What if the drugs had affected the baby? She had felt the baby move, but perhaps something else was not right. Charlie sat down abruptly in the other chair, pressing her legs together and looking across the table at her sister.

"Yes, something's wrong," she said crossly. "My bladder feels like a water balloon, I'm about to wet my pants, and I'm pretty sure we've been kidnapped, and not for the reason you think." She

311

cast a desperate glance around the room, then met Waverly's eyes. "This isn't about money," she said grimly. "I think we're in big trouble."

Charlie related the facts to Waverly as simply as she could, stating the main points of her story baldly and truthfully. She told Waverly about the women in the back of the transport truck, about Kinga and Simona and the long drive to Belgrade. She told her about the threat to Monica, about Sandra Ling and Charlie's decision to testify, and about the man outside her apartment. When she was finished she took a deep breath and crossed her arms over her stomach, waiting for the explosion.

But Waverly surprised her. She didn't say anything, just scrutinized her sister for a long moment. "Why didn't you tell me this before?" she asked quietly.

Charlie shrugged. "Because I knew you'd make me come back to the US, leave my work and my own life. And I want to help these women. I feel like I have to testify. I'm tired of running. If I don't help them, who will?"

Waverly regarded her sister gravely. "You're either much braver than I am or much stupider. I can't decide which."

Charlie gave her a dry smile. "Probably both."

"You put the baby in danger. You put me in danger." Waverly frowned. She fixed her sister with a hard stare. "You should have at least told me. We could have made a decision together." She glanced at Charlie's stomach, her baby tucked safely inside, and her mouth trembled for a moment. "I understand why you feel you have to stay. I don't agree with it and I don't like it, but I do understand. But now what? What if something happens to the baby?"

"I won't let it," Charlie said with more conviction than she felt. Instinctively her hand went to her neck, to the thin chain and solid little medal sitting under her shirt. She touched the image of St. George, trying to summon courage. Her heart was pounding too fast and she felt dizzy, probably a combination of the drugs and fear. She had been foolish to try to fix this on her own. She should have let other people help her, confided in them. It was too late now. No one had any idea where they were, including Charlie and Waverly. She glanced around the small, neat room, gauging any chance of escape. Nothing presented itself.

What did the kidnappers mean to do to them? That was the pertinent question. Would they simply keep Charlie until after the trial and then let her go? Would they demand some sort of ransom? Or did they want a more permanent end to the situation, one that came with a bullet to the head? She shuddered, feeling suddenly small and vulnerable and very alone. How stupid she had been, thinking she could be a lone cowboy, and now she'd put Waverly and the baby in grave danger as well. Charlie ran her hand over the baby, reassuring the little one that all would be well, but she couldn't summon the same optimism for herself. It would be so easy to make the two women disappear. No one would find their bodies. They could vanish without a trace. Only Ilir knew what had happened, and who knew where he was. Had the traffickers threatened or harmed him? Had he betrayed Charlie and Waverly? She had no idea.

Charlie heard heavy footsteps in the hall, and a moment later the door opened. She sat up, squaring her shoulders against the frisson of fear that skittered up her spine. A giant of a man filled the doorframe. Charlie recognized him instantly. The bald man with the eagle tattoo on his neck, the one who had been eating the sheep's head with his friends. Dressed in combat boots, cargo pants, and a black muscle shirt, he had a nasty scowl below a beetle brow and a handgun tucked in the waistband of his trousers. He was carrying a plastic tray of food. Wordlessly he crossed to where they sat and set the tray on the table. He glanced at them briefly, then stepped aside.

Charlie opened her mouth to ask him a question.

"Save your words. He does not speak."

She whirled to find a dark, slender young man

standing in the doorway watching the interaction. The giant grunted and loped to the door, assuming a watchful, guarded stance. The younger man came into the room. He was about twenty-five, Charlie guessed, with slicked-back dark hair, dressed in a blue Adidas tracksuit and spotless matching athletic shoes. He stopped a few feet away and regarded them with a curious expression. He did not look like a villain, more like a normal guy going out to watch soccer on a Friday night.

"What do you want with us?" Charlie demanded at the exact same moment as Waverly said entreatingly, "I'll pay whatever you ask if you let us go right now."

The man looked from one to the other, a small, surprised smile playing on his lips. He seemed almost amused. "Unfortunately, this is not my decision. I have orders to keep you here." His English was heavily accented but precise. He was obviously educated.

"Who ordered you to kidnap us?" Charlie crossed her arms over her stomach, a gesture of protection, and stared him down. "And why?" She felt a wave of fury spiral up through her body, the ancient fight-or-flight instinct of a trapped animal flooding through her veins.

The young man looked unimpressed by her fierce demeanor. "Because you are of use to us."

"I'm an American citizen," Waverly interjected. "I demand to be released to the nearest American embassy."

"Of use how?" Charlie scowled. "Why are you keeping us here?"

The man shrugged. "Soon you will understand everything." He seemed almost cheerful, which chilled Charlie to the bone. Something seemed very wrong about this situation. She didn't understand what was going on. Somehow she had to convince him to let at least one of them go.

"My sister has nothing to do with this." Charlie lifted her chin, ignoring Waverly's protest, trying to bluff her way out of this mess. "I'm the one you want." She moved in front of Waverly.

The man looked surprised. "You?" he asked, genuinely puzzled, then pointed to Waverly. "No, she is the one we want."

"What?" Both Charlie and Waverly stared at him in astonishment. Never in any of her frantic calculations had Charlie considered this scenario. The kidnappers didn't want her? What could they possibly want with Waverly?

"Yes." The man leaned toward Waverly and tilted his head slightly, looking at her as though she were a rare object of art. "Waverly Talbot, the famous television star of *Simply Perfect*. My aunt and mother are your biggest fans."

Both women gaped at him, stunned. Charlie shook her head, trying to make sense of his words. She was thoroughly confused. Was it possible that they had not been kidnapped by the traffickers, the people who had threatened Monica? It was good news if it was true, but brought with it more questions than it answered. If it was not the traffickers who had taken them, then who were these people and why did they want Waverly?

"Why have you kidnapped me?" Waverly asked tremulously, her expression unsure.

The man smiled slightly. "We need your help."

Their captor refused to say more, insisting that they first eat and rest. The giant guard accompanied Charlie to the toilet, where she took a few extra moments to snoop around the bathroom, learning nothing more than what brand of laundry detergent the household used. She could not tell where they were, not even what country they were in. Depending on how long they had been unconscious, they could be almost anywhere in the Balkans. It was even conceivable that they'd been taken by boat to Italy, although she didn't think so. The back of the laundry detergent box was in several languages, all of them Central European. They were still somewhere in the Balkans; she'd lay money on the fact.

When she got back she was surprised to discover Waverly's purse and suitcase and her backpack lying on their beds. Her Keens and

Waverly's Jimmy Choos were primly tucked under the bedframe beneath them.

"He brought them," Waverly murmured, nodding to the slim man standing next to the giant with the eagle tattoo. She cast a look at their captors and said in a low voice, "So, do you think they're with the Serbian Mafia? Are these some of the men who trafficked those women you helped rescue?"

Charlie glanced over at the two men. The hulking one was standing at attention, staring blankly off into the distance, but she had the impression that the younger man was listening to their conversation.

"We can talk about it later," she said, nodding her head slightly toward their captors, hoping Waverly would get the message and stop talking.

Waverly, however, missed the cue.

"Do you think they're trying to stop you from testifying at the trial?" She was trying to whisper, but it was more of a stage whisper, quite audible. "What happens if you don't make it to Belgrade?"

Charlie rolled her eyes. Her sister would make a terrible spy. "We'll talk later," Charlie hissed, jerking her head at the young man. Waverly finally caught on and nodded, clamping her mouth shut.

The young man interrupted their exchange. "If you need the toilet in the night, Artur will be outside the door to help you." He indicated the hulking guard, who scowled at the far wall. "He doesn't understand English, but he knows the word *toilet.* Do not try to escape. You have nowhere to go, and we will treat you kindly if you help us. Now you should rest. Tomorrow will be a very busy day."

He gestured for Artur to follow him and started to leave the room.

"Wait," Charlie called, desperate to learn anything she could, trying to understand what was going on. "What is your name?"

The man turned. "I am Jetmir," he said. He inclined his head cordially, then left them, locking the door behind him.

Jetmir. Charlie frowned, puzzling over his nationality. It didn't sound like a Slavic name. Not Greek or Italian either. Was it Albanian? His accent had sounded Albanian to her, similar to Arben and Ilir's.

Waverly was sitting on the bed rifling through her purse. "They took my cell phone." She sounded disappointed.

Charlie looked through her bag. Nothing was missing except her laptop and phone, the only things she really wanted to find. She left her purse on the bed and went to the table. Her stomach growled with hunger, and she lifted the foil that was over one of the plates on the plastic tray. Strange that even in the midst of the most extreme circumstances the body still needed sustenance. Many things went on as before—the breath filling her lungs, the steady drumming of her heart, quieter now that there seemed to be no imminent danger. She slid into a chair at the table and rested her throbbing head in her hands. How had this happened? How were they in this place, held captive for unknown purposes, whisked away from their lives in the blink of an eye? No one knew where they were. *They* didn't even know where they were. Everything felt turned inside out.

Charlie and Waverly shared a mostly silent meal of baked peppers stuffed with rice, meat, and tomato sauce. The food was hearty and good, but neither enjoyed it under the circumstances. Charlie ate mechanically, filling her belly, eating for the baby, but her mind was on their current situation. While they ate they briefly discussed their predicament in low undertones, in case Artur was listening outside the door. Unfortunately, there was little to discuss. They didn't know where they were, who had taken them, or why.

While Waverly seemed confused and a little unsettled to discover that apparently she was the reason they had been kidnapped, Charlie was secretly relieved. Whatever this was, it seemed better than being kidnapped by the traffickers. The Serbian Mafia was brutal and ruthless. These people, whoever they were, were at least treating them with some level of decency.

"We have to find a way to contact someone and tell them what's happened to us." Waverly took a sip of water, drumming her fingers on the table, trying to come up with a method of communication.

"Even if we could get hold of someone, we have no idea where we are. We have almost nothing to tell them," Charlie pointed out, dabbing at the sauce from her dinner with a hunk of bread.

"Maybe Ilir got away and is trying to get help for us right now," Waverly said hopefully.

"Or he was in on everything from the beginning." Charlie frowned. "The guy who roofied us was related to him, remember?" She thought of how distant and curt Ilir had been during the drive. It seemed likely that he had been the one to orchestrate their disappearance. A depressing thought, that the one person in the world who knew where they were was probably not in any hurry to reveal their whereabouts.

Waverly pursed her lips. "What in the world could they want with me?" she wondered aloud.

Charlie had been wondering the same thing. "I guess we'll find out tomorrow," she said grimly.

Waverly looked up and met her sister's eyes. In Waverly's, Charlie saw fear mixed with a tinge of curiosity. Neither said anything more. There was nothing more to say.

CHAPTER 22

The next morning Artur brought another plastic tray with breakfast and removed the remains of their dinner. Charlie sat up with a groan as he left the room with the dinner tray. She had slept poorly, alert to every noise, her mind whirling through the long hours of darkness, trying to make sense of their situation, trying to come up with an escape plan and a solution. She had reached no conclusion, just frustrated and exhausted herself until she drifted into an uneasy sleep.

In the bathroom down the hall she showered and changed into fresh clothes. Waverly did the same after her. Then they sat down to a simple breakfast of fresh round bread, cheese, ajvar, and scrambled eggs. Halfway through breakfast Artur brought in two cups of strong coffee. Charlie waved hers away, but Waverly downed hers quickly, grimacing as she swallowed the thick, dark brew. She and Charlie both preferred tea, but coffee was the only beverage on their breakfast tray.

They were almost finished with breakfast when Jetmir appeared, Artur following him like an obedient hound. Their host was looking just as dapper as he had the day before. He was wearing a new tracksuit, this one red, but the same spotless athletic shoes.

"You are refreshed?" he inquired. "Is there anything you need to be comfortable?"

"We'd be a lot more comfortable if you'd tell us where we are and what you want with us," Charlie said boldly. Waverly nodded her agreement.

He chuckled. "Soon you will know everything you need to know. Please get ready now. We are going to meet the man in charge."

Charlie and Waverly exchanged glances. That sounded ominous but possibly enlightening.

With Jetmir leading the way and Artur bringing up the rear, his hand hovering menacingly over his gun, they walked single file through the house. As they passed an open doorway, Charlie caught a glimpse of a narrow kitchen where a tiny, wizened woman in a head scarf and long skirt was stirring a bubbling pot on a gas stove. The woman looked up and glowered at them as they passed. On the other side of the hall was a half-open door leading to a living room. On a black leather sofa sat two large men smoking and watching television. They did not look up as Charlie passed them. She couldn't be sure, but she thought she recognized them from the restaurant in Montenegro.

Jetmir led them through the front door and across a scrubby patch of ground toward a large outbuilding made of brick plastered over with stucco. Charlie looked around her as they walked. There were no other houses within sight. The air smelled sweet and fresh, the morning sun burning off the night's chill. A large, bare vegetable patch lay in the sun beyond the outbuilding. A shiny new Mercedes was parked in front of the building, along with a few older Volkswagens.

Charlie craned her head, focusing on the license plates. Most license plates in Europe had the initials of the country to one side of the plate. She squinted. *RKS,* the plate on the shiny Mercedes read. Republic of Kosovo. The other cars' plates were the same. Kosovo. They were in Kosovo. Charlie closed her eyes for a moment, relieved to at least know what country they were in, but that only deepened the mystery. They had been kidnapped in Montenegro and brought across the border into Kosovo. But why?

They came to a halt in front of the outbuilding. Roughly triple the size of the house, it had a few windows set high in the wall and covered with black material, and a heavy metal door. Jetmir opened the door and ushered them inside.

It took a moment for Charlie's eyes to adjust. The room was a hive of activity. Over half a dozen people were running to and fro inside, heads bent as though on important errands. Her gaze instantly went to a makeshift stage at the other end of the room, illuminated by lights on poles. In front of the stage two men fiddled with a video camera on a tripod. The air was cold in the cavernous room and smelled of stale cigarette smoke and vaguely of horse manure from the garden outside.

"Welcome, welcome, honored guests."

Charlie and Waverly turned in unison to find a balding, rotund man in a dark suit addressing them. His eyes behind wire-rimmed glasses were sharp, assessing. His leather shoes were perfectly polished. He said something to Jetmir, who nodded and fell back a half step, ushering Charlie and Waverly forward. *They're speaking Albanian,* Charlie realized, listening to them. She didn't speak Albanian, but she recognized its soft cadence, the *shh*es and pursed lips. The man in front of them must be the big boss Jetmir had mentioned.

"Welcome to our television studio," he said, gesturing expansively. "I am Erjon." On his left hand he wore a heavy gold ring with a red background and a bold black double-headed eagle, the symbol on Albania's national flag. "Come." He motioned for them to follow him to the stage. "See what we have prepared for you."

They skirted the two men adjusting the video camera and approached the stage.

"Oh," Waverly gasped. "It's my kitchen."

Charlie stared in surprise. Waverly was right. Their captors had tried to reconstruct the kitchen from *Simply Perfect*, but nothing looked quite right. The marble was obviously laminate and not the right color, the refrigerator in the back was only spray painted silver, but it was clearly the *Simply Perfect* kitchen, or at least a cheap knock-off version of it.

"What in the world?" Charlie muttered, more confused than ever. She shook her head, feeling a bit like Alice in Wonderland, as though she'd tipped down a hole and come out in a strange Albanian alternate universe.

"You like it?" Erjon asked Waverly, gesturing to the kitchen and looking pleased. "It is for you."

"Er, thank you," Waverly said politely.

"Please . . ." He invited them to sit down on two folding chairs facing the stage, and he sat down opposite them. "Coffee, tea? *Burek*?"

"We're fine," Charlie said automatically.

Waverly was still staring at her makeshift kitchen, her brow furrowed in puzzlement. She crossed her legs at the ankle, posture correct even as her face displayed a mixture of consternation and confusion. "What is this for?" she asked, voicing the question Charlie had been waiting to ask as well.

Erjon smiled broadly. "Your television show.

We have the kitchen, the cameras, even your costumes." He snapped his fingers, and a young woman hurried over with a rolling rack of bright evening gowns in a rainbow of colors.

"You see, we have thought of everything," Erjon said proudly, motioning to the evening gowns.

"Ah, I see," Waverly murmured, hesitating before reaching out to touch an emerald-green gown covered in sequins. They were a far cry from her usual demure outfits under pretty vintage-print aprons. "But I still don't understand. What do you want me to do?"

Erjon nodded, snapping his fingers. The young woman rolled the rack of gowns away as another young woman appeared with a small cup of thick dark coffee. He took a sip, savoring it for a moment.

"You are here," he said slowly, with gravity, putting the cup down with a *clink* of porcelain, "to help the Albanian people gain unity and freedom."

Waverly and Charlie exchanged a look.

"What?" Charlie asked guardedly.

"You are going to help us bring the Albanian people together, to once again achieve ethnic Albanian unification," Erjon said smoothly. He threaded his fingers together and rested them on his rounded middle, sitting back in his chair, satisfied.

Waverly looked utterly mystified. Charlie stared at him, trying to put the puzzle pieces together. Finally, something clicked into place. She'd read a report on the concept of a unified ethnic Albania a few years before. It was a grand plan to reunite all ethnic Albanians under one country. The problem was that the plan included uniting Albania, Kosovo (whose population was mostly ethnically Albanian and identified strongly with Albania), and portions of land from at least four other sovereign nations. Unfortunately, Serbia, Montenegro, Macedonia, and Greece were not favorably inclined to carve off portions of their national territory and hand it over to a large group of zealous and patriotic Albanians; it was a plan that seemed doomed to failure from the start. So this was who had kidnapped them? Albanian nationalists?

Charlie felt equal parts relieved and baffled. "How exactly is Waverly going to help you?" she asked.

Their host smiled, pleased that they had finally gotten to the crux of the matter. "She is a famous TV star in America," he said, gesturing grandly to Waverly, "and America is a very powerful country. When America wants something, other countries listen. So . . ." He shrugged as though the outcome were obvious.

Charlie stared at him for a moment, trying to follow his logic. "Wait . . . You want Waverly to convince the US to support Albanian reunifica-tion?" she asked in disbelief.

"Yes." Erjon nodded. "Exactly."

"But how will I do that?" Waverly asked. "I'm just a home entertaining show host."

"You will help us by filming your cooking show and showing American people how great Albania is," Erjon explained.

"I'm not that famous," Waverly said in a fit of honesty.

Charlie kicked her in the shin discreetly. Now was not the time to have a sudden spurt of humility. Waverly's supposed fame might be all the leverage they had to work with.

Erjon laughed. "We see you on the television. All America watches the television. You are a famous lady."

Charlie's mind was working furiously, trying to determine the best course of action. Their kidnappers' plan was, of course, ridiculous. To use a home-hostessing show on the Food Net-work to convince the US to back an impossible reunification effort was absurd. But at least it meant that they had not been kidnapped by human traffickers, and if the Albanians wanted Waverly's help so badly, that meant that Waverly and Charlie had some possible negotiating power.

"What do we get if she cooperates?" Charlie asked abruptly. "Will you let us go?"

Erjon nodded. "Of course. When we are

finished making the shows, you are free to leave. You are our guests here."

Charlie calculated dates in her head. They had been taken yesterday, she thought. Therefore, it was probably April 8. Just nine days until she had to testify in Belgrade. And about three months until her due date. Surely they wouldn't keep them long enough for her to have the baby? How long did the Albanians think it would take to convince America to support their plans? It seemed likely that someone would figure out where they were before her due date, but the odds of being released before the trial seemed slim. Nine days was a short period of time to find the missing Talbot sisters, but she had to be in Belgrade by the seventeenth. What could they do?

"And what if she refuses to help you?" Charlie asked. She was testing the parameters, trying to gauge their captor's intentions.

Erjon smiled slightly, looking Charlie in the eye. He leaned back in his chair comfortably and took another sip of espresso, then set it in its saucer. The woman who had brought him the coffee appeared, and he handed her the cup before waving her away. "I hear something interesting from Jetmir," he said in a conversational tone of voice. "He says there are people in Serbia who are looking for you. People who would very much like to find you."

Charlie's blood ran cold at his words. So Jetmir had been listening to their conversation about the traffickers. Erjon's mouth was drawn over his teeth in a smile, but his eyes were hard.

"I have contacts in Serbia," he said softly. "My cousin knows powerful people there, people in that line of work. A phone call from me and they will know exactly where to find you. But we don't want to do this. There is no need for anyone to know you are here." He spread his hands in a gesture of goodwill. "As long as you help us, we will keep you safe."

Charlie swallowed hard and sat back in her chair. So that was the end of the negotiations. The Albanians held all the cards. She and Waverly were stuck, with no obvious way out.

"I'll do it," Waverly said, casting a worried glance at Charlie. "Whatever you want, I'll do it."

"Excellent." Erjon looked genuinely pleased. He clapped his hands, and Jetmir appeared from somewhere behind them. "We start tomorrow," he said, dismissing them with a wave of his hand.

"Are you honestly getting dressed up for this farce?" Charlie asked early the next morning, yawning and stretching on the bed with a groan.

Waverly, who had been up for a half hour already, glanced up from the mirror, her curling iron in her hand. Charlie was not a morning person, never had been, but Waverly loved the early mornings. There was such a sense of purpose and possibility in the morning. Anything could happen when the day stretched before you. Waverly found those early hours to be her happiest and most productive. She often used them to try new recipes and putter around her kitchen, listening to Whitney Houston or Celine Dion, her mother's apron tied over her pajamas.

It was barely light, but a few minutes earlier Artur had brought breakfast and an evening gown for Waverly—a flared emerald-green mermaid cut that looked like a prom dress from the early nineties. He left the dress on her bed and tapped his watch, motioning for Waverly to get ready quickly.

"I'm preparing for whatever the day holds," Waverly responded. "Usually I have a hair and makeup girl, but I can do it in a pinch. And I'd say this certainly qualifies as a pinch." She took a small bite of eggs and carefully wound another piece of hair around the barrel of the curling iron.

Charlie helped herself to breakfast and then flopped onto the bed, balancing a full plate of bread and cheese and eggs on her stomach. "But they're forcing you to do this. It's not like it's a real show."

"Well, I'm a professional," Waverly stated tartly. "This might not be a real show, but if I'm in front of the camera I need to look the part.

I'm *Simply Perfect*'s Waverly Talbot no matter what the circumstances. And right now our circumstances seem pretty dire, and I am doing whatever it takes to keep the people who have captured us happy."

She closed one eyelid and brushed a pearly eye shadow across it. Charlie didn't understand what it meant to have a public image, Waverly thought as she readied herself for the camera. She had been cultivating her public persona for years. She was the consummate professional, even in less than ideal circumstances.

Charlie took a big bite of eggs. "Do you think anyone knows we're missing yet?" she asked.

Waverly carefully applied a coat of mascara to her upper lashes. "Yes, by now Beau will realize we didn't make it to that wedding. He'll know we're missing, but I have no idea what he'll do about it or how he'll find us." She bit her lip, carefully brushing eye shadow across the other lid to match.

Beau was clever and loyal and resourceful. He would work unceasingly to find Waverly, but the problem was that he would have so very little to work with. For all intents and purposes, she and Charlie had simply vanished somewhere between Sarajevo and Pristina. That was a long and lonely road. They could be anywhere by now.

Charlie had said the day before that she thought they were somewhere in Kosovo, based on the license plates, but that still only narrowed it down to an entire country. It was a small country, true, but a large and imprecise region if you were searching for only two people, especially if there was a reason to keep them hidden.

Waverly rubbed a touch of blush below her cheekbones to highlight them. She was working hard to remain calm, to summon the Zen-like serenity she tried to channel on the show. She was choosing to ignore so much about her circumstances right now. She could focus on recipes and camera angles because they distracted her from thinking about Andrew or worrying about how exactly they were going to get out of their current predicament.

At least they hadn't been taken by the people who were after Charlie. Waverly shuddered at the thought. As long as she did her job like their captors wanted, it seemed there was a good chance things could still turn out well. She glanced at her sister and her unborn child, feeling the responsibility for their safety settle on her shoulders like a lead blanket. She couldn't exactly orchestrate a rescue, but she could do her best to keep them safe until they were rescued or released by the people who had taken them.

And who knows, she thought, trying to think of anything positive about their current situation, anything to keep her panic at bay, if they were rescued, this would make a pretty sensational story. She sat back and studied her reflection, then blended the blush into her cheekbones a little more. Maybe she should publicize it when this whole ordeal was over and they were safely home. Perhaps it would prove to be the illusive ratings boost the show needed. Pioneer Woman Ree Drummond had never been kidnapped by Albanian nationalists. As long as they could stay safe until they were rescued, maybe this entire ordeal could actually turn out to have a silver lining. Waverly bit her lip and studied her reflection. First she needed to be very careful and keep their captors happy until someone came to rescue them.

"Junior likes breakfast," Charlie observed, putting her hand to her belly. "He's kicking hard. Ouch." She flinched.

Waverly surveyed her sister out of the corner of her eye. More things to add to the list of items to try not to worry about right now. The baby. How long would their captors keep them here? Charlie couldn't have the baby here, in the middle of nowhere. They needed to be on a plane to the US before she reached thirty-six weeks. Waverly did the math. That left about eight weeks. Surely someone would rescue them before then. Living in this uncertainty and tension for eight weeks was unthinkable. How many cooking shows could they possible want her to tape?

She closed her eyes and practiced a few

breathing exercises her therapist had taught her years before to help control her panic attacks. She pushed all the troubling thoughts from her mind, all the things she could not control. She had become good at not thinking too hard about things, practiced at letting go of anything unpleasant. She employed the same tricks now, breathing in strength, breathing out everything else—her worry over the baby, her fierce longing for Andrew, the strain of being in captivity, the uncertainty of their situation. She did this ten times, until she felt a veneer of calm and poise descend upon her. She knew every bad and difficult thought was still there under the surface, lurking. Nothing had changed, but she could focus on the pinpoints of light, the tiny bits of her current situation that felt positive and hopeful. With the last exhale she opened her eyes, then peered into the mirror and applied Dior Grege 1947 to her lips, making a perfect pucker. She was ready to face the day.

CHAPTER 23

A half hour later, when Artur and Jetmir escorted Waverly and Charlie to the first taping, the outbuilding was buzzing with activity. Erjon met them at the foot of the stage. He was dressed as impeccably as before and smoking a cigarette. It was barely seven in the morning.

"You are refreshed?" he asked, not waiting for a reply. He gestured with the lit cigarette. "Come, we are ready to make the show."

Someone found a seat for Charlie off to the side where she could watch the action but be out of the way. She sat in her leather jacket, shivering a little in the chill, wishing again that she'd brought a warmer coat. A young woman appeared with a blanket and handed it to her. Charlie wrapped it around her legs and belly. It was musty, but at least it was warm.

Up on the brightly lit stage, Waverly was getting a wireless microphone attached to her gown. Charlie kept an eye on the stage but also surreptitiously surveyed the entire room, taking stock of the operation. She counted six people besides Erjon. Jetmir had disappeared and Artur stood by the single metal door, hand on his gun, scowling. It seemed to be his perpetual expression. Off to one corner beside the front entrance was a little room where Erjon and others went in and out. It looked like an office or a command center of some sort. Charlie made a mental note to check it out. Maybe there was a telephone there.

Realistically, though, what good would it do to call anyone? What could she say? "We're alive and being held probably somewhere in Kosovo." There were thousands of miles of land, hundreds of villages. If she could get a look outside at a nearby town or at a piece of mail with an address . . . She shifted uncomfortably, trying to come up with some halfway decent plan. Her mind had been running full tilt since they'd awakened from being drugged, her thoughts going round and round like a hamster in a wheel, but so far it was getting her nowhere.

Onstage Waverly was being introduced to a stunningly beautiful young woman wearing a sequined silver evening gown with a slit to the knee, towering high heels, and a glittering crown and sash. Charlie leaned forward, intrigued by the spectacle.

"This is Antigona." Erjon proudly introduced the young woman to Waverly. "She is Miss Kosovo. She will help you host the show."

Waverly and the young woman looked each other up and down in a silent mutual assessment.

"Oh, this should be interesting," Charlie murmured, amused despite their current difficult circumstances. Waverly did not like to share the spotlight.

"And how is she helping me exactly?" Waverly asked with a frosty, polite smile.

Erjon explained, "Each show you will make an American food, and Antigona will make a food from Kosovo, a traditional Albanian food. Then we will compare them." He clapped his hands. "So America will see how excellent is Albanian food and culture. You see?" He seemed very confident about this plan.

Antigona was adjusting her sash and casting bored looks around the room, perched on her high heels like a lovely water bird about to take flight.

"What are you going to cook?" Waverly asked her. The girl gave her a startled look. She had very large dark eyes and a long oval face that was almost too pretty to be real.

"She doesn't speak English," Erjon told her. "You will tell the American people what she makes and how good it is."

Waverly looked skeptical. "Does she cook? She certainly doesn't appear to eat." She looked the slim young woman up and down critically.

"Yes, yes," Erjon said impatiently. "She is Kosovar Albanian girl. Of course she cooks. All Albanian girls cook. So they can take care of us men." He laughed heartily at his own joke.

Waverly huffed at this display of female disempowerment but appeared to regain her composure after a warning cough from Charlie.

"Fine. What is she going to make? What did you say her name was, Antagony?"

"Antipathy," Charlie murmured under her breath, wishing Andrew were here to witness the scene. They would amuse themselves by coming up with variations on the girl's name. She missed her brother-in-law and wondered again what was happening between Waverly and him. Waverly had said he was heading to his fishing cabin in the Adirondacks. Would he even know they were missing? She hoped so, and that he was doing everything in his power to find them. She tried to imagine what that might be but failed. Maybe Andrew had previously untapped reservoirs of heroism and cunning, an edge of James Bond to him. Maybe he was at this very moment miraculously zeroing in on their location.

She entertained a brief fantasy of Andrew bursting through the doors of the outbuilding and freeing them, sweeping them away in a helicopter he'd parked directly on top of the garden plot. But strangely, when she played it out in her head, it was not Andrew who broke through the door. It was Johan Kruger. She shook her head, trying to dismiss the image of Johan sucker-punching Artur in the nose, but it lingered, giving her a warm little glow in her stomach. What she wouldn't give to see him come through the door in real life.

Onstage they were about to start filming. A young woman with a makeup kit dabbed at Antigona's forehead with pressed powder. She approached Waverly, but Waverly shook her head. On the fake marble island in the forefront of the cobbled-together kitchen sat an array of ingredients, mixing bowls, and measuring cups and spoons. The cameraman, a skinny young man with acne, who looked barely out of his teens, gestured for silence, and Antigona took up her position next to Waverly behind the island.

"Action," Erjon called, waving his hand. "Now cook!"

Over the next hour Waverly whipped up a batch of simple buttery sugar cookies dipped in sugar and lemon zest, and Antigona made a similar Albanian cookie called *kurabie*. Antigona proved to be a quick hand in the kitchen, and Charlie enjoyed the spectacle of watching the two women try to out-dazzle each other and fight for dominance at center stage.

Although Waverly was filming the cooking videos under duress, Charlie knew her sister couldn't resist the allure of the camera. Once the filming started, Waverly acted as though she had forgotten all about being kidnapped and forced to cook in a sham kitchen in an outbuilding some- where in Kosovo. She ramped up the *Simply Perfect* Waverly Talbot charm and made those butter cookies look like the best thing on earth. Which was probably why they were in this situation to begin with. Waverly's star power had convinced their captors that she could sell anything, even Albanian unification.

Charlie sighed and massaged the back of her neck where a muscle was knotted from stress. It was so hard to sit there and do nothing, just wait for a rescue that seemed far away and improbable. If only Waverly could charm her way out of their imprisonment and back to freedom. Determined to at least gather information, Charlie looked for a chance to snoop around.

While the cookies baked, the show took a short break. Erjon joined his cooking stars on the stage to explain the next section. All eyes seemed to be focused on the front, so Charlie seized the opportunity to stretch her legs and further her investigations. She wandered the length of the outbuilding, taking her time so that people turned back to their work and ignored her slow meander. The outbuilding was damp and cold and smelled like a curious mixture of baking lemon cookies and cigarette smoke. Charlie closed her eyes briefly and apologized to the baby for the secondhand smoke, determining to find some fresh air as soon as possible.

At last she reached the office door at the opposite end of the room from the stage. She peered inside. The small space was brightly lit with a fluorescent light and cluttered with papers scattered over a large metal desk that took up most of the room. The young woman who was serving as the show's makeup artist was seated at the desk in front of a computer screen. She looked up and caught sight of Charlie, her eyes widening in alarm.

As the girl rose to intercept her, Charlie caught a glimpse of the computer screen. It was a news update from NBC News. Waverly's face was plastered across the screen with the caption *Celebrity Chef Vanishes.*

The young woman moved to the door and blocked Charlie's view of the computer, looking at her suspiciously.

"WC?" Charlie asked innocently, pretending that she had not seen anything.

The young woman came out and shut the door to the office behind her, then called for Artur to escort Charlie to the toilet. It was a squatty potty attached to the outside of the building. In the smelly dimness of the closet-size space, Charlie awkwardly squatted, her rounded belly throwing her off balance. She braced herself against the side of the small enclosure, elated by the headline she had glimpsed. *Celebrity Chef Vanishes.* So they knew Waverly was missing, and it was headline-worthy news. Waverly would be pleased to hear that. Undoubtedly, then, Andrew knew they were missing, and Charlie's colleagues at Care Network most likely did too. This was good. It would have been better if the headline had said *Celebrity Chef's Location Pinpointed,* but still, at least they were on the radar. Cheered by the thought, Charlie struggled to her feet and headed back to see if Waverly was finished filming.

"Of all the stupid, half-baked ideas . . . ," Waverly huffed as Artur led them around the perimeter of the yard. Charlie had petitioned Erjon to let them have some fresh air after filming was done, and he had agreed to fifteen minutes if they stayed on the property and with Artur at all times. "And that pageant princess . . . She kept stepping on my toes on purpose so she could get more camera time."

They rounded the tilled garden. Charlie inhaled the earthy scent of turned soil and fresh country air. It was a sunny day, and it felt wonderful to be away from the stuffy, smoky confines of their room and the outbuilding.

"I missed the last part," Charlie confessed. "What did they have you do when the cookies were done?"

Waverly rolled her eyes, stumbling over a clod of earth. "That was a complete farce. I had to taste my cookies, then taste her cookies, and say how great they both were, and how similar. Erjon said I could like mine, but I should be more impressed with hers. Like she can bake a better cookie than I can." Waverly sniffed. "Mine were lighter. She overworked hers."

They cut across the narrow strip of grass at the back of the house and headed into the scraggly orchard they could see from their window. Charlie glanced back at Artur and moved a little farther away, taking Waverly's arm. She didn't have any idea how much English he could understand, but she wasn't taking any chances.

"I saw something today," she said, lowering her voice. "Look, is this an apple tree?" she said in a louder voice, stopping to admire a twisted apple tree covered in tiny new green leaves. Artur plodded along behind them morosely. When they stopped he paused to light a cigarette. Charlie took the opportunity and moved around the tree, giving them more privacy. "I saw a news alert on a computer screen in the office," she whispered urgently. "It was your face on the screen. They know you're missing."

"Who knows?" Waverly asked, her face brightening.

"All of America by now, I'd guess," Charlie murmured. "It was on MSNBC."

Waverly gripped her hand hard. "Oh, this is good news," she exclaimed, relief bubbling in her voice like champagne. "So they're looking for us?"

"Yeah, but it may not be enough. Listen." Charlie pointed up at the tree, pretending to be explaining something about it to Waverly. Artur wasn't even looking at them. He was fiddling with a lighter. "We have to get word to someone outside somehow. We can't just wait until filming is over. It could take weeks at this rate. I'll miss the trial date."

Waverly nodded. "And you have to be on a plane back to America before you're thirty-six weeks along. You can't have the baby here."

Charlie grimaced at the thought. "Agreed. So here's what we have to do."

Artur was watching them and smoking, his face impassive.

"What are these apples good for?" Charlie asked loudly.

"These are cooking apples, I'll bet. Too tart to make applesauce. Unless you add a lot of sugar," Waverly answered with equal volume.

Artur took a long drag on the cigarette and sighed in a tired way.

"We have to try to figure out where we are in Kosovo," Charlie muttered, glancing at their guard. "Anything to narrow down the search. And then we have to get a message to someone outside."

Waverly looked at Charlie askance. "And just how do you propose we do that?" she asked.

Charlie lifted her chin. "I don't know yet," she admitted, "but we don't have much time."

CHAPTER 24

Artur knocked on the door at five thirty the next morning, rousing Waverly from a particularly delicious dream. She and Andrew had been breakfasting in Paris, eating *pain au chocolat* on a balcony overlooking a winding street in the Latin Quarter. For a moment after Artur's sharp knock on the door, Waverly allowed herself to drift back into a half sleep, trying to recapture the magic of the dream. Paris in the spring, the sun warm on her face. She looked down onto the street, savoring the last crumbs of the buttery pastry, when a little girl passed below the balcony, holding on to a woman's hand. Waverly could only see the top of the woman's head, but the child looked up, and Waverly gasped. It was the same girl—round, dark eyes, hair tousled by the breeze, and that strawberry birthmark perched on her right cheek.

"Wait," Waverly called, leaning over the balcony, trying to get her attention as the girl turned away, and then another loud knock on the door woke her. Abruptly the girl, the balcony, the sun, and Paris disappeared. Across the room Charlie groaned and rolled over but didn't rise.

She was growing rounder by the day; her belly stuck out like half a small watermelon under the blanket.

Waverly blinked awake as Artur came into the room with the breakfast tray, closely followed by two young women. She recognized one of them from the day before. The girl had been helping Antigona with her makeup. Now she carried the same large makeup kit in an orange plastic box and had a banana-yellow satin evening gown slung over her arm. The other girl was bristling with assorted hair-care products, a hair dryer, curling iron, and straightener. Wordlessly they began arranging their supplies and plugging in various implements while Artur unloaded the breakfast tray onto the table. Charlie turned toward the wall and pulled the blanket over her head.

"Good morning," Waverly said to the girls.

They glanced up. "No English," the makeup girl said, smiling apologetically.

"I can do my own hair and makeup," Waverly said, but the girls just looked at her blankly. Waverly sighed. "Okay, well, let's get this over with." She slid her feet into the ugly homemade slippers and gestured for the women to begin.

Twenty minutes later Waverly was sitting in one of the plastic chairs in the very form-fitting, very vivid yellow gown, being beautified within an inch of her life. Her hair was piled on top of her head in an elaborate updo, and she could feel her eyelids drooping under the weight of fake eyelashes. Charlie sat at the table in her pajamas chewing a slice of bread spread with adjvar and watching the proceedings with interest.

"How do I look?" Waverly asked.

"Well, I'm pretty sure astronauts can see that dress from the international space station," Charlie observed.

Waverly sighed. "I was afraid of that."

Someone knocked on the door and one of the girls called out a welcome, pausing with a tube of blush in her hand. The door opened, and Jetmir poked his head inside.

"Ah, good, you are almost ready," he said. He came into the room, looking Waverly up and down approvingly. "Very beautiful, like Albanian bride now."

Waverly frowned, unconvinced. "Was yesterday's hair and makeup not good enough?"

"You are a beautiful woman," Jetmir said smoothly. "We want you to look successful, like a TV star, so everyone can see that we treat you good, that you are happy here."

"But I'm not happy here," Waverly countered, blinking her false eyelashes. "I'd be happy if you'd let me go."

Jetmir laughed as if she'd said something funny. "When we are done you will go free. But first you will help us. And today you will contact your television friends. The show from yesterday is ready."

Waverly sat up straight in the chair. "What do you mean, 'contact my television friends'?"

At the table Charlie gave a cough and shot her sister a warning look.

"We have made the show very good and now it is ready. Today you will contact your friends in America and get them to put it on the television."

Waverly's mind was racing. Could she actually speak to anyone? What could she say that would help someone find them? The thought of hearing Beau's voice made her feel like crying. She pulled herself together. They might only get this one chance. She had to make it count for Charlie and the baby.

"Fine then," she said calmly, not betraying her inner turmoil. She waved a hand at the young women working on her. "When I'm done here I'm happy to help."

As it turned out, Waverly did not get to call anyone. She and Charlie were taken to the outbuilding, and Waverly was given a printed statement to read in front of the camera. Erjon sat to one side, Artur towering silently behind him and watched the filming closely. The prepared statement was full of grand sentiments about the idea of Albanian ethnic unification and assured the watcher that Waverly was being treated like a queen. It requested that Beau and the Food

Network immediately air the episodes they would be sending. And then Waverly reassured them again that she was happy to be helping such a worthy cause and that there was no need for alarm. She was safe and well.

As the cameraman videoed her, Waverly read the last line of the prepared statement and took a deep breath, mustering her courage. On the way over to the barn, she and Charlie had only had a moment's whispered conversation, but they had agreed that if she could, she must try to give as much information as possible. She laid down the paper and looked straight at the camera. Her heart was pounding in her chest. The cameraman was still filming. Good. She smiled her most dazzling smile and said very quickly, "Please also let Charlie's friends at Care Network know that she is just fine as well, especially her colleagues Dr. Johan Kruger and Arben. Let them know that we are both happy and well."

The cameraman stopped filming abruptly at a sharp command from Erjon, and Waverly sat back in her seat. Her evening gown was wet under the arms with nervous perspiration. Would the message go through or would they edit it out? Would Beau contact Johan Kruger and Arben?

Erjon approached her with narrowed eyes.

"You read the paper only," he said sternly. He pointed a finger at her. "Nothing else."

Waverly looked at him innocently. "I was just

letting Charlie's work colleagues know that she is safe too. You want them to know that she is okay, otherwise they might really make a fuss looking for her. And you don't want that, not if you want to tape all the shows and have them run on TV."

Erjon frowned, considering her words. Apparently deciding that she had not said anything worth editing out, he nodded at the cameraman and then gave Waverly another stern look. "Next time you read the words on paper. That's it." He wagged a finger at her.

Waverly nodded, dropping her eyes and trying to look appropriately chastened. "I understand." Secretly she was elated. It wasn't much, but if Beau received the message and was smart enough to contact the men she had named, it was a step in the right direction. If Arben could find Ilir, wherever he was, they might figure out what had happened to Charlie and her and where they were being held.

Erjon clapped his hands. "We send this message now. Let's get to work."

Using the e-mail address for Beau that Waverly supplied, Erjon and his crew sent her video message first, closely followed by the first episode they'd filmed the day before. Antigona arrived as they finished sending it, dressed in another sequined gown, this one a spring green, and after a quick break for coffee and cigarettes they began filming another episode.

Antigona made *flija*, a traditional dish that reminded Waverly of a stack of pancakes or crepes smeared with cream cheese between each layer. The flija was served sweet with jam or honey, or savory with cheese, adjvar, and pickled vegetables. In return, Waverly made French-style crepes stuffed with cream cheese and spiced apples.

In the moments before filming started, Waverly wiped off the bold pink lipstick the makeup girl had used and quickly applied her signature color, thinking of her mother as she did so. Her mother had seemed like such a pillar of strength to Waverly's childhood self. She couldn't remember Margaret Talbot ever being afraid of anything.

Waverly took a deep breath, needing the reassurance and strength of Margaret's legacy. She glanced over at her sister, ensconced in a folding chair with a mug of tea, her belly swathed in a knit blanket. Waverly wanted to be that strong for her baby. She wanted to be that strong for her sister as well.

When they were little their father used to call Waverly his rose and Charlie his wildflower. But roses were deceptively hardy, Waverly had discovered. They looked delicate, but they could be surprisingly tough. She needed to channel that now, to be tough and smart and strong. Charlie and the baby needed her. She rubbed her finger across her teeth to remove any lipstick stains, then plastered on a dazzling smile and went to stand in her fake studio kitchen to make crepes and mark time until they could be rescued or find a way to escape.

That evening after the filming for two episodes had wrapped up, Erjon appeared and motioned for Waverly just as Artur was leading her back to the house for the night. Charlie had gone back earlier to eat supper and rest. Waverly sighed. She couldn't wait to take off her outfit and slip into her pajamas. The high heels were pinching her toes dreadfully. Erjon waved her over and showed her an e-mail on his smartphone. Waverly's heart jumped a beat. It was from Beau.

> I got both videos. Unfortunately, the Food Network's schedule is full, but I posted the first episode to YouTube and expect it will get a lot of views. Keep up the good work. We're keeping it up on our end.
>
> —Beau

Waverly stared at the words, trying to discern their full meaning. It sounded as though Beau had gotten her clue. She fervently hoped so. Perhaps even now he was making contact with

Johan Kruger and Arben. Perhaps their rescue was brewing at this very moment.

Erjon tapped the screen and said disapprovingly, "Not on American television."

Waverly hesitated, trying to think of a way to spin the news. "No," she said finally, slowly, "but this might be better. YouTube is even bigger than cable television. More people watch it, from all over the world."

Erjon eyed her skeptically. "Huh," he said noncommittally. He glanced at the message and back at Waverly. "Maybe," he said again, his voice chilly with warning. "Remember, if you don't help us, I cannot promise to keep your sister safe."

Waverly swallowed hard. "I've done my part," she said firmly. "Let's see what happens next."

Charlie was sitting propped up on one of the twin beds in a cozy nest of blankets trying valiantly to focus on the Steinbeck novel she'd brought with her for the *Simply Perfect* road trip. She was waiting for Waverly, eager to hear if there were any new developments, and kept reading the same few sentences over and over. She just couldn't maintain interest in *Cannery Row*. All she could think about was how to bring about a rescue. She wondered if Waverly's hint to Beau had worked, and if so, was anyone even close to figuring out what had happened to them and where they were being held?

When Waverly came back to their room, Charlie waited until Artur left them alone, then eagerly demanded any new details. Waverly kicked off her shoes, sat down at the table, and told Charlie about the last episode's taping while she picked at her dinner. After eating just a few bites, she pushed her plate aside with a sigh. She rose and moved across the room to the mirror hanging on the wall and surveyed the bright yellow evening gown, pulling a face.

"Can you unzip me?" she asked. "I can't stand to be in this thing a minute longer."

"Sure." Charlie pulled the zipper down, and the dress puddled to the floor.

Waverly arched her shoulders and groaned with relief. "That's better. It was hideously tight. I've spent all day feeling like I'm being slowly squeezed to death by a banana boa constrictor."

"Beauty hurts. Isn't that the saying?" Charlie gave her a wry smile and returned to her cozy nest in bed. The dress truly was awful.

Waverly slipped into her pajamas, a periwinkle paisley-patterned set, and knelt on her bed in front of the mirror. She ran her fingers through her hair, still perfectly formed and sprayed into submission, and winced as her fingers caught in the curls. She pulled her hair back from her face with a headband and opened her makeup bag, taking out a cotton round and a bottle of makeup remover.

Charlie watched her sister, struck by the familiarity of the gestures. How many nights had she stood brushing her teeth in the cramped bathroom in Aunt Mae's farmhouse and watched Waverly perform this simple bedtime routine? A thousand? More? It made her feel like a teenager again, in a moment erasing all the distance between them. Waverly was just home from cheerleading practice. Charlie had finished her AP paper on *Wuthering Heights*. They were still two peas in a pod, together through thick and thin.

Charlie shook her head, coming back to the present in a rush. They were not teenagers anymore, sleeping in their matching twin beds a scant few feet from one another in the white gabled room, close enough to touch but dreaming different dreams.

Charlie studied her sister as Waverly gently and methodically swiped the cotton round over her skin, taking off the layers of foundation and blush. Without makeup she looked tired and a little pale. There were crow's feet at the corners of her eyes, Charlie noted with a pang. They were growing older, both of them. So many years had passed already. So many choices. So much they could not undo.

"What are you thinking?" Waverly asked,

breaking into Charlie's reverie. "When you frown like that, you get wrinkles on your forehead, you know."

Charlie sighed ruefully. "Just thinking about how many years it's been since we shared a bedroom. Seventeen. Seems like a lifetime."

Waverly nodded. "But somehow it seems like it was just yesterday too." She peeled off the ridiculous false eyelashes and set them on the bed. They lay there like two spiders. "What happened to us?" she asked.

"What do you mean?" Charlie slipped her bookmark into *Cannery Row* and laid the novel aside.

"I mean, we used to be each other's constants. We were so different, but we had each other to rely on no matter what. And then somehow . . . somehow we lost our way. I don't even really know how it happened." Waverly looked thoughtful. She picked up her hairbrush and began to gently comb out her hair, wincing as it caught the tangles.

Charlie shrugged. "We were on two different continents, leading very different lives. It was a lot of years. I guess we just grew apart."

"Maybe." Waverly sounded doubtful. "But it seems like more than that. Honestly . . ." She tapped the hairbrush against her lips. "Now that I think about it, I think it happened when you left Africa and moved to Budapest. It seemed like you just . . . disappeared."

Charlie's breath caught in her throat. She looked down at the tiled floor, avoiding Waverly's eyes. She felt exposed by her sister's perception. It was true. When she had left Johannesburg, she had run from everything, including her relationship with Waverly. In her hurt and shame, all her former intimacies had been too painful to continue. She had been hiding ever since, until Aunt Mae's death had shaken her from her cocoon of isolation.

"What happened in Africa anyway?" Waverly asked. She opened a small tub of Crème de la Mer face cream and scooped up a pea-size amount, holding it between her fingers for a few seconds to warm it. "Why did you leave? I don't think I ever really knew." She pressed the cream into her skin with the tips of her fingers, gently, like she was touching a bruise.

Charlie opened her mouth, ready to offer a vague explanation, then stopped. She was at a crossroads, she realized. She could easily brush off the question, give a bland, vague answer that revealed nothing. Or she could trust her sister, offer the truth, and see where it took them. It was what she wanted, wasn't it? To close the distance, mend the years of silence? She shut her eyes, took a deep breath, and spoke the words aloud for the first time.

"I left South Africa because the clinic I spent several years of my life planning, building, and funding went bankrupt. My business manager swindled the clinic out of all of the funds. I lost every dollar of my trust fund. And then I was raped."

Waverly gasped, but Charlie continued, not looking at her sister. It felt so freeing to finally say the words. She had kept them inside, dark and hidden and secret. Bringing them into the light felt like taking off a heavy weight. "I didn't want those things to break me. I wanted to be stronger than any act of violence or deceit. But I couldn't. In the end they broke my grand ambitions. They shattered me."

Charlie met Waverly's eyes, her own stark and open. At last she had nothing left to hide.

Waverly laid down her little tub of moisturizing cream and crossed the room in a few quick steps. Kneeling in front of the bed, she gently took Charlie's hands. Her eyes glistened with tears. "Oh, Charlie, I'm so sorry," she said at last. "I'm so sorry that you went through all of that alone. I'm sorry I didn't ask the questions sooner. I wish I could have been there for you. Please forgive me."

Touched, Charlie simply nodded. She couldn't speak. The tears lay just below the surface. She had finally opened the secret spaces of her soul, the parts seared by shame and failure. It felt as though she'd opened her rib cage and shown Waverly her shriveled, pitiful heart, and in Waverly's gaze there was only tenderness and compassion. For the first time in years, Charlie felt that someone truly saw her and knew her. She had ached to be known this way without even realizing it. She had missed her sister.

Waverly was speaking. "No matter what happens with this"—she waved her hand around the room, encompassing the whole strange ordeal of their kidnapping and present circumstances—"no matter what, let's not lose each other again. Is it a deal?"

Relieved, Charlie nodded. "It's a deal." On impulse she held out her fist, her pinkie finger extended. Waverly blinked, then smiled and hooked Charlie's pinkie with her own, reviving their long-lost secret childhood pinkie promise.

"Now you know we have to follow through," Charlie said lightly.

Waverly laughed and pulled Charlie into a fierce hug, and Charlie let herself be embraced. She inhaled the scent of Waverly's cream, lightly floral with just a hint of citrus. She imagined Aunt Mae looking down on them, smiling as her two girls found each other again. So many decisions and days and years had pulled them apart. It had taken extreme circumstances to bring them back together. But now, no matter what happened from this point forward, at least they had each other once more.

After the revelations and emotions of the night before, the next day seemed anticlimactic to Waverly. It almost felt like a repeat of the one before. Bread and eggs for breakfast. Another heavy makeup and big hair session. Another episode taping. Antigona made traditional pickled vegetables. Waverly whipped up a big glass jar of refrigerator bread-and-butter pickles and another of watermelon rind pickles. But something had changed. Despite their continuing circumstances, there was a new closeness and camaraderie between Charlie and her. They would always be markedly different people, but somehow they had bridged the gap of so many years. They were together again. That knowledge lightened Waverly's heart through the long daylight hours of preparation and filming.

Late that night Artur came for them unexpectedly. Charlie was already asleep, and Waverly was working on the next day's recipe, trying to decide on an easy dish involving grilled meat. It was the main ingredient for the next day's show, and she didn't want to be upstaged by her younger costar, whom she'd taken to privately referring to as Antagonist. She stared at the piece of paper and wrote *American hamburgers* at the top. She was also trying not to think about Andrew, wondering what he was doing. Where was he? Had he flown to Europe? Or was he still at the cabin, and if so, did he even know she was gone? Or, horrible thought, was he home, carrying on with his work, content to let the authorities sort out his wife's disappearance? She felt her heart crumble at that thought. No, she needed to focus on the positive, not dwell on the unknowns.

She wrote down the words *caramelized onions* and *balsamic glazed mushrooms,* then paused. Should she do an onion jam or a blue cheese dressing for the burgers? Her thoughts turned from the burgers back to Andrew. He loved his burgers stuffed with Stilton and coated in cracked black pepper. She wondered again if he knew about her disappearance. If so, was he worried? Surely he still cared about her. But maybe not enough to come after her. They were separated, after all. She acknowledged the term for the first time. It was true. They were still married but wanted very different futures. She wrote *brioche buns?* with a question mark. She had no inkling of what this separation would mean long term. She loved Andrew. She believed that he loved her. But what could they do, faced with such irreconcilable visions of the future? Waverly laid the pen down and glanced over at her twin's sleeping form across the room, at the round ball of the baby curled within her belly. It was irrevocable, the path Waverly had chosen. But she had no idea how it would play out.

A pounding on the door snapped her out of her thoughts. Artur poked his head into the room and motioned for them to come with him. Waverly woke Charlie, and a few moments later they were padding behind their silent guard, following the beam of his flashlight to the outbuilding. Following Charlie, who was in her pajamas, Waverly sniffed the fresh, cool evening air. It smelled of manure from the garden and woodsmoke. Gravel crunched beneath their feet, the only sound in the darkness. In the outbuilding the large main room was dark, but a light was on in the office. Artur left them at the door to the office and grunted, gesturing for them to go inside. Erjon sat alone at the computer, studying something on the screen. He looked up when he heard them come in.

"Ah, come." He motioned them over to the computer. "Come see." He pointed at the screen. It was a paused YouTube video of the cooking episodes they had taped the first day. In the video Waverly was frozen with her mouth open, just biting into one of Antigona's kurabies, a strained smile plastered on her face. Antigona was standing in her sequined gown and tiara watching Waverly try the cookie, with an equally strained expression. The video was titled "Waverly Talbot—Captive Cookie Show-down." It already had over a hundred thousand views.

"Oh wow." Charlie gaped at the screen, her expression disbelieving.

Waverly looked at her own frozen wide-open mouth on the video and felt a twinge of annoyance. Of all the things to go viral, a video of her in a forced cookie bake-off with an Albanian pageant queen was not anything she would have chosen. It was fame for all the wrong reasons. She frowned.

Erjon looked pleased. "This is good," he announced. He gestured to the screen. "Many people see it all over the world. This is good." He sat back, satisfied. "We will make more videos. The world is watching. You rest now. Tomorrow we make another video and send it to Beau Beecham for YouTube."

Waverly's heart sank and she exchanged a brief look of dismay with Charlie. It was exactly what they did not want to hear. Erjon showed no sign of letting them go soon, especially not after this new development. Waverly and Antigona were suddenly YouTube sensations, the grand kind of publicity Erjon was hoping for.

Waverly bit her lip, staring at the screen. How in the world were they going to get rescued? Every day the no-fly date for the baby drew closer, as did Charlie's date to testify for the trial. Somehow they had to get away, and they were running out of time.

CHAPTER 25

Andrew shifted his Lexus into drive and carefully bumped down the rutted dirt trail that led away from the tiny log fishing cabin where he'd been holed up for the past two weeks. The cabin was tucked away in a remote patch of wilderness in the Adirondack Mountains, the nearest town miles away. He'd purchased it years ago as his own private retreat, long before he met Waverly. She'd never even seen the place. It was without Internet or cell reception or indoor plumbing, but to Andrew it was perfect, a simple space where a man could listen to the quiet of the forest and collect his thoughts. He rarely used it anymore, but he liked knowing it was waiting for him should he need it. This time he had needed it.

He cast a last look in the rearview mirror before the cabin was obscured by the dense foliage. It had been a good and productive time away. He'd had the time and space to seriously reflect on the current state of his marriage and the trajectory of his life. And he had come to a decision. It was not an easy or simple one, but he was confident it was the right one. Now to share the news with Waverly.

Andrew glanced at his watch, resolving to call her as soon as he had cell reception. He calculated the time difference in his head. Six hours ahead in Budapest, where Waverly had gone to visit Charlie and the growing baby. Their growing baby, he corrected himself. He needed to start thinking differently about the child if this was going to work. It was early afternoon in Hungary and time to call his wife.

As he drove, Andrew glanced at his phone every few minutes, checking to see if he had service. He wound his way toward Interstate 87 and began the four-hour drive home to Greenwich. Finally, his phone made a dinging sound. He had cell reception and evidently a text message. His phone dinged again and again. He glanced at it and almost swerved into the next lane. The screen was filled with text messages.

With a sinking sensation in his stomach he looked for somewhere to pull off the road, forcing himself not to look at the messages while he drove. What had happened while he had been away? Was it Waverly? Was she okay? Or maybe something with the baby? Hoping it was just a work crisis, he pulled into a gas station and slammed the car into park, fumbling for his phone. The first text message he saw was from his secretary, Nancy.

Andrew, I can't get ahold of you and the press is going crazy. What do I say to them? CALL ME!

He scanned the next one, his heart pounding. It was from his sister in London.

Just saw the news. Shocking! Are you okay?

"News? What news?" Andrew muttered, frantically scrolling through the remaining messages. They were all similar—dramatic, concerned, and devoid of any useful solid information. He ran a hand through his hair, distressed, and glanced up at the service station. There on a newspaper stand on the sidewalk in front of the station was his wife's face in full color under the headline *Kidnapped TV Star Still Missing*.

The next few minutes were a blur. Andrew bought the paper, shoving the quarters into the machine and ripping the edition from the stack inside the case. He read the article speedily, greedy for information. His hands were shaking.

She's alive, she's okay, was his first thought, accompanied by a flood of relief so strong it made his knees buckle. He sank down in the driver's seat and read the article again more slowly. His initial relief gave way to a growing sense of disbelief as he digested the scanty lines of the article. Kidnapped. Accompanied by her sister, international aid worker Charlotte Talbot. Held in an unknown location. Viral YouTube videos of cooking demonstrations. International manhunt under way.

Andrew set the paper down in bewilderment, heart pounding. His wife had been kidnapped. It seemed too bizarre to be true. All the time he had been imagining Waverly safely cozied up with Charlie enjoying a break in Budapest, she had in fact been held prisoner in some unknown location. While he had been enjoying cooking his daily catch in a cast iron skillet and reading a bit of Thoreau before bed, content with the silence and the room to think, Waverly was being held against her will and forced to make sham cooking videos by unknown kidnappers.

Was she scared, in distress? Was she being harmed in any way? He closed his eyes, overcome with a wave of emotion. He felt guilty and protective and monumentally worried all at the same time. What was being done to find her? Did the police have any leads?

He picked up his phone, intent on finding out as much as he could, then stopped. Whom could he call? He scrolled through his list of contacts, hoping for inspiration. Waverly's producer, Beau . . . What was his last name? He had to think for a long moment before he dredged it up from the recesses of his mind. Beecham? Was that it? There was no Beau Beecham in his contact list. Why had Andrew never put Beau's phone number into his phone? What about Waverly's assistant, Sophie? He checked his numbers again with a growing sense of helplessness. No Sophie. Why had he never thought to get her number either? It was because he let Waverly handle all the details of her *Simply Perfect* empire. He didn't concern himself with the particulars. Well, now he was regretting not concerning himself at least a bit more.

He gripped the steering wheel and tried to think. It was unlikely he could find out anything useful sitting in a petrol station parking lot. He needed to head for home and regroup. He bought a double espresso, downing it without tasting it, then laid the paper with the color photo of Waverly on the seat next to him and raced for home at speeds roughly double the posted limit. There was no time to waste. He had to find his wife.

As soon as he walked in the door of their house, Andrew tossed his leather overnight bag on the kitchen chair and called the Food Network. For the next hour he worked fruitlessly to reach someone who would give him any information. He asked for Beau, only to be told that he was filming on location in Europe and was not available. He tried to cajole and reason with each person he managed to talk to, but to no avail. No one believed he was actually Waverly's husband, and all cited various confidentiality and legal reasons why they could not give him any information. He finally lost his temper with the last one, swearing elegantly and thoroughly at the stunned woman on the other end before hanging up. It was pointless. All the people who could verify that he was who he said he was were apparently somewhere in Europe trying to find his wife. Meanwhile he sat in his kitchen and got nowhere.

He ran his hands through his hair, exasperated. Unable to think of what else to do, he listened to his dozens of voicemail messages. A few from friends and work colleagues. Most from reporters wanting a statement. He deleted all of those one by one. When he got to the last one, he listened absently for a few seconds.

"Hi, this is Jessica Archer with Channel 9 news out of Athens, Ohio."

Another reporter. He started to delete the message, then hesitated. That name seemed vaguely familiar for some reason. He listened to the rest of the message.

"I'm an old friend of Waverly's from high school. I did an interview with her when she was in Cooksville last fall. Of course we're all just horrified to hear about Waverly's disappearance. I was hoping to talk to you for a few minutes, just to hear your side of things, see how you are holding up. We're all *so* worried. Please call me if I can help in any way. I'd love to hear from you."

Andrew remembered seeing the segment last fall when they had been in Cooksville for Mae's funeral. It had been a brief snippet of airtime, a startled-looking Waverly being accosted over breakfast by a fiercely peppy redhead in a vivid pink suit. But she knew Waverly. He paused, considering. Perhaps this Jessica Archer could help him. She was only a small-town reporter, but perhaps as a reporter she would have special clearance or connections that could get him the information he needed. At the very least she might be able to convince someone who mattered that Andrew was who he said he was. He liked the idea of contacting someone who actually knew Waverly. Andrew scribbled the woman's number down on the corner of the newspaper, right above the blond crown of Waverly's head, and then he called her back, hoping against hope that she would somehow be able to help him find his wife.

Jessica Archer answered her phone on the first ring with a brisk eagerness that took Andrew aback. He stumbled through a hello and briefly explained why he was calling. He tried not to sound pleading or pathetic, clearing his throat and summoning his best London banker voice, the posh and polite method that had stood him in good stead all his adult life. He needed this woman's help but didn't want to grovel.

He needn't have worried. Jessica was very keen to assist Andrew in gleaning any information she could about Waverly, but she wanted something in return.

"I'll even go with you to try to locate her," Jessica said. "But when she's rescued, I want the first exclusive interview with the two of you."

"Done," Andrew agreed promptly, secretly relieved that she had said *when* she was rescued and not *if*. As though it was only a matter of time until Waverly was found. With the help of this Jessica person, Andrew intended to be there when they found her.

"I'll make some calls," Jessica promised him. "See what I can dig up. What did you say her producer's name is? Beau what?"

He could hear her scribbling something down as he spelled out Beau's last name, at least what he hoped was the correct spelling. He really needed to start paying more attention to the particulars of his wife's professional life.

A moment later Jessica hung up with a promise to call him as soon as she had any news. And then Andrew was alone in the huge, echoing house. He looked around at the kitchen—Waverly's mother's apron hung on a hook by the spice cabinet; a wedding photo of the two of them sat in a silver frame by the office nook where her collection of vintage cookbooks was shelved. His stomach rumbled, and he realized he hadn't eaten since early morning.

Getting up, he poked around the kitchen, feeling a little lost. Waverly kept him efficiently and thoroughly fed, and he couldn't remember the last time he'd done more than pour his own scotch. Julia Child's *Mastering the Art of French Cooking* lay on the counter, open to a recipe for crème brûlée. Waverly had scribbled indecipherable notes along the margins. Andrew put his finger on her familiar looping cursive scrawl and blinked back an unaccustomed prickle behind his eyes. He missed his wife. And he was worried about her, worried sick and feeling utterly helpless.

He made himself a piece of toast, fiddling with the gleaming silver toaster until the third slice came out unblackened, and then poured two generous fingers of eighteen-year-old Macallan and sat in his favorite leather club chair in his study.

When Jessica Archer called back just ninety minutes later, Andrew was deep into his second scotch and repeatedly watching the YouTube videos of Waverly on her bizarre hostage cooking show. He paused the video—Waverly, wearing a fixed smile and a sequined evening gown that displayed rather a lot of cleavage, was dipping perfectly round cookies into a bowl of

375

sugar. Andrew tore his eyes away from his wife's face and answered the phone, trying to compose himself. He felt a little woozy from the alcohol, but Jessica didn't seem to notice.

"I can't get anyone to give me any information," she said immediately, "but I have a few leads in Europe. We're going to have to do this the old-fashioned way. Pack a bag and meet me at LaGuardia tomorrow morning at five. We're catching the early flight out. We'll start in Budapest."

CHAPTER 26

Charlie woke in the middle of the night with a gasp, immediately aware of the tightening in her pelvis, low and strong, stronger than she'd ever felt before. She'd been having practice contractions for weeks, gentle little tightenings that lasted a few seconds. This wasn't that. She sucked in her breath, counting the seconds, every molecule of her being focused on the baby and what was happening within her. Was this labor? It was too early. She was barely twenty-nine weeks. She squinted at the clock across the room. Five in the morning. She lay still, tensed, willing it to go away, deeply afraid that something was going wrong, something beyond her control.

"Not here, please. Not like this," she whispered, trying to relax her body. Another contraction squeezed her pelvis, this one even stronger. She looked again at the clock. Ten minutes had passed between the two.

In the bed opposite her, Waverly was lying on her side, one hand curled under her cheek, wheezing gently. She had endured another long day of taping several back-to-back episodes. Erjon, delighted with the success of the first

YouTube video, had posted two more in the past forty-eight hours, both of which had garnered hundreds of thousands of views. The mood in the studio was increasingly buoyant as the videos went viral, but the crew and Waverly and Antigona were working longer and longer hours. Waverly had come back to the room late that evening with a plate of her own deluxe American hamburgers with homemade mayonnaise and onion jam and Antigona's grilled cevapi and fresh kajmak for Charlie.

Charlie shifted the turgid ball of her stomach, trying to get comfortable, trying to relax. She clutched the medal of St. George, making a valiant effort to calm down and encourage her body to stop whatever it was doing. She was breathing fast and shallow. What if she was in labor? She couldn't have the baby here. Would a twenty-nine-week-old baby even survive without a sophisticated NICU? She shut her eyes and concentrated on breathing slowly, deeply, trying to consciously relax the muscles of her body. She was shaking with fear. Her thumb pressed hard into the little metal knight and the dragon he fought as she tried to control her emotions, to convince herself that everything was going to be okay. It had to be, for Waverly, for the baby inside of her. She couldn't allow herself to think of any other outcome. She tried not to think about the baby, how tiny and vulnerable he still was. The thought of something happening to him pierced her, sharp as an ice pick to her heart.

"Stay in there, pal. It's not time to come out yet," Charlie whispered. She was answered with another contraction, ten minutes after the last.

She lay counting the contractions for an hour before she finally woke Waverly. At her explanation, a brief look of alarm flashed across her sister's sleepy face. Waverly scrambled to sit up, but she schooled her features almost immediately. It was getting light outside. Artur would bring them breakfast soon. There was another day of taping planned, this one focused on cabbage leaves.

"What should we do?" Waverly asked, stumbling from the bed and hovering over Charlie.

"I don't know," Charlie admitted. "I think we need to tell Jetmir as soon as possible. Maybe they'll let me go to a hospital. I need to get checked out."

Waverly bit her lip, looking worried. "Okay, I'll fetch him. You try to relax."

Charlie snorted. "Yeah, right. I'm trying, but it's not working."

Waverly pounded on the locked bedroom door, calling loudly for Artur. A moment later he poked his head in, wearing his perpetual scowl. "Jetmir, Jetmir," Waverly demanded, pointing to Charlie on the bed. "Baby. Emergency."

Artur frowned and withdrew. They heard his heavy steps moving down the hall. A few moments later Jetmir appeared, yawning sleepily. A heavy stubble covered his normally clean-shaven face, and he scrubbed a hand through his hair, zipping the front of his tracksuit. He came fully awake when they explained the situation, however, and immediately called Erjon on his cell phone. He spoke in rapid Albanian for a moment, then listened carefully, nodding often.

When the call was finished he turned to Charlie. "We will bring someone to help you," he said. "I will get her now." He took leave of them, promising to return quickly.

Waverly perched on the edge of the bed beside Charlie, hands clasped between her knees. "Oh, I hope they hurry." She glanced sideways at her twin. "This is not how I imagined it going at all."

"You and me both," Charlie said dryly, then winced as another contraction tightened her body. "Still ten minutes apart." She tried to keep her voice even and calm, but panic was beginning to squeeze her heart. She had to protect this baby. She had to somehow make everything okay.

"Well, they're not getting any closer together. That's good, right?" Waverly said, smiling encouragingly.

"It shouldn't be happening at all," Charlie muttered. "It's too soon."

Waverly hesitated, her hands fluttering over her

sister's belly. "Do you mind?" she asked. Charlie inclined her head, an invitation. Waverly cupped her hands around Charlie's stomach, fingers splayed over the round dome.

"Hello, baby," she said softly. "We want to meet you but not just yet. You need to stay in there awhile longer. You'll see the wide world soon enough, little one." The baby pressed against Waverly's palm, a hard knob of knee or elbow jutting under the dome of skin.

"Oh." Waverly looked startled. "She's really in there, isn't she?"

Charlie grinned in spite of herself. "Yeah. Wild, isn't it? You think it's a girl?"

"Well, the doctor thinks so, and I keep having dreams about a little girl, so I think it might be." Waverly cocked her head, looking a little wistful. "I envy you, you know."

"For what?"

"Getting to carry her inside you for so many months. You're making a human, every fingernail and tooth bud. It's amazing."

"But it's your baby," Charlie said gently. "I'm just the factory."

"No." Waverly shook her head. "You're far more than that. You get to create a life. That's a miracle."

Charlie flinched as another contraction squeezed her. "Well, this miracle maker has to pee like a racehorse. Can you help me up?"

Charlie was just struggling to sit up, Waverly supporting her, when the door opened and Jetmir appeared, followed closely by a wizened, tiny woman. Charlie recognized her immediately— the cook from the kitchen. Her heart sank. This could not possibly be who they were bringing to help.

Jetmir smiled as he made the introductions. "This is Valbona. She don't speak any English, but she has had twelve children, so she can help you."

Charlie and Waverly stared at the toothless, wrinkled woman in horror. She scowled back at them, arms crossed over her sagging bosom, iron-gray wisps of hair straggling from beneath a head scarf.

"Oh dear Lord," Waverly intoned under her breath.

"Seven of her children are still alive," Jetmir added helpfully.

Charlie blanched at his words. "We have to find a way out now," she murmured to her sister, her face stricken. "We're out of time."

Waverly wrinkled her nose at the pungent vinegary brine as she lifted another pickled cabbage leaf from the large glass jar. Antigona's eyes were watering as she expertly rolled a leaf around a small mound of minced meat and herbs. Waverly did the same, gingerly tucking the ends under, wrapping it as snug as a baby in a bunting. As she worked she kept up a seemingly effortless patter of conversation, narrating her actions, offering tips. She had been doing this sort of thing for so long that it came as second nature. Sometimes she could talk to the audience while thinking about something else entirely.

She glanced up at the red light of the camera, aware that every nuance and gesture would be plastered on YouTube before evening. Was there any way to get a message out? She had been horribly distracted all day. She'd burned her hand while frying the meat, and it throbbed, the bright red welt stinging from the salt and vinegar in the brine. All she could think about was Charlie and the baby. Charlie had been resting since early that morning when the contractions started, and so far there had been no change, but Waverly was petrified. So was Charlie, although she wouldn't admit it. They were both trying to put on a brave face and be strong for each other. Valbona had brewed a foul-smelling concoction of herbs into a tea and pressed it upon Charlie. As soon as she was gone, Charlie had covertly dumped it out the window and gone back to bed to lie flat and count contractions.

Her sister was doing all she could at the moment. Now it was up to Waverly. She had to get them out somehow. But no grand escape plan had occurred to her. So she dutifully rolled cabbage leaves around the meat, filled the silence with cheery prattle, and tried desperately to concoct a strategy for rescue or escape.

She started from her thoughts when Antigona bumped her hand. Waverly moved a few inches away, giving the other woman more space. Antigona liked to be center stage. Waverly sighed and rolled another cabbage leaf. Antigona bumped her hand again. This time Waverly looked up. The young woman was looking at her with wide doe-eyes through a fan of fake eyelashes. She looked like a doll with perfectly painted lips and a glittering tiara.

"Baby need help?" Antigona asked in a low voice, keeping her eyes on the cabbage leaf in her hand.

Waverly stared at her. "What?"

With a loud clatter Antigona dropped a spoonful of meat filling on the floor behind the island. With an exclamation of dismay, she bent over, making a furtive gesture to Waverly to follow her. Waverly ducked down behind the island as well, confused.

"Baby need help?" Antigona asked again, quietly and insistently, meeting Waverly's eyes.

Waverly nodded her head tentatively, her eyes filling with tears. "Yes, the baby needs help," she whispered.

Erjon called to them from the front of the stage, demanding to know if everything was okay. Antigona answered in a flood of Albanian, waving him away over the top of the island. She hunkered down, balancing precariously on her absurdly high heels, and reached into the bodice of her dress, drawing a cell phone from the sweetheart neckline and pressing it into Waverly's hands. Their eyes met for a brief moment, an understanding passing between them, bridging age and culture, the language of one woman helping another in need. Surprised, Waverly snatched the phone and stuffed it down the front of her sequined peach gown, the only hiding place she had on the skin-tight ensemble. The cell phone was still warm from Antigona's skin.

"Thank you," Waverly whispered in gratitude.

Antigona nodded, blinking once and again. Her eyes were moist. "I had baby," she said sadly. "Three days." She counted out the number on her pink manicured fingers. "He died." She reached over and clasped Waverly's wrist for a moment, her fingers strong and sure, then rose and straightened her dress, smoothing the wrinkles from the front. Then she picked up another cabbage leaf as though nothing were amiss. She did not look at Waverly again.

The taping dragged on interminably. Waverly finished rolling the cabbage leaves with shaking hands, stumbling through the prepared speech at the end, overwhelmed with the secret of the little cell phone lodged in her cleavage, a glimmer of hope, a chance of escape. At last the episode finished, and she asked for a toilet break. Erjon motioned her toward Artur.

"But then we make another show. This time dessert and good Albanian coffee."

Waverly quickly agreed, anything to give her a few minutes of privacy. Artur accompanied her to the toilet. She made herself walk sedately to the outside squatty-potty, although her insides were quivering with fear and anticipation. So close. They were so close . . . She paused, pretending to adjust her shoe, and quickly memorized the license plate number of Erjon's Mercedes. At this point anything was better than nothing. Maybe the information would help.

In the dank confines of the toilet she pulled the cell phone from her bodice. It had a jeweled case covered in glittery fake gemstones. She checked the time. Just after four p.m. In the dim light she almost missed it, but then she stopped and squinted. A tiny slip of paper was protruding from the edge of the case. She pulled it out gently so as not to tear it and stared at the single word of Albanian written in a feminine, looping scrawl. Waverly frowned, puzzled. Was it the name of a town? Their location? She had no way of knowing. Other than the license plate number it was all she had to go on. She would send it in the hope that it would help someone find them. With shaking hands Waverly sent the first text to Beau.

CHAPTER 27

Early the next afternoon Charlie was dreaming of Africa. She was sitting in front of the medical clinic, a squat building painted a cheerful yellow. There was grit between her teeth and between her toes. A long line of mothers holding babies snaked around the building, waiting for her to weigh the infants and measure their heads. Although she had not been back to Africa since the terrible incident, she returned often in her dreams. Her heart was still there, in the shantytown clinic where she had spent so many strenuous, bittersweet hours, in the empty field where her parents had lost their lives, their plane falling from the clouds in a streak of smoke beneath a wide-open sky.

She was reaching for the first baby, a fat, gurgling child with dimples at his knees, when someone grabbed her by the shoulder and shook her firmly. She opened her eyes and squinted at the figure looming above her head, disoriented. All of a sudden she was not in Africa at all. She was lying in a bed in a dim room, early-afternoon sunlight slanting across the floor. And Johan Kruger was standing beside her, his strong hand on her shoulder. He bent over her, his expression concerned.

"Charlie? Charlie, are you okay?" Behind him two policemen stood in the doorway, armed with rifles and stern expressions. She struggled to sit up, trying to orient herself. Kosovo. She was in Kosovo, and the baby . . .

"You," she exclaimed, thinking for a moment she was imagining him rescuing her again, and then astounded to see him in the flesh. "I'm having contractions," she blurted out. "And I'm not far enough along to have this baby. I'm only twenty-nine weeks. Can you help me?"

Johan frowned. "How long have you been having the contractions, and how far apart are they?"

"About thirty-six hours. They're twenty minutes apart now, but they were ten to start with." She looked around, still a bit groggy and confused. "Where's Waverly?"

"Don't worry, she's fine. She's in good hands. The police and her producer are with her. They've rounded up all the people on the property and she's identifying them. She'll be back any minute. Just lie still." Johan gently pushed her back into a prone position.

Charlie lay down, feeling almost giddy with relief. They were rescued. The reality dawned on her slowly. It was going to be okay. "How did you find us?" she asked again. "Did you get

Waverly's texts?" She felt like laughing and crying both.

"Yes," Johan confirmed. "She was able to give us the name of the nearest town and a license plate number. It took a bit of time to get here, and we had to coordinate with the local police, but they tracked down the owner of the car and finally we located you. There are a lot of people who have been wondering where you are. Do you mind if I examine you?" Johan gestured to her stomach and Charlie nodded.

Johan dismissed the police officers in the doorway, washing his hands in the bathroom and locking the door when he came back in. He placed his hands on her belly and pressed gently. He asked her a few questions and observed her through a contraction. He was all business, courteous and professional, but Charlie felt herself blushing furiously as he performed his examination. Usually very little about the human body embarrassed her, but then, she had to admit, she'd never had a raging crush on her doctor before.

She focused on the ceiling, on a water stain in one corner, trying not to feel self-conscious. A dozen times since their abduction she'd imagined Johan rescuing her, breaking down the door with his beefy shoulders. She'd never imagined him doing this, however. His warm hands on her skin felt strangely intimate. He finished his examination and pulled the blanket up over her belly again, then stood back and met her eyes.

"I think it's safe to move you, but you need to be checked out by an obstetrician," he said. "The baby seems to be okay, but we should get an ultrasound to make sure." He paused and looked down at her.

"What's the date today?" Charlie asked.

"The fourteenth of April."

Charlie nodded, calculating in her head. "First let's make sure the baby really is okay. That's the most important thing, but if he is, I have to get to Belgrade as soon as possible."

Johan fixed her with a curious look. "Why? What's in Belgrade?"

"I have to testify in a trial." When she told him the details, he listened intently, looking grave. "So you have to be there on the seventeenth?"

Charlie nodded.

"Sounds like we need to get you to Belgrade, then," Johan said briskly. "It's probably the closest place to get you and the baby checked anyway."

Charlie cocked her head, listening for any noise outside. "Is everything really okay out there?" she asked.

Johan stuck his head out the door and asked a question to the police officer. He came back a moment later. "They've detained all the suspects now. Your sister is just fine. She'll be here soon."

He poured a glass of water from the pitcher on the table and handed it to Charlie. She took it, surprised. It touched her, that simple gesture of care. It had been so many years since a man had taken care of her. Shane had tried, but he had not really known what she needed, and truthfully, she had not let him. She had been impatient with his attempts, fumbling and misguided. But with Johan it felt different. He was capable of caring for her, of giving something she could accept, that she needed. She guzzled the water greedily, suddenly parched.

"Is there anyone you want to call to let them know you're all right?" he asked.

Charlie thought about it for a moment. "Is Andrew with you? Has he contacted you?" It had just occurred to her to wonder where he was. Surely he was somewhere close by. It was, after all, his wife and his unborn child who had been kidnapped, not to mention his sister-in-law.

"Andrew?" Johan raised an eyebrow, looking puzzled.

"Waverly's husband."

"I don't think so, no." Johan looked apologetic. "I'm sure we can contact him. Is there anyone else you want to contact about what is happening with the baby? The father maybe?"

"Just Andrew," Charlie said. "He's the baby's father."

Johan looked startled. "Does your sister know?" he asked cautiously.

Realizing how the statement sounded, Charlie laughed. "Waverly knows. It's their baby. I'm carrying it for them. Well, technically it's a sperm donor's baby. Waverly can't get pregnant, and I've got a good set of ovaries I wasn't using, so . . ."

Johan stared at her for a moment, processing her words. She thought he looked a little relieved.

"That's very noble of you," he said finally.

"Yeah, well . . ." Charlie shrugged.

Johan studied her, his eyes serious. "It's a selfless act, Charlie. The Maasai do something similar. No woman is barren. If she can't have children naturally, another woman will offer to bear a child for her. That child will be the barren woman's. A bit more earthy than your process, I'd imagine, but the same result. Everyone who longs to be a mother gets to be one."

Charlie brushed away the compliment, embarrassed. She handed the glass to him, and he refilled it, drinking the second glass himself. She watched his throat move as he drank. The gesture was strangely intimate, his mouth where hers had just been. She looked down at her hands, willing herself not to blush. This was ridiculous. She was a grown woman, pregnant with her sister's baby. And mooning over a handsome doctor like a sixteen-year-old schoolgirl.

She distracted herself, placing her hands over the baby. He shifted under her skin, stretching and wiggling his tiny fingers. She laughed from the fluttering movement but also with the sweet sensation of relief. They were rescued. For now the baby seemed to be staying inside. "Everything's going to be okay, pal," she murmured, reassuring herself as much as the baby.

She heard voices in the hall and recognized her sister's. The door flung open with a crash and then Waverly was there, falling to her knees beside the bed in her sequined evening dress the color of an eggplant, half crying and babbling about the rescue, almost hysterical with relief. She smelled of frying oil and hair spray, and she hugged Charlie and the baby so hard the baby kicked at the restraint. Charlie patted her sister's stiff hair, reassuring her that all was well, while Beau and Johan watched the happy reunion.

Waverly pulled back. Her mascara was running down her cheeks, but she didn't seem to care. "You're all right?" she kept asking. "And the baby?"

"We think the baby's fine, just needs a checkup, and your sister needs to rest," Johan assured her. Waverly looked from Beau to Johan, beaming through her tears. She managed to still look radiant despite the pink eyes and wet cheeks. "You saved us," she said. "I don't know what we would have done without you. Thank you."

"Our pleasure," Johan said simply.

Beau shifted from foot to foot, a bashful hero. "Anything for you, Boss," he said. "You're the brave one. We never would have found you if you hadn't given us the information."

"I had help," Waverly said, her voice softening. "A very courageous young woman helped us get rescued." Waverly hesitated, looking at Beau. "Where's Andrew?" she asked, her expression hopeful and a little timid.

Beau looked down. "I haven't heard from him," he admitted finally. "I don't know where he is." He looked at her apologetically.

Waverly took a deep breath and squared her shoulders. "Well then," she said, but her voice caught on the words. She said no more. Charlie reached out and took her sister's hand, squeezing it in solidarity. She didn't know what was happening between Waverly and Andrew, but she knew it was hurting her sister. Waverly did not respond. Her hand lay limp in Charlie's grasp, the cold diamond of her solitaire engagement ring pressing into Charlie's palm.

The next few hours were a blur. Waverly and Charlie gave detailed statements to the chief of police, who deigned to do the interview in the bedroom so Charlie could remain lying down. He was a granite-faced man who treated them kindly, if a bit gruffly. He was a father of a daughter about their age, he explained, and a grandfather too. He was deeply embarrassed that the kidnapping had happened in his country. When he understood about Charlie's contractions and the need to get to a hospital in Belgrade, he made the remaining questioning go as quickly and smoothly as possible.

Partway through the interview process, Johan received a phone call. When he hung up he waited for a pause in the interview and updated them both. "When Waverly was texting us she mentioned that you suspected Ilir was the one responsible for drugging you and bringing you here. We passed that information to the police in Budapest, and I just got a call that they've arrested him. He confessed to everything. He's being charged as an accomplice in your kidnapping."

The news of his arrest should have come as a relief, but it made Charlie sad instead. Ilir with his laughing eyes and endearingly cocky swagger. He was young and idealistic, easily swayed by men more calculated and powerful than himself. He had gotten caught up in something that would cost him dearly.

By evening they were on their way to Belgrade in one of Care Network's minivans, Charlie's backpack and Waverly's roller safely stowed in the back. Only their cell phones were missing. Charlie shrugged it off, stating that she'd just get another phone in Budapest, but Waverly fretted about the loss of her iPhone. Before they set off she asked to borrow Beau's phone and sent one text, then handed it back with a troubled look on her face.

Johan drove, Beau navigated, and Waverly sat in the middle seat, while Charlie lay as comfortably as possible in the backseat. They stopped at a tiny store at a crossroads, and Waverly and Johan gathered supplies, coming out with their arms full of snacks and bottles of water. Once more on their way, Waverly made sandwiches from fresh white bread and slices of salami. Beau munched on a package of potato chips and told them about the media frenzy surrounding Waverly's abduction.

"As soon as that first YouTube video was posted, it went viral. Your face was on every television station and every newspaper in the country. And now that you've been found, it will only intensify, at least for a while. We're keeping your location a secret for now while the kidnapping investigation is under way and because of Charlie testifying, but CNN just broke the news a few hours ago that you've been found alive and unharmed." Beau gestured to his phone. "I just checked my e-mail, and Ellen DeGeneres wants to interview you as soon as you get home. So does *Good Morning America*." Beau waved his empty potato chip packet grandly. "With all this publicity, the Food Network is going to want to renew for at least two seasons, I'm guessing." He grinned. "I'm telling you, Boss, you couldn't have gotten this much media coverage if we'd spent a million bucks. This was golden. You were one of the top hits on Google last week."

Waverly looked pleased and handed Beau another salami sandwich. "Well, I did my best," she said. "A professional is always a professional, no matter the circumstances. Charlie did very well too," she said graciously. "It was a team effort."

Waverly was trying to be strong, to pretend that she was just fine, but Charlie could sense the sorrow and worry that lay just beneath the surface. Charlie herself was feeling much better. Reclining on the backseat, she devoured two sandwiches and an entire packet of potato chips, suddenly ravenous with relief.

It was a long drive, more than six hours, and they drove through the night without stopping. Beau dozed off after a few hours. Johan drove silently, seemingly wrapped in his own thoughts. At Charlie's request he put on some music, a favorite blues rock playlist of his, and the soulful sounds of Eric Clapton and Tom Petty and the Heartbreakers played softly against the background hum of the tires on the pavement. Waverly put her back to the side window and stretched her legs out across the seat. She was still wearing the gaudy cocktail gown, her hair half falling down in waves to her shoulders. She leaned her head back against the window and closed her eyes.

In the darkness Charlie could just make out her sister's outline, the pert nose, the downturned mouth. She seemed so sad.

"You okay?" Charlie asked, keeping her voice pitched low so Johan couldn't hear them, already knowing the answer.

Waverly shook her head. "He didn't come," she said softly. "I thought . . . I thought he would come, but he didn't even contact Beau. How could he not at least call Beau and ask about me? I texted him just now from Beau's phone, but he hasn't responded." She sounded hurt and a little bewildered.

"What's going on with you two?" Charlie asked, shifting, trying to get comfortable against the seat.

Waverly sighed. "I wanted something so badly and couldn't take no for an answer," she admitted finally. "I didn't listen to what he wanted. And by the time he was able to make me hear, I'm afraid it was too late." She sounded so resigned.

"Was it about your career?" Charlie asked.

"No." Waverly didn't elaborate.

"Oh." Charlie laid her hand on her stomach, over the baby, understanding dawning. She had a queasy feeling in the pit of her stomach, the sensation of falling from a solid place into thin air. She had noticed how unenthusiastic Andrew had seemed about the plan, but Waverly had seemed sure enough for both of them. Charlie had assumed they had come to some agree--ment privately. Apparently not. But what did that mean, then? Did Andrew not want the baby? What would Waverly do, raise the child by herself?

"What are you going to do?" Charlie asked, hoping her sister had a strategy, a plan to make things come out right.

Waverly shifted on the seat, leaning her head against the window, looking out at the darkened countryside whizzing by. "I don't know," she finally admitted.

But this baby was coming whether they were ready or not. And Charlie suddenly felt very unready.

CHAPTER 28

Belgrade, Serbia

Waverly came fully awake with a start in the early hours of the morning as they pulled into the parking lot of a darkened, squat concrete office building. "Where are we?" she asked, peering out the window. She had been dozing, thinking of Andrew and the night he proposed to her. He'd hidden the ring in a gorgeous bunch of gardenias and then when the time came could not locate it. He'd been flustered, down on one knee rummaging among the blossoms for the silk ribbon with the ring attached. She had thought it was adorable. Now it made her feel like crying. What was she going to do? She missed him so much, the longing felt like a sob caught in her throat. She shook her head, trying to bring herself firmly back to the present. She swallowed hard. "Is this the obstetrician's office?"

Charlie nodded. Johan had called in a favor to a doctor he knew, who had agreed to see them as soon as they got into town. They were going to check on the baby.

They left Beau sleeping in the front seat and

401

filed quietly into the darkened office building through a side door. Inside they all shook hands with the doctor, a gruff, heavyset man in a rumpled white coat. Johan laid his hand on Charlie's arm as the doctor led the way to the examination room. "I'll wait here for you."

Waverly noted how his hand lingered on Charlie's arm, how Charlie leaned in ever so slightly to his touch. She smothered a little satisfied smile. It had been too long since Charlie had let someone care for her. It had been too long since she'd had someone to lean on. Charlie's fiancé, Shane, had been sweet but too soft. Waverly had only met him briefly the one time Charlie had brought him back to the US from Johannesburg, but the impression he'd left had been one of idealism and a dreamy sort of optimism. Hardship would have snapped him. Charlie had been the strong one in that relationship. But Johan projected a solid, steady calm. He was a man to trust in a crisis, to depend on. He was an oak tree, strong enough for her sister. Plus, he was quite good-looking in a clean-cut sort of way, with those broad shoulders and that delicious accent to boot.

Waverly followed Charlie and the doctor, taking a seat by the exam table in a clean but worn exam room. Charlie pulled down the top of her jeans and lay back on the table. The doctor asked her some questions, then squeezed gel from a tube onto her stomach. And then Waverly realized she was about to see the baby. Her stomach did a quick little flip. Nervously she gripped the arms of the chair. In a moment she would be seeing her child for the first time.

The ultrasound screen flickered black and white, the image wavering indiscernibly for a second. And then all of a sudden there was the baby, a clear profile—little lips and nose and forehead. She was sucking her thumb, seemingly relaxed.

The doctor zoomed the ultrasound wand around Charlie's stomach, then said, "All is okay. No problem. Baby is good."

Waverly released a breath she hadn't even realized she'd been holding.

Charlie nodded, looking immensely relieved too. "Can you tell if it's a boy or a girl?" she asked.

The doctor furrowed his brow, moving the wand to a different position and studying the image for a moment. "A boy. It is a boy. See, here." He pointed.

The little dark bump looked indiscernible to Waverly, but the doctor was certain. Charlie grinned. "I knew it. I knew it was a boy."

Waverly blinked, taken aback. In theory she did not care about gender. Girl or boy, either was fine, just as long as the baby was happy and healthy. But still she felt oddly disappointed. She had been so certain it was a girl because of her recurring dreams. She had bonded somehow with that little dark-haired girl. Now she was faced with the reality of this child, a boy, not the little girl whose face she had been dreaming about over and over in the past few months.

Charlie rested her hands gently around her belly, cradling the child. "So he's okay? Nothing to worry about?"

The doctor shrugged. "We cannot predict early labor, so he could come at any time, but he is stable. Rest and avoid stress. You will be okay."

While Charlie wiped gel from her stomach and dressed, Waverly sat quietly in the chair. The doctor had printed out a photo of the ultrasound, and she studied it, tracing the contours of the baby's face, his little thumb stuck in his mouth. Looking at his face, she tried to swallow her disappointment. He was healthy and well. That was all that mattered, she told herself. But it was not all that mattered, not to her, not if she were honest. For the first time Waverly felt a tiny niggling of misgiving in the pit of her stomach. Charlie had known it was a boy, while Waverly had been imagining a different child altogether. That fact, coupled with Andrew's strong misgivings, were making her feelings about the baby complicated. She wanted him, of course she wanted him, but when she looked at the baby's face she felt no recognition whatsoever.

He was a little stranger in her sister's belly.

She tucked the photo in her purse and tried to put away her doubts.

They piled back into the van.

"Where are we going?" Charlie asked as they turned out of the doctor's office parking lot and headed back toward the outskirts of Belgrade. The early morning was still black around them and chilly, the streets almost deserted.

"Somewhere safe," Johan said. He didn't elaborate. From the passenger seat Beau gave a wheezy snore and shifted deeper into sleep. Charlie nodded, seemingly satisfied, and settled back against the window, closing her eyes. In a moment she was also asleep, her head tilted back, mouth open a little.

Waverly remained awake. She reached into her purse and touched the ultrasound photo. She thought of Andrew and that disastrous breakfast at the Paradise Hotel. *I love you, my darling,* he'd told her, *I will always love you. But we do not want the same future, and I don't know what we can possibly do to change that.*

She had thought he would come around, that she could somehow convince him to change his mind. But it looked as though she was wrong. She bit her lip, imagining her world devoid of Andrew. It was unthinkable. His presence in her life was her bedrock, a steady point from which all else in her life radiated. If he were absent, what would she have to stand on? How could she possibly raise a child without him? Had she made a mistake?

No, she told herself firmly. She could not think like that. What's done is done. There was the reality of the baby, alive, healthy, and coming in a few months or less. This was the child she had longed for and cried for. It did not matter that it was not the child she had been dreaming of. He was her responsibility, her blessing. In a few months he would be in her arms. Indeed, the nursery was already set up, the beautiful Restoration Hardware crib already made up with Egyptian cotton sheets in a pale buttercup hue. She could not abandon the baby any more than she could imagine her life without Andrew. She was truly stuck.

The ride took a little less than twenty minutes. Johan pulled up to a quiet, dark house and switched off the ignition.

"We're here." He opened the driver's door. "Wake Charlie, will you?"

With a sigh Waverly untangled her legs from the sequined evening dress and slipped her feet into the uncomfortable matching high heels. Johan did not wake Beau. "The fewer people who know about this place the better," he said when she asked if she should rouse him. Waverly gently shook Charlie. "We're here," she whispered, although she had no idea exactly where *here* was. She thought they were still somewhere in Belgrade.

Charlie stretched and yawned, then clambered awkwardly out of the backseat, following Waverly down the narrow concrete walkway to the front door. They appeared to be in a residential area, with rows of tidy, darkened houses sleeping behind gates and fences. Somewhere a dog barked and another answered it. Otherwise all was silent. The house was large and traditional looking, with white walls and a red-tile roof that sloped down over a wide porch. Johan knocked lightly on the front door, and from somewhere in the recesses of the house a light sprang to life. After a moment the door opened and a dark-haired woman poked her head out, eyeing them. Behind her an enormous Great Dane nosed his head around her hip. Waverly took an instinctive step back, but the dog merely looked at them with mild interest.

"Where are we?" Charlie asked.

"This is a safe house," Johan answered them, greeting the woman in halting Serbian. "It's for women who have been rescued or escaped trafficking. You'll stay here until the trial is over." He ushered them into the front hall and closed the door behind him. "No one knows you're here, and we need to keep it that way for the safety of the other women." His voice was sober. "This is Vesna, the housemother. She'll look after you. Tell no one where you are. Do you understand?"

Charlie nodded and yawned hugely.

"That won't be hard," Waverly muttered. "Neither of us has a phone, and frankly, I haven't had any idea where I am since we left Sarajevo."

"Good." Johan smiled tiredly. "Let's just keep it that way for now."

The next morning Waverly and Charlie arrived early for breakfast after spending a very short night in twin beds in a spartan but functional room. Vesna had handed them towels, pointed out the communal bathroom and the dining room where breakfast would be served at seven thirty, and left them alone. Fatigued, they had not even bothered to shower but had fallen into their beds, desperate for sleep.

A little after seven, showered and somewhat refreshed, Waverly trailed Charlie down the stairs, looking around curiously. She could hear movement and voices in other rooms but saw no one else. The house was large and spacious with beige tile floors, wide doorways, and minimal furnishings. The scent of toast drifted up the stairs, buttery and enticing, and Waverly's stomach rumbled. It had been many hours since the salami sandwiches in the van. They entered an open dining/kitchen area with two long wooden tables and a bay window overlooking a fenced backyard. The Great Dane from the night before was outside and standing at the window, pressing his enormous muzzle to the glass, eyeing them. There was only one other person downstairs when they arrived, a petite girl with a dark auburn ponytail. She wore glasses with thick yellow plastic frames. She was standing over a toaster with a bag of sliced bread.

"Kinga," Charlie exclaimed in delight.

The girl looked up, dropping the bread she was buttering on the counter. "Charlie?" She hurried over to them, kissing Charlie warmly on each cheek in the traditional Hungarian manner. "What are you doing here?" she asked, smiling broadly. "Are you here for the trial? It doesn't start for several days." Then she glanced down at Charlie's rounded stomach and exclaimed in surprise. "You're pregnant? I didn't know!"

Charlie shrugged. "It's a long story. We got into some trouble and just got out of it. We're lying low for a while. And yes, I'm pregnant. Also a long story. Kinga, this is my sister, Waverly."

Kinga offered her hand, still a little buttery, and Waverly shook it. "Pleasure," Waverly murmured, confused. How did Charlie know this girl?

"Kinga is the one I was telling you about, one of the women I helped in Serbia," Charlie explained.

Waverly narrowed her eyes, trying to remember

the details associated with that name. "Oh, the one who's going to court."

Kinga nodded, a look of apprehension flashing across her face. "Yes, soon."

"Are the other women still here?" Charlie asked.

Kinga shook her head. "Only Simona with her daughter. All the others are back in their own countries now."

Waverly glanced back toward the dining area as several women came clattering down the stairs and took seats around the table. Someone let the enormous dog in, and he wandered from person to person, sniffing and greeting each in turn. Kinga and Charlie were engaged in conversation, and Waverly looked around, wondering what to do with herself.

"Is there anything I can do to help with breakfast?" she asked, interrupting them. Kinga looked at the plate of toast she'd left on the counter. "We have to make more toast," she said.

"Here, allow me." Waverly took the bag of bread and set about toasting more slices. She smiled at the irony. If only her television audience could see her now, toasting white bread and slathering it with margarine. She wrinkled her nose in distaste at the margarine tub and put two more slices into the ancient toaster.

Vesna came into the kitchen and set out yogurt, cereal, and apples on the large center island. A few of the women and children gathered around the island, filling plates and returning to the dining room. Waverly kept busy and stayed out of the way. There appeared to be about seven or eight women living in the house and at least three or four children of varying ages. Waverly buttered another two slices of toast, turned to put them on the plate on the island, and then froze. A little girl, her back to Waverly, was feeding a piece of toast to the Great Dane. She was small, maybe four or five years old, and her curly hair swooped in dark whorls against her scalp. She was wearing a pink shirt and leopard-print leggings. Waverly caught her breath as the girl turned, laughing as the dog licked her hands and face. Somehow Waverly knew even before she saw the pale red birthmark in the shape of a strawberry high on the girl's right cheek. This was the child she had been seeing in her dreams.

An olive-skinned young woman with short dark hair took the girl's hand and led her near where Waverly stood gaping at them. The little girl turned and looked at Waverly with wide, dark eyes. She looked too serious for her age, her expression solemn.

"Charlie," the woman said.

Charlie looked up from her conversation with Kinga. "Simona," she exclaimed, hugging the woman. "And who's this?" She bent down awkwardly, her belly sticking out between her and the little girl.

"This is Nadia, my daughter," Simona replied in heavily accented English. She placed her hand on the girl's head, looking proud. "My mother sends her here to live with me. It is safer for her to be here with me before the trial, and my mother is very sick. Cancer in her stomach."

"I'm sorry about your mother, but very happy to meet Nadia." Charlie smiled at Nadia.

"And you, you are pregnant?" Simona asked, gesturing to Charlie's stomach.

"Yep, due in July," Charlie said, placing her hands on the baby. She didn't offer any other explanation, just turned and introduced Waverly to Simona.

"Hello," Waverly murmured, unable to tear her eyes away from the little girl. She was astounded to see the girl from her dreams standing before her. No one seemed to notice her reaction, however, and after a few moments breakfast resumed as usual. Waverly took an apple and a small cup of yogurt and sat at a table but didn't eat a bite. All she could do was stare at the little girl, her mind whirling.

Nadia ate a few spoonfuls of yogurt and then fed the rest to the dog, her eyes sparkling with mischief as he licked off her spoon. She laughed, the sound high and bright, and Waverly marveled at the child standing in front of her. How was it possible that she had been dreaming of this exact little girl for months? And what in the world did it mean?

CHAPTER 29

The next few days were busy with preparations for the trial. Kinga's was first, but the judge had scheduled Simona's only a few days later. The two women were growing increasingly anxious about facing their perpetrators in court.

Sandra Ling, a pencil-thin Asian American woman with crisp pressed business suits and a glossy pageboy haircut, came each afternoon to meet with Kinga, Simona, and Charlie. They sequestered themselves in the small front office where Sandra drilled them in the finer points of winning a court case.

Waverly spent the time trying to be useful and keeping herself occupied. She helped Vesna plant a large garden in the backyard and volunteered to prepare meals. If her hands were busy, her mind was less prone to wander toward Andrew and questions about the future. Why had he not come for her? What did his silence mean? He had not responded to her text on Beau's phone. Her apprehension grew with each passing day.

Nadia was often at her heels. The first day Waverly had been reluctant to interact with the little girl, unsure how to reconcile the girl from her dream with the reality of Nadia's presence. It was not her own daughter Waverly had been dreaming of, that much was certain. It was someone else's daughter, a living, breathing child. Waverly had no idea what to make of it. Her dreams, like so much else in her life at present, seemed like a conundrum.

For most of the first afternoon she tried to ignore the girl, but every time she turned around, there was Nadia, watching her with those dark eyes, following her every move. She was quiet and sober, intent on Waverly's actions, but when she caught Waverly's eye her face lit up and she laughed, a high, sweet giggle that seemed to fill the room with joy. After a few hours of trying to pretend she didn't see the child, Waverly gave in and motioned her over to where she was mixing up batter for muffins.

"Here, you can add the strawberries." Waverly handed her a bowl filled with ripe chopped strawberries. Nadia grinned and started scooping up pieces of fruit and eating them as fast as she could, her eyes darting to Waverly's face.

"Save some for the muffins," Waverly admonished with a smile, even though Nadia didn't speak any English. She pointed to the bowl of batter and then to the strawberries. Nadia understood and helped tip the remaining strawberries into the muffin batter. Her hands and mouth were pink and sticky with strawberry juice. Waverly handed her a wooden spoon, instructing, "Now you can help stir them in gently. Don't overdo it, though. Nobody likes smashed strawberries."

From that moment on, Nadia didn't leave Waverly's side except to go to bed at night. The second morning of their stay, Waverly taught the little girl how to plant squash, making a mound of dirt and pressing the seeds into the soil, not too deep, not too close together, as Vesna had shown her earlier. Waverly's mother, Margaret, had loved to garden and had passed on some of her knowledge to her daughter, but it had been years since Waverly had grown anything more than a decorative pot of herbs in her studio kitchen windowsill, and even those she had not tended herself. Waverly wore a pair of bright orange rubber gloves to protect her hands. It wouldn't do for the star of *Simply Perfect* to have dirt under her fingernails. Dirt didn't film well.

Nadia squatted next to Waverly, her brow furrowed in concentration as she dropped seeds into the little wells of dirt with strong, brown little fingers. She spoke very little, just an occasional word in Bulgarian. Mostly she watched Waverly, trailing along behind her like a tiny shadow clad in bright pink.

Waverly liked the company. It kept her mind from her troubles. For lunch she taught Nadia how to make a cheesy potato casserole. They peeled potatoes together, giggling as the peels curled over their hands and fell to the floor. Then Waverly whipped up a batch of browned butter brownies, letting the little girl lick the spoon. It felt so simple and homey and right, working together in the rhythm of the kitchen. It reminded her of afternoons spent helping her mother prepare for a party. Waverly even let Nadia try on her Dior Grege 1947 lipstick, dotting it on the little girl's full lower lip.

"Very glamorous," Waverly told her, lifting her up to look at her reflection in the mirror. Nadia looked at herself, her eyes shining. She pointed to Waverly and then to her own reflection. "*Krasiva*," she said. Waverly nodded. Although she had no idea what the Bulgarian word meant, she felt the girl's delight.

Working in the beige-tiled kitchen of the safe house, Waverly felt as though something was coming full circle in a way she could not even articulate. She did not think about returning to America, although of course that would happen after the trial ended. She did not even think about the show. She tried unsuccessfully not to think about Andrew, but she missed him dreadfully, the ache like a stone lodged painfully in her throat. She just allowed herself to focus on the tasks before her, on the simple, homey pleasures of doing a job well. She baked and stirred and measured and imparted her kitchen wisdom to her tiny accomplice, doing the only things she knew to do to mend her broken heart. It had worked when she had lost her mother. She wanted it to work now when it seemed she might be losing her marriage as well. She thought of the text she'd sent to Andrew. She was stung by his silence. Perhaps he really did not care. She would not grovel, and so she did not attempt to contact him again.

A few afternoons later Charlie accepted a glass of cold homemade cherry juice from one of the other women at the safe house and headed across the sunny backyard with a sigh of relief. After a grueling day in court giving her testimony, she was relishing the simplicity of a late-afternoon cake-and-punch birthday celebration for one of the children living at the safe house. Dotted around the yard, the ladies of the house sat on blankets spread on the grass, cups of cherry juice in hand, enjoying the mild weather. They were waiting on the other half of the refreshments; Waverly's simply perfect vanilla cupcakes were still cooling from the oven. The giant dog, Boris, was sprawled out in the sunshine, panting and happily surveying the tranquil scene.

Charlie wandered over to the newly planted garden plot and surveyed the orderly mounds and rows. The evenings were still cool in April, but the late-afternoon sun was almost too hot on the back of her neck. A neighbor was cutting grass, and the sharp, living scent drifted across the garden on a slight breeze. She took a sip of the cherry juice and glanced at her drink. Bright red cherries bobbed cheerfully in their own juice, laced with enough sugar to make her teeth ache. She held on to the cup, closing her eyes and enjoying a moment's peace. She was immensely glad her testimony was over.

The actual trial was a blur. When she thought of her time testifying it came back to her in fragments. The smudged fingerprint on the glass of water provided for her as she testified. Her own voice echoing dully in the quiet courtroom, baldly outlining what she had seen that January night. Sandra's eyes narrowing in on the defense attorney like a hawk as he tried to trap Charlie with carefully worded questions. Charlie concentrated on simply telling the truth, fixing her eyes on Kinga's pinched, upturned face, on Simona sitting near Kinga, squeezing her hands together so tightly her knuckles turned bone white. Charlie focused on the questions, remembering Sandra's admonishments to speak plainly, calmly, to tell the facts. At last her testimony was done.

Charlie sighed and opened her eyes. She had done her part, but in the end she knew it might not make any difference. The trial promised to be both lengthy and excruciating for Kinga. The Serbian legal system, Sandra had explained to them, did not favor the victims or make a court case against human traffickers easy to win. Kinga faced an uphill battle at every turn.

Still, Charlie reflected, she was glad she had testified. At least she had stood with Kinga and spoken the truth, spoken out against the injustice that had been done to the young woman. Her decision to testify was a stake in the ground, a declaration to the world and to herself that Charlie Talbot would not be bullied or cowed into submission any longer. Whatever the outcome of the trial, Charlie felt as though she had found herself. She had stopped running and turned to face her dragons. In doing so she found that she had faced her own fear and won.

She reached up and touched the medal of St. George beneath her blue cotton maternity shirt. "Thank you," she murmured. She had no idea if St. George had any hand in her newfound valor, but she was grateful for the infusion of courage, whatever its source. She felt once more comfortable in her own skin. This was who she was meant to be, bold and strong, not cowering, not avoiding the truth no matter how hard it was.

From across the yard Kinga spotted Charlie and gave a little wave, coming over to join her. She held a cup of cherry juice and seemed fragile, as though if Charlie prodded her she would break.

"You okay?" Charlie asked quietly.

Kinga hesitated. "I just . . . keep thinking about

what happens after," she said, hunching her shoulders as though to protect herself. "Even if I win it isn't really over. Sandra says I can go home after the trial, but I'm afraid to. My family knows what happened to me. And if I do win I'll have put my cousin in jail. I'm afraid my family will hate me." Behind her yellow frames her eyes filled with tears.

Charlie didn't know what to say. She couldn't just offer a blithe assurance, because Kinga was right. Sandra had told her privately that often families blamed the victims of trafficking unjustly, faulting them for being stupid enough to be trafficked, ashamed of them if they ever returned. There was no guarantee that Kinga's family would see her homecoming as a happy event.

Charlie touched Kinga's shoulder in sympathy. "I'm sorry," she said, wishing she could somehow make it okay. No woman should have to endure the things she had endured. At her age, Kinga should be occupied with boyfriends and hipster bands and a real job in Berlin, not the finer points of the Serbian legal system or whether the man who had sold her into slavery would get off with a bribe or on a legal technicality. Not whether her family would blame her for the injustice and cruelty she had suffered. It wasn't fair. Life so often wasn't fair.

Simona came out from the house and saw them

standing by the garden. She started toward them, but her cell phone rang. Charlie watched as she pulled the phone from her pocket, checked the number, and frowned. Darting a look around her, Simona answered the call, skirting the garden to the narrow strip of yard by the fence, putting distance between herself and the others. Curiosity piqued, Charlie strained to hear her conversation across the garden plot. The girls were not forbidden from having cell phones, but they were strictly forbidden to contact the outside world while at the safe house. Simona was flouting the rules by taking the call. Kinga was still talking, but Charlie stopped listening. All her attention was on Simona. She had an uneasy feeling that something was amiss. Simona's trial against her traffickers was scheduled to start in a few days, and the young woman had been growing increasingly nervous and irritable as the date drew closer.

Simona was speaking Bulgarian, Charlie surmised from the snippets of the conversation she could catch, and she was not happy. Charlie caught the tone of her voice and her expression. Equal parts angry and afraid. Simona listened to the conversation on the other end of the line, her face tight. Her hands were balled into fists and her face was dark as a thundercloud. A moment later she hung up the phone but didn't rejoin the party.

"Everything okay?" Charlie called to her, cutting Kinga off in the middle of a sentence.

Simona shook her head as though chasing off an annoying fly. "Yes. It was nothing."

Charlie watched her carefully, waiting to see if Simona would elaborate. "You sure?" she asked finally.

Kinga eyed them both curiously.

"Just a warning to be careful," Simona said at last. She wouldn't look at Charlie. She just stared out across the garden at the other women with a thoughtful, troubled expression on her face, then turned and went into the house.

"She likes you."

Waverly whirled from the kitchen island, a spatula of pink frosting in her hand, surprised to find Simona standing beside her. She had not heard the other woman approach. Simona watched Nadia smear gobs of pink cream cheese frosting across the top of a vanilla cupcake. They were late in finishing the dessert for the afternoon birthday celebration, but the cupcakes were just now cool enough to frost. Nadia was helping Waverly decorate them for the party that was already in full swing in the backyard.

"She's a lovely little girl," Waverly observed. "So bright and such a quick learner." She watched the child, her heart squeezing just a little at the thought of leaving. Charlie was done

423

with her testimony for Kinga and would testify in a few days when Simona's trial began. Then there would be no reason for them to stay at the safe house any longer. She'd grown very fond of Nadia over the last several days. She would miss her when they left.

Simona crossed her arms and nodded, not taking her eyes from her daughter. "You have children?" she asked.

Waverly shook her head. "No." She didn't elaborate. Even with the baby Charlie was carrying, the subject of her miscarriages was too painful for her to dwell on. She never forgot her babies, but she didn't want to share them with the world. It was too personal, still too raw. Charlie had not told anyone other than Johan about their surrogacy arrangement, and Waverly was grateful for her sister's discretion. She preferred to keep the matter private for now.

"Why? You don't want to be a mother?" Simona asked.

Surprised by the bold question, Waverly hesitated. "I want to be a mother more than anything," she answered honestly, finally. "But we don't always get what we want."

Simona made a small huff of agreement. "I never wanted a baby," she said.

"Oh?" Waverly glanced at Nadia. The little girl was intent on scooping frosting from the bowl onto another cupcake. Her fingers were pink-tipped where she'd been liberally sampling the frosting.

"The first time I was sold, I was seventeen," Simona said quietly. "They took me to Kiev to a brothel. After six months I was pregnant. They would not let the girls keep the babies. They made us get an abortion or they would sell the babies to families for adoption."

Waverly shuddered, glancing at Nadia, her hair in two little pigtails, her tongue stuck in the corner of her mouth as she concentrated on completely covering a cupcake top with frosting.

"So I tried to kill myself," Simona continued. "I tried to jump out the window one night when a customer was smoking a cigarette with the window open. Six stories. I wanted to die. But he stopped me. He was not such a bad man. When he heard I was pregnant, he helped me escape."

Waverly was speechless. Simona told her story so matter-of-factly, but there were many layers of horror and sadness underlying her words. Waverly imagined her at seventeen, trapped in a life of misery and sexual slavery, pregnant with Nadia and perched on a window ledge six stories up, seeing only one way out. It made her feel sick. Her life was so sheltered, her suffering and worries shrinking to insignificance in the face of Simona's story.

"I'm so sorry," Waverly said at last. She could think of nothing else to say. She had suffered and lost and grieved, it was true. But not like this. No one should suffer like this. It was inhumane. It was almost unimaginable.

A dollop of frosting fell from Waverly's spatula and landed with a splat on the counter. Nadia looked up and saw them both watching her. She smiled, holding up a cupcake to show her mother, chattering for a few seconds in Bulgarian. Simona grunted in appreciation, and Nadia beamed at the attention.

Simona watched her daughter for a moment. "I love my daughter, but this is not the life I thought I would have," she admitted.

Waverly sighed. "So often we don't get the life we thought we would have," she said. She thought of the six pregnancy tests in her closet, the pink lines now faded with time, and closed her eyes briefly. She didn't know what else to say. "She's a beautiful little girl," she added. "You gave her a gift when you chose to have her. You gave her life."

Simona laughed, a bitter sound. "Yes, and for what? So when she is eighteen she can have the same fate as her mother? There is nothing for us in Bulgaria anymore. It is not a safe place for her. There are people who are waiting for us if we go back—" Simona stopped abruptly. "It is not a safe place. No place is safe for us," she said bleakly.

"But surely if you win your court case . . . ,"

Waverly protested. She wanted to offer some hope, but as she spoke she remembered Charlie telling her about the rampant organized crime and corruption that allowed human trafficking to flourish in the region. Perhaps Simona was right. Perhaps there really was no safe place for them back in their own country. She shivered, suddenly worried for Nadia. What would happen to the little girl? Waverly picked up a cupcake and expertly frosted the top. The party was still going on outside, and the women and children were waiting for the treats. Still, in light of their current conversation, frosted cupcakes seemed pointless, almost flippant.

"Do you know anyone who can help you?" she asked instead, twirling the spatula through the frosting to make a perfect swirl. "Anyone who can keep you and Nadia safe?"

Simona shook her head. "There is no one." She turned and looked at Waverly for a long moment as though weighing and measuring something internally, then turned back to look at her daughter. "Do you know what Nadia means?" she asked finally. Her face was inscrutable.

Waverly had a fleeting impression that she was being tested somehow. "No, I don't." She cleared her throat. "What does it mean?"

"Hope," Simona said, and for one brief moment her expression was tender as she gazed at her daughter. "Her name means hope."

"It's a beautiful name," Waverly said. "It fits her." She placed the last frosted cupcake on the tray.

Simona nodded. "It's what I want to give her," she said sadly. "But I don't think I can."

"You're doing your best," Waverly replied. She picked up the tray, ready to take it outside to the waiting party. "She knows you love her, and that counts for a lot."

Simona nodded. "Maybe," she said at last, "but I don't think it is enough."

CHAPTER 30

The morning of her trial, Simona vanished. Vesna woke Charlie with the news at just past six, and together they searched Simona's room. Her bed was empty, her cupboard bare. Only a bobby pin and a sock under the bed remained.

And Nadia. Simona had left her daughter. The girl slept peacefully in the other twin bed, clutching a glittery rainbow-colored stuffed unicorn, unaware that her mother was gone. Charlie noticed a folded piece of paper half tucked beneath Simona's pillow. In a bold black scrawl it said only, *Call Sandra.*

Sandra picked up on the first ring and arrived at the house twenty minutes later. Armed with cups of strong coffee brewed by the taciturn Vesna, Charlie and Sandra set to work. In dismay and then in growing resignation they retraced Simona's flight. She had taken money from the grocery petty cash jar in the office. She had used the office computer to look up bus and train schedules out of Belgrade to several points around Eastern Europe—Skopje, Thessaloniki, Bucharest. She was well and truly gone.

Sandra sighed, running a hand through her

sleek pageboy haircut. She looked both worried and exasperated.

"Did she give any warning?" she asked Charlie. "Do you know if something happened to make her run?"

Charlie thought of the phone call in the garden at the birthday party a few days before. She told Sandra about it and about Simona's reaction. "Do you think someone forced her to go?"

Sandra nodded. "It's likely. She probably ran because someone threatened her. She was planning this yesterday. I didn't see it until now."

"She left Nadia," Charlie said incredulously. "How could she leave her daughter?"

Sandra sighed in resignation. "I think she thought she was doing the best she could for Nadia, that leaving her was safer than taking her. And she's probably right." She sighed again. "What a mess."

The door opened and Vesna poked her head in. "I find this by the toaster," she said. She held an envelope out to Sandra, who took it, glancing at the name scrawled on the front. "I need to speak with your sister as soon as possible," she said to Charlie gravely.

"Waverly? Why?"

"Because Simona left something for her."

Standing in the tiny front office of the safe house facing the crisply pressed and steely-faced

Sandra Ling, Waverly stared incredulously at the legal papers in her hand. She pulled the tie of her silk robe tighter around her waist and blinked hard, trying to make the words come into focus. She had been sound asleep when Charlie roused her with the news of Simona's disappearance and the discovery of an envelope addressed to her. Now she squinted at the contents of the envelope, attempting to follow Sandra's rapid-fire explanation. Her mind was still sleep muddled. She had been dreaming of Andrew again. They had been on their sailboat, the *Allegra Day*, on a pristine Sunday afternoon. She had been spreading brie speckled with truffles on homemade parmesan crisps while Andrew handled the lines with a deft hand.

"I don't understand," Waverly said, shaking her head and blinking. "What do you mean she left Nadia to me?"

She heard the words Sandra was using but couldn't quite seem to align them with reality. Simona was gone. That much she could comprehend. Simona had left Nadia asleep in bed. But after that Waverly was having trouble grasping the situation. She glanced at Charlie, who was sitting in an armchair in the corner watching the exchange with unconcealed astonishment. Charlie shook her head, as baffled as her sister.

"Simona named you as legal guardian of her daughter," Sandra said baldly, gesturing to the papers. "She had me draw up the legal document yesterday. She said it was for Nadia's maternal grandmother, to give legal custody of Nadia to her. But she put your name on there instead. Look." She leaned over and pointed to the blank spaces where Simona had scrawled Waverly's name. The document was dated the night before.

"But why me?" Waverly asked in bewilderment.

Sandra raised an eyebrow. "Can you think of someone better?" she asked. "If you were being threatened, if you had to run and couldn't take your child with you, whom would you want to raise her? Someone back in the village in Bulgaria where she might become a target for the same people who'd trafficked you? Would you want to put her in a state-run orphanage? There aren't very many good options. I think she felt you were the best chance Nadia had at a good life."

Abruptly Waverly crumpled onto the ottoman at Charlie's knees. "She picked me?" Waverly asked, her mind whirring in shock. She shut her eyes and tried to breathe deeply in through her nose and out through her mouth. It wouldn't do to have a panic attack just now. She needed to focus.

As she breathed in and out in a measured cadence, slowly she began to see the pieces drop into place before her in her mind's eye. Her repeated dreams in which Nadia asked Waverly to come for her. All the unlikely events that had led them to this place and time. It was no accident, Waverly was sure. She had no idea how it was all happening. It defied rational explanation, but somewhere in her gut, in the space far past logic, where there was simply intuition and response, Waverly felt the slow and steady swell of rightness, of inevitability. It felt warm and full, like a flower coming into bloom, like the sun breaking over the horizon at dawn. This was supposed to happen. It was meant to be.

"Don't be alarmed," Sandra said brusquely. "Of course you don't have to say yes. Unfortunately, I think Simona's mother is in poor health and no longer able to care for the child. I'm not sure about any more distant relatives who might be able to take her. But you can turn the child over to the state system, and they will place her in a suitable foster home. You are not obligated in any way."

Waverly looked at Sandra, her eyes wide. "What do you mean?" she asked, clutching the papers to her chest. "Of course I'll take her. She's supposed to be mine."

In the hectic ensuing hours, Charlie attempted to make herself useful. Sandra handled the details of postponing the trial while she tried to locate Simona. At lunch, to the women of the safe house Sandra spoke optimistically of this simply being a delay. Once Simona was found the trial could proceed as planned, she said, but in private she was more realistic.

"She's gone. And she'll stay gone until she wants to reappear, if she wants to reappear. I don't anticipate that we'll see her again," she confessed to Charlie, giving a weary sigh.

Waverly spent the day with Nadia, and Charlie popped in to see them when she wasn't helping Sandra. Upon discovering that Simona had fled, they had all agreed to tell Nadia that her mother had gone on an extended trip. They did not know when she would be back, but in the meantime she was to stay with Waverly.

At breakfast Waverly broached the topic of her mother's disappearance with Nadia while one of the other women in the safe house translated her words into Bulgarian. Nadia accepted the news with no obvious concern. She was used to her mother not being around and didn't seem bothered by her unexpected absence. Waverly let her help make apple crumble for lunch. The little girl clearly adored Waverly, watching her every move and trying to mimic her, copying everything from Waverly's walk to the way she flicked her hair from her cheek. She didn't want Waverly to be out of her sight and whimpered if she left the room.

Charlie sat at the dining room table with a mug of chamomile tea balanced on her rounded belly, watching the two of them make the crumble, and wondered how in the world Waverly was going to navigate this unexpected life change. The baby gave a kick, and Charlie smiled despite the sobering circumstances. He was alive and well in there. "It will be okay, pal," she whispered to him. "Things will work out somehow." But she couldn't see the way forward, just the messy reality of their present predicament.

"What are you going to do?" Charlie quietly asked her sister as they cleared the plates from the table, helping a few of the women in the house clean up from lunch.

"I don't know," Waverly answered. They watched Nadia feed Boris the last of her apple crumble. "But I know this is the right thing to do. I've never been more sure of anything."

"What about Andrew?" Charlie asked. They had not spoken of him since the car ride from Kosovo. Charlie didn't think he'd been in touch with Waverly. Indeed, he seemed to have vanished. "If he isn't excited about one child, what's he going to think about two?" She placed her hands protectively over her belly.

Waverly pressed her lips together in a thin line. "Right now Andrew isn't my biggest concern."

But Charlie could tell she was lying. Waverly was worried, and rightly so. It was one thing to bring a baby into a stable, loving marriage. It was quite another to be a single working mother and raise a newborn and a four-year-old who didn't speak English. That thought was daunting enough to cow even the hardiest soul. Frankly, it seemed like a recipe for disaster.

Charlie sighed, wondering for the thousandth time just where her brother-in-law was and why in the world he was so silent. A few dozen times she had considered asking to borrow Sandra Ling's phone and texting him, but had stopped herself each time. She didn't want to get in the middle of Waverly and Andrew's marital complications. If he was choosing not to contact Waverly, then nothing Charlie said would make a difference. It was their marriage, and they needed to work it out between them. Besides, she didn't want to break the safe house rules about contacting outside people. It was probably best to just let things be until they were back in Budapest.

Late in the afternoon Charlie was in her room trying to rest. Waverly had taken Nadia into the backyard to play with Boris, and Charlie slipped upstairs to put her feet up and read for a few minutes, but she couldn't seem to concentrate. The world felt turned completely on its head. Even the baby seemed cross, kicking her repeatedly in the ribs and kidneys. She had to go to the bathroom every half hour. She sighed. A couple more months and he would be here. But what did that mean now? Born into a world that looked quite different from what any of them had imagined when they had started this entire escapade. She found herself feeling surprisingly protective of him. Nadia was a darling child, and Charlie was relieved that she would have a stable, loving home with Waverly, but it still left her wondering about the baby. Where was his place in all of this?

Downstairs she heard the doorbell ring and the muted sounds of Vesna talking with someone. Curious, she listened for a moment before recognizing the deep voice and Afrikaans accent. Johan. The baby did a little somersault, and her heart leapt at the same time. She had not seen Johan since he'd dropped them off at the safe house. He had sent a message through Sandra the next day to say that he was returning to Budapest and would come to pick them up after Simona's trial. Now there would be no trial, but he was here as promised.

She bolted upright and tried to style her messy hair with her fingers, pulling down her maternity top over her belly and feeling foolish at the blush rising in her cheeks. A moment later there was a knock on her bedroom door.

"You're looking well," Johan said, eyeing her with a professional scrutiny as he came into the room at her invitation. "Has the baby been behaving himself?"

"Yes, but you've missed a lot of drama," Charlie replied. She filled him in on the new developments.

He leaned against the doorframe and whistled. "Sounds like quite the morning. And I'm afraid I'm not going to make it any easier. I've come for you and your sister. You both have visitors at the Care Network drop-in center downtown."

"Who?" Charlie asked, startled.

Johan looked rueful. "Beau swore me to secrecy about Waverly's visitor, but I'm afraid Ursula came with me. She wants to talk with you."

Charlie's stomach dropped. "Oh." She had a sneaking suspicion that she knew what Ursula wanted to talk about. It had been more than two weeks, and the decision about staff cuts had probably already been made. "Let's get this over with," she said, fishing under the bed for her shoes.

When Waverly, Charlie, and Johan arrived at the drop-in center, Beau was not there yet, but Ursula was waiting. Johan took Waverly on a tour of the center, keeping her out of the way while Charlie met with her boss. Nadia had stayed behind at the safe house under the watchful eye of Vesna, bribed with a cookie and cartoons to let Waverly out of her sight.

Charlie and Ursula sat in two uncomfortable folding chairs facing each other in the drop-in center's main room. One of the center staff had made them both coffee. Charlie held hers, not drinking it.

Ursula leaned forward earnestly, her pale blue eyes boring into Charlie's. "Charlie, we are glad to hear you are safe. We were all so worried for you," she said.

Charlie was surprised. Ursula's concern seemed genuine.

She continued, "And what you are doing, testifying for these women. It is a brave thing to do."

"Er, thank you . . . ," Charlie stammered, taken aback by the compliment. She had never received an iota of positive feedback from Ursula before.

Ursula smiled, a brief curling up of her lips, and then started into what seemed to be a rehearsed speech. "Charlie, you have given many good years of service to Care Network, and we appreciate your hard work, but after reviewing all of the staff positions—"

"I quit," Charlie interrupted her.

Ursula stopped talking abruptly, her mouth snapping shut like a nutcracker. She looked surprised. "What?"

Charlie took a deep breath. The words had flown from her mouth unbidden, almost of their own volition, but she did not take them back. Once she spoke them, she knew it was the right choice. It was scary to take that step with no idea what came next. She had very little financial reserves and had to pay her rent and fund her necessities somehow, but it felt liberating. "I'm turning in my resignation from Care Network," she repeated.

Ursula raised her eyebrows but didn't interrupt.

"I've enjoyed my time here and the chance to do good and necessary work," Charlie continued, "but I can't keep my position, not after what I've seen and experienced in the last few months. I feel I need to put my efforts toward directly helping women in vulnerable situations. Please consider this my two weeks' notice."

"Well." Ursula sat back with a grudging look of respect. "I accept your resignation. We will see you in the office on Monday, and you can begin turning over your duties."

She stood, and Charlie followed suit. Ursula extended her hand to Charlie. They shook. "I wish you success in whatever you choose next," Ursula said stiffly but sincerely.

"Thank you," Charlie responded. She was still stunned by what she'd just done. The notion had been percolating for months, ever since that night in the Serbian village. Finding Kinga in the back of that transport van had relit a fire in her belly, one that had lain long dormant since that traumatic night in Johannesburg.

"Well," Ursula said crisply. "I had better be going."

Charlie rested her hands on her belly and

watched her former boss walk away. She knew she had just made a momentous decision, of course, but the reality was only slowly starting to sink in. How would she pay her bills? How could she afford to stay in Budapest? And Johan, what would happen with him? The thought about Johan came unbidden, somehow more pressing than even her sudden unemployment. It surprised her that she would care so much.

Ursula pushed through the glass door and out onto the sidewalk, brushing past a small knot of people approaching the drop-in center from the street. Charlie glanced up as they reached the door and froze. Beau was standing on the other side of the glass, reaching for the handle. Behind him, peering over his shoulder, was a redhead in a raspberry-colored trench coat and sunglasses. Was that Cooksville's hometown star reporter, Jessica Archer? Charlie gaped at the wholly unexpected visitation, almost missing the third person standing just to the left of Jessica. Andrew.

"Andrew?" Waverly gasped. She couldn't believe her eyes. Her husband was standing in the doorway of the drop-in center, peering around the room with a worried frown. His eyes lighted on Charlie, and he started toward his sister-in-law.

"Andrew," Waverly called again. Andrew froze,

glancing up at her voice. When he saw Waverly his face cleared in an instant, suffused with relief. Waverly made a small sound, something between a sob and a laugh.

Andrew gave her a tired smile. "Darling." He held his arms out to her and she flew into them, burrowing her face into the lapel of his suit coat. He clasped her around the shoulders and pressed his cheek into her hair. He was rumpled and unshaven, she noticed right away, and smelled vaguely of stale cigarette smoke. Andrew was never rumpled, nor did he smoke. He was always perfectly pressed, even at the end of a long business day. Her cheek scraped against the stubble on his neck. She didn't care. She had never been so glad to see anyone in her life. She clung to his neck as though she were a drowning woman and he was the life preserver. She was vaguely aware of other people standing awkwardly around the room, watching the reunion in fascinated silence.

"Where have you been?" Waverly demanded.

Andrew pulled back to look at her, gently gripping her arms as though to keep her close. His eyes were pink-rimmed. He looked exhausted. "Trying to find you," he said. "I didn't know what happened to you for days after you were taken. I was at the cabin and didn't have Internet or cell coverage. And when I got home and saw all hell had broken loose, well, it took a devil of a time to track anyone down who could tell me anything." He drew a shaky breath. "Turns out I should have been paying more attention to your work contacts. I didn't have anyone's number, and the Food Network stonewalled me and wouldn't believe I was who I said I was. I called and called your cell phone, but I couldn't get through. I was so worried about you, my darling. Petrified."

Waverly folded herself into his arms again and buried her face in his chest. "I thought maybe you weren't looking for me," she confessed. "I texted you as soon as we were freed, but you didn't respond."

Andrew looked confused. "I'm sorry, darling. I didn't receive the text. I wish I had. As soon as I found out you were missing, I never stopped looking for you. Are you all right? Truly?" Andrew pulled back a little, scrutinizing his wife's face, running his thumbs over her cheekbones and down her jaw as though to reassure himself that she was there in the flesh, safe and sound.

"I'm fine," Waverly assured him, beaming at the warmth of his attention. "And Charlie and the baby are safe too. It's a boy, by the way." She said the last part a little shyly, unsure where he stood on the subject of the baby. She didn't mention Nadia. There would be time for all of that later. She didn't know how they would navigate what came next, but in her heart she knew they would do it together. Andrew had come for her. That was all that mattered now.

"I'm so glad you are all safe and well," Andrew said. He glanced over at Charlie, his eyes resting for a brief second on the baby. "Jessica helped me find you." He gestured to the reporter, who was standing off to the side with Beau, taking photos of the touching reunion. "She got us to Budapest, and after some sleuthing we located Charlie's workplace and met up with Dr. Kruger, who finally put us in touch with Beau. They agreed to drive us here, but no one would tell us where you were, not until today."

Waverly pulled back and looked at Jessica for the first time. "Jessica Archer?" she asked in astonishment.

The reporter was tapping notes into her phone while keeping an eye on the happy couple. "The one and only," she said.

"You helped Andrew find me?" Waverly asked.

"Well, I am a reporter," Jessica said dryly. "I have a trick or two up my sleeve."

"No doubt," Waverly muttered, smiling prettily. "Well, thank you for whatever you did to help Andrew find me." She turned back to Andrew, dismissing Jessica, who kept tapping notes into her phone in an unruffled manner.

"They're keeping a pretty tight lid on you two on account of the security concerns," Beau volunteered. "Until after the trial. I think the network thought Andrew was a reporter or something. He and Jessica managed to get hold of the good doctor here"—he jerked a thumb at Johan—"and that's how they finally found me."

Waverly glanced at Johan, noticing him for the first time as well. Charlie appeared to be trying very hard not to look at him. Her cheeks were flushed. Waverly smothered a smile and buried her face in Andrew's chest again, wrapping her arms around his neck as though she would never let go. It was all going to be okay, she sensed. Somehow it would all turn out right.

With Andrew and Waverly locked in a long embrace, Charlie felt as though she were intruding on a private moment. She headed toward the staff kitchen at the back of the building, looking for a drink of water. Beau followed, trailed by Jessica, who kept snapping photos of the happy couple. Johan fell into step beside her. He raised an eyebrow.

"So that's Andrew—mysterious husband and father of the baby?"

"In the flesh," Charlie replied. She glanced back at the newly reunited couple, smiling. She was deeply glad and relieved to see her brother-in-law. Andrew and Waverly were standing very close together, their foreheads touching, looking deep into each other's eyes. Waverly was crying.

She was a beautiful crier, glistening and dewy, not splotchy and swollen. Andrew couldn't stop touching her—the curve of her cheek, her shoulder, brushing back a wisp of hair from her brow.

"Quite the happy reunion," Johan commented, following Charlie's line of sight.

"Yeah," Beau interjected, holding his Samsung aloft as he filmed the scene. "This is going to be ratings gold."

Jessica appeared to also be filming on her smartphone.

"Stop that." Charlie swatted at Beau's phone. "Not everything has to be used for a ratings boost."

"Says the woman whose career doesn't depend on ratings," Beau said, but he stopped videoing.

Jessica just moved closer to get a better shot.

"Former career," Charlie corrected.

Johan looked at her in surprise, and Charlie smiled ruefully at the memory of her very impulsive resignation.

"Did she really fire you, after everything you've just been through?" he asked.

Charlie shook her head. "I quit before she could. I couldn't go back to putting condoms on bananas, not after everything I've seen in the last few months. The work I was doing was good, but it's not enough anymore. I need a change."

Johan nodded in understanding. "Fair enough. What are you going to do?"

"I don't know yet," Charlie said over her shoulder as she headed down the hallway to the kitchen. "Something to help women like Simona and Kinga." She badly needed a shot of whiskey, but a cup of water would have to suffice. "First I'm going to have this baby, and then I'll figure out the rest."

CHAPTER 31

Y ou don't have to leave. You could stay the night." Andrew rolled over in the disheveled king-size hotel bed and gave Waverly a shy smile. Waverly cupped his face in her hand, reveling in the rasp of stubble across her palm, the warmth and familiar smell of him—Earl Grey tea and the peppermints he kept in his pockets.

Johan had taken Charlie back to the safe house after Andrew's surprise appearance, but Waverly had opted to go back to the hotel where Beau, Jessica, and Andrew had taken rooms. Before leaving them Jessica had extracted a promise of an exclusive interview with both Andrew and Waverly after breakfast the next morning. Waverly suspected that Jessica viewed Waverly's ordeal as a golden ticket to national recognition.

Putting all thoughts of the opportunistic reporter aside, Waverly stretched languidly and yawned, feeling sleepy after their surprising and delightful reunion. She would have liked nothing better than to stay, order room service, and curl up next to her husband as though the events of the past month had been nothing more than a bad dream. But she couldn't. There were things she had to tell him. She had to explain why she couldn't stay with him at his hotel, why she had to return to the safe house that evening. She had to tell Andrew about Nadia.

"So the baby's a boy?" Andrew interrupted her train of thought. He rolled onto his back and laced his hands behind his head, gazing up at the ceiling. "I've never had a son before. I could teach him to play baseball." He paused. "Or cricket." He looked as though he might be enjoying the thought.

Waverly turned to him in surprise. "Does that mean you want the baby?" she asked cautiously. They had not talked about anything after their initial meeting at the drop-in center. They had been too eager to be with each other, desperate for the other's touch, a reassurance of sorts, a pledge that they were still together, still committed to one another despite the harsh words and silence and distance of the past weeks. Now that they were reunited, there were pressing and important matters they needed to discuss.

"I watched all the videos of your captive cooking show on YouTube," Andrew said, not directly answering her question. "I watched them over and over. I couldn't get enough of watching you."

"Why?" Waverly asked, surprised.

Andrew shrugged. "Partly to convince myself that you were really okay, but that wasn't all. It was something else too." He paused. "You were so brave. There you were, trapped in that ghastly place, forced to do things against your will, but you were so poised, so unbowed. Beau told me that you smuggled a cell phone in your dress. He said you were invaluable to the rescue."

Waverly looked down at her hands. "Charlie was having contractions too early. The baby could have been in trouble. We didn't know what was happening. It was Antigona, the Albanian woman in the videos, who helped me. She smuggled a cell phone to me, and I was able to reach Beau with information that allowed the police to find us."

Andrew reached for her hand, clasping it in his own. "I realized something before I heard that you'd been rescued, before I even knew that you'd been taken against your will."

"What?" Waverly asked, her breath catching in her throat. She waited, sensing that what he had to say was important.

"That I cannot live without you. I can't, and I don't want to. And when I heard that they had found you, that you were alive and unharmed . . ." He stopped, blinking hard, his voice thick with emotion.

Waverly bit her lip, tears springing to her eyes too. Her cool, calm British husband never showed this much emotion.

"It was the happiest moment of my life."

Andrew met her eyes, his own serious. "So if you want this baby, if this is what you really want, then I will love you and love him as much as I possibly can. You are strong and courageous, my darling. And you will be the most amazing mother to our child."

Waverly shut her eyes and nestled against her husband's bare chest, listening to the beating of his heart beneath her ear, her own drumming a rhythm of gratitude and expectation. She was daring to believe, to hope, that it could be all right. But first she had to be honest with him about everything. She placed her hand on Andrew's chest and took a deep breath, then raised her head and met his eyes. "Darling, there's something else I have to tell you," she said.

His gaze was calm and even. "All right," he said mildly.

"What would you say if I told you we also have a daughter?" She kept her eyes on him, feeling her pulse quicken.

Andrew furrowed his brow quizzically. "Besides Katie?" he asked, referring to his daughter with his ex-wife.

"Besides Katie," Waverly confirmed. "Her name is Nadia." And then she explained.

When she was done he was quiet for a long moment, staring out the window at downtown Belgrade, considering. She held her breath.

Would he change his mind? It was a monumental thing to ask of him, she knew, to be a father to a child who was not his own. He had agreed to a baby who at least had some biological relationship to them through Charlie. But for him to adopt a four-year-old whom he had never even laid eyes on, who did not even speak his own language . . . It was asking for the moon. And yet somehow she had the courage to ask it of him. She could feel the rightness of it in the core of her being. It was meant to be.

The minutes stretched long as she waited in nervous anticipation for his response. Watching her husband's face, those calm, gray eyes fixed in the distance, Waverly had the impression that Andrew was somewhere far away, that perhaps he was saying farewell to another life, the life he had once thought he would have. Finally, he looked up and met her eyes. His expression was frank and open. "It's not what I expected," he said slowly. "But I'm willing to pursue this if you are sure it's the right thing."

Waverly felt the prickle of tears, relief seeping sweet as honey through her veins. "It is," she said with fervor.

Andrew reached for his trousers and shirt. He slid the shirt over his shoulders and buttoned the cuffs, then turned to Waverly. "I'd like to meet our daughter."

• • •

Two days after Andrew's unexpected appearance, Johan drove Charlie back to Budapest in one of the Care Network minivans. Beau had flown back to the US that morning to finalize plans for Waverly's upcoming interview on the *Ellen DeGeneres Show* and *Good Morning America* amid a wave of positive publicity. The Food Network had been in contact. They had renewed *Simply Perfect*'s contract for another two seasons and wanted to discuss Waverly doing a two-part Christmas special based in Budapest.

Jessica Archer had left on the same flight as Beau, armed with her exclusive first interview with Waverly and Andrew and a very determined look in her eyes. She had confided to Charlie that she had plans to barter the interview for a ticket out of her Ohio small-town newsroom.

On their way out of Belgrade, Charlie and Johan stopped by the apartment that Waverly, Nadia, and Andrew were renting to say good-bye. When Waverly ushered them into the ornate living room with soaring ceilings and tall windows overlooking a verdant green park, Nadia was sitting on Andrew's lap on a tufted leather sofa. She was giggling as he patiently braided a Barbie doll's blond hair. The little girl nestled back against Andrew's crisp button-down shirt, watching intently as he added a bow to the hairdo.

"She adores him already," Waverly said, giving her husband and Nadia a fond look. "And I think the feeling is mutual."

Andrew glanced up and raised his eyebrows at Charlie, the merest hint of a smile curving up the corners of his mouth. "What's a five-letter word for an unexpected outcome?" he queried.

Charlie laughed. "Happy?" she guessed, ribbing him a little. Then, because she couldn't resist playing the game for real, she guessed again. "A twist."

"Indeed." Andrew nodded. "Right on both counts."

Nadia tugged at his wrist, pointing to a pink, sequined Barbie ball gown. Andrew slid the doll's legs into the gown and expertly fastened the Velcro.

"We're both staying in Belgrade as long as we can," Waverly explained, watching Andrew and Nadia with an indulgent expression. "I'll have to go back to the US in the next couple of weeks, but Andrew's taken a leave of absence and will stay here until Nadia's paperwork is sorted out and she can travel to Connecticut."

"Don't foreign adoptions usually take months or even years?" Charlie asked.

Waverly nodded. "Often, but we've hired the best adoption attorneys in the US, Serbia, and Bulgaria to sort out all the legal details. And Andrew just spoke with Senator Rigbsy—

they golf together—and he assures us he'll do everything in his power to move things along as well. We think this is a special case and will go more quickly."

Charlie and Johan stayed only a few minutes. They wanted to reach Budapest before rush-hour traffic snarled the city streets.

"You'll call the instant you think you're in labor?" Waverly asked yet again, turning to Charlie as she led them to the grand front door. "I'll be on the first flight to Budapest as soon as I get the call."

"As soon as I know I'm in labor, I'll call you," Charlie assured her. Because of her delicate condition, the Serbian doctor had advised against her traveling by plane, so the original plan to have the baby in the US had been abandoned. She would have the baby in Budapest, and Waverly would fly over as soon as possible, then return to the States with the baby after he had been issued an American passport and the legal paperwork surrounding his official adoption by Waverly and Andrew was completed.

It was not how any of them had imagined the situation, but given all the variables, it seemed like the most straightforward option. Waverly needed to return to the US to ride the wave of publicity for as long as it lasted to help secure *Simply Perfect*'s future. That, coupled with the unknown length of time Nadia's adoption process would take, meant that she was not free to wait on the birth of the baby in Budapest. Better to come after he had arrived and then take him back with her after his paperwork was in order.

Waverly laid her hand on Johan's arm. "Take care of her, will you?" she said earnestly. "I feel so much better knowing she has someone trustworthy to turn to."

"I'll do whatever I can," Johan assured her.

"Good." Waverly squeezed his arm. "You'll be in good hands with Dr. Kruger," she told Charlie, shooting her sister a sly, satisfied look.

Charlie ignored the comment and its thinly veiled prompting. Waverly had made it abundantly clear that she thought Charlie and Johan would make an excellent couple. Charlie agreed, but she wouldn't give her sister the satisfaction of admitting it. Not yet. She wanted to see what happened between them after her return to Budapest, and there were so many uncertainties now after her resignation from Care Network. All she knew was that she did not want to see Johan Kruger walking out her door. Beyond that, she had no idea what could happen.

"Be careful," Waverly said, clasping her sister in an unexpectedly fervent hug.

"I will." Charlie returned the embrace, feeling a dart of sorrow. She would miss Waverly. She was suddenly reluctant to leave her sister. It felt as though they had just found each other again.

Waverly pulled back and searched Charlie's face. "Thank you," she said finally. "For everything. You're the bravest person I know. You and St. George have more in common than you think. You are my hero, my Red Cross Knight."

Charlie dropped her eyes, embarrassed. "You didn't do so badly yourself," she said. "If I had to be kidnapped by Albanian nationalists, I couldn't have chosen a better partner."

Waverly laughed and Charlie joined her, the humor tinged with fondness and relief. Waverly caught Charlie's eye, holding her for a moment. "Call me and tell me how you are," she requested.

"I'll send an update every day," Charlie promised.

"And don't wait too long," Waverly said as a low aside. She made a slight gesture toward Johan. "I know a good thing when I see it. I hope you have the good sense to see it too."

Charlie gave her a cryptic smile but said nothing. She followed Johan out the grand front door to the minivan, turning to Budapest and whatever lay ahead.

A few weeks later Waverly was in her kitchen in Connecticut working on a new recipe idea, a variation of the Hungarian cold fruit soup with pears and mascarpone cheese, when Sophie brought in the mail.

"A letter for you from Budapest," her assistant said, laying the plain white envelope on the granite countertop. Waverly wiped the pear juice from her hands and picked up the envelope, noting Charlie's bold, angular handwriting and the row of ornate stamps marching across the top.

She opened the envelope with a paring knife and slid out a card. It featured a massive bouquet of bright pink roses and a lengthy sentiment entirely in Hungarian. Inside Charlie had written,

> It's garish. And I think it might be a get-well card.
>
> But Happy Mother's Day.
>
> You're the best mother I know. Here's to the future.
>
> Love,
Charlie and little pal

Touched, Waverly reread the card with a laugh that turned into a stifled sob. *Here's to the future,* Charlie wrote. That phrase struck Waverly. For so long she had been trying to recapture the past sweet days of their childhood, trying to recreate and preserve what had been lost, the life and home she had longed for with a broken heart for all these years. But there was no more need. Her home was full with Andrew and Nadia. *Simply Perfect* had been renewed for another two seasons. She would not trade the reality of the present now for any other life, any other way.

She propped the card up on the counter so she could see it as she cooked, then turned back to the pear soup. Under her breath she was humming a little tune. For the first time in as long as she could remember, she felt perfectly content.

CHAPTER 32

Early July
Budapest

At 11:03 p.m. on a night in early July, Charlie awoke from a restless sleep, coming to consciousness fully in an instant as a gush of warm fluid soaked her pajama bottoms. She switched on the light and struggled to sit up, already reaching for the phone.

Waverly was in the middle of a happy hour with business colleagues in New York City but picked up immediately. "Is it time?" she asked breathlessly.

Charlie winced at another contraction, this one stronger than before. "Yeah, I think so."

"I'll get the earliest flight out in the morning," Waverly promised. She sounded so excited, almost panicky. "Call me as soon as you have news."

"Okay, I will." Charlie drew a sharp breath as another contraction hit.

She hung up and dialed the after-hours hotline of the private clinic where she would be having the baby. The young Hungarian woman who answered took her name and information and promised to immediately call the staff into work. They would be waiting for her when she arrived. Then Charlie made one final call. Johan answered on the third ring, his voice rough with sleep. When he heard who it was, he rallied immediately. She could hear him rummaging for his clothes as she told him it was time.

"Have you called a taxi?" he asked. "Or do you want me to come for you?"

She had only intended to tell him she was in labor, but at his offer she felt an instant rush of relief at the thought of his presence. "Could you come get me?"

"On my way."

Hurriedly she pulled on her birthing clothes—comfortable lounge pants and a dark tank top. She tucked the thin silver chain with the medal of St. George under her top. She had not taken it off since Waverly had given it to her. She paused for a moment, rubbing the worn medal, breathing a prayer for courage and protection. She needed it now more than ever.

Grabbing her hospital bag and the coconut water and fruit she'd kept stocked in the fridge for the past week, she stood by the front door, ready and waiting. She felt strangely calm. Her warmly lit apartment, the darkness outside the window, the stillness of the square outside, felt almost surreal. She was intensely aware of what was going on in her body but strangely detached from her surroundings. She was moving through the motions as though in a dream or underwater. Every four minutes she would stop for a strong contraction, wincing and blowing out air as her clinic's birthing instructor had taught her in the few sessions they'd had together to prepare for the birth.

Five contractions later her door buzzer rang. Johan was there, standing outside, his hair sticking up at the back, an anxious look on his face. She handed him the hospital bag and for a moment he clasped her hand, searching her face. He was taking her pulse. She could feel his fingers pressing on the inside of her wrist. The contractions were becoming more intense and closer together.

"How can I help?" he asked.

"Stay with me." She had not intended to ask him, had not even known that she wanted him to until this very moment, but she needed his calm presence, his steady, strong hand, and the reassurance that all would be well in the midst of such a new and unknown process.

"Of course." He looked a little surprised and relieved.

In the dimly lit and luxurious birthing suite of the private clinic, outfitted with a gigantic birthing tub, soothing dark wood accents, and a panoramic view of the Danube and Castle Hill,

Charlie, Johan, and the midwife settled in for the duration.

The labor progressed slowly. Several times through the long hours the midwife rubbed Charlie's stomach and hands with essential oils, the pungent scents of geranium, clary sage, and jasmine rising in the warm, dark air. Charlie cupped her hands around her nose and breathed in the oils, visualizing strands of light flowing through her nose down into her abdomen and out, expanding to fill the room. Dawn broke over the city, the Danube like a sheet of mother-of-pearl, the sky behind the castle blushing peach and rose.

Charlie was calm and focused and a little afraid. It was not so much a sensation of pain as it was of intense pressure, a primordial force moving outward and downward through her body. She was in its grasp and had no control, just carried along with it in its inexorable progress. She clasped Johan's hand through the most intense contractions, unaware of the pressure she exerted until she saw the red gouged crescents from her fingernails on the backs of his hands.

Time became elastic. Charlie had no idea how long they had been in that space. It felt like minutes or forever. There was no sense of hurry, no outside world, only the slow bloom of her body in an age-old act of bringing forth.

When the contractions grew so intense that

Charlie begged for relief, the midwife turned on the shower as hot as it would go, urging her under the spray. Charlie didn't let go of Johan's hand, and without a moment's hesitation he walked into the shower too, pausing only to shuck off his shirt and socks and shoes. Charlie stood under the stream of hot water as it pounded her lower back and rested her head against Johan's bare shoulder, the medal of St. George dangling between them. The water soothed her muscles, dulling the intense edge of the contractions and allowing her to rest. She dozed for a few moments, standing up, her face against his shoulder, and he held her, the steam from the water billowing around them and beading on their hair and eyelashes. She did not feel awkward with Johan seeing her here at her most vulnerable. She trusted him and needed him, and that was enough.

When Charlie finally pushed the baby into the world, Johan sat by her shoulder and held her hand, his strength giving her courage when she needed it most. There was a flurry of activity around the hospital bed where she lay—doctor, midwife, and neonatologist all crowded around, and a moment later she heard a loud and indignant wail. Euphoric, sweaty, and out of her head with fatigue and exhaustion, Charlie lay back, panting, and grinned. Johan gripped her hand hard. He was grinning too.

"It's a boy," he said, peering at the baby as

the doctor held him up. "And he's a fine little fellow."

The doctor laid the baby on Charlie's chest. He was just beginning to turn pink, still slippery and angry. He screwed up his face and wailed. Charlie put her hands around his little skinny body and looked into his face. *Oh, it's you,* she thought, surprised. He had been there all along, bobbing in the warm, placid darkness of her womb. Somehow she knew him already. "Hi, pal," she whispered. She was aware of doctors and the midwife, of Johan beside her, but she only had eyes for her son.

"Mine," she whispered, and the word scared her. He could not be hers. He was promised to another, and yet there was no denying the feeling coursing through her. When she looked at his face, she knew with a certainty that went to her core: he was hers. For a moment, just for a moment, she ignored the fact that in a few weeks he would be flying away from her to his new life with his intended parents. For a moment she simply went with her gut. She was his mother. He was her son. It was simple and elemental and undeniable. And impossible. But she did not think of that. She simply looked at him, his tiny old-man face and fringe of hair so pale it looked white, at his wrinkly fingers and skinny chicken legs. She had never known such a big love.

The neonatologist examined him, taking him

for a few minutes to clean him and weigh and measure him.

"He's a handsome little chap," Johan said admiringly as they took the baby away. "You should be proud."

Charlie nodded. She couldn't take her eyes from her baby. Even across the room her eyes followed his every move as the doctor examined him. "I didn't know it would be like this," she said slowly. It felt like a confession, although she wasn't sure what exactly she was confessing.

"Like what?" Johan asked.

"Like falling in love."

Johan looked at her intently. His eyes were pink with fatigue and he was sporting a dusting of stubble like cinnamon sugar along his jaw. She had a sudden urge to rub her face against it like a cat. *That's just the hormones talking,* she told herself, trying to corral her emotions. She was exhausted and elated and suddenly ridiculously attracted to the man who had just seen her give birth. She almost laughed at the absurdity of the last sensation. She'd probably put her relationship with Johan firmly and forever in the friend category by making him sit with her through labor and delivery. It was something that many husbands were not able to do. And yet she had asked it of this man, a friend but not a partner, not even a lover. In retrospect it was extraordinary of him.

"Thank you," she said. "For staying with me."

He met her eyes, his own gaze intent. "It's an honor." He opened his mouth as though he were going to say something more, but then the doctor interrupted, handing her the baby. He was now clad in a tiny pair of white pajamas and a white cotton cap that tied under his chin. His eyes were closed, and he looked thoroughly disgruntled. He stopped crying, though, as soon as Charlie touched him. She snuggled him close and marveled at how warm and impossibly small he was.

Now that the major event was over, she felt peaceful and serene. And tired. She yawned, and a nurse appeared at her side in an instant, motioning for the baby. Charlie didn't want to give him up, but she was so drowsy. Another nurse helped her across the hall into the spacious recovery room with a queen-size bed and velvet pillows and an ornately frilled bassinet positioned beside the bed. She was asleep before her head touched the crisp cotton sheets.

"Oh, he's gorgeous," Waverly cooed, bending over the bassinet. The baby looked up at her solemnly. It had been twenty-four hours since his birth. A storm on the East Coast had delayed Waverly's flight, and she had just arrived in Budapest and come straight to the hospital from the airport.

"May I?" she asked Charlie, gesturing to the baby.

Charlie was sitting in a chair by the bank of tall windows looking out on the Danube and the Széchenyi Chain Bridge. She winced and gingerly shifted position, feeling sore all over and strangely out of sorts. "Of course."

A nurse entered with a breakfast tray and set it before her. It was loaded with fruit, pastries, yogurt, orange juice, and cornflakes. While Charlie started on her breakfast Waverly lifted the baby, cradling him a little awkwardly. "I've been taking parenting classes from a private instructor," she confessed to Charlie, "so I'll know what to do with him."

Charlie dropped her gaze to her cereal. She forced herself to take another bite of cornflakes, but they tasted like cardboard.

"Oh, you're such a handsome little fellow," Waverly cooed. "And so calm. I believe he understands everything I'm saying." She held him a little away from her and peered into his face. "I think he's got Mother's eyes, but it's definitely your nose and chin. Whatever the combination, he's just perfect. Nadia is going to love you. Yes, your big sister is so excited to meet you."

Nadia's adoption paperwork had been processed in record time, and she was adjusting well to her new life in Connecticut with the help of a sweet Bulgarian nanny and a private English tutor.

Charlie kept chewing, trying to swallow the hard knot lodged in her throat. It had been stuck there since the birth, since she had first held her son. It was not getting smaller.

Waverly glanced at Charlie, cradling the baby against her chest. She looked perfect despite the long flight and travel delays. She was wearing a new color of lipstick, Charlie noticed briefly, a brighter pink hue that suited her better than her usual Dior shade. "How are you feeling?" Waverly asked. "Tell me about the birth. I want to know everything."

"I'm fine," Charlie said briefly. She did not want to share the details with Waverly. They were hers and hers alone. "It was long and intense, but good," she said at last.

Waverly looked disappointed at the scant information. "Was Johan with you the whole time?" she asked.

Charlie nodded. She smeared butter on another bite of croissant. "I couldn't have done it without him," she said honestly. "He was what I needed."

"Have you seen him since the birth?" Waverly asked. "I'd love to thank him in person."

"He's probably still trying to recover," Charlie said, dodging the question. It galled her somehow to think of Waverly thanking him for helping with the baby's birth, as though Charlie were just the birth vehicle. Which was precisely how she had explained it to Waverly way back in the beginning when she'd thought up this crazy scheme. Now she was feeling something quite different. And she didn't know what to do about it. Trying to distract herself, she stared at a huge bouquet of white roses on the dresser, a congratulations and thank-you from Duncan and Kate, who were now dating thanks to Charlie's meddling.

Waverly was rocking the baby and humming softly, gazing down at him with an adoring expression.

"Did I tell you we're thinking of naming him Arthur?" she asked. "After Grandpa Arthur? Arthur Talbot Ross. It has a nice vintage ring to it, don't you think? We've decided to give him my last name as well as Andrew's. I wanted to do it as a way to honor Mother and Daddy, and Andrew agreed."

Charlie made a face. "Sounds like an old man to me," she said. She tried to say it lightly, but it came out more sharply than she intended. Waverly looked wounded.

"I'm sorry," Charlie sighed. She set down her coffee cup. "It must be the hormones talking. I'm just grouchy."

The baby began to cry, a high, thin hiccup of distress, and Charlie jumped to her feet, instinctively reaching for him before she even thought. "Give him to me," she said urgently. It was not a request.

Waverly slowly handed him over with a look of confusion. Charlie clasped the baby to her, skin to skin, and shushed him gently. He immediately calmed, making tiny snuffling sounds. Charlie looked up. Waverly was watching her carefully, a look of understanding dawning on her face.

"What would you name him?" Waverly asked softly. "If you could."

Charlie bent her face over the baby, refusing to look up, refusing to acknowledge what they both knew to be true. "Alexander," she said at last. "I would name him Alexander. It means defender of mankind. And George, for St. George, our patron saint of courage. And Robert, in honor of Dad. Alexander George Robert Talbot."

The next morning Waverly arrived at the clinic bright and early. Charlie and the baby were being discharged, and she had come to collect them. Despite jet lag, Waverly looked fresh and rested, wearing a shell-pink blouse with a huge bow at the neck and a pair of sand-colored trousers. In contrast Charlie was disheveled and unwashed, still wearing her lounge pants and a tank top. The baby was sleeping in the bassinet. Charlie sat in an armchair nearby, watching him, jealous of every minute she had with him.

"We can't leave the hospital until you give

them a name for his birth certificate," Charlie said. She avoided looking directly at Waverly.

"I'll go see them then and get it sorted out," Waverly said. "We'll have you back home soon."

Charlie said nothing. She had not slept well. She'd sat up through the night holding the baby and trying not to think about what was coming. The thought of her arms being empty, of his little body jetting a continent away, was agonizing. And yet what could she do? It was what she had signed up for. She had agreed to carry him, to grow and house him and then birth him for her sister. This was not her baby. Except somehow she could not convince herself of that.

"I talked to Andrew last night," Waverly said. "I thought we'd agreed on Arthur, but now he seems partial to Liam. So I don't know which we'll choose. I'll have to call him back before I sign anything. It's later there now, but it can't be helped. I sent him photos of the baby. He thinks he's just perfect. So does Nadia."

"Good," Charlie said flatly.

Waverly sighed. "Do you want to talk about this?" she asked.

Charlie set her jaw. "There's nothing to talk about," she said.

Waverly said nothing. Charlie could feel her sister's eyes on her. She hated every moment of this day. She felt like screaming or crying or both. She clenched her jaw and leaned away from her son, trying to practice letting him go. Except she couldn't seem to move an inch away from him. It was absurd, this bond she was feeling. She had no partner, no job, a precarious future. She was a terrible prospect as a mother. What could she possibly offer him?

She had thought this would be a straightforward process. She had never wanted a baby, had not had a maternal streak in her. But that was before. Before she'd carried him and talked to him and nurtured him for those long months. Before she'd looked into his little wrinkled face and felt their bond as mother and child. He was her little pal, and she could not think of her life now without him. Except she had to. She couldn't take the baby away from Waverly. She had no choice.

"I'm going to call Andrew and then go sort out the birth certificate." Waverly sighed. "I'll be back." At the door she turned. "One question," she said.

Charlie waited.

"Would you keep him if you could?"

Charlie made a sound, almost a whimper. She did not answer.

Waverly nodded. "I thought so." She left the room.

She was gone for almost an hour. When she returned Charlie did not look up. The baby was awake, and Charlie was sitting in bed holding him, cradling his little body against her stomach and gazing at his face as though trying to memorize every square inch of him. His eyes were shut, but he was moving his limbs, his actions jerky and uncoordinated.

"All the paperwork's in order," Waverly announced. "We can leave when you're ready."

"What'd you end up naming him?" Charlie asked reluctantly.

"See for yourself." Waverly set a document in front of her.

Charlie skimmed the lines in Hungarian until she got to the name. Her eyes widened. "Alexander George Robert Talbot." She looked up at Waverly, puzzled. "What about Arthur and Liam?" she asked. "Weren't those your top picks?"

"It wasn't our decision to make," Waverly said gently. "Andrew and I are in agreement."

"What do you mean?" Charlie asked in confusion.

Waverly shook her head. She took the document from her sister and pulled a chair close to the bed. "Charlie, let's be honest with each other." She met her sister's eyes. "This is your baby. We thought it was mine, but we were wrong. He belongs with you. My child is waiting for me at home. Nadia is the child I am supposed to have. And Alexander is your son. It's as simple as that."

Charlie opened her mouth to argue but found

that she had no words. Her eyes welled with tears. Waverly took her hand and Charlie squeezed it, overwhelmed by this gift, by the responsibility and rightness of it. She put her cheek against the soft fuzz of the baby's head and breathed in his sweet, milky scent, her heart swelling with a love she had not anticipated, a love fiercer and stronger than anything she'd felt before.

"Hello, Alex," she whispered. And just like that she was home.

EPILOGUE

December, five months later
All Saints Episcopal Church
Baltimore, Maryland

E very new life, every child is a blessing to the world," Father Alderson intoned. "As such, these young ones we are baptizing today bring joy and life with their presence on earth."

In the chapel of their childhood church, Charlie and Waverly stood together to dedicate their children. In Charlie's arms Alex began to squirm and screwed up his face, prepared to let loose with a mighty wail. He didn't like the bow tie she'd put on him. It was a present from Kinga who, after winning her trial, was building a new life in Stockholm. She had made the tie herself.

Charlie jostled Alex, hoping to stave off a full meltdown. Across the baptismal font Waverly and Andrew stood with Nadia perched on Andrew's hip. She was wearing a green crushed-velvet dress with a stiff petticoat and black patent leather shoes, her hair in perfect plaits.

The chapel was smaller than Charlie remembered. It was still beautiful, decorated for

Christmas with gleaming oak and real evergreen boughs, and it smelled the same—the scent of fragrant evergreen spice and sap and the beeswax candles burning in their holders beneath the stained glass windows. The chapel had looked cavernous and so very solemn when she was little. All Saints was the church their parents had been married in, the church she and Waverly had been baptized in as babies, the church they had attended every Christmas and Easter as a family until their parents' death. Now it seemed fitting that they have their own children baptized there too. Charlie had asked Waverly and Andrew to be godparents for Alex, and they in turn had asked Charlie to do the same for Nadia.

The chapel was empty except for the priest and the six of them—Waverly and Andrew with Nadia, Charlie with Alex. And standing beside Charlie was Johan. He reached out and took Alex from her, making a face so that the baby laughed suddenly, a peal of joy that rang from the rafters. The priest faltered in his prepared speech, and Charlie threw a grateful look at Johan, who winked in acknowledgment.

It had been a whirlwind courtship, but they had so much history, so much they shared, that it had not seemed rushed to either of them. In April they were planning a simple wedding at Waverly and Andrew's house. It would be catered by *Simply Perfect* and followed a few weeks later by a reception in South Africa for Johan's family and friends. And in June they would relocate to Boston, where Johan had accepted a job heading up a health program for urban youth. At the same time Charlie would begin a part-time position as a coordinator at a trauma and recovery center for sexually exploited women and girls. Initially, when they had been offered both job opportunities in Boston, they discussed the future at length. In the evenings as Alex slept, they sat together sketching a possible future that felt exciting and new.

"I've never lived in America. I'm up for the challenge. I think I could learn to like American football," Johan said thoughtfully.

"Boston's a great city," Charlie agreed, "and I like the idea of being so close to Waverly, Andrew, and Nadia. If I take this coordinator position, I could work part-time doing something I'm passionate about and still be home with Alex part of the week. It feels like the best of both worlds."

After a few days of deliberation, they accepted the jobs.

"We baptize this child, Alexander George Robert Talbot, in the name of the Father, and the Son, and the Holy Spirit. Amen." The Reverend Alderson sprinkled a few drops of water on Alex's head, and the baby looked surprised, then began to wail.

Then it was Nadia's turn. "We baptize this child, Nadia Margaret Mae Talbot Ross, in the name of the Father, and the Son, and the Holy Spirit. Amen," the priest intoned.

Nadia stuck her thumb in her mouth and flinched as he sprinkled her and water ran into her eyes. Andrew wiped it gently away with the cuff of his dress shirt.

Charlie had chosen the name Robert to honor their father. Waverly had given Nadia the middle name of Margaret in tribute to their mother, and Mae in honor of Aunt Mae. Their parents were so close in this moment. Charlie could feel their presence in the empty pews. They were not there in body to celebrate their daughters' joy—two new grandchildren and a future son-in-law— but they were there in spirit. Margaret in her good pearls and Dior Grege lipstick, dabbing at her eyes with a handkerchief. And Robert, his laughter booming from the rafters at the antics of his grandchildren. Aunt Mae was present too, watching them all with a satisfied smile, wearing her best polyester housedress, the one with the mint-green pussy willows on it.

Their parents and Aunt Mae were proud of both of them, Charlie sensed, standing there in the church. Proud of who they were and who they were becoming, proud of the choices they had made, proud of the life they were building.

Waverly met Charlie's eyes across the baptismal

font. Hers were glittering with unshed tears, but they were happy tears. Charlie understood. She and Waverly had come full circle. They had finally gained what they had been looking for all these years. Family. Love. A sense of place. In the process they had uncovered a truer version of themselves.

This is the life we were meant to lead, Charlie thought, looking around her with a sense of gratitude and satisfaction. Her eyes lighted on Alex snuggled into Johan's arms, on Nadia resting peacefully against Andrew's chest. She turned and saw Waverly, the sunlight streaming through the stained glass window over her head, lighting her hair like gold. Charlie felt a swell of gratitude for her sister, for the twists and turns of their lives so far, for the unexpected joys of their children and their men, and for the journey that had brought them back together. They were the Talbot sisters once more.

It is enough, Charlie thought, savoring the moment and all it promised for the future. *It is more than enough.*

Discussion Questions

1. Waverly and Charlie both experience significant loss as adolescents and also as adults. How do these losses affect their life choices and relationships? Are the effects positive or negative?
2. Courage is a central theme of the story. How do Waverly and Charlie exhibit courage? What other characters show courage?
3. Which characters do you see choosing to love sacrificially in the story? How do they show sacrificial love?
4. Is Charlie's offer of surrogacy sacrificial or selfish? Why?
5. Aunt Mae's motto is "Whatever the Good Lord puts in your hand you give back to others." How do characters live out this motto in the story?
6. The idea of motherhood is a central theme in the story. What different ways is motherhood portrayed? What do you think about these portrayals?
7. The legend of St. George and the dragon is a recurring element of the story. How does this legend influence Charlie's choices?

8. By the end of the story, Charlie and Waverly are reunited as sisters. What choices do they make to help mend their relationship? Do you think they could have done more? Why or why not?

9. Is there a time in your life where hurt, loss, or secrets hindered a close relationship? Was it ever restored? Why or why not?

10. How does Charlie's choice to rescue Kinga and Simona impact the rest of the story? Do you think she made the right choice to first rescue the women and then to testify in the trial? Why or why not?

11. One of the themes of the story involves human trafficking and injustice. Have you seen or experienced injustice in your life? What do you think needs to be done to challenge injustice in our world?

12. What is an issue of justice in the world that you are passionate about? What have you done or can you do to bring about change in this area? Is it something you need to have courage to do?

About the Author

Rachel Linden is a novelist and international aid worker whose adventures living and traveling in fifty countries around the world provide excellent grist for her stories. She holds an MA in Intercultural Studies from Wheaton College and a BA in Literature from Huntington University, and she studied creative writing at Oxford University during college. Currently, Rachel lives in beautiful Seattle, Washington, with her husband and two young children. Rachel enjoys creating stories about hope and courage with a hint of romance and a touch of whimsy.

A Note from the Author

Dear reading friends,

While Kinga and Simona exist only in this story, the reality is that tens of thousands of Central European women are victims of sex trafficking each year. During my time living and working in Central Europe, I encountered many of these women in my daily life—in the popular tourist districts in European cities, in my local Budapest metro station with their pimps loitering nearby.

In Moldova I sat and ate cookies and drank homemade cherry juice with women who had escaped sex trafficking. As we shared about our lives, I looked across the table and realized that these were just women, regular women who had been trapped in horrible circumstances, exploited and abused for profit and pleasure. Several were mothers of young children, like me. We had a lot in common.

Many complex factors allow trafficking to flourish, from broken families and early abuse to global economic supply and demand worth billions of dollars, but at the center of sex trafficking are simply humans, mostly women.

Mothers, daughters, sisters, friends. As the director of the rehabilitation house in Moldova told me, "We're not about causes. We're about people."

Faced with the enormous and horrendous reality of human trafficking and sexual exploitation, it is easy to become discouraged. How can we possibly end it? I firmly believe there is hope. The fight for justice is not an impossible fight. And it is our privilege and responsibility to do our part.

Therefore, I am thrilled to be a supporter of an amazing organization, Hope Dies Last, a justice ministry that reaches out creatively to trafficked, marginalized, and exploited people across Europe. Based in Budapest, HDL partners with other anti-trafficking organizations in Europe, creating resources and addressing the root causes of human trafficking and sexual exploitation. I know the HDL staff personally and am consistently impressed by their integrity, creativity, and compassion.

As part of my commitment to justice for exploited women, I support Hope Dies Last and the fight against human trafficking in Europe. You can learn more about their work at www.hope dieslast.org.

Let's do our part to see justice become reality. This is a fight we can win!

—Rachel

Acknowledgments

Writing this book has been a labor of love. Budapest and Central Europe are an often overlooked but truly amazing city and region in Europe. I so enjoyed including in the story many aspects of the wonderful experiences I've had living there for the past five years. It's also been a solemn privilege to write about several issues dear to my heart—motherhood and miscarriage, and human trafficking and modern day slavery.

So many people both in Central Europe and in the US have contributed their time, wisdom, and experience to make this story shine. I want to thank each of them. A great BIG thank-you to . . .

My wonderful former editor, Karli Jackson, who helped give this story wings and my also wonderful and capable new editor, Kimberly Carlton, who guided it safely home! Also marketing whiz Kristen Golden and publicity queen Allison Carter as well as Amanda Bostic and the rest of the excellent Thomas Nelson team. All of them consistently exhibit such professionalism, dedication, and kindness in this publication process. I am so grateful!

My super agent, Chip MacGregor, whose practicality, wry humor, unflappability, and wisdom are truly invaluable. Chip, I'm so glad you're in my corner.

My wonderfully honest and wise test readers—Sarah Smith, Adelle Tinon, Sarah Wolfe, Amy Strobach, and Carmelita Egan. Their constructive criticism and keen insights made this story stronger.

My Central European friends and colleagues who provided specific expertise in various areas. Any remaining errors are my own! Of special note, Misha Mihaylova who helped with all things Bulgarian, Belinda Chaplin for her aid with Serbian, and Florin and Florina Mereu who gave valuable linguistic insight on the correct way to demand silence in Romanian.

The Hope Dies Last folks who provided excellent and heartbreaking information regarding human trafficking in Europe. Your work is inspirational and so necessary. I am always positively challenged by the work you do. I'm glad to also call you all friends and am so proud to be partnering with you!

My dear Albanian and Kosovar friends for their warmth, gracious hospitality, and indomitable human spirit. Your friendship is a gift.

Last but most importantly, my precious family. My husband, Yohanan, who is my strongest supporter, an insightful editor, and a thoroughly good man. Thanks for introducing me to central

Europe and then inviting me on this crazy adventure of a life we've chosen! You are my favorite. And for Ash and Bea. You make our lives and the world a brighter place.

Center Point Large Print
600 Brooks Road / PO Box 1
Thorndike, ME 04986-0001 USA

(207) 568-3717

US & Canada:
1 800 929-9108
www.centerpointlargeprint.com